I0732282

PLAY SMART
WORK FOR IT BOOK #5

ALY STILES

1—TRAINING

NASH

There are three things you have to understand:

1. I'm desperate.

2. Desperation makes people do strange shit.

3. Gouging one's eye out with a butter knife doesn't pay well or I'd be doing that instead.

I stare at the whiteboard in the shrinking conference room. At least it isn't the six-inch binder in front of me. We're on page something after fourteen and before ninety-seven. I know this based on how I zoned out for good at page fourteen and there's a scheduled break at page ninety-seven. We're definitely not on break.

"And what do we call the room that contains the servers?"

I pull my gaze from the luxurious white nothing to rest it on the instructor. He's staring at me with wide eyeballs about to burst from his head. He also wears a toothy grin that makes me suspect the stain on his polo shirt might not be ketchup.

"You're asking me?" I say, pointing to my chest.

He adds a vigorous nod to his killer-clown face. "Yes, Nash. What do we call the room that contains the servers?" He says this in the same tone an adult would use when asking a toddler if *it's ever okay to bite our friends?*

"Um. The… server room?" I respond dryly.

He claps once and juts a finger at me. "Exactly. The server room! Turn to page twenty-seven while we review a list of all the features of the server room."

Wait, we're only on page twenty-seven?

A puff of air expels from my lungs as I drop my forehead to my fists. This can't be real. I angle my head just enough to check on the other intern, but she's glued to *Chad* like he's some business mastermind and not a pompous idiot who asks questions like, "What do we call the room that contains the servers?" Hang on, is she actually taking notes?

My roommate Marcos warned me about this place when he asked his girlfriend to get me a job at Reedweather Media, her father's company. What he didn't warn me about was my direct supervisor, Chad Smith, or the fact that I'd be competing with another intern for some permanent position I don't want. If I had to guess, his negligence is related to the fact that he and Nate are tired of covering my portion of the rent and had no interest in lending me the ten grand I need to buy the recording equipment I've been drooling over since Abram Fletcher of Redburn told me it's mine if I want it.

And I *want* it—badly enough to turn to page twenty-eight, it turns out. Is that a diagram of a toilet?

I glance up, and sure enough, our boss is demonstrating flushing. If he wipes his ass, I'm out. Speaking of, the brownnoser beside me shoots up her hand.

"Yes, Paige," Chad says, crossing his arms in a bold display of instructor-ness.

"Is the soap in the dispenser a liquid soap or a foaming variety? I don't see it listed."

I stare at her in disbelief. She's not even being facetious. Her fingers hover over her keyboard, waiting to transfer this information to her laptop. What could *possibly* be the context for referencing that in the future?

Never mind. I don't want to know.

Chad scrunches his brow and taps his chin. "That's an excellent question, Paige. It's the foaming variety, but I'll make a note to add that revision to the training manual."

Paige adjusts in her seat with a self-satisfied smile and… no freaking way. That was a distinct *gotcha* look that just blasted my way. Oh shit, she's for real.

I straighten a bit and study her more closely. Her prim and proper business attire meant, like this manual, I lost interest the second my eyes grazed her stuck-up silhouette. But apparently, a direct challenge is enough to awaken the cynic in me, because suddenly I'm seeing way more than some expensive tailored business costume. Vibrant dark red hair twisted in tight curls frames pale skin without a single freckle or blemish. Well, except for a beauty mark on her left cheek that is *not*, and I repeat, *not* kind of sexy. (Fine, it is.)

Bright hazel eyes flash with confidence and indignation when they turn on me. Even her pen and leatherbound folder are pretentious and irritating. I snagged my writing utensil from the bulletin board in the lobby of our apartment building on my way out this morning.

She flips her curls over her shoulder and fires an eye-dart as if daring me to engage. I arch a brow in response, loving the way her pretty eyes narrow with disdain. She wants to play? Fine. At the very least, messing with Chad Smith will give me something to do that doesn't involve memorizing bathroom protocols.

I raise my hand, smirking at Paige's surprised flinch.

"Yes, Nash," Chad says, pointing at me—I guess to distinguish from all the other Nashes in the room.

"While we're on the subject, I don't see anything in the notes about whether or not the toilets are high-efficiency and-or water-conserving models. I think it's very important to be cognizant of our environmental impact, even in the most mundane of tasks." Yes, that last sentence was entirely sculpted to make Paige Goody-Two-Shoes react with flabbergasted concern the way she is now.

That's right, my friend. I'm bored, not an idiot.

Her eyes blaze as she shoots up her hand again.

"Yes, Paige," Chad says, his voice now strained. I must have rattled him. Clearly, he's concerned about whatever bombshell is coming next that will blow up page twenty-eight of his precious manual.

"While my *colleague*, here, makes an excellent point"—she says *colleague* like *I'm* the one who decided not to disclose the soap viscosity—"he always has the option of relieving himself at his home before and after his shift. I presume an environmentally conscious activist such as my counterpart has a high-efficiency-water-conserving toilet in his personal residence."

"You want me to hold it for nine hours?" I ask, turning to her.

"Your bodily functions are none of my business," she quips.

"I mean, you're the one who brought it up, so it kinda makes me think you're interested in my bodily functions." I toss a flirtatious half-smile just to piss her off more.

She huffs and straightens in her chair, focusing back on Chad who looks like he's lost a limb, not control of a conversation about toilets.

"People! Can we calm down? Please!" He waves his hands in frantic motions toward the floor in what I'm guessing is a "calm down" gesture if we're supposed to do the opposite of what he's doing. "Look, you both have raised some very important questions. How about we take five minutes while I investigate, and you…?" He makes the cryptic hand-flapping motion again.

I give him a confused look just for fun.

And we what, Chad? Sit on the ground? Worship the whiteboard? Fan ourselves?

I know I shouldn't even as I do it. But… well…

Hand.

Up.

"Yes, Nash," he sighs out in exasperation. I taste Paige's ire when I swallow a smile.

"So, where exactly do we stand on the toilet situation for this break?"

His eyes grow into giant orbs just as steam wafts from the woman beside me.

Hell yeah. I am so down for this. I may have no interest in a pointless internship, but I'm *extremely* interested in messing with an Ivy League princess.

And Chad.

* * *

I'm leaning against the wall outside the conference room, enjoying some precious seconds of training-free solitude, when an older man with slicked-back hair and a slicker smile screeches to a halt in front of me. He turns abruptly, and I cringe at my second killer-clown grin of the morning. What's with this place and weird smiles?

"Well, hello, my young friend! Reed Reedweather the third. Nice to meet you." He shoves his hand in my direction, and I straighten from the wall.

Reedweather? As in *Reedweather Media*, the place where I'm currently employed? Guess this is the big boss.

I take his hand on instinct, wincing inwardly when his fingers clench around mine in an uncomfortably tight grip. With our hands clamped together, his eyes narrow and bore into me with disturbing intensity. I stare back, blinking through several rounds of whatever is happening right now. When he finally lets go, I flex my fingers and shove them back in my pockets.

"Hello, Mr. Reedweather. Nash," I say.

"Just Reedweather." There's that smile again, this time with a hint of confusion.

"Okay?"

"No Nash."

"Huh?"

We exchange another long, awkward look.

"My name isn't Reedweather-Nash. Just Reedweather," he explains.

I squint back. "Um." Is there a re-start button for a conversation? I shake my head, clearing everything that just happened, and point to myself. "I'm Nash Ellis. That is *my* name."

"Oh!" he laughs out, clapping my arm. "Right, right, my boy. Nash-el-is. You must be one of the new interns." He looks damn proud of himself for putting that together. "I'm sorry I missed your introduction this morning, but you're in good hands. Chad is one of our best and brightest." Well, that's alarming. "It wasn't so long ago he was just a young pup like you."

I tilt my head, having no idea what any of that means. I settle on: "Okay" with a tight smile. He seems to like that and claps his hands.

"You look like quite the interesting fellow, Nash-el-is."

"Thank you?"

"Are those… what do they call them?" He tugs on his earlobe, and I resist the urge to say "ears." This conversation is already confusing enough.

"Gauges," I say instead.

"Ah, quite the rebel, aren't you?" This comes with what I think is supposed to be a conspiratorial wink. Is that a rebel thing?

"And those too." He points to my forearms, now exposed from rolling up my sleeves in that stifling conference room. I'm going to assume he's referring to my tattoos and not a shirt.

"You a bike boy, Nash-el-is? I used to ride them all back in the day. Hot and heavy, if you know what I mean." Another wink, which makes me fairly certain that I don't know what he means. Also, what's a bike boy?

"Um. No, actually. I'm not." I don't think? His eyes narrow again.

"But the…" He points to his forehead, and now I have no clue what the hell is going on.

"The… head?" I ask.

"Ah." He crosses his arms and leans back. "Is that what they're calling them now?"

"Yes?"

He purses his lips, studying my face with aggressive intrigue for a passing hallway chat. "You know, there was a time when establishments like this wouldn't have permitted the…"—he waves his hand at my face—"and the…"—

now at my arms. Can he not use nouns or something? "But here at Reedweather Media, we believe in what we call, *Rapid Inclusivity.* Have you covered *Rapid Inclusivity* yet in your training?"

Shit, more chapters to dread? I lie with a nod.

"Excellent! Yes, my boy. We open our hearts and arms to all types, even the unorthodox ones such as yourself. So *welcome,* Nash-el-is. You're our first ever bike boy." I can't even argue since I still have no clue what that is. "And who knows, maybe one day I'll get myself a *head.*"

He winks again and continues on his way with a smug gait.

I stare after him, scratching my own head. When my finger brushes my eyebrow piercing, I almost choke.

Please let me be there when he walks into a body-piercing shop and asks for a *head.*

* * *

Back in the conference room, my amusement fades. Chad must have decided our training wasn't boring enough and has added a slide presentation to explain our first official project as interns. At least it doesn't involve toilets.

As usual, MBA Princess over there is vigorously typing notes. She even types like she thinks we get points for our button-pushing ability. I pick up my pen and write the word *Groundhog* with several bold underlines on my notepad between us just to mess with her.

To my utter delight, she peeks over and startles in her chair. She stares at the word for at least ten seconds before studying her screen, then back to my notes. I add *Rapid Inclusivity* with a heart around it. Her eyes widen and narrow. I draw a stick-mouse wearing a top-hat, and she huffs in indignation when she realizes she's being played. It's everything I can do to keep my snort inside.

"Something funny?" Chad interrupts, his gaze lasering in on me. I lift my head from where it was resting on my fist.

"No, sir," I say. "Just taking notes." I hold up the pen in my hand, and Chad's expression transforms from annoyed to suspicious.

"If that's true, then perhaps you'd like to make the first suggestion?"

I clear my throat and straighten in my chair, sliding my attention to the screen to figure out what's going on.

Wait.

I squint at it, suddenly mad at myself for missing whatever this is. Because, that, right there, is magic.

"A… mermaid?" I say, slanting my head. No. Not a mermaid. A peanut with a tail fin? Do peanuts swim? Damn, where's that conversation re-start button?

"Not just a mermaid. We're launching an entire Mer-Nut campaign," Chad clips out, totally serious.

"I'm sorry. A *what*?" I rip off the top page of my notepad so I have more real-estate for whatever is about to go down.

"A Mer-Nut campaign," he repeats with some measure of irritation. "You and Paige will be working together to develop a comprehensive plan for our proprietary Mer-Nut brand representing Sandeke Telecom's Warp Speed Internet Service."

He waves at the screen impatiently like that's a sentence people say all the time. I stare back at it, but I still only see swimming peanuts. Hang on, is one of them wearing a monocle? Also, the king Mer-whatever doesn't look like a peanut, but I can't place that particular legume. Is it possible this underwater kingdom hosts a diverse array of tree nuts? I suppose that fits Mr. Reedweather's *Rapid Inclu-sivity* narrative. I scan the crowd of Mer-things looking for any being that could be considered a "bike boy."

"We need print, digital, and television ads, along with developing a line of Mer-Nut merchandise to create buzz. To our knowledge, this concept is completely original and has never been used before." An aquatic nut community? Seems like a valid claim. "You will find all of this information, as well as a variety of resources to get you started in the second half of your binder."

I flip to the tab helpfully labeled "Mer-Nuts." Sure enough, smaller versions of the weirdness on the screen clutter the page in front of me. I turn the page to find what looks like a human wizard in a pointy rainbow hat staring back at me. Now I'm even more confused—and strangely delighted. The next page contains a detailed map of an underwater community, meaning Mer-Nuts have an entire civilization and socio-economic system. This might be the stupidest thing I've encountered in my twenty-four years, which makes me love it all the more. And I thought this job was going to be boring.

I glance over at my counterpart who doesn't look nearly as pleased.

2—CLASHING

PAIGE

I dip my spoon into my yogurt as I glower at my laptop screen. For the record, my eyes keep drifting over the top to skim the guy at the neighboring breakroom table for purely cynical reasons. The fact that Nash Ellis has stunning blue eyes that practically glow from his face is completely irrelevant. In fact, it's disturbing how his thick dark lashes provide such a stark contrast to his luminescent irises that it almost looks like he's wearing eyeliner. Okay, it's possible *disturbing* is a strong (inaccurate) word for the effect, but I'm in no mood to be generous.

There's an arrogance to Nash that has gotten under my skin in record time. He clearly has no interest in being here, while I've worked my ass off for this opportunity to climb my way through the prestigious Sandeke Telecom Empire. Sure this internship sucks and our boss might be one of the most inept people I've ever met, but my journey to becoming a CEO of a multi-million (billion?) dollar company has to start somewhere. If I have to pretend to be interested in toilets and whatever this weird Mer-assignment is, so be it.

As a confident, accomplished woman in a man's world, I spend a lot of time pretending. Pretending not to be angry when my achievements are devalued or flat-out stolen. Pretending not to be offended or embarrassed when I'm forced to endure sexist jokes or even direct harassment. Pretending I don't want to throw a right hook when someone calls me *sweetie* or makes a comment about my appearance instead of my skills and intellect. Pretending I don't want to scream when some man tells me I *need to smile more.*

My grip tightens on my spoon. Cue new subject, please.

I divert my gaze back to my laptop and open the folder Chad said contained electronic versions of all the information in the binder. Why he killed a tree to print what was already on the server, I have no idea. I caught Nash's smirk when Chad made that announcement so I know he was thinking the same thing. Maybe that's what I hate the most about Nash. He's clearly intelligent but seems intent on making sure no one knows that. Wasted brains are not something I tolerate well.

I lift my eyes over the screen again, and sure enough, he has his head on his folded arms as if he's napping. All I see is a curtain of dark medium-length hair draped over a toned, tattooed forearm. Oh, and did I mention the gauges and eyebrow piercing? All of them are small, but still. With his black jeans and plaid button-down shirt rolled to the elbows, he looks more like a roadie for a rock band than a future executive. Not once have I seen him open the laptop Chad gave him this morning. What is he even doing here?

As if sensing my critique, he raises his head and blasts me with an electric blue stare. The corner of his mouth ticks up in amusement, and I snap my attention back to my screen, heat spreading over my chest and into my cheeks. I sink further in my seat, hoping he can't see my blush from his vantage point. I don't even know why I'm blushing. It must be an allergic reaction to irritating people. (We can ignore the fact that I didn't blush once in Chad's presence.)

Crap, he's getting up.

I pretend to be concentrating on this folder of—I can't tell yet—as he approaches my table. He then proceeds to lean over and check my screen before pulling out the chair across from me.

Rude! Who does that? What I'm doing on my laptop is none of his business. Also irrelevant to this situation is the fact that his flagrant intrusion may have reminded me that he smells really good. He doesn't seem like a cologne kind of guy, so I can't figure out what that distracting scent is. Body wash? Shampoo? I shudder and force my thoughts to anything other than Nash Ellis in a shower. Which, of course, is now triggering unhelpful curiosity about other piercings he may have.

"Whatcha doing?" he asks, lowering himself to the chair.

I flick a dismissive glance at him. "Working. You should try it." I hate that I can sense his wry smile without even seeing it. Gah! That's going to be annoying.

"We're on break."

"And what's your excuse for the rest of the morning?" I ask, looking up.

Ugh. Big mistake. His eyes light up with a competitive spark I feel in my bloodstream. I live for the chase, so if he's planning to challenge me for this job, he's in for a hell of a ride. Plus, there's the strange effect of his annoying symmetrical face. Seriously, what's up with that? It's like he pierced his brow just to distinguish the left side from the right side. No one should be that good-looking. It's unethical.

I glare back at my screen.

"I took notes all morning," he says.

I hear the smile in his voice, so I know he's referring to the doodles and random words he kept jotting down to distract me. Along with Groundhog, some odd stick-animal, and Rapid-something, he also kept scribbling a bunch of other completely unrelated sentences that read more like lines from poems. I don't think *those* were meant for me, though, since he wrote them on one of the pages deeper in his notepad and kept covering it up when he finished. I will never, ever admit that one of them actually struck me in the gut.

"Let the waves of darkness break, and take, the pain below, purged by the undertow…"

Even that annoyed me. Stupid pretty, intriguing words that were so much more enticing than the strange Mer-things we were supposed to be talking about. Also proves my point that this boy has zero interest in the topic at hand.

Once again: *Why. Is. He. Here?!*

"You scribbled doodles and wrote poetry. Pretty sure that doesn't count as work unless you're in preschool," I reply, squinting at my screen again. What *is* this folder supposed to be? There's a map of an amusement park and the beginning stages of a proposal—evidenced by the word "Proposal" typed at the top of a blank page.

"Lyrics."

I slide my gaze back to the intruder. "Huh?"

"It wasn't poetry. They were song lyrics. Specifically." He shrugs like it's totally normal to be writing song lyrics during a training session on your first day of employment at a new firm.

"Why are you writing song lyrics instead of paying attention?" My glare returns when his face gets all smirky again.

"Why are you watching me write song lyrics instead of paying attention?"

Somehow I manage to swallow my growl and focus back on my work. "By the way, feel free to jump in and help with this project anytime," I quip without looking at him.

"We're on break."

"And your breaks are different than your working hours how?" I arch a brow and dare another look.

This time his sly smile does something to my stomach I don't like… because I really like it. Ugh.

"A rollercoaster," he says finally.

"Huh?"

The smile grows into a grin, and I harden my stare.

"Look at us. We already have a rapport."

My glare becomes a squint. "What are you talking about?"

"I say a word. You say *huh*. Let's try it again. King Chester Chestnut."

"Huh?" Crap. "I mean, excuse me?"

His look of pure triumph is two seconds away from getting covered in a cup of half-eaten yogurt. I ball my fingers into fists to keep from getting fired on my first day. After an agonizing moment of letting his smuggery sink in, he leans forward and braces his forearms on the table.

"The folder you're looking at. It's the planning phase of a cross-promotional venture with an amusement park to sponsor a rollercoaster featuring one of those weird Mer-whatevers. Pretty sure it's some dude named King Chester Chestnut."

Wait. What? On so many levels—*what?*

"How do you know that?" I snap. I'm also praying he's wrong because what the hell?

He shrugs and leans back. "I looked at it before we left for lunch."

"I didn't even see you open your laptop!"

"Okay? Well, I did. I was curious what kind of machine they gave us. Of course, it's a piece of shit. We won't be able to do much with it from a graphics and recording standpoint. I'll bring mine tomorrow."

"Recording standpoint?"

"The song we're going to write to go with the Mer-crap. I didn't see anything about original music but I'm, like, ninety-nine-point-nine percent sure we won't find an existing track to license that's appropriate for this campaign."

"Is that what those undertow lyrics were for?"

His amusement fades, his gaze lowering abruptly. Hmm. Interesting.

"No. That was something else," he mumbles, picking at a scratch in the table.

I shouldn't have mercy on him but those haunted blue eyes suck all remaining snark out of me when they lift hesitantly. Besides, how the heck did he figure the amusement park thing out so quickly? I've been sifting through these files our entire lunch break and still haven't found enough evidence to draw that conclusion.

"So what's a musician doing as a marketing intern at Reedweather Media anyway?" I ask.

He seems to clear the cloud from his head and shrinks back in mock offense. "What makes you think I'm a musician and not a marketing *nut*? Pun intended."

I roll my eyes and focus back on my screen. Anything to keep me from rewarding him with a smile. I open the next file and—oh no. He was right. Grinning back at me is a schematic drawing of what looks like the front car of a rollercoaster. There is definitely a creepy looking Mer-Nut king sketched out in blueprint lines and measurements. Beside the designer's logo is the title "Chester_Chestnut_Car_1 – Rev 1.0."

I think I do a great job pretending I didn't just die a little on the inside.

* * *

I usually take the elevator to my apartment on the fourth floor. Today? Stairs. Hell, I'm not positive I won't turn and march back down them when I reach my floor just so I can stomp back up again. I *hope* I'm disturbing the neighbors. Especially Mrs. Hammond who thinks the entire building wants to hear her rehearse for her imaginary opera debut. Someone needs to tell her she's not a soprano and drawing out vowels does not make a word Italian no matter how hard you roll the Rs.

Val looks up from the small breakfast table by the window when I burst through the door and slam it shut behind me. I'm a tad more gentle with my laptop case and my blazer which happens to be my favorite because of the way it accents my eyes. But everything else in my path, fair game—including my brother who pulls the studio headphones off his ears and loops them around his neck.

"And how was the first day?" he lilts out with faux cheerfulness.

I glare back as his lips twist up in a smirk reminiscent of a certain annoying intern. This deepens my scowl.

"It was glorious, *Perceval*," I say, lashing back with his given name. "How was… whatever it is you do?"

He shakes his head, clearly not up for a fight which disappoints me. I could use a good round of verbal sparring, and there's no one better at it than my younger brother.

"It's called producing."

"Whatever," I mutter, grabbing my water bottle from my bag and joining him at the table.

His recording gear has officially taken over the entire right side of our tiny apartment. I don't know what most of it is, but my talented brother can do a lot with a laptop, guitar, small keyboard, and a handful of electronic box things. He tried explaining it to me once. He never tried again.

"So let me guess, not the corporate utopia you were hoping for?" he says.

I cross my arms and try to block images of schematic drawings of soap dispensers from my mind. "They taught us how to use toilets."

He laughs, thinking I'm joking. His smile fades when he sees I'm not. "I don't understand."

"Exactly."

"But…"

"Exactly. And that's nothing compared to what happened after that. We're being put on the most asinine project you can imagine. Wait. No." I hold up my hand. "You can't imagine it. It's beyond imagination. And the worst part? I have to work on it with this horrible other intern."

I don't like his smile. It doesn't match the appropriate level of indignation he should be displaying on my behalf.

"Horrible, huh. Let me guess, this person isn't up to your unreasonable standard of perfection? You know not everyone is going to be a level-one genius like you, right?"

My glare returns which widens his annoying smile. "Yes, if you must know. He's… Well… no. He's actually… I mean…" Crap. How to explain Nash Ellis?

I study my brother in the filtered light from the window. Dark longish hair, two-day scruff, torn graphic tee that's *supposed* to look like garbage, tattoos every-where… it's the one on his cheek at the corner of his eye that finally made our parents formally disown him. Not kidding, they put it in writing and had it served to him like some weird divorce notice. Our parents are a whole other discussion.

Anyway, all this is to say that my brother is… basically Nash.

My scowl scowls. "Never mind," I mumble.

He lifts a brow, amused. "Hmm. Interesting opinion on the topic."

"I don't *have* an opinion," I snap.

"No? Then that would be the first time ever."

"I hate you."

His irritating grin widens. "Yeah? Is that why you're blushing right now?"

"What?! I am not," I say, crossing my arms.

"No?"

"No! If I'm flushed, it's because of anger."

"At me or him?"

"Both!"

"So you *do* have an opinion on this guy."

I point at him. "I refuse to take your bait. Your opinion on my opinion is irrelevant. Besides, what about you, smartass? I'm guessing your day was all rainbows and sunshine?" Probably not Warp-Wizard-hat rainbows, though. Lucky bastard.

His smile fades as he tugs the ends of his hair like he does when he's distressed. Uh-oh.

"Better to just stick to your day," he grunts.

My mood shifts as I search his face. "What's going on? One of your magic music boxes stopped working?"

His mouth tips up in a weak smile as he shakes his head. "Nah, nothing about that. Just…" He blows out a breath at my stern look. "Mom and Dad are on my case again."

My fist tightens around my water bottle. "What happened this time?"

He averts his gaze and reaches for his headphones with a shrug.

"No way," I warn, staring him down. "Talk."

God, I hate our parents. How can they not see how amazing and talented their son is? Their life-box is so freaking small and restrictive.

He releases a long exhale and swipes his phone off the table. After scrolling through it, he pushes it toward me. My stomach tightens as I pick it up and focus on the screen.

"You have to be kidding me," I mutter. Have I mentioned I hate our parents?

I look back up, my heart breaking at the expression on his face. He shrugs again but I see the pain in his eyes.

"They're demanding repayment for your one semester at Yorkshire?" I ask in disbelief. I knew our parents were bitter that he didn't submit to their chosen path, but this is downright vindictive. Borderline ruthless.

Wait, now that I think about it, Dad *did* wear that eyepatch after his laser surgery. And didn't Mom buy a matching outfit for Polly, her precious Maltese so they could sit maniacally on the "nice" chaise for the Christmas card photo?

O.

M.

G.

Our parents *are* ruthless.

"They're saying it was a loan and they're calling it due. I have two months to pay it back or they'll sue."

I don't even know what to say as blood boils inside me. "How the hell are you supposed to come up with that kind of money in two months?"

"They know I can't. This isn't about the money," he says quietly. "You know that."

I shake my head, refusing to believe even they could be so cruel. And this is a brain that's accepted Mer-Nuts are a thing.

"They're monsters, Val. You get that, right? This is a reflection on *them*, not you."

His gaze drifts to mine before he lowers it again. "I mean, it's just thirty grand. No big deal, right?" He huffs a dry laugh as he grabs the headphones and readjusts them in place. I let him go this time, watching for anything else in his body language I should be worried about.

Val Andrews is the sweetest, smartest, most driven person I know. So what if he doesn't want to devote his life to the family empire like the rest of us. It doesn't take a PhD to see he's not wired for KPI Reports and… whatever Reedweather Media is turning out to be. Believe me, corporate America can only handle one angsty musician, and right now that slot seems to be filled by Nash Ellis.

Rhonda and Burt Andrews are on notice. You mess with my brother, you mess with me.

"We're going to figure this out," I say in my stern big-sister voice. "They do *not* get to dictate our lives anymore."

My brother looks up with those big brown eyes I vowed to protect with my life since they made his a living hell.

By the power vested in me by the Mer-Nut state of Macadamia, I hereby declare:

Game. On.

3—PIVOTING

NASH

I look up from my guitar at the clatter of the front door. Marcos shoves it open, his face spreading into radiant glee when he spots me on the couch.

"You? Are a dick," I say, pointing at my roommate as he kicks the door closed behind him.

"That's no way to thank your best friend for getting you a job," he teases.

I've never gone to blows with *my best friend*, but there's a first time for everything. My fingers clench around the neck of the guitar to be safe.

I've been playing and writing since the second I got home in an effort to cleanse my head of today's nightmare, so far to no avail. I don't think there's enough music in the world to appease the corporate Cerberus that is Chad Smith, Reed Reedweather, and Paige Andrews. Somewhere that ancient Greek hellhound is merrily tormenting the eternal souls of vanquished interns.

There's *maybe* a twenty percent chance I go back tomorrow.

"You didn't get me a job. You sent me through a wormhole to Hell," I say, strumming through the progression I've been working on. Even that cool variation on the 6 isn't cutting it tonight. I play through the minor chord a few more times, hoping there's magic in repetition. Nope. Still can't erase images of swimming tree nuts.

Marcos snickers and drops to our armless armchair.

"You must have met *Chad*," he says. "He was my intern opponent when I was there. Who'd you get?"

My gaze snaps to him in surprise. "Wait. Chad Smith?"

He nods.

"That's my boss."

Marcos' eyes widen three sizes as his jaw drops. "No…" he whispers. He shakes his head as if he just lost the ability to comprehend words. That is, until he abruptly awakens all sleeping hellhounds with a burst of exuberant laughter. I've heard the word "chortle" before but never witnessed it until this moment.

"No… no way," he gasps out. Yep, he's legit laugh-crying. "I'm sorry, man— just… one sec." He wipes his eyes, trying to catch his breath. "Oh my god. Does Eva know?"

"As in your girlfriend Eva who got me this job in the first place?"

He nods again.

"I don't know, Marcos. *Does* she?" I clip out, returning to my music. Seems like something he would know. Probably *did* know when he hooked me up. I'm not buying any of this ignorance bullshit. Or a birthday present for him next month.

"Dude, I'm sorry," he says, clearly trying to regain control. "I shouldn't have laughed. I mean, having Chad as a boss… I can't even… wait, is he still obsessed with nuts?"

I look over in surprise. "When you say nuts…"

"As in, actual nuts. When I was there he based his entire creative campaign around edible nuts. The dude was obsessed."

I let out a breath, shaking my head. "Great. So, want to explain to me what the hell a Mer-Nut is?"

Wrong question.

Marcos loses his shit again, and I roll my eyes through another round of hilarity as I wait for my best friend to finish relishing in my misery.

"Wait… you're…" He coughs and wipes his eyes again. "You're telling me that stupid Mer-Nut campaign got greenlighted?"

My sardonic look tells him exactly that apparently, and he blows out a shaky exhale. "Shit, Nash. I swear, I had no idea Chad was going to be your boss. I just assumed it would be Eva like when I worked there."

"Well, guess what. It's not," I say dryly.

Marcos is obviously trying to suppress his amusement. It does nothing to mitigate the situation.

"Who's the other intern? Are they cool at least?"

I legit grunt as I start through the verse chords again. "Nope. Try a smarter, cuter version of Chad. So yeah, I guess the female equivalent of you."

I sense his attention and look over to find a disturbing grin on my roommate's face. Clearly, he heard something different than what I said.

"What?" I ask.

He shrugs with an even wider smile, and my eyes narrow. "Nothing. Just, you kind of love me, so by the transitive property, that would mean you love her."

I don't know why I even asked. There wasn't going to be an answer I would have liked.

"Um. No. Check your math. This girl is all the things I *don't* like about you."

Why is he still grinning like he knows something I don't?

"Okay," he says.

I arch a brow. "Okay?"

He shrugs. "Whatever you say."

I huff and turn back to my strings. Doesn't he have important business shit to do? "I'm serious, dude. It goes both ways, trust me. Hell would freeze over before that woman would give me a second look. *I'm* everything she hates about everything."

"You know what they say about opposites."

"They end up killing each other? Wait, what are you doing?" I ask when he pulls out his phone.

"Texting Eva to find out what the hell is going on."

"About Paige?" I ask in alarm.

Marcos crosses a triumphant look to me. "Paige, huh? So our corporate siren has a name."

I make the executive decision to change the title of this song to "Ode to Roommates Thrown Out of Windows."

"You're ridiculous," I mutter.

He snickers and settles back in his chair. "Speaking of ridiculous, did you meet Reed Reedweather yet? He try to get you to smoke a cigar and drink scotch at his desk?"

My gaze shoots to him again and maybe the slightest hint of a smile threatens my dark mood. That question shouldn't have made any sense to me, and yet strangely, none of those words came as a surprise.

"No, but I might have convinced him to get his eyebrow pierced."

Marcos smirks. "At least he can probably pronounce your name. Nash is pretty hard to screw up. He could never get mine down. Still hasn't, even though I've been dating his daughter for over a month now."

"Oh, you mean, Nash. El. Is? I keep picturing seashells every time he says my name for some reason."

His eyes widen again, and yep. Cue the obnoxious merriment.

"Have I mentioned I hate you?" I mumble, turning away to pick through a lead line I'm thinking about for the intro. I'm definitely not asking him about the "bike boy" thing.

"Oh hey," he interrupts a few seconds later. "Good news. Eva says not to worry. They're pivoting tomorrow."

I narrow my eyes at him. "Pivoting? What's that? It doesn't sound good."

He grins. "It is. Unless you were really looking forward to immersing yourself in Mer-Nuts for the next two months."

* * *

Lottery players everywhere, take note. I *did* show up the next day. Mostly because Marcos told me he'd kick my ass if I embarrassed his girlfriend by quitting on day one and Nate said he'd join him because I'm already three months behind on my portion of the bills.

Besides, I'm dying to know what "pivoting" is.

It doesn't take long to find out when I approach my workspace and see Paige seated at her side of our conjoined desks with a stiff back and a grave expression. I'm thinking she just found a crease her iron missed, until I hear the heated voices coming from Chad's office.

"They're mine! I trained them!" he hisses.

"They're not *yours*. This isn't a dodgeball team," Eva replies in a bored tone. "Besides, you wasted an entire morning teaching MBA grads how to use a toilet."

"It was one chapter!"

"No one over the age of three should need any training on flushing, Chad."

"Well, it makes that loud noise and can splash on your pants if you're not careful!"

"None of that changes my previous statement. Also, you can stop yelling."

"Besides, pretty sure that Nash guy isn't MBA material," Chad grunts.

I'm strangely flattered by that.

"Yeah? *Pretty sure* he's still qualified to use a toilet."

"I'm going straight to Reedweather."

"Please do. Actually, while you're there, let him know I finally got the budget from Sandeke Telecom and I'll be pulling Nash and Paige off the Mer-Nut campaign to put them on the band partnership project."

Band partnership? Okay, now she has my attention.

"This isn't right! You know how hard I worked on that proposal. It's what got me this job!"

"Yeah, I wouldn't brag about that if I were you."

Two seconds later, Chad huffs away from his own office, his light blue polo shirt flapping in the wind as he storms by. I noticed yesterday how the sleeves of his shirts seem unusually wide while the waist is unusually tight. It's like he asked the tailor to make his clothes fit as awkwardly as possible.

Paige and I watch him disappear toward the bathrooms he so loves before turning back to find Eva hovering in front of us. Her gaze passes over me briefly in recognition before she resumes her professional demeanor. You'd never know I just saw her in her sweats making out with my roommate three days ago. Marcos always says she's a badass in the office, so I'm not surprised. Paige looks like she's ready to make out with her as well.

Wait.

I shake my head to force away the inappropriate image.

Well, maybe just tuck it away for later.

"Nash?"

I blink up at Eva who's giving me an impatient look. Paige is looking plenty glib with her laptop and weird binder clenched under her arm.

"You coming?"

"Oh. Right." I push my chair back and get up as well.

Eva hesitates when I start toward them and directs her gaze to my desk in an obvious message. Shit, my laptop. I pull it from the charger and then grab the handle of my messenger bag that has my personal computer. Eva looks surprised that I have anything besides that one broken pen I brought yesterday. She clearly doesn't understand what I'm willing to do for top-of-the-line recording equipment.

"This way, please," she says, waving us behind her.

We follow her through the maze of cubicles and desks, past the Accounting Department, through the Copy Department, and around some dude who definitely just minimized an active game of solitaire. I can't tell which department he is because he doesn't have a smarmy "World's Best *Whatever*" mug on his desk identifying it.

We finally reach another office similar to Chad's, and she motions us inside. After closing the door, she waves us toward a table by the wall. We've just taken our seats when we're interrupted by a loud knock.

"Excuse me," she says, crossing back to answer the door.

I've never seen a human deflate the way this one does when she pulls the handle.

"Eva," a familiar voice says in a low, solemn tone. "May we join you?"

She sighs and steps back, and even Paige frowns when Mr. Reedweather and Chad enter the office like we've been impatiently awaiting their arrival.

"I brought Chad up-to-speed on the Redwood campaign, so he's ready to take point on that."

Redwood campaign? Is that in the "band" or "nut" category? Could go either way.

Eva pales, her gaze settling on the two men in what I can only describe as alarm.

"Actually, I was thinking it'd be best if Chad focused on his… Mer-Nuts… while Nash and Paige worked on the band partnership campaign. And remember, we're not calling it the Redburn campaign. This has nothing to do with them."

Redburn? What the…? Now I'm *really* confused and glance around for hidden cameras. Do they know I'm buying Redburn's equipment? Wait. I vaguely remember something about this from a few weeks ago when Marcos and Eva were pestering me to hook them up with my friends Abram and Kaitlyn. It had something to do with…

Fu-uck.

Corporate espionage!

Please tell me that shit isn't still going on and that's why I'm here. If these people think I'm using my connections to help them be cheating douchebags, they're in for a rude awakening. When Eva crosses her gaze to me, my heart rate picks up. Marcos is so getting a pop in the jaw tonight. Wait, um, a kick to the groin. Much safer for my hands.

"Right, right. Of course," Reedweather says, waving her off. He starts toward the table and pulls out a chair. "Except not, because I want him on this project instead."

Chad shoots his hand in the air, and I think he's swatting an invisible wasp until Reedweather points at him. "Yes, my boy?"

"We could combine both into one super campaign!"

All life drains from Eva's body. "I don't think—"

"Well! What a fantastic idea," Reedweather says. "Such an excellent example of *Fused Amalgamating*, as they say."

Fused Amalgamating? Whoever "they" are shouldn't be in charge of saying things. In related news, Eva seems to have less enthusiasm for amalgamating when it involves fictional ocean communities.

Her gaze crashes into mine, pleading, but I'm not sure what she wants me to do. Trust me, her boyfriend's strategic business genius did not rub off on me. I rock spreadsheets and reports about as well as Marcos adjusts the EQ on a keyboard plugin. To clarify, that's a step above "I don't even know what that means."

But she's persistent, and despite previous grumbling, I happen to kind of love her boyfriend like a brother, so…

"Can Mer-Nuts sing and play instruments?" I ask. "I mean, there's the terrible underwater acoustics issue and… lack… of… arms," I explain when Eva's eyes widen in silent reproach.

I shrug. Seem like valid arguments to me. *Are* there rules for Mer-Nut debates? Chad and Reedweather must agree when the excitement leeches from their faces.

"Excellent point, my young friend," Reedweather says in a grave tone. "Perhaps—"

"Whales sing!" Chad interrupts. "Dolphins too!"

"Do they, though?" I ask, tilting my head.

"Yes! They do that sonar whining thing!" He shoots a look to Reedweather, who nods with all the confidence of the marine biologist he clearly is.

"So… we're thinking the way to sell our internet service is through blasting consumers with… sonar whining?" Paige asks slowly.

Her gaze brushes mine with a flash of understanding and possibly… encouragement? Hang on, are we actually vibing right now? Also, how is that scenario harder for me to accept than singing Mer-Nuts?

Two days in, and this place has already effed me up beyond repair.

"Another excellent point, my dear," Reedweather muses, even adding a dramatic chin stroke. I don't miss how Paige tenses at the patronizing address. It kind of makes me want to stroke our boss' chin with my fist on her behalf.

Because that's not patronizing.

Whatever. I'd do it anyway.

"Paige is right," I say. "I've been a musician most of my life, and I'm almost positive the market for sonar whining is non-existent outside of the marine wildlife community."

Chad perks up. "We could—"

"No," Eva snaps, staring him down. "We are not recognizing marine biologists as a consumer subset just so swimming peanuts get their day in the sun."

"They'd die in the sun," Chad mumbles, glowering at the floor.

Reedweather smacks his palms on the table, drawing this unnecessary argument to a long-overdue end. "Great! Then it's settled. Best of luck to you all!" He offers a broad, encouraging grin before pushing up from his chair and crossing to the door. "My dream team," he adds, twisting on his heels to finger-gun each of us.

Hold up. Is *that* pivoting? Can't be…

Business shit is so confusing.

4—SMOLDERING

PAIGE

His leg keeps brushing mine. His arm too as our chairs inch closer and closer for some reason. He also taps a pen on his full lower lip when he's thinking which may or may not be kind of hot. Okay, *very* hot because it turns out Nash is as intelligent and gifted as I suspected. Just, not in a way that was remotely helpful until now.

I could kick some universe ass for miring us in the *one* project that requires all of his expertise and none of mine. How the hell am I sitting at a particle board desk watching *this* guy own the planning meeting? The worst part, every annoying thing about him is turning me on. I clamp my legs together like that's suddenly going to make him not smell like a sexy temperate rainforest and look like the freaking Greek god of irresistible bad boys. He's even wearing a tighter t-shirt today, and let's just say his previous plaid button-down wasn't because he had anything to hide. The boy is… achingly beautiful. Also, exasperating. Exasperatingly beautiful.

"For the hundredth time, Tek Tonik is not an option," he says, rubbing at his eyes in frustration. I've seen a lot of that too. It's a known symptom of working in close proximity with Chad Smith.

"They'd be perfect for this," Chad continues, completely ignoring any voice that isn't his. "Huge name, international appeal—"

"We don't even offer this service internationally. Warp Speed is only available in U.S. metropolitan regions," I point out, if only to keep the two men from going to blows. I don't think my girl parts could handle watching Nash dominate in a street fight right now. Unless… would he take his shirt off to fight? Strictly a logistical consideration.

"And Tek Tonik is not a *band*," Nash repeats for what I count as… yep, he's right. The hundredth time.

"So how were they playing my cousin's wedding?"

Does incompetence explode brain cells? We're about to find out as I hold in my snort while Nash holds in his desire to punch our boss. I reach over and place a soothing hand on his knee before he ends up in jail. Except… crap.

Nash flinches at the contact, his gaze shooting to mine in surprise. Sparks rip through me when his frustration morphs into a different kind of heat. The way he shifts closer makes it clear he felt that surge of electricity too. That he *enjoyed* it. The side of his thigh is now completely fused to mine, triggering invisible, forbidden currents neither of us seem urgent to tame. I pull my hand away with a protective eye-roll, but the haughty smile lingers on his lips.

Fine. You're freaking gorgeous. Can we move on?

"I guarantee he wasn't playing your cousin's wedding," Nash says to Chad, while still looking at me. *Probing* me. Exploring and daring me to… what? Smack him? Sure. I'm game.

Focus, Paige.

But now my blood seems to think a corporate office is the appropriate place to throb in inconvenient body parts. Where is his pooling right now? He taps his pen as his gaze drops to my chest which means… he's concentrating. Hard.

Gah!

"I have video!" Chad argues, drawing us back to reality. Thank the heavens for Chad.

(Well, *there's* a phrase for the record book of firsts.)

Nash finally seems to refocus as well and directs his attention to safer targets. "I don't doubt you have video of a wedding cover band playing some of Tek

Tonik's catalog. He's an elite producer and DJ with credits on half the dance tracks blowing up the clubs right now. But I'm telling you, your friend *Kyle* is not going to *hook us up* with a dude who could build a house out of his platinum records."

"Cousin," Chad mumbles. "Kyle is my *cousin*."

Nash releases a long exhale and scrubs at his eyes again. "Okay, look. We've already wasted an hour on this. If Sandeke Telecom wants a top-level name for a promotional partnership, we need to stick to mainstream artists who hit the same demographics we're targeting. They also have to be willing to sell out." He casts a hard look at Chad. "That means no fringe genres, no social activists, and definitely no international producers."

"What about Jarvis McKinnley?" I say.

Nash glances over with an expression similar to the previous one he blasted my way. The one I need him *not* to blast my way if I have any hope of staying focused.

"Larinda Scott's ex?" he says to himself. "That's genius."

His blue eyes flash with respect when they settle on me.

I manage to compact my giant grin into a casual smile and even add an indifferent shrug like a badass. "Brighthouse is our biggest competitor, right? If they're partnering with Larinda, who better for us to team up with than her ex?"

"It would be a two-tiered warzone," Nash says, waking up his laptop. It must be his personal one because the background is some dark artsy goth-looking thing with illegible script littered throughout an intricate, morbid design. My Sandeke one is blue.

But the program he fires up is not for spreadsheets or word-processing. It's for… I have no clue. It looks like something I've seen my brother use.

"What are you doing?" Chad and I ask simultaneously.

I cringe, doubly annoyed by the delight on Nash's face when it angles toward me. There's nothing I like about the fact that Chad and I shared a brain for three seconds.

"It's recording software," he says, focusing back on his screen. I'm surprised he let me off the hook so easily, and I find the tiniest part of my conscience switching sides on the Nash Ellis is an Asshole Debate.

Chad's brow scrunches as he leans in from the other direction to stare at the screen. "What software are you recording?"

"Huh?"

Chad waves at the screen. "You said you're recording software. Looks like squiggly lines?"

Nash's mouth opens to respond, then closes again. I see the moment his brain gives up.

"Yes," he says dryly. "That is what it is. It's a squiggly line recorder." He turns back to the screen, his jaw ticking so slightly I have no doubt Chad missed it. In fact, our boss looks pretty damn triumphant over there basking in his masterful computer sleuthing skills.

In real work news, Nash has now opened up several rows of "squiggly lines" and is pulling a small hard box from his laptop bag.

"Hearing aids," Chad explains to me when Nash opens the case. Does it even count as mansplaining when it's so blatantly wrong?

Nash fires another annoyed look at Chad and shakes his head in irritation. "Custom IEMs," he corrects, pulling out the clear earpieces and unwinding the cord. I've definitely seen my brother with those. In-ear monitors or "ears" as he calls them, and he treats them like crown jewels. I touched them once just to see if I'd be transported to some mythical land.

"For hearing, though, right?" Chad asks.

"Hearing music, yes."

"So..."

Nash doesn't engage in the pointless debate and shoves the silver cable into the headphone jack on his laptop. He fits the clear earpieces into his ears and zeroes in on the screen like he's immediately forgotten he's in an office and other people exist.

Within seconds he's a different person.

And his face…

I recognize that look well, the bliss of an artist engaged in the one thing they live for. I've grown up watching my brother's face ignite like that in a way nothing else could replicate. Except, Nash getting lost in his art has a different effect on me. It's mesmerizing how his hands work the track pad in a smooth symphony with the rest of his senses. Touch, sound, sight, his entire essence is wrapped up in whatever he's doing, and suddenly I see him in a different way than I did just an hour ago, a minute ago. Is this what I look like when I'm developing a marketing campaign, or when I'm brainstorming solutions to a problem?

If so, I look… profound. Fascinating.

Whole.

And there's something else. Something older and darker that filters to the surface the longer I watch him. A shadowed history that breathes words like, *"Let the waves of darkness break, and take, the pain below, purged by the undertow…"*

I study the tattoos on his right arm, noticing the unsettling images for the first time. There's a macabre beauty to the art. Dark and light twisting in a harmony of warring stories. Who is he? What brought him here? If it's anything like the hard path that formed my brother, he's probably bursting with surprises. In fact, somehow I *know* he is.

Maybe I was wrong about him. Maybe—

He straightens abruptly and rips the right earpiece out.

"This is going to take me a while if you two want to work on the boring business shit."

Have I mentioned how much I hate Nash Ellis?

* * *

I practiced my tirade. Scripted it out and edited it to perfection like everything I do. I even took a bathroom break halfway through my torture session with Chad to dry run the appropriate facial expression for its delivery: part irritation, but not full-blown anger. Nash can't know how furious I am that he's stolen this project and relegated me to… Chad-level.

But the second I return to our desks and collide with rapturous blue eyes, I forget all about my expertly honed fury. His smile alone makes me take the earbud he hands me (not a custom one this time because *apparently* he's considerate enough to realize that wouldn't have worked for my ears. Zero points for that.)

(*Fine.* One point.)

I shove it in and give him an impatient look.

He made you spend two hours with Chad and argue about global crises like which shade of magenta makes the best font for a slide presentation. Answer? None. Fonts should never be magenta.

"Wait, what is this?" I ask several seconds into his creation. I try for casual, but there's a hint of awe in my voice. Of course he picks up on it, and his smile lifts.

"Our campaign pitch. Four of Jarvis McKinnley's hits mashed up and remixed into a full-length radio release. It's just a rough idea, of course. Our real version will be better. We do a video trailer with the research data and talking points woven into sequential scenes of millennials being cool and doing cool shit non-millennials wish they were doing. That way we can pair the strategic plan directly with an emotional experience that's much more likely to have an impact. I've never met the guy, but I have a feeling Jarvis will be swayed by pretty pictures more than bar graphs."

I open my mouth to respond but… "So… not a slide deck?"

"A what?"

I release the annoyed look I've been hoarding. "A slide presentation. How we're *supposed* to pitch a campaign."

He makes a face. "Really? Sounds kinda basic, no?"

"It—"

I stop myself. Holy shit. This song-mash-up-whatever is good. *Really* good. And combined with a surprise video trailer?

Geez. And he did this in a couple of hours under the influence of a boss whose greatest achievement was inventing a fictitious species that never should have been invented?

I shake my head, staring at his screen as the song comes to a shiver-inducing end. Wow, I do *not* want to hear any of his original music. (I do.)

A lot.

Double shit.

"Hmm. Interesting idea," I say, pulling out the earbud.

His face falls, and *maybe* I feel badly for downplaying his genius. But then I remember I just sat through a fifteen-minute explanation of why boiling eggs for egg salad is different than boiling eggs for other things. I didn't even know there were so many reasons to boil eggs.

"You don't like it?" he asks, a flicker of doubt in his eyes.

I'm surprised by the flash of insecurity. I guess I thought… I don't know. Cocky musician? Self-assured artist?

Your brother is neither of those things.

I search Nash's face, finding neither of them in him right now either. Well, that's annoying.

With a sigh, I hand his earbud back to him. "I love it. It's really good. And it could be interesting to pitch a trailer instead of a slide presentation." I cast a dramatic look toward Chad's office door. "We'd just have to clear it with *him*."

Nash smirks. "If you're on board, leave that part to me."

* * *

It seemed like a good idea. A no-brainer. Nash wanted to work on his mashup which is now going to be a full remix. Except his "midi controller" is busted, whatever that is. Also, something with a speaker. Or was it a monitor? Is there a difference?

Regardless, I texted Val who said he has all of… *it*… and we're welcome to use his gear. This led to a remote bromance with me in the middle transferring musician lingo from my coworker to my brother via my fingers and phone. I typed at least a thousand words and I only recognized half of them. In the end, it made way more sense for Nash to come over tonight and work with Val and his equipment here.

What I hadn't anticipated was the effect of watching my brother come alive in the presence of someone who shared his passion and spoke his language fluently. For the record, I did *not* almost tear up when Nash made Val's face glow with long overdue praise for his talent. It was just a stray eyelash. Probably.

"Dude, that's sick. Where'd you get it?" Nash asks several minutes into our "work" session that has yet to involve any work. He hands the studio headphones back to Val, whose eyes light up with excitement.

"It's this guy who makes his own plugins. All original stuff you can't get anywhere else. You should see the library of Arp effects."

"Are they expensive?"

"Not too bad. Not as much as the Remotescapes stuff."

Nash grunts. "I just spent two hundred bucks on a cello plugin and you can't even adjust the cutoff."

"Oh shit. Have you tried the—"

"Um, hello?" I interrupt, waving at them. "I'm still here. Can you guys share recipes later? We've already wasted a half hour."

Val shoots me an irritated look, and I widen my eyes right back at him. We're here for a reason, and I don't need to be near Nash any longer than necessary tonight. I already have to endure him all day. His gaze lifts and grazes mine in amusement. So glad my impatience entertains him. You know what would entertain *me*? Working.

"The boss has spoken," Val mutters. He holds up the cable for the big desk speakers and waves toward Nash's laptop. "You can use my monitors so both of you can hear what you're working on."

"Thanks, man. Really appreciate this," Nash says, settling into the chair Val just vacated.

"No problem."

"Hey, maybe we could collaborate sometime," Nash says.

"Yeah? Okay, sweet." My brother is beaming again as he leaves the kitchen to head toward his bedroom. *Beaming.*

But any gratitude for my coworker dissolves when I look back to meet his entertained face.

"How is that your brother?" he asks.

"What do you mean?"

"He's actually pretty cool."

I glare at him, yanking another chair from the table as his lips tip up in an amused smile. Damn, he's cute. And so freaking annoying.

I park the chair beside him and offer the most impatient expression I can muster. "You have your precious mini controller now. We going to work or what?"

His lips lift even more as he studies me in that irritating way of his, like he's the only one in on some hilarious joke in his head. A head which is currently covered in a black beanie, I might add. It's May. Who wears a hat in May? Just because it makes the ends of your dark hair curl up beneath it in a (very) flattering way does not make it appropriate seasonal wear.

Now I'm even mad at his hat?

There's no way we both survive this internship.

"Sure. But it's a *midi* controller," he says.

"Same thing," I say, waving him off. "Wait, that's just a piano keyboard thing."

"Yeah. Also called a midi controller."

"What does it do?"

"Controls midi."

I squint at him, and his smile grows.

"Smartass."

"Come here. I'll show you," he says, relaxing into his chair. He turns on the speakers—sorry, *monitors*—and I inch my own chair toward him so I can see the screen. Maybe a little too close because soon I'm in direct scent and body heat range. He must feel the effect as well when that smile returns and he settles even closer.

I pretend not to notice the distracting sensation of his firm thigh against mine.

"This thing actually doesn't make any sounds," he says, pressing on some of the keys of the keyboard that's not a keyboard. "It's just triggering software in the computer to make the sounds."

"So you're not actually playing, just… programming?"

His smile this time isn't smug. It's genuine, and it turns out I like that one quite a bit. "Yes, exactly. I mean, I'm still playing the root of a melody, but then I can apply any sound I want to it. A piano, a violin, percussion, synth sound, what-ever you want. Each row here is a different track with different notes and sounds, and once you layer them on top of each other, you start assembling your masterpiece."

"Wait." I squint at the collage of minuscule rectangles. "So essentially, you're converting music into data points. In theory, you could copy and paste the same thing over and over without having to play it again, right?"

His genuine smile becomes a genuine grin and… whoa. That's a thing I'm having trouble being mad at.

"Yes. In fact, you can even move the notes around in the program and make them different notes if you want to alter the melody. The midi controller is basi-cally just another fancy computer accessory like your mouse or, well, the other kind of keyboard."

"So is that what you'll do with Jarvis McKinnley's songs?"

"Not exactly. I won't be altering any of the original tracks, just cutting them and adding to it. So really—" He's interrupted by his phone and sighs when he reads the display. "Hang on," he says to me. Rude? Sure. Also a relief because I was starting to forget he's a rude, obnoxious slacker.

"Yeah, what's up?" is his cultured greeting. "I'm working." His brow furrows at the response. "Hilarious. I'm serious. I'm doing actual legit work for my legit job. A job *you* made me take… Right now? We're kind of… No, I know, but why would she need to talk to *me*?"

He groans and leans back in his chair, pressing a fist to his forehead. "Fine. Okay, but… I said *fine*. Be there in a half hour… I'm across town, dude. What do you want me to do? Just… thirty minutes, okay?"

I'm good at pretending. I think I do a great job of pretending I'm not disappointed when he hangs up and says he has to go.

5—RECRUITING

NASH

My roommate Marcos is intelligent. Like, ridiculously so. Full-ride to pretentious schools and top-honors-level intelligent.

Or so I thought, because suddenly he doesn't understand basic human words like:

I.

Don't.

Want.

Any.

Part.

Of.

Your.

Spy.

Shit.

"At least think about it," Marcos says, pretty much begging at this point. Typically, I'm the one begging so this reversal is a fun twist and the only reason I'm still sitting here.

See, just because he and his girlfriend lived out some kinky corporate espionage fantasy a few weeks ago, doesn't mean the rest of us want to sneak around collecting boring documents no one wants to read even in non-spy format.

"We're not asking you to do anything different than what you're doing now," Marcos argues in yet another attempt to dispute my opinion that he's smart.

I cross my arms and lean back against the armless armchair. "Uh, last I checked, pretending to work for Larinda Scott, while really working for Sandeke Telecom, while really working for *you* is not what I was doing this morning. I'd rather play with Mer-Acorns."

Are acorns nuts?

I pull out my phone to check while Marcos and Eva bore their gazes into me like they can telepathically convince me this isn't a terrible idea.

"Denver Sandeke wants to send in a spy to cheat, yet again, and we need it to be someone we trust," Eva says. "Someone who will help us sabotage *both* exploitative, duplicitous companies."

"And that person you 'trust' is *me*?" Yeah, I need to seriously reconsider my generous assessment of my best friend's girlfriend as well.

"Nash, come on!" Marcos says. "You were tailor-made for this. Who better to pose as an industry professional than the one person in our inner circle who is actually an industry professional? Plus, you know pretty much everyone. This will be cake for you."

I grunt and cross my arms. "The last time you said that I ended up locked in a conference room being forced to think things like, *what would a Mer-Nut eat?*"

Even Mr. Serious can't stop the corner of his mouth from ticking up as he cocks his head. "That's actually a great question. What *would* a Mer-Nut eat?"

Eva smacks his chest, and he forces away his smile when her eyes narrow at him.

"Brighthouse stole this idea from us by also cheating," Eva says, clearly not interested in Mer-Diets. Her loss. "We have a chance to find out what Bright-house is doing, while also thwarting Sandeke Telecom who think they're gaining another unfair advantage over their competition. This is the perfect opportunity to pit two behemoths against each other in another step toward mutual destruction."

Hmm. This is starting to become less spy and more superhero. Strangely, that development is warming me to the idea. In this scenario, I'd be "Bike Boy," of course.

"What's so funny?" Marcos asks. His *begging face* is back to *irritated face*.

"Nothing. Are acorns nuts?"

His *irritated face* is now *exasperated face*. My work here is done.

I push up from the chair.

"I'll loan you the money for that sound mixing board or whatever," Marcos blurts out.

I freeze, turning slowly to face my roommate. His gaze locks on mine, blue-green eyes pleading with the force of a brother who's earned a lifetime of favors. This is really that important to him?

And suddenly, I'm back in the rec room of the Bellevue Group Home for Boys, shaking and terrified as only one person stands between me and the bullies who decided early on I was the weakest link. The one person who claimed me as family when no one else on this planet would. I don't owe Marcos a favor. I owe him my life.

With a heavy sigh, I drop back to the chair and lean forward. "Fine. I'll do it. But I want a cool spy name."

* * *

See, this is the problem with agreeing to help your roommate end corporate tyranny. They seduce you with rainbow promises of changing the world and then inform you that Denver Sandeke is insisting that the Reedweather spy take cover by "getting fired" so no one from Brighthouse will connect them to Sandeke Telecom. Oh, and it has to look real so no one at Reedweather Media will question their sudden absence either. According to Eva, I'm the ideal choice for *that* reason as well since, and I quote, "of all the current Reedweather Media employees, you've made the least impact and will be the least missed."

I'd love to see that on a motivational poster.

Failure: Because sometimes being a zero makes you a hero.

Problem is, for this *one* project, they actually do need my useless, incompetent ass, so I'm still expected to execute our own version of the band sponsorship thing by continuing the Jarvis McKinnley campaign off-hours. Yep, now I get to work *two* jobs I don't want, while being publicly branded "unqualified to flush toilets and operate soap dispensers" or whatever it is the Reedweather Media interns actually do. Just the thought of Paige's gloating face when she finds out I've been fired is enough to make my eye twitch.

"How is this even going to work?" I mutter to Eva as we sit in her office the following morning so she can "terminate" me. (For the record, I perked up at the idea of being *terminated* instead of fired. That's at least badass superhero lingo.) "Won't it be obvious I'm still around when the Jarvis McKinnley campaign actually gets done?"

"No, because you're going to be an unnamed consultant who will funnel everything through me. I'll in turn pass it on to Paige, who will be the face of the campaign."

I stiffen and laser a stare at her. "Hang on. You want *me* to do the work and then hand it over to Paige to get the credit?"

Eva shrugs. "Basically."

"Will she *know* I'm the one doing the work?"

"Of course not."

"Eva."

"Nash."

She waits with the poise of a less important politician standing behind the important one at a press conference. There will be no negotiating on this.

I groan and lean my head on the backrest of the chair. Staring at the ceiling, I try to think of anything worse than this scenario.

"Also, Chad will be your contact for the Brighthouse espionage portion."

That'll do.

"I'm sorry, what?" I say, straightening to look at her again.

"Chad will be the person handling the information you gather from Brighthouse and passing it along to the Sandeke powers that be."

"Chad Smith," I repeat. I mean, there are other Chads in the world, right?

"Correct."

"Is my handler." And other possible spy tasks. Someone has to get coffee and procure spy paraphernalia like those umbrella guns.

"That's a bit dramatic, but sure. If you want to play pretend James Bond, he will be your handler."

"How, though?" I groan. "In what universe is Chad Smith the answer to any question that isn't, *who do we* not *want running this project*? And you're the one who used the word *handle*," I mutter, now pissed at everything, including words.

Her exasperated sigh is oddly reminiscent of Marcos'. Is that a couples thing like ending up with the same hairstyle and preferred candle scent? In related news, I'm single and never dated anyone seriously, so I don't actually know about "couples things."

"I get he's not the ideal choice," Eva says, drawing me back to the world's worst intelligence briefing. "But my father loves him, and that's enough for Denver Sandeke who really doesn't want any involvement in this except a pat on the back for his genius."

"So let me get this straight. Chad is my partner, Paige gets the glory, and *I'm* the one who has to deal with the bullshit from *both* sides of this circus?"

"Pretty much."

"I hate you and Marcos. You know that, right?"

"Yep. And you also love him, so suck it up and go kick some spy ass, James Bond."

I'll be kicking *somebody's* ass.

Also, I'm Bike Boy, not James Bond.

* * *

I plaster my best I-just-got-terminated look on my face as I return to my desk. Halfway there, I remember to switch my smile to a frown because most people think getting fired is a bad thing.

"You okay?" Paige asks, tilting her head in what could arguably be concern. Or maybe anticipation. Pretty sure she didn't expect me to last as long as I did. It would blow her mind to know I was chosen for something over her, even if *technically* it's because I'm the worst at that thing.

"Not really," I say. "I just got—"

"Yo, Ellis. You ready to go undercover and take those Brighthouse fuckers down?"

Wow.

Paige's eyes narrow in confusion as Chad lifts his fist for what I'm assuming is the customary spy/handler fist bump.

"Undercover?" Paige asks.

"Shh!" I hiss at Chad.

"What's going on?" she says, directing her hazel gaze at me. I shudder at what that look would do to me if I actually liked her. Which I don't. At all.

I blink to clear my head and fire a glare at Chad once I remember we're now super-secret spies and he blew our cover literally twelve seconds in.

"Nothing. Just…" Shit.

Chad widens his eyes and covers his mouth in another unhelpful spy reaction. Man, I'd love to play poker with this dude. He probably sends screenshots of his cards every round.

Paige looks testy when I turn back to her. Love her or hate her, the woman is razor sharp. Hell, she probably would've figured this weak plot out in an hour anyway. And suddenly…

No, Nash. You're not seriously considering this.

My eyes drift to Chad, who I'm not entirely convinced knows what a spy actually does. Back to Paige who would have a plan mapped out, indexed, and filed in the time it'd take Chad to find his way out of a bathroom stall.

Yeah. I'm doing this.

I glance around to make sure no one's paying attention before leaning close to Paige. "Can you take your lunch break now and grab coffee with me?"

She tenses, her cheeks flaring an adorable shade of pink. Her eyes dart to mine, just inches away and blistering with the last thing I expected to see in her potent greenish-brown irises: fire. Bold and burning as her gaze sinks to my lips.

Wait… Hang on…

No freaking way.

My heart rate picks up as my own focus slides to her full mouth, and suddenly I forget why I'm even hovering like this. I breathe in the sweet scent of vanilla and something floral as my fingers clench the back of her chair, my other hand braced on her desk. I have her trapped between my arms, almost a foot away, but mere millimeters in my dick's measurement system. Because he seems to think she's right up against—

"It's a secret," Chad whispers at our ears, making us jump. How did he get to our side of the desk so fast?

Paige twists her head toward him, and I swear she looks as disappointed as I am.

"Obviously," she mutters. Her attention returns to me. "And sure. I can take my break. Now?"

Has she always smelled like an intoxicating mix of vanilla and lavender? Have her lips always been so full and shiny? God, they're practically edible, and suddenly I'm picturing them caressing the tip of a pen. A straw. My aching di—

"Unfortunately, I won't be able to join you. It's Wednesday," Chad informs us.

Right. We're at work.

"It's Wednesday?" I repeat.

Chad nods and straightens. We watch in silence as he stalks back to his office, clearly satisfied with that exchange.

Okay? Well, thank god it's Wednesday, I guess.

* * *

The Bluesy Bean is one of my favorite spots to chill. Not only do they have good coffee. I've done some of my best writing in the small seating area at the back of the café too. Kaitlyn Parker turned me on to this place about a year ago. I guess she used to work here back in the day and still stops in whenever she's in town. They even named a cappuccino after her when she made it big as a songwriter. I ordered it once, but the Kaitlyn Kappuccino is just a regular cappuccino with a K carved into the foam.

Right now, my favorite table in the back has *two* occupants, however: me and an overachieving redhead who's pretending she's not checking me out every five seconds. Then again, I've been on the same covert observation schedule. At present, I'm glued to the image of her perfect lips on the cup, as sexy and distracting as I imagined. When the tip of her pink tongue slips out to collect an errant drop on the rim, I force my attention to the stupid portfolio she carries to center myself.

This woman is an all-American Ivy-League princess. Probably comes from money and privilege. The polar opposite of you and your broke, orphan ass. In other words, zero chance, overzealous dick. Stay in your pants.

But she's making it hard with the way her gaze keeps tracing my tattoos and piercings. Like I'm Bachelor Number Four on the list of Dudes Your Parents Would Never Let You Date. It's hot, being the forbidden fruit, especially when her fingers tighten around her cup as if she's trying to distract them from grabbing *me*.

What part would she explore first? With clothes or without? Where would we be when she finally gave in to temptation? Bedroom? Living room? Office... My blood fires hot at the growing dirty wish-list.

"So is there a reason you brought me here?"

And she's back.

I offer a familiar shrug to return the favor.

When she rolls her eyes, I know equilibrium has been restored.

"Nope. Just looked like you could use a break. Your brain…" I motion toward her head. "It was emitting all this smoke and shit. Safety hazard."

Double eye-roll for that. I didn't even know that was possible.

"Come on, Nash. I only get an hour." She crosses her arms, then must remember she needs them to eat the bagel she ordered. I don't even try to hide my amusement as her brain trips into hyperdrive to figure out how to rebound from that misstep.

"You want me to feed it to you?" I ask with a smirk.

"Huh?"

I grin.

She glowers.

"I meant, *excuse me,* not *huh,*" she says, untwisting her arms from the anatomic puzzle. "As in what confusing thing are you talking about now?"

"Your bagel. You were trying to figure out how to eat it since you crossed your arms out of spite."

Her eyes widen. "How did you…"

"Am I wrong?"

Her hunger must finally win out over pride when she goes in for the bottom half of her bagel. Interesting. My bagel-eating technique also starts with the bottom portion to save the best part for last. Maybe successful partnerships have been built on less.

She legit grunts as she shakes her head. "No. Just… How did you know that?"

I lean back with my mug. "I read people well."

"You do?" she asks through a bite. "Because you come across as the opposite. Like, completely oblivious to the world around you."

Ouch. "Just because I can read a person or situation doesn't mean I care about it."

My statement comes off as more bitter than I intended, but I guess that's what happens when you find yourself in a situation there's no way you should be in. For example: a lunch date with Paige Andrews.

But she doesn't snap back at me like I expect. Instead, she lowers her bagel to the plate and studies me. "Interesting philosophy. Know what I'm reading in *you*?"

I try the eye-roll to see what all the fuss is about. Okay, yeah, I get it.

"I'll tell you," she continues. "I think you *do* care. I think you care a lot. You just pretend not to because you've been hurt in the past."

I let out a dry laugh. Hurt? God, she has no idea. It's also none of her damn business.

"And?" I say in a bored tone.

Her expression darkens. "*And* maybe if you stopped pretending to be a lazy, apathetic moron you'd actually accomplish something."

I flinch and look away. Wow.

Harsh? Yes. Correct? Also yes. But what she doesn't understand is that not all of us grew up with self-esteem cheerleaders and chocolate chip cookie chats about our hopes and dreams. Some of us had that cookie snatched out of our hands by Billy Stanton while his friends looked on and dumped the rest of our lunch in the trash. Some of us cried ourselves to sleep every night from cold or hunger or fear, only to get bullied even more for it. Some of us grew up in a world that didn't give a shit about what you could or could not accomplish. We learned early on that no one gives a fuck about you so why the hell should you give a fuck about them?

Read people? Yes. That's just survival. *Care* about people? That's stupidity. There's only one person on this planet I trust, and it's not the person sitting across from me.

"Sorry. That came out wrong," Paige mumbles, going back in for her bagel as if you can retract a statement like that.

"Did it?" I ask, testing her with my gaze. "Because it sounded like it came out exactly how you feel."

She meets my cold stare, blinking through what looks like genuine regret.

Regret. Another thing that means jack shit.

"I already said I was sorry. I shouldn't have said that."

"That doesn't change the fact that you think it."

She studies her plate, but now that old wounds have ripped open, I'm suddenly spiraling into a completely different mission. I don't even know what, but nothing seems as important as explaining *why* I'm a lazy, apathetic moron.

When she opens her mouth to continue, I brace for the fight.

"I don't think that," she says quietly.

My retort freezes on my tongue.

Thick lashes blink over her wide eyes as she searches my face. "I think you're intelligent and incredibly talented. I'm upset because you hide that from the world and pretend to be the opposite. It's like you don't *want* to be special or succeed at anything."

That was not the response I was expecting. Not even close. Rocked, I don't know what to say. I avert my gaze and pick at the edge of a napkin.

"Don't you ever dream?" she asks softly. "You're a musician. An artist. You're so talented, have so many connections. Why are you here doing nothing? What is it you want from life?"

I look up again, suppressing a pinch in my chest at the sincere, ridiculous question. I'd even laugh if my head wasn't such a mess right now.

What do I want? Not to hurt. That's it. I just fucking want to not hurt.

But no one's interested in that conversation, least of all some woman who hated me an hour ago. With a deep breath, I suck all the poison back inside. Swallow it. Absorb it into the marrow of my being and do what I do best, apparently— transform into a lazy, apathetic moron.

"We got off-track," I say in an even tone. Not a trace of the pain remains.

Not a trace of the pain remains.

Nice. I file that for future song lyrics.

"The reason I brought you here was to talk about why I was *really* in Eva's office all morning. I'm not supposed to share this, but since Chad already did, I kind of don't have a choice. Besides, I actually think you might like this project and be able to help." Somehow I bet she'll love the Mission-Impossible-James-Bond thing way more than I do.

Her brow is furrowed in lines I can't distinguish from the previous conversation, so I keep going before she can direct us back to that atomic wasteland.

"They're going to tell you I was fired this morning. I wasn't."

6—PLOTTING

PAIGE

There are people you figure out in five seconds. Chad. My cousin Stephanie. Her boyfriend Josh who once said raisins are grape seeds and "the state of Alaska is a hoax." Then there are people like Nash who you suspect will never be solved. *Can't* be solved because they operate on a level—in a world—you don't understand. Instead of figuring him out, those five seconds of analysis make it clear you know nothing about him. Maybe no one does.

"Let the waves of darkness break, and take, the pain below, purged by the undertow..."

How much is he hiding? A whole damn lot.

And me? I'm hopelessly attracted to challenges.

The fact that we can't stand each other only adds another layer of intrigue that now has me studying his beautiful, complex existence as he leans over his laptop on the coffee table at his apartment.

After the Bluesy Bean confession, we both decided we needed way more debriefing time, and I reluctantly agreed to meet him at his place after I got off work. Well, maybe *reluctantly* is a strong word. And maybe I don't hate the plain white t-shirt he's wearing that shows off even more of those sexy tattoos I want to know everything about.

"You okay?" he asks, his lips curving up in an annoying smirk I want to smack off his face. Or… remove… in… other ways. I feel the burn in my cheeks as his gaze wanders over me, very clearly revealing—and enjoying—that he caught me gawking.

"I'm fine," I mutter. "Just bored. How long does it take to download that plug or whatever?"

"Plugin. And a while. It's an entire suite."

Perfectly symmetrical lips twist up further at my eye-roll.

"Because it seems like you're spending a lot of time staring at me," he says casually, focusing back on his screen.

"What else am I supposed to look at while we literally do nothing?"

"I didn't say you had to stop. Or that I didn't like it," he adds with a delicious rasp that also gets me warm. Did I mention his voice? Yeah, I'd do anything to hear him sing. My gaze drifts to the guitar leaning against a stand beside the couch. Probably his. Definitely his. Is that why his hands are so beautiful? I noticed tonight how perfect the tattoos on his fingers look when he types. Okay, fine, when he does anything. How pretty would they look intertwined with mine?

Ugh. Why the heck does it take six million hours to download a plug-whatever??

"Is that yours?" I ask, nodding toward the guitar.

That smile. Of course it is. But this snarky smirk comes with a flash of shyness that releases all kinds of chaos in my stomach.

"Yeah," he says, then leans back with a stretch solely designed to show off more of his lean, chiseled body. He's not overly muscular, but possesses a sleek perfection carved by vigorous stage workouts and long nights hauling crates and equipment. Great, and now I'm picturing that T-shirt soaked with sweat, clinging to his skin beneath the glare of bright stage lights. Maybe the edge of his dark boxer-briefs peek out just above the waist of those ripped jeans when he's really locked in and unleashing on his guitar.

He must know he's torturing me, and when his fingers lace behind his head and his gaze locks directly on my eyes, I know I'm in trouble. All the hormones in my body are screaming and flailing along with every fangirl who's ever crushed on this boy before, during, or after a show. He's probably used to all the groveling and hero worship, thinking enigmatic hotness is a free pass to be a cocky, arrogant rocker.

Well, not from me. Not a chance.

I straighten on my side of the crusty old couch and pull out my own laptop. There's plenty I can do that's more productive than watching someone watch something download.

I feel his attention as I fire up my computer and open the folder I created for the Jarvis McKinnley project. But as the seconds tick by beneath his stare, the sparks become a steady burn in my belly, an ache for something I've never wanted before. I'm a responsible, intelligent woman. Zero interest in the bad-boy-rebel cliché. Should I decide to share my life with a man, it will be with a responsible, intelligent human being like myself.

This one may be intelligent, but that's the only box he checks on my list of musts for potential mates.

Stable.

Predictable.

Motivated.

Determined.

Yep, he's an X through the rest of it.

"You want to hear something I'm working on while we wait?" he asks.

My brain says no while my lips say, "Yes." In fact, they add, "Is it that undertow song?"

His fingers unlock from behind his head as he pushes up from the couch in what I'm positive is an excuse to avoid my question. He still doesn't respond while he plucks the guitar off the stand and returns to the couch to tune the strings.

When he launches into a slow, absent strum, I'm convinced he's not going to speak at all.

"You think I'm aimless, right?" he says, proving me wrong. "You're so sure of yourself, so driven. So why did you decide to go into business? Of all the possibilities in the universe to make your mark on history, how did you come to the conclusion that working at Reedweather Media was the right path?"

My eyes flicker to his in surprise, but there's no hint of arrogance or judgment in his expression, no anger or disappointment. Just sincere curiosity and a desire to understand something he doesn't.

"I…"

Jarred by his words, I blink and look away. How do you answer a question you've never asked yourself?

After several long seconds, his strumming intensifies into a steadier groove that signals the start of a song. Soon he's lost in the music, and it occurs to me that he didn't wait for an answer. He didn't *want* an answer. That question was for me, not him, and shivers rush over my skin when his haunting, gravelly voice fills the room.

You ask how I'm doing just to hear that I'm fine.

Smiling as I recite that same lie every time

Crying through the laughter

Lying through the cheers

Trying to survive years of being "great."

Do you hear me

Do you see my grave

I'm lying

I'm hiding

I swear I'm still trying to be brave

See this grin? It's for you because mine's a joke that's been choked from lungs torn when my heart broke

Tearing piece after piece for someone to claim

Stain

Beneath the shame of

Tossing them all to be used and abused, crushed and confused

With the fake lips that say

"I'm okay."
No really.
I won't waste your time.
I'm so, so, so fucking fine.

When you call me your friend
I'm just a tragic loose end
A deadly game of pretend
Let's say I'm fine

Hey where'd you go I thought this rope was my hope
Nope, just to choke
like all those times you said I'd cope
Passing nods in the halls like that's all it takes
A quick break, a handshake,
another pat on the back with a smile great,
thanks
so glad we're all okay

When you call me your friend
I'm just a tragic loose end
A deadly game of pretend
Let's say I'm fine

"Yeah, I'm fine."

Nash doesn't look up after the last chord rings out. The raw pain of his song hovers in the air around us as his left hand tightens on the frets. His right arm remains draped over the body of the guitar, pick still clenched in his fingers. His mind is somewhere else, that place where artists go to harvest beauty from the darkness. Everything in me wants to go there with him. Just a glimpse, which would probably be all I could handle. I don't know anything about him, but for some reason, it feels like I know too much.

I expected him to have some talent, but wow. I was not prepared for that. Once again, I'm left frustrated and confused about how someone as well-connected and gifted as he is could be content drifting on the periphery of his potential. He's flipping through corporate training manuals when that kind of genius is bursting inside?

I have so many questions. Nothing about Nash Ellis makes sense without that guitar in his arms, but his story doesn't belong to me any more than I should have to explain why I chose Sandeke Telecom.

With a mist of artist angst still drifting through the room, I decide there's really only one possible response to this scenario.

"Wow. Those Mer-Nuts really messed you up, huh."

Nash looks up, his gaze landing on me with surprise. I hold my breath, searching electric blue eyes until …

Snort-laugh.

"So bad," he says through a chuckle.

I grin and tap his leg with my shoe. "Look at us."

"Huh?"

I smirk.

"Our awesome rapport," he concludes, shaking his head with a genuine smile I'd fight Mer-Armies to keep on his face. What makes this person truly happy besides music? Is there anything?

I feel his attention on me and try to stay cool as it intensifies.

"Hey, Paige?"

"Yeah?" My teeth sink into my lip. My focus settles on those fascinating hands I want to trace and explore just for a few glorious seconds. I bet they're warm and strong and hold so many secrets.

"I was wrong about you."

Surprised, I meet his gaze, heat flooding through me at the way he's looking at me. Maybe I was wrong about him too.

"Oh?" I say.

"Yeah." He waves toward my legs. "You do own a pair of jeans."

He laughs when I shove him.

* * *

"Do you know who that is?" Chad whispers, practically bouncing on his toes.

I follow his eyes through the window of the conference room to a sparkly man chatting with Eva and Mr. Reedweather. Other sparkly people look on in varying shades of bored, and I'm guessing they make up "the entourage." The man seems to be getting along swimmingly with Mr. Reedweather, though, which raises all kinds of red flags.

"Jarvis McKinnley?" I wish I'd guessed wrong when Chad looks crestfallen that I solved the riddle so quickly.

"Yes. And guess who gets to pick up his lunch?"

"You?"

"Nope," he says with a glib look that I finally missed one. "Stacy."

"Okay." I don't know Stacy.

We focus back on the action in the conference room, waiting for our cue to join the meeting.

To be honest, it's a miracle I'm here today. After Nash told me about this supposed plot to spy on our competition, I was so disgusted, I almost called HR to quit on the spot. The FBI would have been my next call. Or is it the Better Business Bureau? I don't know—whatever agency oversees things like corporate espionage investigations—but Nash convinced me I'd do more good by helping him and his roommate thwart the plan than by marching off in a huff. He obviously hasn't seen my "huff" because that sucker can do plenty of damage.

It turns out my coworker's pleading blue eyes have more power over me than I thought, because here I am two days later, still hovering in the halls of a lying, cheating company I want no part of. I told him I'm quitting the second they don't need me anymore. He told me, "Duh."

Reedweather hasn't even curved his hand into a full beckoning position before Chad is plunging through the door toward our guest. I follow behind, maintaining plenty of distance between me and my associate who is now bowing like we just performed the mother of all ballet routines. Even Jarvis looks perplexed. (To be fair, the man looks like the type who might be frequently perplexed.)

"Ah, Chad. Also Paige," Reedweather says, motioning toward me.

I almost bow as well but catch myself in time. Geez. It's like Chadisms are infectious.

"It's so great to meet you, Mr. McKinnley," Chad says. "We are thrilled at the prospect of working with you. We're huge fans!"

"Same," Jarvis says with an absent twist of the lips. I study him as he immediately forgets about us and signals one of the sparkly strangers to discuss something that sounded like "lemon wheels."

From my research, Jarvis is thirty-two, but he seems younger in person. His hair is coifed in that perfect way to look like it's not, his clothing the same. His shoes are expensive but don't remotely coordinate with the rest of what he's wearing, and there's a green bandana around his wrist for some reason.

He looks like he was put together by a committee of gifted stylists who were told to pretend not to be.

Nash pulls this look off way better.

Wait. Where did that come from?

He does though.

Shut up, brain.

You shut up.

Lemon wheels—in addition to distracting your annoying brain from hot musicians—are also a thing people request at random times, it turns out. Within seconds, Jarvis is nursing a plate of lemon slices and a glass of water.

"It's his signature drink," Chad whispers. "It's a room temperature distilled aquatic base infused with Meyer lemon wheels directly from Meyer."

"So… lemon water?"

He glares at me. "No. It's a pure water base that he varies with varying amounts of lemon wheels depending on his needs."

"Ah. So… water with lemon."

Chad gives up on my culinary ignorance and watches Jarvis assemble his concoction like the dude invented the concept of adding lemon to water for a slightly different version of water. In fact, *everyone* is staring with rapt attention as if we've suddenly forgotten he's just some dude here to sing about internet streaming service. Yep, eight people are getting paid to watch a guy drink water.

I so wish Nash were here right now. He'd love this.

When I'm sure no one's paying attention to me, I snap a discreet photo of the tray on the conference table and send it to Nash with a text.

Me: Still no progress on the marketing campaign, but Jarvis has successfully imbibed lemon water. Wait, I'm sorry. "A room temperature distilled aquatic base infused with Meyer lemon wheels directly from Meyer."

Nash: There's so much wrong with that sentence, I'm just gonna let it go. But what's with the bandana on his arm?

Me: No idea. Probably a common custom in the geographic region of Meyer.

Nash: Where they grow the lemons.

Me: Exactly.

Nash returns a laughing emoji, and I can't stop a smile from slipping out.

"Okay, well, if you're comfortable, we'd love to get started," Eva says, drawing the room to attention. By her irritated expression, she's not overly excited about lemon water either. Maybe it's because she's never had *Meyer* lemon water.

What would happen if one used Meyer lemon wedges instead of wheels? Or even non-Meyer lemons? I table those culinary puzzles for later consideration.

"Of course," Jarvis says, taking a sip of his drink. "Can't wait to see what you all cooked up."

"*Cooked*!" Reedweather declares. "I remember—"

"Great," Eva clips out before her father can finish whatever it is that will send us on an hour-long detour about literally nothing. "If you turn your attention to the screen we'll be presenting a fantastic video put together by…"

While Eva shares our carefully sculpted plan to make Jarvis McKinnley the face of Sandeke Telecom, I use the time to survey the scene for useful information like a good spy. A minute in, though, I realize it's harder than I thought to distinguish "useful" information from regular information.

For example: is the fact that Jarvis tunes Eva out exactly seventeen seconds into the presentation useful? Maybe. More useful might be the woman beside him who's been typing notes with vigorous determination the entire time we've been here. An assistant maybe? Either way, she's the one we need to be talking to if we want information.

Not useful: Chad's recitation of Jarvis McKinnley's entire discography when Eva asks for feedback. Also, Jarvis' response of, "Yeah… probably… four?" until the woman beside him whispers something and he changes his answer to, "Thank you."

Useful: the bandana appears to be representing support of some charitable cause and/or small sovereign nation.

Not useful: Mr. Reedweather insisting on a ribbon-cutting ceremony to celebrate this momentous partnership even though no one in the room has scissors or a ribbon.

Useful: Stacy, who shows up with lunch *and* scissors and a ribbon.

Not useful: Nash's text with a video of a cat trying to get into a hammock. No spy points for that one, but it's so flippin' cute.

In fact, I re-read the evidence that he was thinking about me in a non-work context at least ten times on the ride home.

* * *

"What is that?" Val asks, the second I walk in the door.

I squint back, even peeking behind me for a clue. "What's what?"

"The thing on your lips."

"There's a thing on my lips?" I reach up and run my finger over them in search of the offending blemish.

"It almost looks like… I don't know… a smile?" His grin breaks at my hard stare.

"Hilarious."

"I don't know about *that,* but mildly amusing seems fair."

"Dork," I say, dropping my laptop bag by the island.

As usual, Val is stationed at the table, buried in a fortress of music crap with his headphones on. I glower at the mess in the rest of the apartment. Maybe I need to map out the kitchen so he can see where the sink and garbage bin are.

"He's growing on you, huh?" Val says without looking away from his screen.

"I don't know what you're talking about."

"Uh, yeah you do. And it's not a dig. I have a bro-crush of my own."

"You're crushing on Nash too?"

He looks up with a smug glint, and I cringe at the slip.

"So you *do* have a thing for him."

Yeah, that's definitely a Grade-A gloat on my brother's face.

"No! I didn't say that."

"You literally just said that."

"But I didn't mean *that.*"

"So what did you mean by 'too?'"

"It was a universal 'too.'"

"Ah. Like the royal 'we.'"

"Exactly."

"So *we* have a crush on Nash."

"Yes. I mean, no. I mean, gah! I hate you."

"Except you don't," he says with a grin.

I spin away and focus on the sink I've just filled with that slacker's dishes.

"Hey, so you know how I'm part of that project with Jarvis McKinnley? What do you know about him and Larinda Scott?" I say solely for the purpose of research and not at all to change the subject.

"They're both mediocre artists who happen to play the game really well."

I turn to him in surprise. "What do you mean?"

By his look, he's as excited about this topic as I was about the previous one. "The fact that they're superstars is total bullshit. Neither has the musical talent to back it up. Where they excel is the marketing game."

"You mean, like getting sponsors and promo and stuff?"

He shakes his head. "I mean they know how to play people and manipulate the media."

I tilt my head. "Wait. Are you saying they're just acting? No way."

He grunts and shoves his chair to the side. "When's the last time you've heard either of their names connected with anything *other than* their contentious relationship? Don't you think it's strange that they show up to all the same events where they have very public altercations, then initiate press releases about it before the champagne is even out of their systems?"

"They're both country music stars. It makes sense they'd be at the same events."

"Sure, some award shows and fundraisers here and there, but look it up. Most people do everything they can to avoid exes they supposedly hate, but not those two. Clubs, restaurants, resorts. Hell, they were both on the same flight to Hawaii two months ago where they just *happened* to get into a shouting match that required flight attendant intervention."

"You think the fight was staged?"

"I'm saying it's *all* staged. They're playing up this feud to help their careers. They live to blow shit up and make headlines. There are even rumors that they're actually still together."

"You can't be serious."

He shrugs. "Believe me or don't, but you're the queen of research so I recommend doing some if you're about to get drawn into that hornet's nest. I'm ninety percent sure you're all being played. Ask Nash. Dude seems to know everything and everyone in the industry."

He does, and I will, believe me. My ire has been stirred at the thought that he might be hiding even more than I thought. Personal crap, fine, I get it. But work-related issues? Not an option. I thought we were on the same team. Co-spies and all that.

Co-spies? Is that a thing?

Whatever. Co-somethings and they should share information. That's just Teamwork 101.

Why would Nash not mention these two telecom giants are about to get swept up in the Larinda Scott/Jarvis McKinnley hurricane?

7—FAWNING

NASH

In a perfect world, I'd have months to cultivate my relationship with Larinda Scott and her team of oily sycophants. There are industry politics to navigate and delicate power balances governed by fragile egos to finesse. It's a perilous game that takes patience, cunning, and luck to master. Some people spend years trying to enter an orbit just for a brush with the star.

In the wormhole of Sandeke Telecom's corporate espionage, I have until lunch.

Larinda meets with Brighthouse later to plan what's being called *The Gaming Thing*, and I have to go from "friend of a friend" to "trusted inner circle BFF" by then. Actually, I'm not even a *friend of a friend*. Kevin Robertson who connected me with Larinda is *not* my friend, just the dude who screwed me over on a gig last year and knew he owed me. It's the only reason I have no problem screwing him back by betraying his recommendation for a spy job. I'd never do that to a real friend.

Then again, I'm starting to think I'm the one who got screwed after spending the last hour pretending to love clothing for tiny dogs, egg-free cauliflower quiche, and something that looked like a hot towel but isn't for a reason I don't fully understand.

Right now my mission has me at a nail salon staring at a rack of colorful bottles as if I know what the hell I'm looking at.

"Thoughts?" Larinda asks, tapping her finger on her bottom lip.

About the concept of nail polish?

"Um…"

"Jasmine Sparkle Blush, right?" She plucks a pink bottle from the shelf, and I relax. Ah, she's choosing one of these for her nails. I don't know why I thought this stage of the process would have more fanfare. Shouldn't there be a giant display of color swatches like the paint section of a hardware store? Maybe a bored employee hovering close by should you have a question about a wall or chair leg they've never seen that coordinates with your personal tastes they know nothing about?

"Oh. Uh, yeah. Or that." I point at the thing closest to my finger and cringe. I've known Larinda Scott for an hour and twenty-three minutes but I'm already positive "Death March" is not her color.

"Kidding," I laugh out at her look of horror.

A wave of relief washes over her face as she shoves my shoulder. "Oh my god, I thought you were serious for a second. You're hilarious. Like, as funny as my friend Tom who's so, so funny. I like your name by the way. Did I tell you that? Kevin said it's short for Nashville. That's so cool."

Oh. Well, it's not but okay.

"Thanks," I say, forcing another smile. "I like yours too." Is that something you say in these situations? By her beaming response, it is.

"Thanks. Mine isn't short for anything," she giggles.

"Okay. I'm sorry." I cringe again when she scrunches her nose. Guess I missed on that one. Where's a Chad training manual when you need one?

"So Kevin said you're friends with Abram Fletcher," she continues.

I shrug, not thrilled about sharing my real self with these people, but positive that link is the only reason I'm standing here. "We know each other, yeah."

Know each other? Understatement of the century.

"I *love* him. He's basically my favorite. I covered 'Hold A Grudge' on my last tour."

Yep. Abram sent me the video along with an eye-roll emoji and the letters W, T, and F.

"I saw clips of it. It was great," I lie. "You really… made it your own." Probably why Abram hated it so much.

She grins. "Oh! You should do this one."

"Huh?"

She pulls a bottle of dark blue polish off a shelf and hands it to me.

Hang on.

"Oh. Uh—"

"That would look *so* good on you. I love what you do with your eyes, by the way."

"What I *do* with them?"

She flutters hers, and I swallow the follow-up questions. Does it matter?

"Thanks," I say, also accepting the blue nail polish, which I subsequently learn is not actually blue but "Midnight Torch." If I'd known one of these was for me, I would have grabbed "Death March." Actually… I turn and swipe that one as well.

"Left and right," I explain at Larinda's second confused look of the conversation.

Her expression brightens. "Yes! Great idea. I love it. Me too."

She studies the shelves again and selects another pink bottle exactly the same as the first. "Bubble Gum Dream," she whispers, waving it between us like we're in on some big conspiracy. If only she knew.

"So I'm itching to pick your brain," she says as two salon employees direct us to a counter. The man waves me to a stool in front of what looks like autopsy tools. I better be getting a bonus for this.

"Kevin says you're a brilliant producer. Now, I know what you're thinking." Zero chance that's true. "*But, Larinda, you have, like, the best of the best already working for you. Why would you want the opinion of someone you just met?*" Damn. I stand corrected. "It's true too. My team is great but… I don't know. They don't get me like you do. We just met, and already it's like we've been besties forever, you know? I'd love your opinion on what I'm working on."

Wow. BFFs already? I wonder if Marcos will be jealous. Nah. He'll probably just be amazed I haven't quit yet.

"Sure, I'd be happy to listen."

"Perfect! Once we're finished here, I'll send you the link. If it goes well, maybe we can work on all of them."

All of them? Crap.

"Can't wait."

I peek around her to see how the rest of her party is faring. They seem totally fine with what's happening to their hands as they chat amicably about another time they were doing exactly this.

"Can I ask you something?" Larinda says, her smile fading for maybe the first time since I've met her. Seriously, the woman *is* Jasmine Sparkle Blush. I'd do anything for a sliver of that sunshine. "Why are you really here?"

Shit. Did not see that coming.

My pulse picks up, nerves coiling in my stomach at her unexpected question. Has she figured me out already? Maybe I've underestimated her.

"What do you mean?" I ask to buy time.

She tips her head, wavy multi-colored hair cascading over her shoulder. "I mean, why are you hanging with me? Kevin said you're big into the modern rock scene, so why would you want to work with a country music star? I mean, you're friends with *Abram Fletcher.* Shouldn't you be besties with him instead?"

A flicker of doubt passes over her face, and I study her more closely. Is she actually insecure? How is that possible?

"I try to expose myself to as much as possible," I say casually. "How do you know something isn't for you unless you experience it?" It's not really a lie. My entire existence is a twisted social experiment. And the story of Abram and me? Not for human consumption.

Her smile returns, and I release a breath.

"I like that. You're so right. There was this time I thought I didn't like fleece sheets, and then I tried them. It turned out I *didn't* like them, but what if I had, you know?" She shrugs and brightens with a thought. "In fact…"

After looking around with another conspiratorial glint, she snatches "Death March" from in front of me and pushes "Bubble Gum Dream" toward my station.

"Let's expose ourselves," she whispers, even adding a dramatic wink that definitely justifies the technician's mild alarm as he glances between us.

I force a return smile.

* * *

So Paige is back to hating me. I don't even know what I did this time, but it's Val who lets me into their apartment after she opens the door just so she can slam it in my face.

He gives me an apologetic look as I follow him to the kitchen, and I do my best to avoid the ire billowing on the far side of the island.

"Hey, Paige," I say brightly, just to make things worse.

She glares back.

"I like your shirt," I add.

That pisses her off more.

"When were you going to tell me about Jarvis and Larinda?" she snaps.

Confused, I look to Val who shrugs. Technically, I'm here to see him, but I was hoping for a quick debriefing with Paige after starting our separate missions. Pretty sure that's off the table unless it involves her hitting me.

"When was I going to tell you what?" I ask, genuinely lost.

She crosses her arms and leans back in a hard stance. "That this whole thing is a sham!"

"I don't…" I look to Val again. He averts his gaze. Did she go to the same spy school as Chad? I thought it was pretty self-explanatory what the point of spying was. "You knew this was all a spy—"

"Not the spy crap! The fact that Jarvis and Larinda's feud is all fake and they're probably using this to play *us* not the other way around."

That's what this is about?

"Of course it's fake. That was the whole point of the plan. I thought… I mean… it was *your* idea to use Jarvis." I squint at her for clues about what I'm missing.

"Yeah, because I thought they hated each other!"

I shake my head. "*No*," I draw out. "If they truly hated each other, this wouldn't work as a double—triple?—agent thing. What makes it brilliant is that their ruse means we can use it against Brighthouse and Sandeke Telecom to take *them* down. I thought that's why you suggested it."

Also, did I just use the word "ruse"? I look around, hoping no one noticed.

Her angry stare glazes over and now I'm not even sure who she's mad at.

"Wait," she says, straightening. "What's that?"

"What's what?"

"On your hands."

I glance down and wince. "Oh. Right. Larinda picked it out." I hold up my blue and pink fingers.

She tilts her head, and I see the hint of a smile threatening her lips. "I like it."

"Really?"

I study my nails, shifting them in the light. They *do* shine in a flattering way.

"Actually, yeah, I do. It's kinda sexy with your bad-boy vibe."

Whoa. Bad-boy vibe? Me? Always thought I was more the tortured artist, but sure. I can work with that.

When I meet her gaze again, I'm surprised to see she's serious about the nail polish. Huh, interesting. My pulse pounds harder as we exchange some silent, heated message my body's interpreting much faster than my brain.

My brain? Still on the sparkly nail polish issue.

"You had something you wanted to talk to me about?" Val interrupts with a hint of impatience.

Right.

I clear my throat, burning beneath the intense stare of his sister. Why is it suddenly a thousand degrees in here? Two minutes into my visit, and Paige and I have already run the entire length of the love-hate spectrum.

My focus ventures back to her, locking on every detail I somehow missed before. Have her full curves always looked so tempting? Her hair so… what's the word for wanting to tangle your fingers in something in a fleeting surge of possession? *Tangle-able?* Also, I never understood the decorative silk scarf thing until this particular one around that particular neck. The way it drapes down her smooth skin and brushes the gentle swell of her—

"Nash?"

"Huh?"

I hear Val's attempt to get my attention, but… damn, his sister is hot. I mean… not *hot*. Just… okay, fine. The sexy nerd thing is totally turning me on right now. And the way she's looking at me? A shiver of awareness runs straight to my groin. Her intense stare, her body language, everything says she wants *me* to be the one to tug off that scarf and slide open a few of those buttons on her shirt. Maybe reach in to massage a warm, soft mound into a small, firm peak. She'd moan as I crowded her against… the island or table? I could totally get her off with just a—

"Yo. Dude. You okay?" Val again. Shit.

I shake off the trance and tear my gaze away.

"You said you needed to talk to me?" By the way his jaw ticks, it's a safe bet he caught me checking out his sister.

"Yeah. I have a job for you," I say before I get distracted again. Val perks up as I hoped he would.

All previous fantasies dissolve as the reality of what I'm about to do settles in. My voice sounded confident just now, but the truth is, it wasn't an easy decision. I wrestled with the idea for a while because this project would have been a huge opportunity for me as well, but for some reason, Val popped into my head and it didn't feel right to hoard it for myself. The guy could use a break, so here I am, doing the right thing.

The. Right. Thing.

I know. Since when was I the dude who did the right thing? That's Marcos' role. I'm the one who doesn't even remember *the thing* ten seconds after it happens, let alone give a shit about it. I have no clue what's happening to me.

"I'm sending you a link to a folder of one of Larinda Scott's current projects," I continue. "It's got a rough mix, along with all the stems. Nothing's been decided or mastered yet. She wants the opinion of *a brilliant producer*. Can you make some notes I can pass on to her? I'm trusting you and your unborn children to keep this confidential."

Val's eyes widen, and I feel Paige's surprise as well.

"Wait, are you...? I don't..." He shakes his head, blinking in confusion. "You... want *me* to help with this?"

"Not want, *need*," I say. "I'm on a time crunch to win her over and have to accelerate the process. I'm already working on the personal thing." I hold up my shimmery nails. "But I also need some professional ammo. I don't have time to focus on both, so I need you to handle that." It's not entirely a lie, and I force away the ache in my chest at giving up such a huge opportunity.

It's fine. You don't really want this anyway. I mean, country music? That's not even your thing. You'd just fuck it up.

It's fine.

So, so fine.

"If she likes what you come up with, I'll give you credit of course. You in?" I ask.

His mouth hangs open as his eyes dart between me and his sister. "I... you want me to work with *the* Larinda Scott?"

I shrug. "You're an amazing producer, Val. It's time the world knows that."

It's also possible his huge grin triggers the slightest thaw in my cold, dead soul. Huh. Giving a shit: doesn't suck. Who knew?

Then I make the mistake of glancing at Paige.

Any anger she had for me when I arrived has clearly shifted into fire of a different, more blood-pounding nature. There's something else in her face as well, a flash I recognize from years ago. It's the same look Marcos and Nate wore when the other boys finally backed off from a barrage of creative insults they threw at me. Their punches and kicks were less inspired, although for whatever reason those scars didn't last as long as the verbal ones.

What I'm seeing now is that same protectiveness, that same relief at someone you love getting a long overdue break from a universe that seems intent on shitting on them.

It triggers a jolt in my chest as I survey her brother in a new light. Maybe there's a reason he and I bonded so quickly. Not all bullies wear their badges as openly as mine did, and suddenly this strange compulsion to do the right thing morphs into an urge to go even further. Almost like I... *care*. Shudder.

I think I might even "care" enough to do something ridiculous.

"You want to see my first tattoo?" I blurt to Val before I lose my nerve. Yeah, this is getting weird. Sharing shit about myself? Not my strong suit, but for some reason, it feels necessary right now. Like maybe my nightmare brought me here to iron out a wrinkle Fate made by mistake.

Val's confusion at my random question matches my own, but it's like he senses his role in a preordained moment as well when he nods.

"Sure," he says.

I can't look at Paige as I grab the back of my shirt to tug it over my head. I'm sure she thinks I've lost my mind and is probably back to hating me again, but this isn't about her. It's about the piece of myself I see in another lost soul who hasn't been filed down to a walking callous yet. Maybe it's not too late for him like it is for me. Maybe he can still heal and thrive and find purpose instead of drifting through an endless blank space like I do.

I turn so he can see my back, gripping my shirt in my fist like it betrayed me by shedding its veil so easily.

"It's a dragon?" Val asks with a hint of uncertainty. Not because it doesn't look like a dragon, but because he still doesn't understand what's happening right now.

You and me both, dude.

"Yeah. But look closely."

"It's filled with words."

I hear the excitement in his voice, and the corner of my mouth ticks up. "Yep. Every bullshit thing anyone ever said to me. Well, the ones I could remember at least."

"Damn," he mumbles. "That's messed up."

I clench my fist, having no desire to go there. I've already gone way further than I should have. "Yeah, but it's the fire he's breathing out that's the real story."

I wait as he looks closer.

"Poetry?" he asks. "Wait, no. Song lyrics!"

My full smile breaks as I turn to face him. "The shit on the outside, what people see when they look at you? That's on them. What's on the inside, what you breathe in and out? That's on you. You can give them the power to poison you and spew the ugly back into the universe, or you can transform it into something beautiful. Incinerate their hate with a fire that is uniquely and perfectly yours."

Fuck.

Where did that come from?

My chest aches with old wounds as my words settle around us. I still don't understand how we even got here. In a million years I wouldn't have seen this moment coming. I don't share shit about myself, and I'm definitely not the type to offer sage advice, mostly because I don't have any. But maybe I'm glad I cracked open the vault when Val's façade brightens with the best thing one artist can offer another: inspiration.

I'm feeling pretty damn good about myself. And then...

"Can I talk to you?" Paige clips out.

Val and I glance over, my stomach twisting at the look on her face. Crap. Here we go.

"Sure," I mutter, following reluctantly as she stomps toward the hallway.

"Don't," she commands when I unfurl the shirt to put it back on.

Confused, I say nothing as she grabs my arm and drags me into a room at the end of the hall.

* * *

"Two things," Paige barks, shoving me against the door.

"Ow. What did I do?"

She looks angrier than I've ever seen her. I thought… I don't know. I was just trying to help.

Her palms press into my bare chest, locking me against the door as her eyes scour every inch of my face. Her gaze drops to her hands where they're fused with my pecs, pale and smooth against the chaos of my tattoos.

"Shut your mouth and listen, Ellis," she says, blasting me with a warning.

"Okay, geez." I hold up my hands in surrender, the shirt dangling like a vanquished white flag.

But then… wait.

Her soft hands slide down my stomach, fingers clawing at my skin in hot streaks. She traces the waistband of my jeans before pushing her palms back up to hook behind my neck. Stepping forward, she scrapes her body against mine and settles close. So fucking close. What the…?

I harden against her, hissing in a breath when she rolls her hips for more intense friction. She stays braced against me, pulsing just enough to trigger a sharp, exquisite ache at each collision.

"One," she says, gazing at my mouth with raw hunger. "The fact that I'm incredibly attracted to you right now in no way sets a precedent for future encounters."

Oh shit. I fight to keep the amusement from my face because now I can't tell if she's angry or not. It would be just like her to be mad at me for turning her on.

"Two. I'm making the assumption based on circumstantial evidence that you are single and at least mildly attracted to me. If that's not the case, please make the correction now in an explicit way."

I can't stop a half-smile at that one, though, and her eyes narrow on me.

"Mmm… How explicit? Ow!" I say through a laugh when she grips my hair and tugs my head back. She doesn't let go, clutching hard while she searches my eyes in the scorching silence. The solid heat of her body buzzes over my skin as I watch her struggle between wanting to kiss me and smack me.

I'd take a hard dose of both right now.

"Not that kind of explicit," she snaps. "You know what I mean."

I manage a grave nod. "Okay, well, I only need to correct one assumption, Ms. Andrews."

Her brows scrunch. "You have a girlfriend?" she asks, disappointment leeching onto her face. Hell. Yes.

"I'm more than *mildly* attracted to you," I correct.

Her relief lasts just a second before turning to suspicion, as if testing my ability to keep a straight face. I'm trying so damn hard.

"Oh. Well. Great," she says, a flush spreading over her cheeks. "Three—"

"I thought you said two things. Ow!"

Man, I was hoping for that. Her fingers—still knotted in my hair—pull my head down until her mouth hovers over mine. I sense her quick intake of breath before she lifts her eyes to meet my gaze.

"There *were* two," she breathes against my lips. "But then you were an ass so now there are three things."

"How was I an ass?" I murmur, my eyes fixed on hers, my body tense and throbbing for more. I slide my hands around her waist to pull her in. Her right leg tightens behind me as she lifts up on her toes for another firm, torturous graze. Fuck, that felt good.

She licks her lips while staring at mine, and I pull back just enough to torment her. Did she just whimper? She's making it freaking impossible to show restraint right now. I can already taste her. Mint and something sweet.

"All the snide comments," she says.

"Except it's turning you on, isn't it?" I respond in a low voice, brushing her lips with mine again. "You *like* the fact that I challenge you."

"Whatever." She moves in, and I retract.

"Admit it," I say, my grin slipping out.

"You're an ass."

"Yep. And you like it. Admit it." I search her scalding stare, daring her to argue. Her body coils tighter around mine, her lust winning out over irritation, and I'm not sure how much longer I can play this game no matter how fun it is to torment her.

"Fine! Yes. There's something weirdly hot about you being an ass all the time, okay? Now for the third—"

"Don't I get any things?"

I slip my hands under her shirt, and she shudders when I trail my fingers up her sides. She adjusts to urge me on, and I oblige with a slow stroke below the band of her bra. With a sharp breath, she leans further into my touch.

"Argh! Fine! What things?" Her tone is pained, though, and she looks frustrated when I only move my hand a fraction closer to where she wants it.

"Hmm." I squint and stare up like I'm thinking.

"Nash!"

"So impatient."

"I hate you."

"I know. Oh, hey. I've got one."

Her expression turns suspicious again, even as she twists so my hand grazes her breast in a blatant signal. Her chest swells, her eyes pleading until I finally slide my fingertips beneath the lace.

"Nash…" she whines, pressing into my touch. I tease higher, adding a warning glance just for fun.

"My thing is a question," I say.

"Okay?" She groans when I brush her nipple, arching into my hand. I twist gently and cup her breast. I'm not even sure she remembers what we're talking about. Hell, I'm not sure I do either. Damn, she feels good. I start a slow massage and watch her eyelids flutter with each labored breath. She shoves her own hand down my chest in greedy anticipation.

"My question is, why am I the only one naked right now?"

Her eyes flare hot.

"You're not naked."

"Basically."

"You can't *basically* be naked. You either are or you're not. You. Are. Not." She seems incredibly annoyed by that fact.

"Do you want me to be?" I ask, a wry smile leaking out.

Her gaze locks on my lips again as she jerks the waistband of my jeans, separating it from my hips. I arch back to give her more access, tensing when her fingers sink in to tease the sensitive skin just below the hem. Her other hand grips my belt, her thumb caressing the top of my zipper.

"Will you stop that?" she whispers, studying my lips.

God, she sounds like she's in pain. I know how she feels.

"Stop what?"

"The sexy smirks."

"Sexy, huh? I thought you hated me."

"I…"

"So you *don't* want me naked right now?"

"Nash, come on…"

"It's a yes or no question."

I reach down and tug open the buckle, enjoying the tormented look on her face at the invitation. Her fingers tighten around the exposed button and zipper, her knuckles sending tiny shivers over my skin where we connect. Belt hanging open, I lock my hands on my head and stretch further to put my body on display. She looks downright pissed at my cocky grin when she can't help pushing her palms back up my torso to explore every line and groove. I know she can feel what she's doing to me. This, right here? Pure torture.

"Yes or no, Paige?"

She glares at me, her gaze anchoring on my mouth.

"Yes," she grumbles. "Yes! I want you naked. I want you stripped and desperate and hard. Right there." She points to the perfectly made bed a few feet away. "Happy?"

I grin and cup her face to pull her in and finally, *finally* taste that sweet rage. She moans into our kiss, her tongue seeking mine as she drags me toward the bed with her hands anchored behind my neck. She yanks me down on top of her, releasing me to claw at the button on my jeans with one hand, while the other threads in my hair to keep me close. I help her with the zipper as well and kick them off, then climb back to brace over her.

"*Now* I'm the only one naked," I tease against her lips, wet and raw from our kiss.

"Shut up," she says, whimpering when I press into her. Her legs wrap around my thighs, pulling me in for more agonizing contact.

"I'm just saying—"

"Shut. Up."

She forces us around until she's on top, straddling my hips. After pulling off that silky blue scarf, she's about to toss it on the floor when her eyes flash with a wicked thought.

Wait…

She's not…

Hell.

Yes.

She grips my wrist and leans in to drag her lips along my neck.

"Why do you have to taste as good as you look and smell?" she groans. "I hate you so much."

I laugh and coax her back up so I can taste her too. She angles her head to deepen the kiss and accepts the invasion of my tongue. Our fingers entwine and she pushes our laced hands above my head on the mattress.

Her body flattens against me, its heat and firm pressure triggering every nerve and driving another surge of fire through my blood.

"Nash," she moans, pulsing against my erection to the rhythm of our frantic mouths and tongues. "I need more."

"Whatever you want, babe," I murmur.

Oh god. She wasn't lying. Hate tastes fucking divine. I can't get enough, and when her fingers clench mine with each desperate push, I'm done. I'm hers. Whatever she wants. Scarf, ties. Freaking handcuffs and a blindfold. I don't care. We just need to get her naked too and then—

"Paige!"

We freeze and shoot our gazes to the closed door that's rumbling with a knock.

"I'm busy!" she barks at her brother. At least I'm not the only one who gets yelled at.

"I know, but Mom and Dad are here."

She stiffens, her hold loosening on my hands. "What?"

"Yeah. They… please come out."

Oh no. This can't be happening.

"Shit," she mumbles. Her apologetic look does nothing to ease the ache of frustration. Or the throb in my *entire* body.

"I'm sorry," she whispers, brushing her lips against mine. "I have to deal with this."

Groaning, I press the heels of my palms against my eyes. "Are you for real?"

"I know. Just…" She looks conflicted before leaning in for a rough kiss, and soon her hands are back in my hair, gripping hard like she's hate-kissing me again. I don't even know who or what she hates right now, but I love everything about it. For the record, I *only* condone hate-kissing from this point forward.

She groans into my mouth, writhing against me with tantalizing urgency.

"God, I want you so much," she says, fighting herself to pull away again. The look in her eyes when she finally does makes me think there's a possibility she's about to tell her family to eff off.

"I'm right here," I say, trapping her face to keep her close.

But I'm fooling around with the president of the Responsible Adult Honors Society, so of course, her disciplined brain wins out. She recoils abruptly, like it's the only way to sever our connection, and rolls off me. After sliding to the floor, she hovers at the edge of the bed and scans me with a longing I feel in every inch of my groin.

I push up on my elbows, grunting at the fact that apparently I care for the second time tonight. Because this? Sucks.

"Fine," I sigh out when it becomes clear we're finished. "Can you give me a minute to recover and get dressed at least?"

Her smile returns as she studies me with slow, heated precision. "I suppose. Although…"

"Although?"

Hazel eyes flare hot as they burn with all the things she wants to do to me. So, so many dirty, wonderful things. That blue scarf.

Damn.

"Gotta say, Ellis. You may be a pain in the ass, but you are a *hot* pain in the ass."

My own smile slips out. "Ditto."

8—FIGHTING

PAIGE

I didn't really need more reasons to dislike my parents, but interrupting a volcanic encounter with Nash rivals any of the current top four. I'm still on fire from the brief taste of him. The *feel* of him. Hard and warm and wholly mine for those few wonderful minutes. There was so much I wanted to do to him. (The scarf!) Experience. Explore. Share. Give. I'm in physical pain from not having him and I can't even tell if the fluttering in my stomach is from what just happened or what's about to.

If lust was a competitive sport, pretty sure I just made Nationals.

The air is thick with tension when I reach the kitchen—and not the good kind that makes your lady parts burn with hunger for hot musicians. No, this is the kind that makes you sure a branch of the emergency services will be involved in this encounter and you don't even know which one. Personally, I'm pulling for the fire department.

Val leans against the window, staring quietly at the floor. Mom scowls around the room like she's the star of a home improvement show and this is the "before" reel. Dad looks bored, even though he's probably baking plenty of passive-aggressive treats in that cruel head as we speak. Come to think of it, they'd probably co-host that home improvement show and get it cancelled after two episodes.

"We weren't expecting you," I say coldly, brushing past them to go for a glass in the cabinet. No point in pretending they're not demons for their latest attack on Val. Extra demon points for dragging me away from what was about to be a rare win in my pathetic love life.

"That's an interesting fashion choice," Mom says, and I glance down at my untucked dress shirt, currently wrinkled in a suggestive region. My belly quivers from the memory of Nash's beautiful hands skimming up my sides to dislodge it. His scent. His touch. His *heat.* Gah!

Yep, just seconds ago I was feeling the opposite of this.

"It's because the… uh…" I don't actually have an excuse queued up, which turns out to be irrelevant when everyone's attention shifts to the doorway. My relief fades when I see why.

Uh-oh.

"Hey. I'm Nash," he says.

Also in typical Nash Ellis style, he's gone out of his way to make this moment as awkward as possible. My lust competes with dread as I drink in the intoxicating sight of a smoking hot, barely clothed rocker.

I thought he was getting dressed?! Pulling on a pair of jeans and not even bothering to zip them up is not getting dressed. That's top-shelf fantasy material— and inviting a whole shitload of drama I don't need.

I'd be furious right now if I could take my eyes off him. Damn, he's beautiful.

"Who's Nash?" Dad asks, studying our half-naked guest in horror before turning his glare on me.

"He's my, uh…"

"Boyfriend," Val lies.

Nash and I snap a look at him, heat flushing my… everything. What is he doing?!

"Her *boyfriend?*" Dad echoes.

You know he's pissed when he can't form words and just repeats other ones he's hearing. He once told the air conditioner guy, *"there's a coolant leak somewhere and the leak seal isn't working so you'll have to come back and do a three-day shut down to find it so it will just be the four-hundred-twenty-two dollars to refill the refrigerant for now?!"*

The air conditioner guy said "yes."

But I don't know if "yes" is the right answer for this current dilemma. I don't want to contradict Val, but there's no way Nash will accept such a—

"Mr. and Mrs. Andrews, so great to finally meet you."

My snarky friend strides forward with a hand outstretched and a grin I've never seen before. To say that grin is frightening is, well, frightening.

My parents don't even try to hide their horror as they shake hands with my nemesis turned co-spy turned (fantasy?) turned fake boyfriend.

"Paige, what's he talking about?" Mom asks, discreetly wiping her hand on the side of her slacks after touching Nash. Except it wasn't discreet. At all. That snob full-on rubbed her thigh as if he's singlehandedly responsible for history's infectious disease problem.

I wince and peek at my friend/coworker/almost hookup/adversary, but he only seems amused by the whole thing. In fact… Did he just shove his jeans down lower? Yep, I clearly see the delicious tattoo on his hip that was covered just a second ago—right beside the sexy V of his abs my mother has suddenly noticed.

Oh my god. She's openly checking him out.

"It's new," I mutter, wishing I could teleport anywhere but here. "Why the surprise visit? Want something to drink? Is it still raining outside?"

Ah!

"No, thank you," Mom says, her cheeks pink with more than expensive blush. Who needs makeup when you have a hot musician willing to strip in front of you for no reason? For real, does the boy not realize what his annoyingly perfect body does to people?

I survey his smug expression. Yeah, he realizes just fine.

He raises his brows in amusement at my warning look. Ass.

"We're here to see Perceval," Dad says, pulling us back to the other elephant in the room. It's a freaking safari in here today.

"That's kind of inappropriate given the circumstances," I say, shifting my irritation to my father.

"His lack of response to the *circumstances* is why we were forced to come in person." Dad focuses his cool stare on Val. "Since we haven't received a response to our inquiry, we're assuming you've elected not to challenge the claim?"

Val shrugs, still not looking up. "What do you want me to say? You know I don't have the money."

"That's unfortunate," our father says in a snide tone. "You would if you had finished your degree and gotten a real job. I guess we'll have to push the courts to liquidate your assets and garnish your wages—should you ever have any."

He lasers a look at Val's precious recording equipment, and my brother pales, panic flooding his face.

"You can't do that!" he cries.

"We can and we will," Mom says. "Unless you prefer to come home and stop acting like a child with this absurd pipe dream. Really, do you have any idea how embarrassing it is when people ask about you?"

Val flinches, his fingers tightening around the edge of the windowsill.

"You're lucky we're even giving you the option to come home. In my day when children rebelled they ended up in prison," Dad says, crossing his arms.

Hmm. Seems like a stretch.

"Or worse," Mom adds, not to be outdone on the hyperbole.

"So which will it be, son?" Dad says, continuing the bad-cop-bad-cop routine my parents have perfected with my brother. "A long, painful legal battle that you know you'll lose, or a bright, prosperous future?"

"Please don't do this," Val says faintly, tears gathering in his eyes. "I've never asked you for anything. All I want is to be left alone. *Please* just leave me alone."

My heart breaks at the pain in his voice, the fear when he lifts his pleading gaze to us—his *family.* Yes, the people who are supposed to love and support him unconditionally. The people who should be his rock, his foundation.

Not the ones destroying him.

Everything in me wants to lash out at my horrible parents, but I'm afraid of making things worse. I wasn't ready for this confrontation. I need time to think, to prepare. To strategize like I do for everything else. We have to call a meeting, sit down and carefully develop a plan that will allow us to—

"You probably shouldn't *liquidate* his recording equipment. He's going to need that shit," Nash interrupts.

Four sets of eyes dart to him.

"Excuse me?" Dad says, turning his venom on the intruder.

Nash returns a casual shrug, not even a hint of apprehension or concern in his demeanor. I get the sense that boy isn't afraid of anyone. How can you be when your back is covered in reminders of monsters you've already faced?

"The recording equipment," he repeats, waving at the table. "Val will need it for his project with Larinda Scott."

Oh no. What's he doing?!

My parents stare at Nash in disbelief, then their son. After several seconds of silence, Dad spits out an obnoxious laugh.

"You're joking, right?"

Nash tilts his head, eyeing them calmly. "No. I'm Larinda's creative advisor, and I've asked Val to assist us with her current projects."

Creative advisor? Zero chance he didn't just make that up. I groan inwardly at the storm he's brewing.

"I'm sorry, but there's no way Larinda Fucking Scott wants anything to do with our son," Dad says.

"And there's no way you should be permitted to interact with other human beings, yet here we are," Nash returns.

Shit.

Dad's eyes bulge, severely threatening his laser surgery—and his sockets. All our sockets, really. Anything is possible at this point, including exploding eyeballs. Nash Ellis plus Rhonda and Burt Andrews is not an equation the mathematics community has considered yet.

I should have just told my parents I wasn't home.

"There's no way I should be permitted to interact with other human beings, yet here we are?!" Dad roars, storming forward.

Nash doesn't flinch as the older man ducks just inches from his face.

"Correct," he says, then leans past my father to address my mom. "Also, to answer your earlier question, Ms. Andrews, from what I've observed, I'm sure your children *do* know how embarrassing it is when people ask about you."

Thwack.

The room stills, a heaviness filling the air as we stare in shock.

Nash clenches his jaw, stoically absorbing the sting of my father's palm. His cheek blooms with a red print, his eyes fixed on some invisible object on the far wall. I can't breathe as I swing my gaze between him and my father.

"Dad," Val exhales in horror.

The man steps back, his hand shaking like it doesn't understand what it just did.

"You need to leave!" I shout, recovering my vocal cords.

My parents exchange a look, and Dad opens his mouth to speak.

"Now!" I point at the door. I can't read my father's expression as he glares at me, and honestly, I don't want to. Straightening to my full height, I dare him to make more of a scene. After several tense seconds, he shakes his head and stalks to the exit, my mother close behind.

Nash's eyes are hot with anger as he tracks their every step until they're gone.

* * *

"I'm so sorry!" I say, rushing to Nash the second we're alone.

He shrugs off my attempt to comfort him and presses a hand to his cheek.

"It's fine. Forget it," he mumbles.

"It's not fine. It's so, so far from fine. Wait, where are you going?"

I follow him when he starts down the hall.

"To get my clothes."

"We should talk about this. My parents, they're—"

"Let's not, okay?" Stormy blue eyes flash back at me, stopping me in my tracks. I can't even tell if I'm looking at pain or rage. Maybe both. "I'm fine. You're fine. The whole fucking world is fine, so let's just… finish this project and move on with our lives."

A chill runs through me. "Move on? What are you saying?"

He swipes his shirt off the floor.

"Nash!"

I grab his arm, immediately letting go when he winces. Something dark and ominous shadows his features before he clears it and shakes his head.

"I'm saying, we had it right in the beginning. This"—he motions between us—"isn't worth the drama. There are plenty of other guys you can fool around with on the other side of the tracks. I'll upload the latest files on the Jarvis McKinnley campaign when I get home."

"What the hell are you talking about? The other side of the tracks? Nash!"

I march after him, but he's already at the exit.

"I'll text you about Larinda's songs," he tosses at Val before slamming the door behind him.

I stare after him in shock. What just happened? How did I go from having Nash in my bed to being sworn enemies again?

Probably the same way you went from being sworn enemies to having Nash in your bed.

"Well, that went well," Val says dryly.

I spin back and watch as my brother drops to the chair in front of his laptop.

"What am I supposed to do?" I ask, almost frantic. How is he so calm?

He shrugs and unwinds the cable of his studio headphones. "Not much you *can* do."

"There has to be! I have to fix this!"

"Our father *hit him*, Paige. Physically assaulted him. Pretty sure you can't fix this."

"But I still have to work with him!"

"Yeah, that's gonna be super awkward."

I fire a glare at him. "You're not helping."

He's about to respond when he stops and searches my face instead. "Wait. This isn't about work. And that wasn't just a random hookup. You actually *like* this guy."

"What? I do not!" Yeah, I won't win any awards for that comeback.

He huffs a laugh. "Uh, yeah, you do. You want to marry him and have his babies."

I reach for something to throw at him, but the umbrella I snag probably isn't the wisest choice. His smile grows when I lower it back to the floor.

"Also, how did you know we were hooking up?"

"Pretty sure the cockroaches under the fridge knew you were hooking up," he grunts.

"Ew."

"Tell me about it."

I make a face, and he grins. "Well, for your information, it wouldn't have worked anyway because *I'm not worth the drama.* According to him, I was just *fooling around on the other side of the tracks.* Whatever that means."

"It means you're a prissy rich girl and he's—"

"I know what it means," I hiss.

He offers a crooked smile as he yanks the headphones over his ears. Good timing too because a second later—Mrs. Hammond in the Key of Awful.

"You have to be kidding me," I groan, throwing up my hands. She chooses *now* to rehearse?

"Hey, is that a Jarvis McKinnley song?" Val asks with a glint.

I really need to stock up on throwable objects.

* * *

I'm in no better mood on Monday. Nausea sweeps through me from replays of that disastrous encounter with my parents. The argument. The echo of a slap. Even worse is the ache in my chest when I think about those rapturous minutes with Nash right before. His scorching gaze, the adorable smirk that got ripped away from me just seconds later. God, I just want to devour and own him—*hold* him—and now I don't even know if I can get a conversation.

Val insists I can't fix this one, but I don't know how I can't *not* fix it.

"Oh shit," I gasp, jumping back in terror at the figure under my desk. My tea sloshes in my travel mug, my pulse pounding violently as I study the shadow that looks just as frightened.

"Chad?"

I force in a calming breath.

He nods, waving me down. I glance around the office for witnesses before crouching to face him.

"What's going on? Why are you under my desk?"

"Shh!" He lifts his finger to his lips. "It's spy business."

I blink at him. "Huh?"

"Meet me in the conference room in three minutes," he whispers.

"Oh. Um. Sure."

"Great. Just try not to be suspicious," he warns.

You mean, like hiding under someone's desk for god knows how long to deliver a message you could have texted?

"Okay, but why didn't you just message me?" I ask.

Also, we're still squatting on the floor so I feel like we're past suspicious and blatantly in "making a scene" territory at this point.

"We can't have any traceable evidence." His *duh* look clearly ignores everything else about our present situation.

"I highly doubt future prosecutors are going to do jumping jacks over a text between two coworkers about a meeting in a conference room," I point out.

His gaze narrows at me and my spy ignorance. "Trust no one," he warns gravely.

"I… okay," I say, giving up. "See you in three minutes."

"Two," he corrects.

"I thought you said three."

"Yeah, but that was a minute ago."

"But it's just us, right? It could still be three minutes if we start the clock now."

He rolls his eyes. "That's not how this works, Paige."

I don't even have a response for that so I just look around again and offer a weak smile to the employees giving me strange looks as they pass.

"I'm going to stand up now," I tell my co-conspirator.

"Good idea. Go slow. Someone could be watching."

"Right."

I grip the desk to pull myself up.

"And I'll stay here so no one knows we spoke," he whispers.

* * *

I've checked my phone a hundred times since Friday night for a response from Nash. Every time I see a blank screen, my stomach rolls with a fresh ache. Could Val have been right? Was Nash becoming more than a fun nemesis? More than a hookup and steamy crush? Do I have legitimate feelings for him? The thought of not touching him again, not even sharing a smile or banter leaves me feeling hollow. I hadn't even realized what an important part of my day he'd become.

So yes, it's no surprise I'm checking my phone, yet again, on the walk to the conference room. Just the smallest message could put me out of my misery, but alas all I get is a photo of a grape that's shaped like a pumpkin from my uncle.

In other news, Chad is six inches behind me as we stalk through the hall. True to his word, he hid creepily under my desk for two whole minutes while I sat at Nash's old one, because… yeah.

Once we're both inside the conference room, I reach for the partition blinds as he closes the door.

"What are you doing?" he hisses.

"Closing the blinds to the main part of the office so people can't see us."

"But then they'll think we're having a secret conversation!"

"We *are* having a secret conversation."

"Right, but we don't want them to know that. We want them to think this is a regular conversation."

Now, I'm just lost. "Then why couldn't we have a *regular conversation* in your office as soon as I arrived this morning?"

I watch the explanation melt in his brain.

"That's beside the point," he mutters. He shakes off the rocky start to our covert rendezvous and leans forward. "Eva and I heard from our field agent last night."

"Our field agent?"

"Nash," he replies in an annoyed tone.

My stomach tightens as my heart beats faster at his name. So apparently Nash is talking to everyone else, including Chad. Fantastic.

"Oh. Yeah. What did he say?" I manage.

He glances out the window before leaning even closer. Again, why couldn't we just do this in his office?

"Brighthouse is going to sponsor a board game competition, and Larinda will be the host."

"What's a board game competition, and why would a telecom company want to —oh wait. Do you mean an online gaming competition?" Because that would make way more sense.

He shakes his head, but I'm pretty sure he does.

"It's going to be a huge, public event. He says we need to get one of our people entered into the competition so we can sabotage it," Chad continues.

That's a great idea, except: "Isn't there a chance Brighthouse might recognize one of the Sandeke employees? Wasn't that the whole reason Nash isn't supposed to work here *and* for Larinda?"

"Yeah, but he's still working here, just no one knows."

"Exactly. That's my point."

"Yeah, but…"

We stare at each other for a good eight seconds before it becomes clear that this exchange is irredeemable.

"Anyways," Chad says. "No, they won't recognize us because it's all online. Our people can be anonymous."

"Online?"

He nods.

"So they're playing games online?"

"Yep."

"As in an *online gaming competition*?"

I wait for that to click. I can be patient when I need to be.

"That's beside the point," he mumbles.

With a deep breath, I brace myself. "So what's the plan?"

Chad bends close, casting yet another very suspicious-looking glance through the glass wall. If people didn't know we were having a secret meeting before, they certainly do now.

"Tomorrow night. Seven PM. Nash's place. Eva will text you the address."

You don't need it, my brain mutters.

That's beside the point, I mutter back.

9—REVEALING

NASH

Paige shows up first. (Well, technically Eva did since she was with Marcos for dinner, but she's always here so that doesn't count.)

I don't know why Paige's early arrival surprises me. There's zero chance she's been late for anything in her life. I bet if I polled her mom she'd confirm Paige shot out down to the second on her due date. Also, I have no interest in polling her mom about childbirth.

It's been four days since that explosive night at her apartment, and my stomach twists at the sight of her big hazel eyes and dark red hair. So many warring emotions, things to say, and in this moment, all I've got is the fact that her hair is in a cute side braid for the first time that I've seen.

I decide she already knows that and settle on, "Hey."

I step back so she can enter, still fishing for words. "Marcos and Eva are in his room. They'll be out in a few minutes. You're early." She probably already knew that too.

"Yeah, sorry."

Is she nervous? Her gaze digs into me, adding a heaviness to the air around us. Probably has something to do with the fifteen texts I didn't respond to and the storm of warring emotions jerking us around. "I, uh, made a stop first and thought it would take longer."

"It's fine. Come in." I look away as she moves past me, avoiding the awkward subtext we have going on.

Remember just a few days ago when we were about to hook up and then every-thing went to shit?

I had a hard night after that. Fucking brutal when some dude you don't even know triggers painful memories and exposes a lifetime of insecurities and fears. My cheek throbbed the entire ride home, and I don't even know how much of it was internal and external. What I *do* know? People like the Andrews will never understand people like me, and what happened with her father is just a preview of what I'd always be in her world.

No, thank you.

"I know you probably saw my messages," she rushes out. "I understand why you didn't respond, but—"

I hold up my hand. "Don't. I get it. It's fine."

"It's not fine! What happened, it wasn't right and it wasn't fair."

My heart stutters at her apologetic stare.

"Maybe not but it happened, so let's just move on."

"Nash, come on. Please, don't shut me out. Let's talk about this."

"There's nothing to talk about. Just let it go."

Her eyes narrow, and I can tell my resistance is reigniting the fire. I don't care. It's my battle to win or lose, not hers.

"I'm just trying to make things right," she says, her voice wavering.

"It's not your crime to apologize for. You didn't do anything wrong."

"So why are you mad at me?"

"I'm not mad at you." Well, I *wasn't.*

Her mask slips as the frustration leaks out. "Then why are you acting like this?"

Yep. This is exactly why I didn't want to have this conversation.

"Do you have any idea how many times I've been hit over the course of my life?" I ask, studying her with a stony expression.

She winces, her face reddening in the silence.

"You know I don't," she says quietly.

"Yeah, well, I don't either."

Her gaze shoots to me in surprise, and I lean against the wall, crossing my arms. "A fucking lot. But the difference between before and now is that I don't have to stand there and take that bullshit anymore."

"Of course not. I'm so sorry. My family is… It's complicated."

I shake my head and harden my stance. "That's my point. Your family is 'complicated.' *My* family consists of the two guys who live in this apartment, and neither are blood. I don't even have a family in the traditional sense, and after what I saw last night, I'm okay with that. Your parents are assholes, Paige. I will never fit into your world with the—the lawn parties and country clubs and Thanksgiving at Grandma's. I will never understand or accept that as my normal."

"Okay, but if you let me explain—"

"That's what I'm telling you. You don't *have* to explain. The other night was not a shock to me, just confirmation of what this bullshit world is. I know what 'families' like yours think about orphan trash like me. Believe me. No explanation necessary. I've spent my entire life being taught I'm nothing and don't belong."

"Wait, what? Nash, that's not what—"

We're interrupted by a violent knock on the door, and Paige seems way more distressed by the interruption than I am. I don't know what she was about to say, but I have no interest in hearing it. This conversation was over the second her father's palm met my face and reality was literally hammered back into me.

I try to ignore her pained look as I cross to the door. Her distress hurts, twisting something inside that's telling me maybe I'm the asshole right now. A hypocrite. A liar. That, despite my commitment to not giving a shit, maybe I give more shits than I'm willing to admit. Maybe for a few terrifying seconds, when this woman seemed to want me, I started to believe I might actually want something too.

All it took was one slap to prove how wrong I was.

I don't even care who's behind the door right now. I'm just grateful to be spared another raw reminder that caring and connection only lead to pain.

For now, we spy.

I pull open the door and…

Oh.

My.

God.

"Mr. Reedweather?" I ask, staring at him in stunned silence.

"Hello, Nash-el-is," he whispers in a low voice. He leans forward and waggles his brows like I might not recognize him. To be fair I can't remember the last time I've seen someone dressed in a fully buttoned trench coat that wasn't on a crime show. And… is that a fedora? It's pushed so far back on his head I'm positive he's never worn a hat before.

"The pumpkin flies at midnight," he says gravely.

"Huh?"

"The pumpkin!" He adds an emphatic nod that does nothing to help the situation.

"It's a code they came up with," Paige mutters behind me.

I glance back at her in confusion. "A code? I don't…"

"To enter!" Mr. Reedweather hisses. "So you know it's me!"

I turn back to him. "But I know it's you from seeing you."

"Right but…" He grunts in frustration. "You never know who's listening."

"Okay, but we do, because…" I lean out and scan the empty hallway.

No one. No one is listening. No one will ever listen because this is the stupidest spy mission in the history of spy missions. If someone is listening, it's to turn this into a rom-com TV script one day. Or they're just morbidly fascinated and/or confused like I am.

"Um. Sure. Then, I guess, come in." I wave him in, glancing back at Paige for confirmation. She returns a pleading look, but I don't even know what she's pleading for. When I turn back to Reedweather, he hasn't moved. He lifts his thick brows to signal… something.

"The code," he hints under his breath, gesturing with his head again.

"Oh. Um." I look back at Paige but her shrug is supremely unhelpful.

"The pumpkin…" Reedweather coaches.

"The pumpkin?"

He nods, looking pleased. That's good, I guess? The pumpkin. Got it.

But he doesn't move and after several more seconds of awkward silence, he swirls his hand to encourage me.

"Um… the pumpkin…" I scratch my temple, glancing back at Paige who still is not helping. "Flies…?" I draw out, trying to read the man's reaction. When his eyes light up, I know I'm onto something. "At… midnight?"

"Yes!" he cries, thrusting a finger in the air and marching past me into the apartment.

So the code *response* is the same as the code? Pretty sure that's not spy protocol. Also, aren't codes supposed to be nondescript so on the off-chance someone *is* actually listening they don't immediately know the weird thing you just said is a code? Assuming of course, the late May trench coat and awkward fedora didn't give it away. If there's a spy oversight committee, we are so getting audited and fined.

Reedweather's eyes widen and narrow in rapid succession as he takes in our small, cluttered apartment. It's hilarious watching him try to play it cool.

Out of nowhere he says, "This reminds me of eighty-two."

Thinking this is another code, I glance at Paige for interpretation but she looks just as perplexed.

"It does?" I ask for lack of anything else.

His expression turns wistful as he scratches his chin all pondering-like. By the way his eyes shift as he thinks, he's either conflicted by this memory or just realized he's the only one wearing a trench coat.

"That was the year I was poor," he says gravely.

I swallow a choke.

"Oh?" Paige asks quickly, probably so I don't say something to make this worse.

"I was never a bike boy like you, of course, but I know what it's like to struggle. You remember our discussion?"

The confusing conversation we had in the hall last week? Yep, I remember. I haven't been able to cleanse it from my head no matter how hard I try.

"Well, I wasn't entirely honest with you, son. You see…"

We hold our breaths.

"There was a time when station wagons reigned supreme."

Oh.

In a million years I wouldn't have guessed that's how that sentence ended.

"You mean, the car?" I ask, praying there isn't another definition of station wagon because I'm already lost.

"Yes, the car. A fitting metaphor for life, don't you think?" He scratches his chin again which is the only way I know that was a serious statement we're supposed to consider. I call on every poetic neuron in my brain to solve the riddle of metaphoric station wagons.

Those are the cars with the big trunk, right?

We're saved from cryptic philosophical musings by commotion down the hall. Marcos and Eva must have realized it's time to stop making out and join the rest of us lonely people.

Time clearly stops the moment Reedweather sees Marcos.

"Mark-O?" he whispers, his eyes igniting with the luster of the brightest station wagon headlights. "You're at this meeting too?"

"He lives here, Dad," Eva says.

There is no question in my mind that, like "the year he was poor," this moment will be another pivotal event in Reed Reedweather's personal narrative. (No doubt relayed in exquisite detail to unsuspecting victims down the road.)

This is the moment he learned Nash-el-is lives with Mark-O.

"Marcos is my roommate," I confirm.

"Hello, Sir," Marcos says with a nod.

"Well! Isn't this just *Fortuitous Ambiguity!*"

Marcos holds his smile and even adds a shrug, making it look like he agrees with whatever that means. I wish I could pull off fake agreeable as well as he can. No wonder he's so good at this shit. Me? By the uncomfortable looks Paige keeps shooting my way, I look neither certain nor agreeable. It doesn't matter when another knock hammers out.

There's only one person still missing, and I brace myself as I pull open the door to reveal…

For the love of—seriously?

"The pumpkin flies at midnight," Chad whispers in his three-piece suit. He peers over aviator sunglasses positioned low on his nose to blast me with a conspiratorial wink. Geez. The least they could have done is coordinate their spy personas. We're in two different movie franchises as I mumble the bizarre code in response and wave Chad inside.

He doesn't even remove his sunglasses as he squints at each person in the room. Not surprisingly, the individual wearing the fedora and trench coat is the most excited to see him. Chad doesn't reciprocate, however, because his joy is reserved for his former nemesis.

"Marcos," he gasps, lurching forward. Marcos awkwardly returns the fist bump, an agreeable smile still plastered to his face. It's amazing, really, how likeable my friend is. Our other roommate Nate is the same. They both are what you might call "charming." Also, magnetic, good-looking, intelligent, witty, motivated, and even *jacked* from all those hours in the gym to blow off steam.

Yes, being constantly surrounded by their perfection is as annoying as it sounds.

For now, that perfection is being ogled by Chad. For real, the dude is openly checking him out like he's a long-lost lover just returned from sea. Reedweather had a similar starry-eyed reaction when he first arrived, and I'm starting to wonder if Eva wasn't the only one who fell for my roommate during his five seconds as an intern at Reedweather Media.

"No hard feelings about the job, right? We're good?" Chad asks, looking nervous as he tugs the lapels of his tux jacket.

Marcos is currently rocking a six-figure salary in an upper-level management position, working for a guy he respects and a cause he believes in. As a result of that whole mess, he also has a top-shelf girlfriend and mounds of industry respect racked up in a very short time. He and his boss Martin Sandeke may arguably even be friends now. That's quite the feat since after meeting the guy at least ten times, he still doesn't know my name.

My boy is living the dream. Pretty sure he's fine not messing around with that weird-ass Mer-shit.

"Nah. All good," Marcos says. "You were made for that job." He adds a smile that makes Chad—and everyone else—smile back with relief. This situation really can't handle any more variables at this point. Besides, Paige and I already have the awkward-working-enemies slot filled.

Speaking of…

"Okay, great. Can we get started then?" Paige asks. There's definitely a bite to her tone, meaning she's probably stewing about our earlier tiff.

"Of course, of course!" Reedweather says, waving his hand in a circle. He removes his fedora, I guess to signal the official start of our meeting. Chad keeps on the sunglasses, though.

Forty-five minutes later, we've organized ourselves enough to have an actual conversation about business stuff.

"Right, so we need to sabotage this event on Saturday and generate some bad publicity," Marcos says, cutting off a Reedweather monologue about an uncle who either did or did *not* run for mayor of an obscure town in British Columbia. (It was hard to follow since he kept adding random French words for "accuracy.")

"Exactly," Eva agrees. Her gaze rests on Marcos and then me, indicating there's more to this plan than she can say out loud. I'd bet every plugin on my SSD drive that Reedweather and Chad aren't part of the real plan within a plan. Will we have a second meeting later to develop the actual plan? And how do we coordinate that with the official plan? Damn, this is confusing.

Recap. Brighthouse stole Sandeke's big idea. Sandeke now wants to ruin Brighthouse's attempt to execute that idea. Marcos and Eva want to ruin both Brighthouse *and* Sandeke, so… If my powers of deduction have any merit, I'm going to guess she'll want us to drop hints to Brighthouse that this strike came from Sandeke Telecom, which will start the war that will hurt both monster corporations. It's what I'd do anyway.

Crap, what if I'm not as terrible at this spy shit as I want to be?

"Perfect. So now the question is… how do we get someone inside and what is their *mission*?" Reedweather whispers *mission* like he really does think someone is bored enough to eavesdrop on us. I so wish there'd been anything worth hearing in the last hour.

I'm about to joke that we should write *the mission* in invisible ink and eat it after we memorize it when I realize that will send us on a tangent I'll immediately regret. Even worse, they might actually like the idea.

"What if we have someone enter the contest pretending to be a secret spy? He could have an accent and speak in code," Chad suggests.

"That's a great idea!" Reedweather chirps. "His name could be Alan!"

"Or even Roy," Chad says. Reedweather nods slowly, considering.

"What's a 'secret spy'?" Paige asks.

I was wondering that too.

So were Marcos and Eva by their expressions.

"Um, a spy people don't know about," Chad says, squinting at us in irritation. (At least, I think he's squinting. Hard to tell through the sunglasses).

I tilt my head and *definitely* squint back. There's so much wrong with that sentence I don't even know where to start.

Paige does. "Okay, *one*, that doesn't make any sense. Spies by definition are secret, so you can't *pretend* to be something that requires pretending in the first place. And *two*, the whole point of spying is to *not* draw attention to yourself and make people think you're a spy."

Chad deflates, possibly seeing the weakness of his plan. "You're right. The spy should be from Idaho? No one would ever guess they're from Idaho."

Paige shoots me an exasperated look, and I clear my throat. "*Or*," I draw out. "Since I'm already in with Larinda's team and have been officially invited to the event, I could be the spy."

I ignore Marcos who's trying not to laugh at how annoyed I am. Sorry, but not all of us get to spend our spy careers hooking up in closets with our attractive spy partners.

I command myself not to look at Paige or think about hooking up in closets.

Damn, now that's all I can think about.

"But you can't sabotage the event," she says, forcing me to look anyway. Shit. And she's wearing another scarf. Double shit. "You might blow your cover and lose your in. It's too risky."

"She's right," Marcos says. "Paige should go as Nash's girlfriend. She can sabotage it."

I fire a glare at him that screams *What the hell, man?!*

His return look says, *You're welcome.*

My look says, *Fuck you.*

His look says, *You mean* her, *right? Cuz you liiiiike her.*

I roll my eyes and stop looking.

"Yes!" Eva says. "Paige goes in as Nash's girlfriend and the two of you can find a way for her to ruin the event. What do we know about the Brighthouse headquarters?"

I really *really* don't want to get involved in this conversation again but…

"How can Paige be my girlfriend? I thought the whole point of 'firing me' from Reedweather Media was because we didn't want them to trace me back to Sandeke Telecom."

Eva nods. "Right, because you're supposedly working for Larinda, so it would look suspicious if you were also working for a Sandeke company. Your girlfriend working there is no big deal, though."

True.

My girlfriend.

I sigh, out of ideas to stop this.

"You and Paige should hold hands when you get there," Reedweather suggests.

"Make sure you update your statuses on social media," Chad adds.

Yeah, none of this is helping. Paige looks even less excited about the plan than I am.

"Oh! You should make up a story about how you met at a mini golf course." Also Chad.

"Excellent idea, son," Reedweather agrees. "Or even a full-sized golf course. Do you know how to golf, Nash-el-is? If not, I'd be happy to teach you."

"Or even racquetball! I fucking love racquetball," Chad says. "Back in college—"

"Why does she have to be my girlfriend, though?" I cut in. "Can't she just be my friend or a peer?" I was trying for *inquisitive* but my tone probably tipped more towards *indignant*. Paige clearly thinks so when she scowls at me.

"Would you bring a random *peer* as your VIP plus one? Would they even allow that?" Eva points out.

True again.

Crap.

"Fine," I mutter.

"Great! Then it's settled," Reedweather says, clapping his hands. He pushes to his feet and starts toward the door. "Until tomorrow," he adds, turning back and winking at Chad and Paige. Then he looks to Eva. "Until…" His mind works on something. "This Sunday, for brunch?"

"Friday, actually. Rummy night with Mary Lou," she corrects without much enthusiasm.

Ah. Yes. The infamous rummy night. I don't exactly know what happens at those things, but I know it involves stuff it shouldn't. Like giant wooden bears and something called a "scotch robe." Marcos described it to me, and I got more confused and alarmed for his safety.

"And you, Nash-el-is…" Reedweather's face falls when his gaze rests on me. "I don't know, my friend. When will we see each other again?"

He looks stricken. I still haven't figured out why we need to document all of this.

"I can drop by the office next week," I say, mostly to stop the conversation.

"Excellent!" He claps his hands again and opens the door. With a grave nod, he slips through and pulls it closed behind him.

And then we stare at each other.

"Our meeting isn't over, though, right?" Paige asks.

"Did it really even start?" Marcos replies.

Eva clears her throat. "Right, so let's do that."

10—PRETENDING

PAIGE

An hour later, I'm not so sure about the plan for crashing this weekend's event, but I'm very sure Nash still hates me and is acting like a child.

I get that what my father did was reprehensible. But the key point of the story is that my father did it. I'm the one declaring it reprehensible. If Nash gave me two seconds to explain, maybe we could've spared ourselves an extremely uncomfortable mission coming up. We have to pretend to be in love? He won't even talk to me.

You know those story plots where you're screaming for the main characters to have one simple conversation that would clear everything up and save a novel's worth of drama? That's me. Silently screaming at Nash not to make us an exasperating plot device when he storms off for "a thing in Harlem."

I waited behind to talk to him, and now I'm staring at the door, still in disbelief that he left me alone in his apartment.

Alone.

In *his* apartment.

"Hey, so, uh, you need a ride or something?" Marcos asks, studying me as I hover in front of their couch.

Okay, so not *alone* alone.

"Do you have a car?" I ask him, surprised.

"No," he says with a slow grin.

Geez, he's pretty. What is it with this apartment and gorgeous men? Marcos, the sexy executive. Nash, the sexy musician. I don't think I could handle meeting the third one… probably an underwear model.

"So who's your other roommate? You have a third one, correct?" I ask randomly because, small talk—not my thing. Eva left with Chad and Nash since she has an early meeting tomorrow, and it feels awkward to walk out now that we've acknowledged I didn't.

"Yeah. Nate. He should be home any minute." Marcos shoves his hands in the back pockets of his jeans, showing off his trim waist and perfect torso. I wondered what guy would be good enough for an exquisite, intelligent badass like Eva Reedweather.

Right here. This guy.

"Oh yeah. The, um, underwear model," I mumble.

What?!

No!!!! That was fantasy brain, not actual fact. Shit.

Marcos arches a brow, an amused glint in his mesmerizing blue-green eyes. For real, they must have had a freaking casting director fill this apartment.

"Wait, I mean… not that," I say, kicking myself. Crap, I'm so bad at people. Nash and I share that at least. On second thought, no wonder we bombed the communication portion of our relationship. It's a miracle we got as far as we did.

"Not what?" Marcos asks, now looking beyond amused.

"An underwear model," I explain, thinking I can fix this for some reason. "I mean, I know Nate isn't an underwear model. He just was in my head."

Marcos' eyes widen, and then I hear those words with my brain instead of my ears. Oh no.

"You know Nate?" he asks.

"What? No," I rush out.

"So why do you fantasize about him being an underwear model?"

"No, no, no," I say with a laugh. "I don't fantasize about him. I was just... I mean, you all are..." I wave at him, and he cocks his head.

"We're all underwear models?"

"No! Hot, I mean. As in, regular hot, not specifically hot."

"Regular hot," he repeats dryly.

I swallow air down my scratchy throat.

"Yeah, like. Underwear models are a certain type of hot. Then there's, um, athlete hot, and motorcycle hot, first responder hot, lawyer hot..." I stop listing things when I realize I've done nothing in the last two minutes to help this situation.

The side of his mouth tilts up. "So, Nate is in the underwear-model-hot category?"

"Yes! Exactly. I mean, I don't know. I don't know what he looks like."

Marcos nods like he gets it, but he doesn't. He can't. *I* don't even know what I'm saying.

"I see. What kind of hot am I?" By the return of his amused smile, he's not flirting, just curious.

"Oh. Uh. I guess you'd be executive hot."

"Ah," he says. "How do I get to underwear model hot like Nate?"

"He's not! I mean, I don't know if he is, but underwear model hot isn't necessarily more hot than executive hot."

Playful blue-green eyes flash back at me through tousled dark hair, and I feel the heat rising in my chest. I'm probably bright red.

"What about Nash?" he asks. His smile is mischievous this time. It doesn't improve the odds of this ending well.

"Nash?" I sound like I'm pretending I don't know him.

He raises a brow again, probably wondering why I thought that would work.

"Sorry, yes. Um. Nash is, artist hot, I guess."

"Artist hot." He squints like he's thinking. "Yeah, I guess I see it. What with all those tattoos and the tortured genius vibe." His smile grows in sync with my blush.

Tortured genius? Tortured, maybe.

Fine.

Genius too.

So annoying.

"Well…" is my eloquent response.

"You don't agree?"

"No. I mean, yes. I mean… He hates me right now," I mutter.

I look up in time to see his humor fade. Marcos may be witty, bright, and driven, but I've seen enough to suggest he's also compassionate and kind. No wonder Nash speaks so highly of his bestie. Why couldn't my beef be with Marcos Oliveira?

Because you're not crazy about him.

Shut up, Brain.

"I guarantee he doesn't hate you," he says.

I want to believe that, but Marcos didn't see the look in his roommate's eyes when he stormed off—Friday night and just now. *His* good intentions didn't get shot down over and over again when he tried to make things right. All I wanted was a rational discussion about what happened like two mature adults. Instead, he ran away. Again. How does he expect to have any meaningful connections in his life if he bolts at the first sign of trouble?

"Trust me. He does. He won't even talk to me about it," I say.

Marcos sighs with a resigned look and motions for me to sit. Great. Guess the inevitable *Welcome to Nash* conversation is about to go down. For the record, all encounters with Nash Ellis should *start* with that conversation.

"So what happened?" he asks, taking the armless armchair perpendicular to the couch.

"Short version? He defended my brother against my horrible parents Friday night," I begin. "And yeah, he probably shouldn't have said what he did, but he didn't deserve to get hit for it. That's why—"

"I'm sorry, what?" Marcos interrupts, stiffening abruptly.

"Nash didn't tell you?"

"No, but he never says much. He bottles shit up and only lets it out in his music."

His music. Gosh, I love his music.

My heart wilts at the sudden sting of loss.

"Yeah, my dad smacked him."

"In the face?"

I nod, swallowing hard.

"Fuck," Marcos breathes out, eyes dark with anger. "He was even quieter than usual when he came home that night."

My nails dig into my palms as I ward off the ache in my chest. "It shouldn't have happened. I've been trying to apologize, begging him to talk to me, but he won't return my messages and refuses to discuss it. What the hell else am I supposed to do?" My clipped tone betrays my frustration. I'm trying. I really am, but he just keeps shoving my attempts back in my face like a moody teenager.

Marcos studies me in the silence, probably sensing my ire. He lives with him. He must have experienced what I'm talking about. My knee bounces nervously beneath the pressure of his evaluation.

"What has Nash told you about his past?" he asks finally, his tone distant, like he's drawing on truths not in this room.

"Not much," I say. "Just that he doesn't have a family, except for you guys. Oh, and he also showed us the dragon tattoo with all the words and explained its meaning."

Surprise filters onto his face as he sits back. His gaze locks on mine, and I shiver through a rush of unease at his expression.

"Wow. I'm surprised you got that far with him," he says. "He must really care about you."

My heart swells even as I shake my head. "I don't get it. He says he's a loner but he seems to have a ton of friends. He's always out doing things."

"Yes, but no one really knows him."

"Kind of hard to get to know someone who runs away and avoids any kind of real interaction," I say before thinking better of it.

A crease spreads over Marcos' forehead as he seems to run something through his mind. Does he agree or disagree? I can't even tell. I know he loves his friend, but his friend is freaking hard!

After another pause, he settles into the cushion. "All three of us had it bad growing up, but Nash had it the worst," he says. "I struggled with feeling like I didn't belong anywhere, but Nash…" He trails off and shakes his head. "His shit was bad, Paige. Really bad."

A stab of sympathy pierces my frustration as I clench my fists in my lap. Uh-oh. This is going to hurt. I can already tell.

"People mistake his sensitivity for weakness," Marcos continues. "They think because he withdraws into himself and stays detached from the world, he's somehow not as equipped to deal with it as the rest of us. But it's the opposite. That guy has been through hell and understands the cruel, ugly side of living better than anyone. The problem is, that's the only side he got for a lot of his life. I've watched him take hit after hit and still get up every time. He's a freaking warrior, but he lives in a world that's told him it doesn't want him."

Oh god. How about a world that's told him he's a *lazy, apathetic moron?*

My throat closes up as the assumptions I'd made come firing back. What is wrong with me? How could I say something so horrible?

Marcos leans forward and rests his elbows on his knees.

"He can't care about people," he continues softly. "He can't care about anything anymore, because every time he did he got crushed. He's given up on this world —people, dreams, pretty much everything and intends to drift through life in an indifferent cloud. Sure, it will never bring him joy, but it will also protect him from being hurt. You have to trust to get betrayed. Care to be wounded. Want something to lose it."

My chest tightens as I absorb the sting of his words. It all makes sense now. Too much sense, and I feel even more hopeless than before. I wanted to fix things with him? How did I expect to do that when I judged him without knowing a thing about him?

Viewing people through *my* lens can't possibly put *their* world in focus.

"So what do I do?" I ask quietly, wincing at the emotion in my voice. "How do I help him see how special he is and how much I..."

Crap. How much I *what*? There's no point denying how I feel about Nash anymore. My aching heart is reflected all over Marcos' face.

"How much you care about him?" he finishes for me.

I look away and nod.

He sighs and shakes his head. "I'm sorry, Paige. I honestly don't know. Nate and I have had a lifetime to gain his trust. Unless you're willing to do the same, you will probably have to accept your relationship for what it is."

Not enough. That's what our relationship is. Not nearly enough.

"And if I'm willing?" I ask.

Marcos narrows his eyes, his gaze intensifying on my face. "Willing to give him a lifetime? You care about him that much? You barely know him."

"Exactly. And the thought of not knowing him better doesn't feel like an option."

After several long seconds, Marcos releases a breath.

"His music," he says. "If you want to know Nash, you have to know his music."

"You mean the music he doesn't share?"

"You looked him up."

"Of course I did. Know what I found?"

"A few bootlegged recordings of very old shows," he replies dryly, like he expected the question.

I nod and cross my arms. "Exactly. Nothing recent, professional, or directly from him. I even found an artist page someone else created on a social media site listing an EP and several singles but couldn't find the actual music anywhere except those few terrible videos. What happened? I mean, the guy is text buddies with *Abram Fletcher*, for goodness sake. Isn't that alone a career-maker?"

And scene.

I see the moment the vault closes. Marcos Oliveira, the overflowing fount of information on Nash Ellis, suddenly dries up on the spot.

"It's complicated," he mutters.

"Most things are with him," I say, and huff another burst of frustration when it becomes clear that's all I'm going to get.

His expression softens as he searches my eyes. "I can't tell you his story, Paige. Only he can, but I can tell you this. Most people aren't damaged by dreams they never achieve. It's having those dreams ripped away that break us."

* * *

Nash looks nothing like a broken artist on the verge of collapse the following morning when he saunters toward our airline gate with a backpack and a confident stride. My pulse picks up the second I see him coming down the aisle, and I know Marcos was right. This boy may have been through hell, but he's rebuilt himself into an impenetrable pillar of indifference—a ridiculously attractive pillar, judging by the frequent ogling and gaping going on in his wake.

Today it seems like he tried extra hard to remind the world he's untouchable by looking like he didn't try at all. Messy dark hair is shoved under a light gray beanie, making hypnotic blue eyes glow at radioactive levels. A black undershirt, black ripped jeans, and worn leather jacket complete the hot rocker look. No, scratch that. The delicious, tattooed hands peeking out from the sleeves of his jacket complete the hot rocker look. Everything in me wants to scoop his fingers into mine and claim them. He's torture to look at, and I can't keep my grubby eyes off him.

His gaze lands on me from several feet away, and the spark of recognition in his face triggers a strange spike of satisfaction.

That's right, Fellow Travelers. That smoking hot rockstar is here for me.

"Hey. 'Sup. Where's Val?" He drops to the empty seat beside me, blasting me with a scented wave of leather and shower-fresh temptation.

"He went to grab us some water," I reply. "He'll be back soon."

"Cool. You ready to do this?"

"Roger that."

My stomach flutters at the lazy half-smile he shoots my way. It's been too long since I've seen one of those on his lips.

"Is that sanctioned spy terminology?" he asks.

"Can't anything be spy terminology if we're trying *not* to sound like spies?"

His soft laugh almost hurts as he shakes his head and gives me a shove with his shoulder. "Whatever, smartass."

Gosh, I've missed this side of him.

He crosses his legs in front of him and settles into the chair like we're in a living room not an airport. I'm not sure how he can look so relaxed. I hate traveling in general, but especially flying. My nerves are firing into hyperdrive at the thought of boarding a plane in a few minutes. If I'd known this mission required a cross-country journey, I would have declined.

No, you wouldn't have.

Yes, I would.

Uh, no. You wouldn't.

Shut it, Brain. Not in the mood.

"Have you been to L.A. before?" he asks. His gaze lowers to my vibrating knee that's probably shaking the entire cluster of seats. I force it still and grip my messenger bag instead.

"Once when I was younger. What about you?"

He nods. "A lot, actually. Lived there for a while before moving to New York. I'm hoping to meet up with some friends during our off-day tomorrow. You and Val don't have to come if you'd rather chill or do tourist shit."

"I'd love to meet your friends."

"Really? Oh. Uh, cool."

"Why do you seem so shocked?"

He shrugs, another smile seeping onto his face. "No reason. It's just, I figured you weren't into the whole angsty artist scene."

"Angsty artist? Is that what you are?" My tone is teasing, but my question is not, and when he shrugs again, the issue that's been bugging me since the first time I searched his name slips out. "Why can't I find your music anywhere?"

"Because I don't release it," he says matter-of-factly.

"Why not?"

"It's not my thing."

"Not your *thing*? You're a musician. How is making music not your thing?"

"I make music. I just don't share it."

I shake my head, confused by this exasperating, complicated boy. "Why not? It would be easy for you. You're so well connected. I mean, you're besties with Abram Fletcher."

Oops. Said that a little loud and now we're getting all kinds of looks. The other travelers are devouring Nash. It's obvious they think they're about to board a flight with a rockstar, even if they don't know which one.

Nash looks away. "We're not besties."

His confidence has melted into a slight frown that makes my chest tighten.

"Sorry," I say.

"For what?"

"For saying that so loud. Everyone's staring now."

"They were already staring."

It's my turn to be surprised. He noticed that? He never seems to notice anything. *Or maybe he does and just ignores it.* I think back to what Marcos said about protective apathy. How much of his life does he gloss over and bury to guard his heart?

"Well, you kind of stand out," I say to lighten the mood.

His lips twist up. "Do I?"

"Yeah. I mean, it's hard not to notice you." I wave over him and don't like when his smile falters again.

"Right. The tattoos and piercings," he says.

"No. The fact that you're gorgeous."

I expect a resurgence of cocky charm, but his brows pinch together and he anchors his gaze on the floor.

"I worked for him. That's how I know Abram," he says.

"Worked for him?"

"On the crew for Redburn, back when they still toured. I was his guitar tech."

My eyes widen as I study him. Seriously? Wow. That's a huge revelation and yet… it feels incomplete.

"It's cool you kept in touch after all this time. That must have been years ago."

"Yeah, a little over three years."

"Does he keep in touch with a lot of his roadies?"

His gaze snaps to mine. Okay, so maybe my question contained a tad more sarcasm than I intended.

"You'd have to ask him," he says, and I sigh with defeat. Never mind. Guess this is the end of today's frustrating trickle of Nash Ellis information.

"You never answered my original question," I say when it becomes clear that's all I'm going to get. "Why don't you release your music?"

"Why are *you* so nervous?" he returns, trying to change the subject.

Of course he is. God forbid he actually open up about something.

"I'm not nervous," I lie, accepting the subject change anyway. No point pissing him off right before we have to spend hours smashed together on an airplane.

A hint of humor returns to his expression when he reaches over to rest a hand on my knee. "We're getting motion sick from this leg. You're definitely nervous."

Heat spreads through my jeans, and I try to stay casual. He can't know there's a zoo of invisible Disney animals singing around me from his touch. His fingers stay on my leg a few seconds too long, and he pulls away abruptly, as if he got lost in the connection as well and just realized what happened. The crease returns to his forehead, and everything in me wants to reach over and lace my fingers with his.

And kiss him.

And strip him.

And tackle him.

Not gonna happen. He's not interested anymore, remember?

Right. Neither am I.

Liar.

Oh my god, Brain! Will you shut up?!

"Fine. Yes. I'm afraid of flying," I say, straightening when he opens his mouth to respond. "And if you tell me statistically I'm more likely to die in a car crash than a plane crash, I will punch you. Phobias have little to do with reason most of the time."

His smile returns. "I wouldn't dream of it. I was going to say I am too."

My retort withers on my tongue as I stare at him. "You're afraid of flying?"

"Yes."

"But how… I mean, you're so calm right now."

He shrugs. "I may look calm, but I'm not. I'm terrified. I don't like heights or enclosed spaces. Flying is my worst nightmare. Throw in a few spiders and a blackout and you've pretty much got a straight flush of my phobias."

"Wow," I say, shaking my head. "You hide it well. You always seem so relaxed. I guess I thought you were…" I bite my lip to stop the word that was about to come out.

"You always thought I was what?" he asks when I trail off. He looks more curious than angry.

I swallow and force it into the open. "Callous."

He flinches and lowers his gaze.

"Not in a cruel way," I rush out. "Just aloof and indifferent. Like nothing really touches you."

He doesn't respond at first, and I watch his face for clues. Something hit him hard, but he's proving my point with my inability to read him.

"If you can't see it, you can't use it against me," he says quietly.

My heart jolts in my chest.

He doesn't look at me as he gets lost in some distant recess of his head. As usual, a part of me wants to follow him there. The other part is relieved I can't.

And then my own head spins with a realization.

"Is that why you don't share your music? If they can't hear it, they can't use it against you?"

His eyes flicker to mine before darting away again.

That's it, isn't it? That's the key to this man. If we can't see his art, we can't tear it down. His music, his heart, his soul. They're all intertwined into the core of who he is, and my stomach drops at the memory of what Marcos said.

"Most people aren't damaged by dreams they never achieve. It's having those dreams ripped away that break us."

God, what happened to this guy?

It's a moot point when Val returns with a couple bottles of water and a dopey expression on his face. He hovers a few feet away as if waiting for permission to approach royalty. If I weren't still so shaken by this latest Nash Ellis insight, I'd laugh at the way my brother fanboys over our friend.

"Hey!" Val says. "You're here."

"I am," Nash replies, light returning to his face. He shifts in his chair to make it obvious Val can take the seat beside him.

"Water?" Val asks, holding out one of the bottles as he joins us.

"Wait, wasn't one of those for me?" I ask, giving him a hard look.

He returns a sheepish smile. "We can share."

"It's fine," Nash cuts in, patting a bottle shoved into a pouch on the side of his bag. "I'm good. Thanks, though."

"Oh, okay. Great. Um, so, what row are you in?" Val asks, sounding nervous. "Oh. Wait. Fourteen. Duh. You and Paige are together, right?"

Nash leans back, more amusement spilling onto his features. He's definitely picking up the weird bro-crush happening right now.

"Row fourteen, yeah. Sandeke Telecom booked our flights together."

"We booked mine separately," Val says, wincing the second the words come out. "Obviously," he mutters.

"Well, I'm glad you were able to come," Nash says, and my heart warms at the way Val perks up.

"I've always wanted to see L.A. Thanks for letting me tag along."

"You never thanked *me* for any of this. I'm the one who invited you," I say, and Val gives me his familiar irritated-brother look.

"We'll make sure you see whatever you want," Nash says. "In fact, I have some people I'd like you to meet."

"Really?" Val's face lights up. "Like who?"

A smug smile settles on Nash's lips, and I'm starting to think the *callous, indifferent pillar of apathy* is actually kind of enjoying this inadvertent mentorship of my brother.

"We'll see who's around," Nash says with a mischievous grin.

11—BONDING

NASH

"What do you mean you only have one room available?" Paige hisses at the desk clerk with impressive vitriol. *Vitriol.* There's an underappreciated word. Has anyone ever used that word in a song? Has anyone ever used that word *ever* in regular human interaction?

These are the questions I'm pondering while Paige argues with a computer. The poor hotel employee operating it keeps making bug eyes at the screen as if willpower alone will make an extra room available. We considered another hotel, but it was already late, our ride had already left, and we already had reservations here—tomorrow, apparently.

"I'm sorry, Ma'am. We have you checking in Friday night, not Thursday. Today is Thursday," he adds, not without a flair of… vitriol.

Oh boy.

Paige stiffens, her eyes narrowing on the young man. "I'm well-versed in basic calendar science, thank you very much," she snaps.

I toss the guy an apologetic shrug.

"It's true," I say. "She's awesome at calendars."

Paige fires an eye-dart at me.

"What?" I ask. "Just last week I was all, *'When's Tuesday?'* and you were all, *'Yesterday.'*"

Her scowl does not appreciate my support. "You're not helping."

"How exactly would I help?" I ask. One, because I live to piss her off, and two, I'm actually curious. "I mean I could hack the computer and make it *look* like there's another room available, but that would be super awkward when we bust in on some dude pleasuring himself in the shower."

"Gah! I hate you." She swipes the keycards off the counter.

"And thank you," she barks at the hotel clerk.

I actually think she meant that sincerely. Paige's "agitated filter" makes everything come out like a professional wrestler hyping up a crowd. Believe me, I got plenty of it on the plane when her nerves about flying transformed into irritation about everything I did, from resting my arm on the armrest to breathing air at an unacceptable rate.

The car ride was no better. I could do nothing right, but strangely it didn't bother me. It was kind of cute, actually. I knew she was just projecting her insecurities, and as she yelled at me for buckling a seatbelt without untwisting it first, it occurred to me that Paige Andrews is my foil in every way. She's all passion, while I'm cool composure. She's a motivated, high-achieving perfectionist, while I'm... not. She's naïve in a lot of ways, privileged and innocent to the struggles of life, while I was world-weary and jaded by the time I was twenty-one.

Maybe that's why she fascinates me. Maybe every abrasive interaction we have leaves a small piece of our strengths in the cracks of the other's weaknesses. She could use some chill, fun, and new experiences. I could use some, well, everything, probably.

Also, for the record, she doesn't like the way I keep gum in my pocket, crinkle the wrapper, or chew it. Come to think of it, she might just have an issue with gum. I file that away for future ammunition.

For now, I watch her cute butt stomp toward the elevators with the massive suitcase she insisted on transporting herself because, and I quote, "the wheels can stick and it can get *tricky*." I assured her I've never lost a game of wits to a suitcase. That earned me another laser glare.

As we follow behind, Val and I make a silent pact to let this tantrum fizzle out instead of stoking the flames, but man do I love stoking her flames.

In all the ways.

"I can't believe this," she says, after giving the floor-seven elevator button the beating of its life.

"The prospect of sharing a room with us is so horrible?" I ask. "There are two beds. It's not like we have to sleep together."

She looks at me like I just said something entirely different. Wait, is the flush on her cheeks even from anger? Her sudden fire looks dangerous, and I pull my gaze away, not liking the way my body ignites in response. I know she wants to hook up again, but she doesn't understand reality like I do. My heart can't handle another blow, and the fact that I'm denying myself something I so clearly want is evidence I'm doing the right thing in keeping my distance.

I care too much. I don't know how it happened, but I'm terrified the next time we're in bed together it's going to be more than sex for me. I'm going to want something I can't have, will never have, because no amount of someone's strengths can fill the crevices carved into my soul.

And suddenly, I'm just as pissed at that damn computer. Why couldn't it have an extra room? You know what? I'm mad at the floor-seven button too.

Val and Paige look puzzled when I pound it again for no reason.

"You have to wait for all the lower floors, honey. They go in order," the lady behind us explains with a patient demonstration of numbers.

I smile back my thanks, and yank out my phone when it buzzes.

Abram: We still on for tomorrow?

Hell yeah, I type back.

10 at the studio? We can grab lunch after and I'll show you the equipment if you're still interested in buying it, he responds.

Me: Totally interested. Paige and her brother will be with me too if that's cool.

Abram: Of course. Just glad to see you. Kaitlyn's still in town for that awards thing also.

Me: Sweet. Is Martin with her?

Abram: Nope. All clear.

Yeah, Abram and Kaitlyn's significant other aren't exactly besties.

"We've got plans tomorrow," I say as the door opens on our floor.

"With your friends?" Val asks.

It's obvious he's fishing for names, which makes it even more fun when I say "yeah" and start down the hall toward room 709. No way I'm missing the chance to watch the kid shit his pants when I introduce him to Abram Fletcher and Kaitlyn Parker.

The room itself is clean and modern when we arrive, just… small. It would've been a tight fit for two, but three? Especially when one of those occupants is a vibrant, intelligent woman you can't stand and are also incredibly attracted to. Said woman is now rolling her massive (and apparently "devious") suitcase through the door, then stops.

"This won't work," she says.

"It has to work," Val says, pushing past her. He drops his hiking backpack on one of the beds and throws himself on the mattress beside it.

I've stayed in a lot of hotels over the years, and "two beds" often means two queens. Sometimes two full beds, but this one? Neither of those things. I didn't even know they made adult beds this small.

"It's fine," I say, urging Paige and her suitcase inside. "You and Val can take the beds. I'll sleep on the floor."

"You're not sleeping on the floor," she growls. "Val and I will share."

"Yeah, no," Val says. "There's barely room for one person, definitely not two. It's fine. I'll take the floor. I'm the third wheel anyway."

"Not a chance," Paige says. "Not with your back problems."

"That hasn't bothered me in weeks."

"Yeah, because you've been careful! I'll take the floor."

"You can't take the floor. Your allergies…"

While they argue, I drape my jacket over a chair, pull the extra blanket from the closet, and spread it out on the carpet between the window and furthest bed. I grab one of the pillows from the pile on the mattress and test out my makeshift sleeping arrangement.

"What are you doing?" Paige asks suddenly, hand on her hip in all kinds of antagonism. She definitely doesn't like the way I lie on blankets on floors.

"Resting."

"I already said this wasn't happening," she snaps, waving over me.

"Well, you're not the only one who gets a say."

"It's not fair, though!"

"What's not fair?"

"This! You shouldn't have to sleep on the floor while we get the beds."

"What does fairness have to do with it?"

"Fairness is always relevant."

I squint, curious about her world where fairness is always relevant. Sounds nice.

"Okay, look," I say, pushing up to my elbows. "I appreciate the sentiment, but it's not necessary. I've slept on crates, concrete, asphalt, van floors, truck beds, tile, carpet, grass, the backseat of every kind of vehicle you can imagine—if it exists, I've slept on it. I promise a night on a soft blanket won't kill me." I add a smile for reassurance, but my humor fades at her expression. "What?"

All traces of anger are gone as she studies me.

"Nothing," she says quietly. "You… Um, okay. If you're sure."

"I'm sure." But it doesn't seem like my assurance is easing whatever's troubling her.

I pop up from the floor to end whatever this is and help her haul her suitcase onto the bed. Her tension eases at the sight of the cornucopia spilling out when she unzips it. Uh, she knows we're only here until Sunday, right?

"I'm gonna go find food," Val says, moving toward the door. "Got one of the keys."

"Sounds good." Paige is still focused on her suitcase.

The door clatters at Val's exit, and I watch as Paige extracts three hangers' worth of outfits from her bag.

"What are those for?" I ask. I'm not sure I've ever packed anything on a hanger, let alone three in one shot.

"The Gaming Competition. Obviously."

I survey the rainbow of fabrics she's currently aligning in the closet.

"You're wearing three outfits for that? Do you always do costume changes at events?"

She shoots back an impatient look like *I'm* the irrational one in this exchange.

"Of course not. I'll only wear one."

"But you brought three?"

"Right, because I don't know which one I'll wear."

"Hang on, you pack clothes you *might* wear? Do you also pack toiletries, snacks, and other supplies that are in the questionable category?"

"Of course. Everyone does."

"I don't."

"Not surprised," she says. "Just don't come crawling to me when you realize you forgot something."

A smile works its ways to my lips. I know I should let this go, shut up and brush my teeth to settle in for the night but…

"And what do you think you have in that bag, that I'd want to borrow?"

My gaze lands on the lacey undergarments tucked in the corner of her suitcase. Her cheeks get hot when she catches on, and she snaps the lid closed.

"This is exactly why I didn't want to share a room with you."

"Yeah?" I shove my hands in my back pockets with a smirk. "The only reason?"

I know everything in her does *not* want to reward my cocky stance with open lust, but everything in her does exactly that. My grin spreads at the same pace as her scowl.

"I don't know what you're talking about. I'm going to change."

She rips the lid back off her suitcase and begins fishing through the contents. I shake my head in amusement and haul my own bag to my sleeping area.

"Shit," she whispers to herself.

I glance over to see that her fishing has turned into full-on trawling.

"What's wrong?"

Her glare is equal parts for me and some travel god that screwed her over.

"Nothing," she says, turning back to her belongings.

Hard to believe that when she dumps the densely packed contents onto the bed.

"Forget something?" I ask.

"It's fine."

"Maybe I—"

"I said it's fine!"

I'm about to snap back when I notice the tremor in her lip. Wait. Is she about to cry? Over forgetting to pack something? Or is it sharing a room? Or flying? Or…

Fuck.

"Hey, what's going on?" I ask, coming up beside her.

She shakes her head, obviously holding back tears.

"Paige."

"I'm fine." Her voice is quivering.

Silent tears break free, and I pull her in with a sigh.

Her arms tighten around me as she settles into my chest, releasing heaven knows how many pent-up fears and frustrations. Seconds tick by, minutes, while I guard her close, letting her purge whatever this is into my shirt. Not gonna lie, it feels good to hold her. To be… necessary.

Closing my eyes, I breathe in the berry floral scent of her hair, loving how her hands grip my shirt like she's holding on for dear life.

"What's wrong?" I say gently.

I feel the scrape of her head as she shakes it again.

"It's so silly," she whispers. "I know it is. It's just…"

"Just what?"

"I don't like traveling."

"That's obvious," I say with a chuckle.

A choked laugh bubbles from her as well, and she pulls back enough to rest her forehead against my chest.

"I don't like not being in control," she continues faintly. "Not knowing things. Feeling ignorant and…"

"Vulnerable?" I finish when she doesn't.

She looks up at me, wide hazel eyes wet with just that. And suddenly it all makes sense. How did I miss this when all the signs were there from the beginning?

Paige is all confidence because she only surrounds herself with the safety of what she knows. It makes her incredibly strong in every facet of her life, which is structured around her expertise. All well and good, but what about all the amazing things she's missing by locking herself in a comfortable bubble? What if the things she wants most—the things she needs—are in the risks she won't take?

"There was this kid at the group home. Billy Stanton." I release a harsh laugh at the memory. "He and his friends made my life a living hell. They'd constantly tease me, attack me, steal from me, whatever they could do to prey on me because I was small and sensitive and easy to injure. Fighting back just made it worse, and when Marcos and Nate stood up for me, the assholes turned their violence on them too."

"Nash…" she whispers, leaning back to study my face. I look away and focus on the far wall.

"You know what's worse than being bullied and terrorized? Watching it happen to someone you care about on your behalf. Knowing their suffering is because of you. It broke me, Paige—being vulnerable. Being so weak the only two people who gave a shit about me got hurt. By the time I ran away for the last time at seventeen, I was ready to face life as a statue. I couldn't let myself be vulnerable, and the only way to do that is to not care. Not try. Not dream or hope or love. I lived for whatever second was in front of me and that was it. Maybe I am a *lazy, apathetic moron* but it's the way I learned to survive."

She winces, and I don't think her hard stare is meant for me this time. "You're not any of those things. I shouldn't have said that. I'm sorry."

Something flickers in my abyss, the faintest light, and I swallow hard. "It's okay. Everyone thinks that, not just you. It's… Anyway, my point is, being vulnerable is scary. I get it. I do the same thing to protect myself, but it's different for you."

"What do you mean?"

"You have a safety net I never did. You have the luxury to try because you have the luxury to fail. I can't take risks because I'll have nothing left when it all comes crashing down. I can't afford to dream."

"But that's not entirely true, is it?" she asks softly.

My gaze returns to her at the strange tenderness, and now I'm not sure which of us is comforting the other.

"You did care about something," she continues. "You did dream once."

I brace through a rush of pain. How does she know about that? I've done everything I can to erase that fractured piece of myself.

"Yeah," I breathe out. "For a minute."

I pull away and immediately feel cold without her against me. It's familiar, the cold, so I'm surprised when a warm hand wraps around mine. Our fingers lace together, and I study the contrast of her smooth skin with my messy tattoos.

"What happened, Nash? What happened to your music?"

I close my eyes, forcing air into my lungs again.

"Nash?"

What happened to your music?

You could tell her. You could let someone else share your pain.

You could be vulnerable.

After a long pause, I squeeze her palm and release her. "What did you forget to pack? We'll go track it down."

* * *

In addition to dredging up painful memories and almost freeing dangerous confessions, sharing a room has led to another problem. It turns out the thing Paige forgot was her oversized sleep shirts. The solution seemed simple at the time, but has since turned into Problem Three.

"Thanks for the shirt," she mumbles as she shuffles out of the bathroom in nothing but the graphic tee I lent her. Her smooth, flawless legs are on full display with the slightest hint of blue satin panties showing beneath the hem of my shirt. Val is still off searching for food, which means there's no third wheel to temper the chemical reaction flaring up between us when we see each other.

I'm not helping matters by wearing only my boxers, but as we've established, I don't pack extra. I can tell she's trying not to look at me, which makes the whole thing hotter. Her gaze keeps flickering in my direction, then darting away. I'm faring no better in my attempts to ignore her bare arms, shoulders, and legs—all so silky and exposed, begging to be touched.

It's agony watching her walk around in nothing but a t-shirt—*my* t-shirt—and it's only going to get worse from here. With her brother inches away, I'll have to watch her slide into the sheets above me, wearing my clothes as if this is some alternate dimension where I could date a woman like Paige Andrews. I'll have to watch her adjust *my* shirt over her bare breasts and stomach when it rides up. I'll have to fall asleep imagining *my* fabric caressing her skin while she inhales my scent over and over again with each soft breath.

I've never been so jealous of a shirt.

But that's pain for later, because right now I have to watch her watch me trying not to watch her as every damn nerve ending in my body roars to life.

"You're staring," she says, challenging me with a direct look.

"So are you," I counter.

I feel her virtual touch every place her gaze lands. My arms, my chest, my stomach, down to my boxers still waiting for their turn in the bathroom. Coincidentally, this also means she's visually stroking the growing hardness beneath said boxers. Her teeth sink into her full lip, her eyes locked on my groin.

"You sleep naked?" she asks. Her voice comes out hoarse, and she clears her throat.

I can't stop the smile at her arousal. At least I'm not the only one suffering.

"You're wearing my sleep shirt. Plus, per your own logic in your room the other day, I'm not naked."

"Practically," she says.

"There is no practically when it comes to nudity," I remind her. "You either are, or you're not."

In other circumstances, she'd have a snarky response, maybe an eye roll, but her comeback seems snared by the idea of me naked.

"Hey, my eyes are up here," I say, motioning with two fingers toward my face.

I grin when her cheeks turn red.

"Sorry," she mumbles. "You can use the bathroom now if you want."

I could. That would also mean slithering by her in our crowded room. Which would lead to an inhalation of her clean, freshly showered aroma. Which would lead to direct blood flow to a zone I'm already trying to restrict.

For the sake of overworked capillaries, I say, "It's fine. I'll wait until you're done."

"I just said I was done."

"No, you said 'thanks for the shirt,' 'you sleep naked,' and 'practically.' And then of course the present discussion. At no point did you say you were done."

Her eyes flash with indignation as I shrug. Hey, at least they're not (eye-)fucking me anymore.

"Why do you even know that?" she says.

"I have a good memory."

"And you know that's what I meant."

"Really. Which of those statements meant you were done?" I tilt my head and add a casual stretch just to stoke the fire more. Except my stance also stokes other things—in both of us—when her gaze drops to my boxers again.

And now… fuck it.

"I'll use the bathroom," I grunt, uncrossing my arms and making my way toward my duffle bag. Pretty sure my dick can't handle any more coaxing at the moment. As usual around this woman, he's been up and ready for business long before my brain.

Swiping the toiletries from my bag, I steel myself for the battle to come. She's blocking my path between the end of her bed and the dresser. How is she still messing around in her suitcase? She had the whole thing repacked in five minutes before her shower.

She straightens when I pass, doing everything she can to avoid contact. Somehow we do, and I'm grateful as I reach the bathroom unscathed. Seriously, brushing your teeth isn't supposed to be hard.

Hard.

Ugh.

When I return, though, she's *still* in the way, this time facing forward as she stares at the television.

"Anything good on?" I ask, hoping to distract us from the fact that, despite the earlier semantics debate, we *are* practically naked.

"Did you know a group of crows is called a murder?"

Not sure which is stranger: the question or the fact that I did know that.

Also, she's watching an infomercial for dish soap, so now I'm somewhat alarmed.

"So much to know about crows, huh," I say dryly, angling to slink past her.

"Birds in general," she says, lifting her gaze to mine.

I suck in a breath, paralyzed by the look in her eyes. She steps forward and closes the gap between us, trapping me against the dresser. We just hugged the crap out of each other a few minutes ago, but this? Not a hugging vibe.

So, so not hugging.

"What else about birds?" I ask in a low voice. Weird Hail, Mary but let's go with it.

Except her eyes flare with heat at the rasp in my tone, and my entire body hardens in anticipation. She inches closer, grazing my front as my ass presses into the drawer.

"There are ducks that sleep with an eye open," she says in a husky voice no one has ever used to utter that sentence.

"Yeah?"

Her palms spread over my chest, her fingers sinking into my pectorals in a clear message. *This is happening. Now.*

"Yeah," she whispers, pushing her hands up and around my neck to wedge her body against mine. "Want to know another fun fact?"

"Sure," I force out.

"I want to kiss you."

She searches my eyes. Usually, she's all orders and demands, but right now she's need and desperation. Even as we hesitate, our hips rock slowly against each other, like our bodies have already surrendered.

Press.

Hold.

Thrust.

Harder.

Grind.

Release.

Press.

Hold.

Hold, hold, hold. She gasps and adjusts to sink down and anchor her center on my hardness. If she moves even a little…

Fuck.

I close my eyes, incinerating from the inside out.

Why wasn't there another room?!

"I…" *want to kiss you too.* So much.

Her lips are right there, soft and eager.

"Nash, please. Please," she begs, gripping the back of my neck so tight I can feel her hunger.

Paige Andrews. Begging.

There's no defense against that.

I give in with a groan, crashing into the dresser when she collapses against me. It's like her entire body seeks to devour every part of mine as we writhe against each other, clawing and clutching, rubbing hot friction with each buck of our hips. Her hands roam freely while I suck on her lips, her chin, her neck, anywhere I can reach. She moans when I grip her wet hair and back her toward the bed.

We fall in a graceless collision, and I position myself over her, my arms caging her in on both sides.

She smells amazing, tastes even better, and feels like… god, she feels like a fantasy. Like a flame that's too hot to last. It will burn out soon, but for now, I let it consume me.

She spreads her knees so I can nestle between her legs, my hips already pushing through thin fabric that's doing little to block the climbing fury of our lust.

"Nash," she gasps out, locking her ankles behind me. She pulls me into her, bucking over and over until the pooling sparks in my groin blister into flames. I'm tense and primed, hot and aching with every torturous surge of pleasure. Over and over.

Throbbing.

In pain.

Shit. I can't…

Her hands slide down my back, beneath the waistband of my boxers to grip my ass. With another moan, she grinds hard, forcing us even tighter and…

"I need everything this time," she pleads. "All of you."

Screw it. We can deal with the consequences later.

I reach for the hem of her shirt and tug it toward her head, already anticipating the tight heat of her wrapped around me. It will feel like the bliss of heaven and fire of hell all at once, an intoxicating blend of miracle and mistake. And I need it. Every blaze, just burning, burning. Hotter and hotter.

She reaches between us to slide her palm over my hard, eager cock. Up and down, massaging me to the brink of surrender when…

The door bursts open.

Val! Fuck. We must not have heard the click of the keycard.

I tense and roll off his sister, my heart racing. I was actually starting to like the guy. Of course I'd mess it up. This crap is exactly why I didn't want to pursue things with Paige. Caring just breaks shit.

Paige pushes up, doing her best to tug on her shirt and straighten her hair. If not for the tension in the air, it would be hilarious because even "fixed" she's still practically naked, wearing *my* tee. My boxers are shoved suspiciously low as well, and I try for a discreet adjustment that has the opposite effect when it attracts Paige's gaze.

Yep, there's no chance of cleansing the "about to hook up" vibe from our situation. All we can do now is hold our breaths and brace for the fallout. I've been here more times than I can count, staring down the barrel of a metaphoric gun about to face my punishment for pursuing anything that could make me happy. It comes in all forms. A bully's fist. A guardian's tirade. A rockstar's traitorous… never mind. Doesn't matter. I'm ready for all of it. Anything.

Except that.

A grin?

"You know there's this sophisticated system hotels have developed for situations like this," Val says, amused.

We just stare at him.

He plucks the small door hanger off the handle. "For next time," he says, waving the "Do Not Disturb" sign at us.

12—NETWORKING

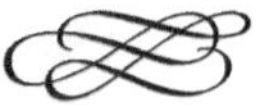

PAIGE

I dreamt about him. Of course, I did.

After the rollercoaster that was our scorching collision last evening, I spent the rest of the night picturing Nash on the floor below me, wondering if he was sleeping or thinking about me too. Was he imagining his hands all over my body? Mine on his? Was he craving what would have happened if Val hadn't returned and stopped what probably needed to be stopped?

Because it was a mistake. I know that. He knows that. The entire freaking universe (except for my brother) knows that. Nash and I make absolutely no sense together and most of the time he doesn't even seem interested. It's always me, throwing myself at him like some pathetic groupie until he gives in—to scratch an itch, maybe? Doesn't matter because I already know he regrets it. He immediately withdrew into his silent, brooding-artist self after that.

So yes. It needed to be stopped, but it would be super awesome if my heart got the memo. And my body. Also, my lady parts that keep swelling and tingling with need for hard, hot skin and deep, explosive pressure that… ah!!

Nash enters the hotel lobby for this morning's continental breakfast, and Val waves him over to our table like the traitor my brother is. I don't miss how Nash's eyes stay locked on Val, avoiding mine even when he mumbles an obligatory greeting to me.

We kept our distance this morning, with him pretending to sleep until Val and I left for breakfast. Once it was safe, he must have gotten up and showered because twenty minutes later, here he is, looking and smelling like a men's razor ad. Hair wet, chin and cheeks dusted with dark, unshaven scruff that makes you want to brush your fingers over the surface while sucking on his minty lips. (Obviously, this is the "before-the-painfully-good-looking-dude-uses-the-amazing-razor" part of the commercial.)

Val and I have almost finished eating, but we wait at the table while Nash gathers his food and joins us. I'm surprised by his meal when he sits down. Something about him made me think it would be piled high with donuts and bacon, but instead, he returns with a mound of mixed fruit, bowl of oatmeal, and cup of coffee.

"No bacon?" I ask.

Yet another mistake when I'm blasted with a stunning blue gaze I feel throughout my entire body. Why does he have to be so friggin' beautiful?

"I'm a vegetarian," he says casually.

Of course, he is. Why wouldn't he be the opposite of what I assumed?

"You sleep okay?" This question feels safer until he looks at me again.

Heat flares low in my belly, pooling in my core as his intense stare answers for him. *As well as you, I bet.*

"Yeah," he lies. The redness of his eyes tells the real truth. "You?"

"Yeah," I lie back, my gaze still locked on his.

"Okay. Well, that's it for me," Val says, slapping his hands on the table. "You kids have fun. I'll be up in the room."

Some part of my brain is warning me to follow, or at least keep Val here as a buffer. These sparks snapping between us can't be healthy, but Nash looks and smells like every fantasy ever right now. Seriously, if there was an instruction manual on how to form the most tempting, off-limits super-crush, this guy would be the deconstructed illustration on page one.

Insert deadly blue eyes (step 2)

Attach lean, sculpted arms and torso (step 3)

Dust skin with sexy tattoos and piercings (step 7)

Add silky dark hair long enough to grip in heated desperation (step 8)

Yeah… I'll save steps 4-6 for my next shower.

"Sounds good," I say to Val. "We'll be up soon."

"We need to head out in an hour," Nash adds as he pokes a piece of cantaloupe.

"Great." Val takes off, and now I have no choice but to focus on the tired, complex, tantalizing artist in front of me.

"Where are we going today?" I ask, deciding conversation is better than wallowing in my lust.

"Don't tell Val, but I'm taking him to meet Abram and Kaitlyn at a big studio."

His tone is casual, and my heart floods with warmth. Not only do I love the idea of Val meeting his idols, but also Nash who so nonchalantly made it happen. It almost hurts how sweet he is without even knowing it. Taking the floor while others get the beds, his observation about my suitcase meltdown and easy embrace to mend it. I liquified last night when he literally gave me the shirt off his back. No hesitation, no expectation of a reward, just a mundane gesture like he was holding the door or pulling an item off a shelf for someone. And yet, somehow I know he'd deny it if I accused him of being selfless. He's too kind to realize it.

His right hand rests on the table as he stabs at more fruit with his left, and I watch his relaxed fingers, itching to caress them. They'd be warm. I know that. The relief of touching him would feel like inhaling a soft spring breeze. It would feel right, even though it shouldn't.

"You're left-handed," I say.

He nods. "My whole life."

His lips twist at my sardonic look, and even his kind-of-smile is cute.

So annoyingly cute.

I study my empty plate.

"Paige, about yesterday…"

I pull in a deep breath at his hesitant introduction. *Please don't say it. Please, please, please.*

"It was a mistake, and I'm sorry."

Dammit.

"I'm the one who threw myself at you," I mumble.

He doesn't respond, and when I dare to check his face, I find the dreaded creased brow. I still don't know what it means on him, but it's becoming a familiar feature.

"It can't work. I mean, come on. It's obvious," he says, meeting my eyes. "You and me? Really?"

I swallow the pointless protest. He's right. We both know it.

"Yeah," I say. "We're too different."

"You would hate my world. Even worse, you'd hate having me in your world. What, are you going to bring me as your plus one to the annual Sandeke Telecom holiday party?"

I shrug with a wry smile. "Could be fun."

He shakes his head, adding a lip-twist of his own. "And what about when your dad and I go to blows at Thanksgiving at your Grandma's house? Would that be fun too?"

My humor fades as I scan his expression for the real meaning behind the joke that doesn't feel like a joke.

"Thanksgivings at Grandma's suck," I say after a painful silence. "They're catered and tense and probably more sterile than the Sandeke Telecom parties. A good fight would liven things up."

His sad smile should make me feel better, but it does the opposite. It feels like a goodbye. Like a seal on an agreement, I don't want to make.

"I'm gonna grab a bagel for the road," he says, pushing up from his chair. "You need anything?"

I shake my head, watching as my super-crush drags my heart across the dining room floor.

* * *

If Nash was tempted to share our secret destination with Val on the drive over, it's thwarted by an incoming video call from Chad. To my phone. Because Nash didn't answer his. Seven times.

I ignore Nash's emphatic hand gesture and take the call because, despite what he seems to think, we're still on company time on a company-sponsored trip. We're supposed to be working, a fact that seems to have slipped the minds of my companions. It's bad enough we're about to spend the day doing the opposite of that. We definitely can't ignore the little work that intrudes on our slacking.

"Paige! Thank god!" Chad cries the second we connect. "Is Nash okay? I've been trying him all morning. He isn't…? You know…" His expression falls, and I glare at my irresponsible coworker.

"In the car right next to me? Yep, he's here." I flash the screen toward Nash's sour face.

"Oh, okay, whew. I was worried his cover had been blown."

By Chad's dire expression, we're chasing nuclear intelligence from a despotic regime, not a sunny, pop-country star whose most punishing retaliation would be a mean-face.

"No, he's fine and still… covered."

Covered? Whatever.

Nash shoots me a *huh* look, and I shrug. He could have answered his phone and used whatever adjective he wanted.

"Tell him I need an update for my weekly report."

I glance over at Nash. "Chad needs an update for his weekly report."

"Oh! And tell him to answer his phone next time."

"Chad says to answer your—"

Nash grabs the phone from my hand with a hard expression. I return a sweet, triumphant smile.

"Nash! Thank god!"

"What do you want, Chad?" he asks in a resigned tone.

"You haven't checked in for a while."

"I haven't checked in at all."

"Precisely. You're supposed to check in daily."

"Who decided that?"

"That's just basic protocol."

"Protocol for what?"

"Work trips. And spy trips. All trips, really."

"Pretty sure it's not," Nash says in a bored tone.

"Well, I need information to file this week's report."

"Have we even been doing this for a week?"

"No. It will be the first one. That's why it has to be good."

Nash's brain visibly gives up the fight. "What do you want to know?" he sighs out.

"Everything you have on Hummingbird."

"Like, a specific one or any hummingbird?"

"No, not the bird! *Larinda!*" Chad whisper-shouts, annoyed by this entire exchange as well.

"You gave her a codename?"

"Of course! We all have a codename!"

"We do?"

I peek at the screen to see a Polo-shirt-wearing handler who looks as exasperated as expected when their head spy is unaware of basic spy-protocol like daily check-ins and codenames.

"Yes! Did you not get my text?"

"Yeah, but I didn't—wait, you *texted* all the codenames? Doesn't that defeat the purpose of having codenames?"

"Only if someone sees it," Chad says. "Anyway, Larinda is Hummingbird, you are Dragonfly, and Paige is Dragonfly 2."

"I…" Nash crosses a frustrated look to me, and I motion for the phone.

"Hey, Chad," I say, once I'm facing our eager boss again. "No news on Hummingbird. Dragonfly is in motion and… *Dragonfly 2*… is also in motion."

Val covers his mouth with his hand to hide a laugh as he pretends to stare out the window. The driver keeps looking in her review mirror, like she's debating whether or not to call the cops.

Chad nods gravely and appears to be writing something. "So Operation Hummingbird is a go?"

"It's a go."

"Excellent." He writes something else, then focuses on me again. "Keep up the good work, Dragonfly 2. And tell Dragonfly I like his disguise. He looks exactly like a poor starving artist."

Val snorts a laugh as I dare a quick glance at Nash. His lips quirk up, and he shakes his head in silent amusement.

"Yours is great too," Chad adds. "I like the ugly shirt. It makes you look more like someone he would date."

I swallow my response to the critique of my favorite shirt, while trying to ignore the boys who are doing nothing to hide their humor anymore.

"Thanks," I mumble. "Have a great day."

I hang up and give the others a hard stare.

"Oh, come on. Obviously, he's wrong," Nash says with a glint that always puts me on edge. "I'd never date a woman in that shirt."

He and Val laugh as I shove him.

* * *

The mood takes a different turn when we arrive at our destination. Val's expression morphs into wonder the second we stop in front of a sleek, modern building.

149

"This is… it's…"

Nash erupts with a grin at my brother's reaction—and Val hasn't even seen the real surprise yet.

"Framework Studios? Yep," Nash says, leading us toward the entrance.

He pushes a button outside the wide glass doors, and a receptionist buzzes us in.

"Nash?" the woman says the second we enter the lobby.

His grin turns deadly, and I'm not remotely jealous at the way she shrieks and throws herself into his arms. I definitely don't care that those arms tighten around her like he's just as happy to see her.

"Hey, Delia. It's good to see you," he says in that not-at-all-sexy rasp he has.

"I can't believe you're actually here! How have you been? How's New York?"

"Colder," Nash says, and the woman giggles. *Giggles!* Even worse, it somehow makes her adorable instead of flighty, like it's obvious the sound originated from a heavy crush and not an empty brain. Nash sure seems to eat it up. He continues smiling while she hangs on his arm.

"Are they here?" he asks, glancing down a long corridor behind us.

"Yep. They said to send you back when you got here."

"Studio Three?"

"Yep. Will you be in town for a while?" Thick fake lashes blink over striking green eyes. Geez, even the most seasoned sailor would be tempted into death against the rocks if this were a Greek Myth and she was a mermaid.

Stop it, hormones. You're being weird and random again.

"No. Just a couple days," Nash says with a hint of regret. I can't tell if it's sincere or if he's just trying to be polite. Then again, he's not known for his etiquette, which means… grr.

"Aww," the woman whines. "Well, you look good, Nashville. Really good."

Wait. Nashville? What is that? Also, she was *definitely* not being polite. She does think he looks "good, really good" based on the way she's still drooling and stripping him with her mermaid gaze.

"We're gonna head back, but it was great seeing you," Nash says, pulling away and starting toward the hall.

"You too, sweetie!" she calls. "Don't leave without saying goodbye."

"Never," he returns, tossing her another grin I want to snatch off his face and lock in a vault so he can never share it with another woman.

Jealous much? In the words of beautiful, mermaid receptionists: Yep.

I even add a mental giggle to test it out. Nope, not a fan.

"You okay?" Nash asks as we move down the hall. "Your face is all scrunched up."

I work to un-scrunch my face. "Yeah, I didn't like the giggle."

"The giggle?"

"Never mind."

"This place is amazing," Val says. "How many studios are in here?"

"Eight," Nash says.

"Can we see one?"

"I think I can arrange that." He adds a mischievous smile I would also kidnap and lock away in my brain vault.

You'd think getting a long, boring tour of crap you don't care about would be the perfect cure for a raging crush, but as Nash points out all the features, rooms, and equipment we pass, it becomes clear we're on his turf now. Talk about seeing the world through someone else's lens. He struts around with a confidence I suspected but never witnessed in the murky maze of the corporate office. And here I thought he was a clueless slacker. He may not mesh well with my world, but he's the king of his.

And it's hot. Not even artist hot, but legit *hot* hot. Now I want to lock all of him up for myself.

That's illegal. And mean.

I'm aware, thanks.

"Wait here," he says, stopping in front of a door with a plaque that says "Three." I peek through the window to see a small room with…

Oh my god.

I sense Val's sharp inhalation as Nash types something on his phone. The man in the booth straightens from a conversation with a guy behind some cockpit-looking equipment. A smile spreads over the man's lips when he checks his phone, and he says something to the seated guy.

Then he turns around.

"Oh shit, it *is* him. That's Abram Fletcher," Val whispers as the superstar himself moves toward us. "No way."

I steal a glance at Nash who looks damn proud of himself for orchestrating this moment.

"There he is," Abram says to Nash, opening his arms for what I think is a hug. It turns into some bro-punch-handish thing. They seem cool with whatever just happened, though, so I guess that's good.

"Hey, man. Missed you, dude," Nash says, clapping one of the biggest stars in the industry on the arm like they're close relatives.

Why isn't Nash a household name again?

"You too," Abram replies with a genuine smile. He's sporting a short, neatly trimmed beard and now I'm stuck with a mental image of him in his underwear thanks to the ads plastered all over the country a couple of years ago. Oh hey, an actual underwear model. Yay for that.

"When are you coming back to L.A.?" Abram asks.

"I just did," Nash says.

Abram grunts as Nash steps to the side and waves at us. "These are my friends Paige and Val. Val is the kid I was telling you about."

Hang on.

Uh-oh.

Crap, my brother is dead. I watch his spirit sputter from his body and drift toward the music-production heavens.

"Oh yeah! You're helping Nash with Larinda's stuff, right? Nash says you've got talent," Abram says. To my brother. Abram Fletcher just told my brother he's talented. Now I'm dead too.

"Um… yeah… I mean, yes… I mean…"

I nudge Val's foot with mine to snap him out of his stupor.

Nash and Abram just look amused.

"I didn't tell him this was happening," Nash explains to Abram.

"Ah," Abram says with a chuckle. "Understood."

"So what's up, man?" Nash says. "Are Ruthie and Charlie around?"

"Nah. We're just tracking vocals today. Kaitlyn and Leo should be back any moment, though. They were grabbing coffee in the lounge."

"Okay, great. Haven't seen Leo since I ran sound for Tenderleaf in Miami. How's Mona doing?"

"She's good. Off in London to give some presentation at a symposium on… something you won't understand or care about. What about you? Still with that girl from Just Hands?"

His gaze settles on me, making it clear he knows I'm not "the girl from Just Hands." My presence means he shouldn't have asked that, but he did anyway, because he's Abram Fletcher and gets to ask any question he wants.

For the record, I'm no longer a fan of "the girl from Just Hands," which now makes me not a fan of Just Hands. (I still like that one song about the thunderstorm, though. I'll just have to listen to it with a grimace from this point on.)

"Am I *with* her?" Nash asks, frowning. "We went on, like, two dates."

Oh. Whew.

Because I really like Just Hands.

"Right. She said you were together. She tried to get into the green room with it."

Nash makes a face. "Shit. When was this?"

Abram shrugs. "I dunno, a few months ago?"

Nash shakes his head. "Sorry, man. I didn't even think she knew we were friends."

"Well, she knew." Abram swats Nash's arm in a comforting gesture. "Don't sweat it. Not your fault."

I study Nash's expression, understanding his situation in a new light. Superstars like Abram are probably used to this crap. Social climbers come with the territory of being rich and famous, but what about the nobodies that surround them? How often has Nash been used for his connections like this? No wonder he guards his secrets so closely.

"So tell me how the fuck you ended up working with Larinda Scott of all people," Abram asks.

Nash clears his throat, and it's my turn to be amused as he struggles for a response. "It's complicated," he says.

"Not gonna lie, I'm kind of offended. You ditched me for *Larinda Scott*? Really, dude?"

Nash rolls his eyes at Abram's teasing. At least I think he's teasing.

"It's not like that and you know it. If I could have stayed, I would have. I just…"

"Yeah, I know," Abram says, squeezing his arm.

The mood darkens again, and I realize a rescue is in order. I cast a glance at Val, but he's still floating in a parallel meeting-your-idol plane. I guess this one is on me.

"How did you two become friends anyway?" I ask Abram.

Nash shoots me a confused look, probably because he already told me, but I'm curious about Abram's side of the story. Maybe his version will even include a verb.

By Abram's chuckle, I might be in luck.

"Oh man, it's the best story."

Nash's glower is just as promising. "Don't," he warns.

"What? It's a great story," Abram laughs out. He turns to me, making it clear Nash is losing this one. The winners? Everyone else, because I can already tell this will be awesome. "So we're on tour, right? I mean, I knew he was good with guitars, but what I didn't know was how hot he was naked."

Told you. This is already my favorite story ever.

Abram's snort when Nash glares at him makes it clear he enjoys tormenting his friend as much as I enjoy anything that involves Nash naked.

"You really don't have to tell this story," Nash says.

"He really does," I say, leaning forward.

"Right, so I'm already running late when I enter the hotel lobby and see my guitar tech in a heated argument with the hotel staff, while wearing a bathrobe."

"I'm sorry?" I can't imagine Nash in a bathrobe. Or arguing heatedly.

"Yep," Abram continues. "It turns out our boy here had gone down to use the sauna and forgot his key—"

"My key was *stolen*," Nash cuts in.

"Right," Abram says. "His key was *stolen* by the magic key fairies and the staff wouldn't issue a new one without his ID."

"It was," Nash mutters. "Les pulled a prank to get me back for Chicago."

"Anyway, the best part is, your boy here wasn't even upset about being practically naked in a hotel lobby; he was mad that this whole debacle made him miss line check and he was about to miss soundcheck as well. The venue was just across the street, so I told him it would be fine with me if he went over in the robe. Turns out that was what he was most worried about. So we did."

"You did a soundcheck in a robe?" Val asks.

The slightest smile flickers over Nash's lips. "Maybe."

"Hopefully you didn't have to run any cables," Val says with a smirk.

"You kidding? One of the haze machines was acting up, so this guy was climbing trusses and everything," Abram says, slinging an arm around Nash.

"It was a stepladder with maybe four steps," Nash says dryly.

Abram rolls his eyes. "Whatever. Seriously, though. The whole thing was badass. Not many people would've had the balls to do what he did. I ended up giving him my shirt when no one had anything he could borrow."

I see the spark of admiration in Abram's eyes. It matches the look in Nash's. Brotherly bonding over a bathrobe. Whatever works, I guess.

"I'm assuming you eventually got back into your room?" I ask.

"Yeah," Nash says. "We sorted it out after soundcheck. Pretty sure they didn't want me running around the stage in my underwear."

"Well, it sounds like it all worked out," I say. "Good to know this whole story had an H.E.A."

They exchange a dark look. Oh no. There's more. There always is with him.

"Yeah," Nash says quietly. "Hey, so—"

"Whoa, is that *the* Nash Ellis?" a voice calls from behind us. We turn to see another good-looking man and attractive woman exiting one of the artist lounges.

"Leo, Kaitlyn, hey," Nash says, probably just as excited to end this conversation as he is to see his friends. "I was hoping you'd be around."

"You know me. Always around," Leo says, going in for another one of those hug-back-slap-shake things. The woman who must be Kaitlyn settles on a regular hug which seems warm and affectionate.

"Hi. Leo DaVinci." The guy holds out his hand to Val and me.

I think he's joking about his name, but his expression remains serious. Leo DaVinci. Okay. Um, his parents must be interesting.

"Leo is also Abram's girlfriend's brother," Nash explains, while we exchange handshakes.

"Yep, although oddly enough Mona hooked up with my boy here in spite of me, not because of me," Leo says.

Wait.

Leo DaVinci has a sister named *Mona*. "Let me guess, you have another sister named *Lisa*?" I joke.

Four serious expressions stare back at me, along with a mortified one from my brother.

"Yes," Val hisses.

"Oh," I say through the awkward silence. "Um, right. Nice to meet you."

After several excruciating seconds, Abram, Nash, and Kaitlyn snicker, and I breathe a sigh of relief when Leo joins them.

"We're just messing with you," Leo says. "I mean, not the name part. That's legit. It's what happens when your parents are DJ Tang and Exotica."

I swallow my embarrassment and shrug. "It's fine. Our parents are Rhonda and Burt and named him Perceval."

"Perceval?" Leo asks.

"I go by Val," my brother mumbles.

"Dude, I got you. Believe me," Leo says, patting his shoulder.

"Just Kaitlyn, here," the woman I kind of don't hate says with a chuckle. "I feel so boring."

"Like you could ever be *boring*," Nash snorts.

They exchange a grin that melts Nash's face into a blast of affection. He's more relaxed in this moment than I've ever seen him. These are his people, and here's another hint that his line about not fitting in or caring is bullshit.

Here is where he belongs and this is what he cares about.

"Hey, if you all are done playing the Cool Nametag Game, you mind if we finish tracking these vocals so we can grab lunch?" Abram asks.

"You want to hang with us in the control room?" he directs to Nash.

"Yeah, man. Of course," Nash says.

"You ready to see the promised land?" he adds to Val as Leo, Kaitlyn, and Abram disappear into the room.

"Yeah, for twenty-two years," Val says.

Nash smiles and waves him toward the door. "Hope you got your shit together, because your day is just beginning."

* * *

I can't decide which is better: your dreams coming true, or watching someone you love's dreams come true.

Nash wasn't kidding about Val's day. After he had his mind blown by whatever magic was going on in the control room, he had it completely obliterated when Abram asked if he wanted to jam a little before lunch. Leo had to take off, but Abram, Kaitlyn, Nash, and Val are now rocking out on the other side of the glass, while I look on with Control Room Guy. Phil, I think his name is?

"He's something special, huh. It's a damn shame."

I look down in surprise at quiet Maybe-Phil. It's the first thing he's said since the musicians left us alone in awkward silence.

"Who's special? Abram? It's a shame?"

The man glares at me like I'm an idiot. To be fair, in this world, I kind of am.

"No. Not Abram. Nashville."

"Nashville?"

Again with the *why are you stupid?* look. "What kind of friends are you again?"

"No, I know. But he goes by Nash. Why do people keep calling him Nashville?"

"Everyone called him Nashville back in the day. I mean, look at him."

I do, and my stomach goes tight. He's always beautiful, but out there, lost in music with three other musicians who breathe it like he does, he's... transcendent. There's no other word for it. Happy in a way I've never seen. Even seated beside one of the biggest rockstars in the world, I can't take my eyes off him. The way his fingers glide over the strings like that guitar is another appendage, the way his gravelly voice sends shivers over my skin as it breezes through the studio headphones we're wearing. He's playing his original song, "I'm Fine," like it's an international hit, not some musical journal entry he messes around with in his living room. And suddenly, it feels wrong. Everything, just, disordered. The universe doesn't make sense when a person like that isn't sharing music like this.

Phil-ish pulls one of the headphones from his ear like he wants to say something, so I do the same.

"We called him Nashville because the kid *is* music. You see it, right?"

"Yes," I say, gazing through the glass at the breathtaking, complex, exasperating puzzle I want to solve. Heat spreads through my entire body, passion like I've never felt before. Not just sexual tension, something else. Something bigger and transformative. What makes *me* come alive like that? Nash's question in his apartment that night floods back.

"Of all the possibilities in this vast universe to make your mark on history, how did you come to the conclusion that working at Reedweather Media was the path worthy of you and your talents?"

I hated the question, because I hate questions I can't answer.

"Yep, it's a damn shame," Maybe-Phil mutters, drawing me back to our awkward bonding.

"Why do you say that?" I ask. "Because he doesn't want to be a recording artist?"

"Is that what he told you?" the man asks with more than a hint of irritation. "That's his story now? He doesn't want it?" He shakes his head. "Stupid kid. Talented, stupid kid."

"So he *did* want to record at one point."

"Wanted to? He could have been huge if that asshole hadn't ruined his career."

My blood goes cold. "Which asshole?" He can't mean Abram. I mean… right?

The man sends me a suspicious look like suddenly he's not sure I actually am friends with Nash. He's not far off. We're here as coworkers. We almost hooked up because of a superficial attraction as coworkers. He spends so much time with me because we're coworkers.

Right?

Right.

"Tyler. Obviously," Phil-Guy says. "Pirate Orgy?" He squints at me like I've probably never heard of music either, and I force a smile.

Okay, yes, I know Pirate Orgy. Who doesn't? And maybe I've even heard their lead singer is an asshole. What I didn't know was that he had a tie to my fr —*coworker*. If I can't get any more info out of Phil-Whatever, I'll be doing another full-scale internet search tonight.

"Right. Tyler ruined his career," I say with what I hope is an appropriate amount of *duh-I-knew-that*.

He glances at me again as if he suspects I didn't know that.

By his tight smile, he must realize he screwed up and gave me new information. Shifting in his seat, he pulls the headphones back over his ears in a definitive end to our conversation.

I lean forward and study the quartet through the pristine glass again.

Nashville. It's not okay that that boy is a has-been at age twenty-four. It's not okay that he's not making music full-time, period.

I know I shouldn't, but I can't help myself.

While Nash releases his soul into a studio that should own him instead of shun him, I pull out my phone and open a search app.

Don't do this, Paige. This will end badly.

Yes. It will.

So badly.

I type "Tyler Pirate Orgy and Nash Ellis" into the search field.

13—RECONNECTING

NASH

Paige has been acting weird. Well, weirder than usual anyway. Talk about a buzzkill. After an amazing half hour of recharging my soul with Abram, Kaitlyn, Val, and my guitar, we returned to the control room to confront a brooding Paige Andrews. I thought that was *my* role in our little duet, so I'm not sure of the logistics if both of us are broody.

Lunch has fared no better, with Paige glowering at everyone from our server, to the couple at the table beside us, to Abram Fletcher who probably isn't accustomed to being glowered at. The expressions reserved for me are even more cryptic. I can't begin to interpret the rainbow of facial cues I'm getting from across the table.

Worst part, I don't know if she knows she's being thorny. And maybe horny? Is she trying to kick me or caress me with the foot that keeps crashing into mine under the table? At least, I hope it's her foot. I look at Abram who's in deep conversation with Val and Kaitlyn. He doesn't look like a dude who's playing footsies with me at the moment.

"You okay?" I ask her.

"Fine, why?"

"Um, because, *that?*"

"Because what?"

"*'Fine, why?'*" I mimic with what I'd consider very accurate Paige snappiness. "You've been irritable since the jam session. Were you mad that we left you? I just thought… I mean, for Val—"

"The jam session was amazing," she says, one hundred percent snappily.

"Oh." I clear my throat. "So, what is it then?"

"Nothing. I don't know why you think there's a thing."

"There's clearly a thing."

"Unless you're referring to my delicious chicken Caesar salad, there is no thing."

I'm no detective but her demeanor doesn't seem related to a chicken Caesar salad.

"Okay, whatever," I say, focusing back on my regular Caesar salad. It's far from the best I've ever had but at least it's not yelling at me.

"Why did you really quit music?" she blurts out.

The crouton I just swallowed lodges in my throat when I look up again.

"What?" I croak.

"You heard me." Her eyes narrow with what maybe *is* chicken-Caesar-salad ire? "I saw you in the studio," she continues. "I saw the way your soul bloomed while you were playing. How can you tell me music isn't your life when it's who you are?"

"It *is* my life. I make my living through music."

Well, "make a living" might be a stretch. Marcos and Nate would argue my "living" is pretty far from made at the moment.

"No, you make a living helping other people make music."

"I still make plenty of my own. Just because a passion doesn't pay the bills doesn't mean it's any less valuable."

She quiets, and my heart races as she studies me. Can she read the lie behind my excellent point? I'm not wrong, except by implication. I think she's about to concede when the hardness returns to her features.

"But your passion almost did pay the bills, didn't it? You had a record deal."

Any remaining appetite I had drains away. If she knows that then…

I clench my fist and draw in a stuttered breath.

"You had a record deal and a hit single. You even toured with Pirate Orgy. So three years ago you wanted to *make a living making music.* You can tell me your version of what happened or let me believe what I read."

I meet her gaze, my stomach rioting against this conversation. Abram looks over as if he senses something's wrong. He's always been perceptive like that, which is even more reason why I can't do this right now. Not because he doesn't know the story but because he knows it better than anyone.

"Not here," I say, silently pleading with her. "Please, just… not here."

Her expression softens, but the sudden pity is even worse.

"Then where?" she asks, making it clear she's not letting this go. And honestly, what choice do I have? She already thinks she knows. She's ready to judge and weigh in on my life just like everyone else. I can let her believe the bullshit floating around or tell her the truth.

"Hey, man, you good?" Abram asks.

I look over, wincing at the concerned wrinkle in his brow—and Kaitlyn and Val's.

Then again, maybe this is the perfect place to release the demons. At the very least, a public setting should prevent any fistfights from breaking out.

Abram stiffens abruptly, ending the debate. I breathe easier at the flash of irritation in his face before he plasters on his stage smile. For one of the first times since we've become friends, I'm happy to be interrupted by gushing fans.

Except the woman who approaches has her eyes locked on someone else.

Me.

"Nash?"

Shit.

"Ophelia, hi. It's good to see you," I lie.

I feel Paige's curious, then irritated reaction when the woman rounds the table for a hug. It's the same response she had when Delia greeted me at Framework Studios. I never even went out with Delia, but I have no doubt that Paige now thinks I've slept with every person in L.A.

Why do you care what she thinks?

I don't. I can't. I won't.

My gaze brushes over her smooth, sharp features. Why do I have to be so attracted to her wrath? It's a dangerous reality when we're wired for constant friction.

Friction. All the hot, wild friction.

Yep, she's made every word in the English language a dirty word in my head.

Meanwhile, Ophelia is going in for the kill, and I have to accept the awkward hug as Abram looks on with a smirk.

"You never returned my text," she says, swatting my chest.

"Yeah. Sorry, I, uh," *told you I wouldn't.*

"It's okay. I'm just teasing. Oh, hey, Abram. Hi, Kaitlyn. What's up?"

They nod back but I doubt she notices when her attention rests on Val. "I don't know you," she says. "Hi, I'm Ophelia."

She holds out her hand, and I try to keep a straight face at Val's confusion as she struggles to figure out who he is and how he's important.

"Hi. Val," he says.

Even Abram's eyes ignite with humor.

"Are you a musician too?"

"Yeah," he says. "Not at the same level as these three, though." He adds a self-deprecating smile that has the opposite effect. Ophelia is actually checking him out. Interesting.

"I'm an actress," she says.

Technically.

"Yeah? Anything I've seen?" Val says like a good new acquaintance.

"You know the girl who dies at the beginning of Halloween Revenge Six?"

Val sucks in his lips as he definitely lies with a nod.

That was Ophelia.

"That was me!" she cries. "I know, it's hard to tell because of all the blood and the darkness. Oh, and the fact that they only showed my severed torso. It wasn't really severed of course," she adds in a whisper, as if no one would have guessed they didn't actually mutilate a cast member for the masterpiece that is Halloween Revenge Six.

"Wow," Val says with a tight smile. "I bet you… had to wear a lot of makeup."

"So much! It's not easy staying completely still while you're pretending to be dead, either."

"I'd imagine not. Bet that took lots of practice."

"Yes, but Nash helped me train by watching TV while I'd lie on my kitchen floor for hours. Right, Nash?"

I don't even know how to answer that, so I just say "Yes."

She grins and focuses back on Val. "So you're a good friend of Abram's?"

"Oh, I…"

He looks nervously at Abram who answers, "Yep."

Val's eyes widen as his cheeks flush—a lot like his sister's do, actually.

"Yeah," he echoes. Can't blame him for his shock. It's a lot to process, but the fact that he's hesitant about it is exactly why Abram probably likes him. My old friend has zero tolerance for bullshit, which is why I had no problem introducing him to a humble, authentic kid like Val. I knew he'd like him because I like him and Abram and I are basically the same person—minus every fact about our past, present, and future.

We *do* both have tattoos and hate bullshit, though.

"And this is Paige," I interrupt, waving at the excluded member of our group. "My girlfriend."

I reach for her hand all boyfriend-like, and she flinches when I capture her fingers. She quickly relaxes into the hold, however, even threading our fingers in an almost believable couple's maneuver. Maybe fully believable when Ophelia's scowl locks on our hands.

"Nice to meet you," Paige mumbles.

"Nice to meet you too," Ophelia mumbles back.

Yeah, that exchange won't make the shortlist for a Hallmark card.

Paige sends me a questioning look, and I try to communicate "I'll explain later" with my eyes. I must have said, "I'm in love with this woman and want to spend so, so many years of wedded bliss with her" instead because her hazel irises are all kinds of *I hate you* right now. Then again, her hate is hard to distinguish from her lust.

"Okay, well, I'm obviously interrupting, so…" Ophelia's gaze lingers on Val who returns a polite smile.

"Nice to meet you," he says, also very politely.

"Yep," she says with fake enthusiasm when she realizes no one is going to stop her from leaving.

Also won't be a Hallmark card.

"Ex-girlfriend?" Paige asks once Ophelia continues on her way. She releases my hand, and I shove it under the table to rest on my lap.

"Thanks for playing along. Didn't want to reopen that door. And no. We never went out."

"Really? So some woman you didn't go out with was upset you didn't text her back?"

"I mean, we went *out* just not dating went out."

She squints at me, and I feel the heat of Abram and Kaitlyn's stares as well. I send them a pleading look, but their return amusement doesn't help.

"Like, we physically went to specific locations together, but never *dated*."

"How many specific locations?"

"Oh, um… I don't know. Seven? Eight?"

"So you went to seven or eight specific locations with this woman and don't consider that dating? When does going to specific locations with someone become dating?"

It's a good question and my friends' attempts not to laugh are really, really not helping at this point.

"I guess… number… nine?"

Geez, I'm just bombing my Hallmark audition today.

Her brows knit as she considers my bulletproof theory.

"I see. Well, I can say from the other person's perspective, if I went to a specific location with a guy seven or eight times, I would expect a return text."

"I told her *not* to text me, though."

"Ah. So you formally broke up with her?"

"I didn't have to break up with her. We weren't together."

"You were, though. Seven or eight times with someone is together."

"No, it's…" I try Abram and Kaitlyn again. "Tell her. It's not, right?"

Abram shrugs. "Dude, I fell in love with Mona in less than a week so maybe you want to find a different ally."

"Yeah, Martin and I were pretty insta-love, too, once we finally got to know each other," Kaitlyn adds. "Sorry, my friend. When you know, you know."

"Right," I say with a grunt. "Val? Come on. Help me out, here."

He scratches his temple with an apologetic look. "Does the number even matter if one of you thinks it was dating?"

"It's not dating! Hanging out with someone is not automatically dating."

"Did you kiss her?" Paige asks.

Geez. How did we get here?

"Yes," I say. "Of course."

Her eyes narrow. "More than that?"

"Why are we talking about this?"

"Because!"

"It was a long time ago. What does it matter?"

"It matters because your philosophy on dating still affects the present."

"I've gone to seven or eight specific locations with you and we've more than kissed. Does that mean we're dating?"

Oh shit.

Her face reddens as the table goes still. An awkward energy bubbles around us, and I scour my brain for a suitable recovery.

Calculators.

Fish sticks.

Koala bears.

Tiny dogs in strollers?

Nope. My brain's got nothing.

Abram clears his throat and three sets of eyes shoot to him. "So, uh, about that recording equipment… should we go take a look at it now?"

"Yes," Val rushes out. "Let's look at it for at least the next ten hours."

The world doesn't suck for five whole minutes. In fact, it's pretty darn glorious as I gaze at my dream 16-channel interface and two top-of-the-line vocal mics.

"Oh, shit. Are those Denton U 89s?" Val asks, leaning down to inspect my future children.

"Yes, sir," I say.

"I think he's in love," Abram says to Kaitlyn.

"What're ya gonna name 'em, buddy?" he directs at me in a sing-song tone. I can *hear* the exaggerated eyelash fluttering.

I'd glare back but then I'd have to stop ogling the equipment I've wanted since… forever.

Abram didn't have a chance to grab it from his friend before our meeting today, so here we are at "Dino's" studio where it's lived while we wait for my finances to improve. If all goes well, these beauties will be mine in a couple of weeks. Marcos promised he'd lend me the money once this spy shit wrapped and I helped him save the world or whatever.

"Wait. That's it?" Paige asks, waving at the three items on the counter. "This is what all the fuss is about? Two microphones and a little stereo?"

Sacrilege.

"This is an AudioStar Comet X16 interface, not a *stereo*," Val says. "It's the flagship AudioStar recording interface. Do you have any clue how good the A/D and D/A conversion quality is? Plus it comes with amazing plugins you can track through with near-zero latency."

"Right, so, that means…?"

"Imagine your ultimate dream clipboard," he says. "Leather binding, built-in calculator, monogrammed pages with those tiny calendars—"

I smirk as Paige shoves her brother. "Hilarious."

"It means your boyfriend here is going to have some pretty sick tracks in the near future," Abram says with a smirk.

Paige narrows her eyes at him, probably because of the boyfriend comment. Or the fact that she knows I won't share those sick tracks with anyone. Or maybe she just doesn't like reflections on the near future. With Paige, it's probably all three.

I'm about to respond when Abram and Kaitlyn's gazes lock on something behind me for the second time today. I really need to start facing in the opposite direction.

I turn and… oh no. No way. *How?!*

"Well, would you look who's back in town. Heard you were stopping by. Your little vacay in New York finally over? How long's it been, *Nashville*?"

I glare at the very definition of a "human trash bag" as Mona once called him.

Tyler.

Here.

In front of me while I was just considering sharing our joint horror story an hour ago. Somewhere The Fates are cackling and toasting themselves.

"New York is great," I say. "Especially, since you're not there."

Tyler sneers at me before settling his attention on Abram. "Hey, man. Great to see you. Been a minute."

Abram glares back. "What do you want? Why are you here?"

"What? I can't stop by and say hello to some old friends when they're in town?"

"Oh, we're friends now?" I fire back.

My blood is boiling, my stomach rolling with each second in this asshole's presence.

"We're in the middle of something," I say.

"I can see that."

He studies Paige with a leering grin, and my fingers curl at my side. I've never wanted to punch someone so much in my life. Actually, not true. I'll put this moment at number eight, although Tyler also holds positions one through four so... I'll figure that math out later.

"Hi, I'm Tyler," he says, holding out his hand to Paige.

She studies it with a look of disdain that slightly eases the tension in my coiled fist. "Good to know. Makes it easier for the police report."

Abram chokes on a swallow of water from his bottle as Kaitlyn and Val snort a laugh.

Tyler's cocky grin falters, and he shoves his rejected hand back in his pocket. His companions have joined him and now it's a full-on buffet of awkward silence and icy stares.

"How's the roadie circuit?" Tyler says, focusing back on me.

"Great. How's the D-list?"

"I wouldn't know. Riding the charts has been fantastic, in case you're wondering what that's like. As you can see, we're working with Dino Fornelli. But I guess you're still an overhyped lapdog. Does he let you follow him to the potty too?" He nods to Abram in an obvious (jealous) message.

I rub my chin in mock agreement. "Yep. That's me. Most overhyped roadie on the planet. I cleaned up last year at the Awesome Roadie Awards. Best Guitar Restringing Technique, wasn't it?" I ask Abram who snickers.

"And Best Black Jeans," Kaitlyn adds. "You should have won Best Parking Lot Football Player too. You were robbed."

I laugh and turn back to Tyler with a shrug. "So much hyping going on with roadies these days. It's ridiculous," I say, shaking my head.

"Whatever," Tyler mumbles. "I'd say we missed you but I don't think anyone noticed you left. Let's go," he tells his band of followers.

I don't recognize any of the faces that scowl at me as they pass, which makes it hard to care that they're scowling at me.

"Asshole," Abram says once they're gone. "Sorry. I had no idea he was working with Dino or I never would have brought you here. You okay?"

I shrug, suddenly feeling weak and tired and so damn depleted as the protective adrenaline drains away.

"Yeah, I'm fine," I lie. "I'm just gonna run to the bathroom quick."

"Nash," Kaitlyn says, reaching for my arm.

I pull away and offer a tight smile.

"Really, I'm fine. Just need a minute."

I'm not.

I'm so not fine.

14—EXPOSING

PAIGE

He's not fine. In fact, he's the opposite of fine as he stalks away, presumably in search of a bathroom. None of us believes his quick exit is related to a bladder issue.

"Fuck," Abram says, rubbing a hand over his face.

"What do we do?" Kaitlyn asks.

"Let him go so he can get his shit together," Abram says. "You know he doesn't want anyone to see him like that."

God, my heart.

We stare down the empty hall our friend just vacated, none of us sure where to go from here. My instinct is to follow him, even though Abram's right. There's no way he'd want that. My chest tightens at memories of him storming away after my father hit him. The last thing he wanted was to be comforted, and my attempts only seemed to upset him more. Still, the thought of him hurting alone isn't something I can tolerate. How many times has that been his fate throughout his life? When does abandonment and neglect become a programmed choice?

"What really happened with Tyler?" I ask, turning on Abram and Kaitlyn. I'm tired of being in the dark. Tired of half-truths and snippets of stories that only muddy the picture of that layered, injured, beautiful boy.

Kaitlyn and Abram exchange a look, and I step forward with a stern expression.

"I'm serious. Just tell me. I already read the articles. Is any of it true?"

After another agonizing pause, Kaitlyn sighs. "It depends what you read."

Finally! Thank god.

"I read that Nash had a hit single and a big record deal coming and lost it all when allegations emerged that he slept with a label executive to get it."

Shit, it sounds so much worse out loud.

I feel Val's shock beside me, probably the same blow I felt when I first saw the articles. The rest won't sound any better so I leave out the crap about his childhood and trouble at a group home, including a couple of arrests.

But Kaitlyn looks sad, not disgusted. Abram just looks pissed.

"If that's what you read, then yes," Abram says in a sharp tone. "It's all true. Also, none of it's true."

Well, that's not helpful.

Kaitlyn peeks down the empty hallway, worry all over her face. They really, truly care about Nash, and the more I glimpse of his world, the more I see evidence that the guy who claims to push people away isn't as good at it as he thinks. Yet again, I feel this driving need to understand how the person he's supposed to be got shoved so far off course.

"Please," I say, softening my stance. "I just want to understand. I want to help him. He's supposed to be filling the world with his music, not working at some mindless office job. Anyone can see that."

Abram searches my face before shaking his head in defeat. "Yeah. He is. Believe me, we've been trying for years to push him back up but he fell too hard. I don't know if he'll ever be willing to give 'the world' another shot after what it did to him."

"So what *really* happened?" I ask. *Please, please tell me.*

Abram clenches his eyes shut and pulls in a deep breath, like he's in pain over what he's about to say.

"I'm the one who introduced Nash and Tyler," he sighs out. "In a way, this is about me more than anything." His words sound like a broken confession, a lifetime of regret in that one sentence.

"Don't be so hard on yourself," Kaitlyn says, squeezing his arm. "Your intentions were good. Tyler being a human waste receptacle is not your fault."

Abram nods, but doesn't seem appeased. "Not that it matters, but yes, my *intentions* were good. Nash had a ton of talent, Pirate Orgy was just starting to gain traction, and—"

"Because of you," Kaitlyn cuts in with a grunt.

He sends her a sharp look, and she shrugs.

"Fine, yes. I'm the one who basically gave them their start," he continues. "I covered one of their songs at a show as part of a deal I made for… something else… which is what launched them into the public eye." He shakes his head. "So yeah, once it became clear Pirate Orgy was going someplace whether or not they deserved it, I wanted to use that for good and help launch someone who *did* deserve it."

"Nash," I say.

Abram nods. "Yeah. The kid was fire. I mean, he'd be sitting on a crate backstage cranking out music that made you stop in your tracks. I gave Tyler and Pirate Orgy the spotlight, but Nash is the one who deserved it. I don't know, maybe it felt like a way to right a wrong, but when Tyler said they were looking for an opening act, I suggested Nash. The two of them really seemed to hit it off in the beginning." Abram quiets and looks away. "Now we know why."

"What do you mean?" I ask, my stomach dropping.

When he doesn't continue, I look to Kaitlyn, silently pleading with her to continue the story.

"Tyler used him," she says, bitterness in her voice. "Tyler knew Nash and Abram were close. I guess he'd always been jealous about that. Maybe in the beginning it was just about using Nash to get to Abram, but eventually their relationship soured and his motives got even more deplorable."

"Deplorable?" Abram asks, fighting a smile despite the somber atmosphere.

"What? It's a great word," Kaitlyn says.

"It *is* a great word. I just didn't know people actually used it."

"Well, people do," she quips, then focuses back on me. "It's the best word for gross Tyler and his gross motives."

"I believe you. I fully support your word choice," I say.

We exchange a smile before hers falters again. "Right, well, whether Tyler always intended to ruin Nash, we don't know, but at some point he went full-on dark side."

"*Deplorable*, even?" Abram says.

Kaitlyn raises her brows at him, and he cowers playfully.

"Yes. Deplorable," she says.

Abram's humor fades as a fresh shadow skims over his features. "Nash thought they were really good friends," he says in a dark tone. "Things get intimate on tour, you know? You spend a ton of time with people, literally on top of each other, especially when you're smaller and crammed in vans and hotel rooms like Tyler and Nash were. Nash must have confided some stuff, and instead of being the friend Nash thought he was, Tyler leaked it all to anyone who would listen."

"Oh my god," I breathe out.

"Yeah," Abram says. "Dick move. Like, beyond a dick move. The worst part is, he waited until it would do the most damage to Nash. His single just hit the charts, his record deal had just been inked, everything looked like it was finally going to happen for him, and then…"

"Splat," Kaitlyn says.

"Fuck," Val mumbles.

"Yeah. Exactly," Abram echoes.

"So does that mean what Tyler leaked is true?" I ask quietly. "I mean, about, well, you know…"

"That Nash slept his way to the top?" Abram spits out. "First of all, do you have any idea how common that's been in the entertainment industry? I'm not saying it's right, obviously. It's wrong, and I'm glad people are finally starting to talk about it, but even if it *were* true in Nash's case, it's hypocritical bullshit for these tabloid editors and record execs to get all preachy and ruin people's lives over something that happens all. The. Time. Hell, half the vultures on their high horses had probably been involved in their own affair on one side or the other.

"Either way, ethics and logic don't matter once the media's claws sink into someone. The *truth* doesn't even matter. Once the relationship was exposed, the label 'had to act' to save face. They fired the quote-unquote 'executive' and rescinded Nash's offer."

I can barely get the words out. "But he *did* sleep with an executive?"

"He explained the real story and we believe him," Kaitlyn says, her tone gentle like she can read my pain. "Yes, he went out with a woman from the label, but she didn't have any role in his deal. In fact, she wasn't even an executive, really, just a mid-level manager in the accounting department who was only a couple of years older than he was. The paperwork for his deal had already been drafted and was in review before they met at some industry event. I'm not sure he even knew she worked for the same label when they hooked up. Their relationship had nothing to do with his contract, but the timing couldn't have been worse. It *did* look suspicious from the outside, and the real story isn't as lurid and attractive as the other narrative, so that's the one that stuck. Even after the truth came out."

"And by then he'd been so wounded, he didn't have the energy to fight the rest," Abram adds.

The rest.

"You mean, the group home stuff?" I ask, feeling sick all over again.

He nods. "Yeah. Only a monster would use someone's trauma against them, but hey, that's Tyler for you."

"Trauma?"

Abram shakes his head. "*That* part will have to come from him. I don't know how much of what he told me is sharable so I'm not touching that one."

I release a breath but completely understand. In fact, I respect Abram for doing what Tyler should have done, what *anyone* should do when someone trusts you with a sacred piece of themself. My stomach feels like it's trying to crawl out of my skin.

"It was back-to-back, kick-him-while-he's-down blows," Kaitlyn says. "And it was brutal. We didn't see him or hear from him for months. He left L.A. for New York and disappeared. No one knew what happened to him for almost a year. We were so relieved when we learned he was finally showing up at events again, even if it was in the tech booth and backstage."

Memories of his song from last week bubble to the surface. Not just the magic of his voice, but also some of the lyrics that got stuck in my head.

See this grin? It's for you because mine's a joke that's been choked from lungs torn when my heart broke

When you call me your friend
I'm just a tragic loose end
A deadly game of pretend
Let's say I'm fine

He's not fine, though, is he? And neither am I. Or Val. Or Kaitlyn and Abram when it comes down to it. None of us are fine. Sometimes we are, but like so many other things, we often pretend because it's easy. Expected. Safe.

Until it's not.

"Thanks for the story," I say, pushing away from the wall.

"Where are you going?" Kaitlyn asks.

"I have to find him."

"That's not a good idea. He doesn't like sharing his baggage with people," Abram says.

"Yes, well, he's already used to me ignoring what he wants. That's apparently my role in his life, so who better to piss him off and force him out of hiding?"

A smile tugs at their lips.

"Fair enough," Abram says, waving me on. "We'll go find a first aid kit for when you confront him."

I smirk and start down the hall.

My confidence fades as I scan the halls and open doorways for any sign of the guy I'm having trouble "pretending" about anymore. With each step, the pieces of our relationship (and my crush) begin to snap into place. As frustrating as Nash can be, I wouldn't want him any other way. He was right that day in my bedroom. I like that he's not intimidated by me, that *he* seems to like that I challenge him just as much. I never dated a lot because most of the guys I came across wanted me to be less smart, less loud, and a lot softer. I always felt like I had to be something else to be what they wanted, but it's not like that with Nash. I've only ever been myself with him, which means the friction that defines us is becoming a dealmaker, not a dealbreaker. He needs a sledgehammer to get through his walls, and I need someone who will force me to look beyond my own.

We are fire and gasoline, and we've become addicted to the flames.

I freeze at the sight of a figure strewn on a couch in a dim alcove to the right. It hurts to see him like that, slouched against the backrest, his head leaning back to stare at the ceiling. What's he thinking? How long would he have stayed here on his own if I hadn't chased him?

I approach slowly so I don't startle him. He tilts his head in my direction but doesn't respond before gazing back at the ceiling like it's the only picture he can tolerate at the moment.

With a sigh, I close the gap and drop beside him. I shift into the same position and roll my head back to study the ceiling as well.

We sit in silence for a while. I have no words, and he wouldn't share his if he did. I'm okay with that, but I don't like the way his fingers scratch absent streaks in his jeans. I really don't like the tortured expression on his face or the lingering redness of eyes that fought old tears and won.

Reaching over, I find his anxious fingers and lace them with mine. He tries to pull away, but finally relaxes when I give a gentle squeeze that makes it clear I'm not letting go.

"In terms of ceilings, this one isn't great," I say, squinting at the water-stained tiles.

He doesn't respond at first, but when I peek over, his features have softened slightly.

"I used to be afraid of drop ceilings," I continue. "Not even because I feared it falling or something gross crashing through. It was the ceiling itself. Like, the actual tiles. All those little dots and holes? Shudder."

The slight curve of his lips sends a rush of warmth through me.

"I used to be afraid of dandelion seeds," he says. "You know, once the yellow flower goes away and you get the wispy seeds? I hated them."

"Well, yeah. Of course. You could totally get one of those suckers in your eye. Or worse, inhale one which would wedge in your lung and cause pneumonia. I mean, they're practically weapons. Pretty sure they're being researched at secret military bases as we speak."

He offers a soft chuckle. "I can already see the troops in formation, holding up their little stems. 'Ready! Aim! Blow!'"

I laugh and tug his fingers to my lips. I know it's a mistake, but it just feels… necessary. He doesn't pull away, but averts his gaze, and we settle back into our somber truce.

After another long silence, he scrubs at his face.

"Did they tell you?" he asks in a resigned tone.

"I already knew. I told you at lunch I saw the articles."

He closes his eyes. "Yeah," he exhales. "Nice story, huh?"

"The only nice part was the photo of you on stage in that one article. Don't get mad, but even the scandal version of you is hot."

His weak smile tugs at me as he focuses back on picking at his jeans. "Yeah? Which article was that?"

"The one on the website with the round, pointy squirrel."

"Squirrel?"

"I don't know. It had some rodent in its logo."

His face scrunches in thought until he releases a genuine laugh that makes my entire body hum.

"Hang on, you mean *The Tattletale Review*?"

"Maybe? Do they have a squirrel for a logo?"

"It's a rat," he says, still chuckling. "As in, 'ratting' someone out?"

I squint over at him. "A rat? Really? What's with the acorn it's holding? Do rats collect acorns too?"

"It's holding an acorn?"

"I thought that's what it had in its tiny paws, but now you've made me question my entire understanding of rodent culture."

"I find it interesting you *had* an understanding of rodent culture."

"Doesn't everyone?"

He straightens slowly, the cloud finally drifting from his face. "Hate to disappoint you, but I couldn't tell you the last time I've reflected on rodent philosophy."

"Whoa, hey now. I didn't say anything about *theoretical* rodent concepts. I wouldn't dare broach that existential landmine."

His blue eyes sparkle with humor, and I can't look away. How could anyone want to hurt this person? It makes no sense to me.

You wanted to hurt him not so long ago, remember? Heck, you wanted to hurt him an hour ago. Twenty minutes ago. Most of the time, really. It's part of your thing with him, right? Nag and criticize, even if it's because—

Ugh. Shut up, Brain. Go get nihilistic with rodents.

"Most of it's not true, you know, the way they spun what happened," he says, growing serious again.

"I know." I shift and pull one leg under me to face him on the couch.

"Tyler was just pissed that his label offered me a deal after seeing me perform at one of *his* shows. He resented the fact that it came so 'easy' for me. Like he had any clue what I'd been through to get there." He looks away. "The other stuff, though…" His voice trails off, and he shakes his head. "I thought he was my friend. We got drunk one night after a show, started talking, revealing stuff, you know? One thing led to another and yeah, I told him some stuff. Personal shit from my past no one but Marcos and Nate knew."

"About the arrests?"

"Arrests?" he scoffs. "The arrests were the least of it. By the time that came out the damage was done. Besides, that was bullshit too. I got picked up a couple of times for trying to run away when I was fifteen. They found me and dragged me back to Bellevue. That's my *shady criminal past*."

"Bellevue is the group home?"

He nods, his face going dark again. "It was the personal stuff that hurt the most, if I'm honest. Stuff that…" He blinks and drops his gaze again.

"Stuff that made you vulnerable?"

His eyes lift to mine, crashing hard in the hazy light. "I haven't shared anything with anyone since. I can't. He didn't just betray my trust, he fucking broke me, Paige."

Something cracks in my chest, and I don't care about the rules anymore. I lean forward and pull him into my arms, holding tight until he dissolves into me. My fingers thread into his hair as I cling to him, relishing the warmth of his breath on my skin and the steady beat of his heart. All I want in this moment is to hold onto this person until his pain becomes mine. I want to absorb it, siphon it out of him until he's light enough to soar.

I want to be the one he hides *with* not from.

"I chose Sandeke Telecom because I'm weak and scared," I say quietly, staring past him at the wall. He releases me and leans back to study my face. I meet his surprised gaze and swallow.

"You asked why I chose this path? That's why. Because I watched what happened to my brother when he broke from the mold our parents made for us and I wasn't brave enough to do the same. I like business—I'm *good* at it—so it was easy to convince myself I was doing it for me and not for them. But if it were truly for myself, I'd be jumping into a startup company to build an empire I'm passionate about, not become another robot puppet in someone else's kingdom. I've always envisioned myself as a CEO, but it's not Sandeke Telecom or my dad's company I want to run."

I suck in a deep breath and force myself to meet his stare again. "You asked why I felt Reedweather Media was the path worthy of me and my talents but the truth is, it's not. None of this is. I'm meant to carve my own path, to gaze down from a summit *I* conceived and climbed. I deserve that, and you're the one who forced me to confront the truth. I thought I had it all together, but I don't. I'm not fine, either."

I inch closer and reach for his hand again. He accepts the gesture and searches my face as we lace our fingers. I see the understanding in his expression, the compassion. I see a guy who cares.

"I'm living a lie, Nash, and so are you. You deserve so much more than this. The world knocked you down and scarred you, but it didn't break you. You know how I know that? Because despite what you seem to think there are many talented, intelligent, accomplished people who still believe in you. Who *love* you."

I tug his hand for emphasis. "I can't begin to understand what you've been through and have no right to rush your grieving process, but I know for a fact that you're wrong about one thing. You *can* afford to take risks. You already did, and when it blew up in your face, you had a wide net of people willing to catch you.

"But you have to let them. You have to believe you are worthy of their love and support. You do have a family, and whether you become a superstar or end up back on your ass, you will be surrounded by people who love you and want to see you thrive.

"We've all heard your music, seen your talent, and I'm telling you, it's worth the risk," I say into the thick air around us. "Whenever you're ready to try again, we will be here for the highest highs and the lowest lows."

I lean into him again, and his arms tighten around me until we're practically one body. I've never felt so whole, so safe and certain. Most of that speech should have scared the crap out of me, but instead, I find myself cataloging my own life and building a mental family tree of all the people who would support me if I was brave enough to step out on my own. It's more than I thought, and as the list of supporters grows, it becomes clear I haven't been honest with myself about my relationships either. I've always assumed Val followed me around because I was protecting him, but what if it was the other way around? What if I'm depending on his support just as much?

"My hair was shorter then," Nash says, finally pulling back. His pretty eyes blink away a flash of shyness before settling on me. "In the photo on that squirrel website?"

I already miss his warmth against me, the flutter in my stomach whenever we touch. Gosh, he's so special. I can't believe just a couple of weeks ago I couldn't stand him.

"I like it how it is now," I say, tugging on a dark, wavy lock.

His weak smile hurts after the heaviness of the last few minutes. "Thanks. I like yours too."

"Yeah? It's a pain in the butt to deal with." I fluff the curtain of curls springing from my head.

"It was perfect for gripping."

My blood stirs at his sly grin, and crap, I'm in trouble. Why do his lips have to look so inviting right now? His soulful eyes, those mesmerizing tattoos? When every brain cell in my head is demanding we go find the others after this long absence, all I want to do is lock us in a room and ravage him for days on end. No brothers or roommates or intrusive parents. Just me and that cocky smile and mouthwatering body and irresistible wit. I want to hear his music, free and untethered by doubt. Over and over until it's embedded in my soul too.

"Anyway, thanks for the chat," he says, pushing up from the couch. He reaches out to pull me up as well. "Sorry for all the drama."

I force away the disappointment at losing him again. The longing.

"Anytime. That's what co-spies are for."

His return smile almost makes it okay that I may never get to kiss him again.

Just kidding. Nothing will make that okay.

* * *

In the history of terrible ideas that includes a record label passing on The Beatles and someone deciding to put Chad in charge of *anything*, I can't say this is the worst idea of all time.

It sure feels close, though, as club lights flash and seductive bass notes thump through a room of undulating, sweaty bodies. Most of them aren't an issue. It's really just one that's causing problems for me. Added to the *Terrible Idea List* are the two martinis I've imbibed that are starting to make terrible ideas seem not so terrible. For example, I am very, very close to breaking a hard, steadfast rule I've followed my entire life while breaking another rule I set this morning.

See, for an hour and a half now I've had to watch Nash and his sculpted, mesmerizing body move vertically in ways I enjoyed horizontally not so long ago. Several individuals have approached him to dance, and at the encouragement of his friends, he's been allowing them to grind against him in a way that makes me want to go on a dancefloor for the first time ever to throw a right hook, also for the first time ever.

Newsflash: Nightclubs aren't exactly my thing. They're his thing, though, as evidenced by the crowd of people who have clustered around him since we arrived. Worst part? I can't tell if he actually knew any of these people before we got here or if they just saw physical human perfection and gravitated toward it like a cat to a broken cardboard box.

"He likes you," Kaitlyn shouts over the rhythmic thumping.

I cast her a skeptical look and take another sip of my drink.

"Clearly," I shout back. "That's why he's letting a parade of supermodels dry hump him all night."

Kaitlyn chuckles. "Well, he's been watching *you* all night."

"Probably to make sure I'm jealous."

Her expression darkens as she shakes her head. "No. Nash isn't like that. He doesn't play games with people."

185

I sigh at her scolding, maybe feeling a tad guilty for my comment that I know was more bitter than true.

"He's looking at you because he wants it to be you," Kaitlyn continues, making the whole thing ten times worse. Because yes, I know that too. How? He asked right from the get-go for it to be me. I refused. Then said no again when he asked ten minutes later. Then again when he asked a half hour after that.

He's stopped asking, but I've felt his searing gaze all night. Mine's probably burning holes right back with the growing fire inside me from every flex and sway of his body in that tight black tee and perfectly fitted ripped jeans. I also know from the ride over and the few times I let him get close that he smells amazing. A person might wonder why you'd say no to your fantasy when it beckons you with a sexy grin and captivating stare, not once but thrice.

One.

Two.

Three denials in perfect poetic symmetry for the mother of all medieval fables.

The answer is simple: I don't dance. Period.

Not even when it means fusing your tingling, needy body with the guy you've been stripping all night in your head.

So instead of running my hands over taut muscle and hot skin, I get to hover at a table and watch other women do it. Instead of inhaling the dizzying scent of crisp, alpine forests and the mint gum he's always chewing, I get to guzzle alcohol I don't really like, while scream-chatting with a woman I barely know. Even Val is out there having the time of his life. Pretty sure Kaitlyn only came because Abram couldn't and she feared I'd end up hovering at a table by myself if she didn't. She was correct.

The person hanging on Nash right now has her hands all over him. Arms, chest… did she just grab his ass? Jealousy is already boiling inside me when lips that were saying something at his ear suddenly land on his neck. He allows it for just a second before arching away and separating from her with a gentle push. He says something, and she returns what's clearly a pout. She leans in again to respond, but instead of righteous fury, he smiles. *Smiles!* Then, takes her hand and leads her off the dancefloor. Where are they going? Why is he letting some woman he didn't want kissing him take him somewhere else to do heaven knows what?

"You just gonna stand there?"

I tense at the voice that's gruffer and more critical than Kaitlyn's patient attention all night.

I glare over at my brother who shrugs. "He wanted to hang with you, not whoever that is," he shouts. "Why are you here and not with him?"

"What are you talking about?"

"You obviously want him."

"I do not."

"The puddle of drool around this table says otherwise."

"Not to mention poses a safety hazard," Kaitlyn adds.

Hey, whose side is she on?

"Just go!" Val says with a small shove in Nash's direction.

"I can't," I grunt, digging in my heels and returning to my post.

"Why not?"

"Because it's a terrible idea!" I shout back. The martinis add a melodramatic harrumph, complete with a self-assured arm cross. I'd make any cartoon teenager proud.

"Why?"

"Because I'm attracted to him. If I was near him, I'd want to touch him and if I let myself do *that* I wouldn't want to stop. His arms would lead to his chest, then his stomach, then his ass, and ultimately his pe—"

"Okay! I get it. Geez," he says with a cringe. "And that's a bad thing, why?"

"Because it's a terrible idea!"

"So a better idea is to pretend you're not interested and let everyone else flirt with him all night?"

"Precisely."

We watch the woman back toward the wall, pulling him along with her until he's aligned with her itty bity body in her itty bity dress. He leans in to say something, and her arms shoot around his neck to hold him against her. I wait for him to peel away, but he doesn't. I don't know which is worse: watching the guy I'm falling for get groped by another woman or my brother's smug expression about it.

"Yeah? And how's that working out for you?" he calls.

I release some of my venom in his direction before the rest gushes across the room to the couple entwined against the wall. Because, yes. Fine. My position on allowing other women to maul the guy I want (badly) actually isn't working out so great.

Val and Kaitlyn wave me on in encouragement as I slam my water bottle on the table and start toward my co-spy and his barely clothed amour. He's taking this James Bond thing way too literally. There are definitely spies who *don't* engage in amorous affairs at nightclubs as part of their missions. Nash needs to be one of those spies. Right the heck now.

They're not exactly kissing when I reach them but they're not exactly not. I can't tell what they're doing but the slightest hint of relief breezes through me when I see they're not as close as I thought. Nash seems to have his arms braced against the wall not to trap her but to keep his body away from hers, even as she's trying for more.

Or is she?

I expected to find raptured lust on their faces, but instead I see a serious, concerned expression on his and tears on hers. My ire flounders a bit, and I stall my attack as I try to figure out what's going on.

He leans in and says something, which draws a nod from her. She swats at her cheeks and returns a wobbly smile. He lightly pinches her chin and kisses her cheek before pushing away from the wall.

Turning around, he stops in his tracks when he sees me. His face falls, and I don't know how to read the mix of emotions that filters over him. He clearly doesn't know what to do next, so I close the gap and grab his wrist.

"Let's dance," I say.

"What?"

"Dancing." I wave behind me at the sea of bodies demonstrating this ancient ritual.

"You… wait. You want to dance with me? You've been turning me down all night."

I nod. "Yes. Because I don't dance."

"But you do now?"

"No."

"I don't understand. What's changed?"

"My internal—and a few external—organs."

"Huh?"

His brow scrunches, and I notice for the first time how much I like the image of his silver piercing when he does that. I reach up and brush my finger near it, then let my touch drift down the side of his face. My gaze settles on his lips and a sharp wave of desire surges through me.

"I turned you down because you're extremely attractive tonight," I explain. "Dangerously so."

"Wait, you've been turning me down because you wanted me too much?"

I nod again, forcing my attention back to his entrancing gaze. "Yes, and since we agreed we can't have what we want, it felt like a terrible idea to indulge in a sample of the forbidden fruit."

His confusion morphs into amusement. "Do you always have to say stuff in the weirdest way possible?"

I narrow my eyes at him. "Do you always have to be a jerk when I'm trying to be nice?"

"This is you being nice?"

I glare at him and tighten my hold on his wrist. In fact, I take his other one, gripping hard in a way that's not even on the spectrum of *nice*. This hold is demanding and possessive, and when his eyes flare hot, my entire core bursts into flames.

We want him! Give him to us! Now, now, now! it's chanting.

Wait. Why is that region speaking in the plural?

Because there are lots of us parts down here, and we're all in agreement!

Crap. Nash is right. I do say stuff in the weirdest way possible.

Whatever.

I don't give him a chance to answer and start toward the crowded dancefloor. When I check his face, those tempting lips are curved in a smile, and the cocky heat in his eyes makes my insides quiver.

"I don't actually know how to dance," I say when he pulls us to a stop and forces me around. "I…"

Words. I forget those, along with my insecurities, time, and every other law of the universe the second his arms cinch around me and I'm flush with his warm, solid body. Damn, he feels good. Smells good. Looks… I can't look. I shouldn't. I know it's a mistake even as I lift my chin to meet infinite blue eyes that are dark and enigmatic in the flashing club lights. They search mine as our fused bodies pulse to the seductive pound of synthetic bass. My hips graze his, over and over, rubbing and pressing until tiny sparks spread from the apex of my thighs throughout my entire being. For real, I feel raging lust in my fingernails.

We want him! my annoying parts chant through the violent blast of heat.

And suddenly, my brain does too. My heart. My soul.

Yes, five seconds in, I'm desperate to do exactly what I've been avoiding all night.

Kiss him.

Touch him.

Claim and devour him.

I lock my hands behind his neck as we rock to the music. Our bodies swell and retract, grinding a flurry of smoldering embers into raging flames. I can't stop staring at his eyes, his mouth. My tongue slips out to wet my own as if somehow that will satiate this hunger. All it does is remind me how much it won't. Nothing will, not until he's inside me. Until I feel him deep and hot and explosive in a euphoric rush of surrender.

Until…

He. Is. Fully. Mine.

And that's when I remember why this terrible idea was a terrible idea. It must occur to him too, because instead of leaning in to give me what I so obviously want, he pulls back. Instead of anchoring me tighter to his devastating body, he puts more space between us. And instead of feeling hurt, I sigh and drop my hands.

We step back at the same time, shivering from a sudden chill in this hot, sticky club.

"I'm sorry," he says.

I can't hear him, but those words can be spoken in a thousand ways without sound. Right now they're a neon sign blazing above dozens of flickering LED spotlights.

"Me too," I say, fighting the urge to grab him and stop him from running.

For a brief second it looks like maybe he wants me to. Maybe we don't have to be responsible or fair to each other. Maybe we can take what we want in this moment and shove the consequences to tomorrow. Maybe we're missing something and there *is* a magical way for us to make this work. At the very least, maybe this is just basic attraction and we could somehow be satisfied with a one-time indulgence.

You know one night won't be enough with him.

The debate is irrelevant when he pulls out his phone and studies the screen.

Fuck: another word that doesn't have to be a word to be understood.

"Can you get a ride back with Val?" he shouts.

"Sure."

"Okay. I have to run. I'm sorry."

Is he sorry? He looks more relieved that circumstances just thwarted what was bound to be another mistake. Because there's no doubt in my mind as my super-crush stalks away that I would've lost the battle with myself. If not for whatever message chased him away, *I'd* be the one dragging him off the dancefloor this time. Probably toward a dark corner where I'd do unspeakable things to any part of him he'd allow.

I stare after my almost-regret for several seconds, almost relieved that we averted disaster.

15—LOSING

NASH

Well, that went poorly—four words I've heard, thought, and felt often in my life, but never so much as right now while I ride the elevator to Larinda's floor.

Her frantic S.O.S. is barely registering on my frayed consciousness as the fiery essence of Paige still buzzes through me. I never should have asked her to dance or accepted when she finally gave in. She was right. We *had* agreed to end this—whatever it is. But then I saw her standing in the swirling club lights, music pounding around us, and I don't know. Nothing seemed as important as being close to her. She was perfection tonight: frustrating, awkward, and so freaking gorgeous. Factor in her willingness to do something she hated just to be with me? Yeah, I was a goner (even if her explanation was hilariously weird.)

But it shouldn't have happened. We're in dangerous waters as we tread this line between heart and health. It could never work between us and every time I let my heart free it gets broken. Again and again, my delicate artist soul has been crushed, and I just… can't anymore.

I've had to lock away my weakest organ to survive, and I thought I'd been doing an okay job of keeping it hidden. That is, until Asshat Tyler sent me reeling today. Next thing I know, Paige is transforming from hurricane to lifeline, and right there on a ratty couch in Dino Fornelli's studio, thick roots of connection sunk deep into my soul. I realized too late that they belonged to her.

Yes, normally, getting cockblocked by a frantic text at eleven o'clock at night would be annoying, but right now? Thank the heavens a pampered country star is being under-pampered.

"Oh, Nash! Thank goodness you're here!" Larinda says as soon as she sees me.

I don't have a chance to respond before she's dragging me into her hotel suite and slamming the door.

"Hey," I say, lifting a hand to greet the other six people in the room. So this is a group thing?

Larinda chews on her lip as she paces in a silk robe, her hair gathered in a loose pile on her head. She's still in full makeup, and by the grave expression on each face something catastrophic has occurred.

"They just told us I can't wear sequins on camera!"

Or that.

Her tortured gaze lands on me, and I swallow my initial response.

Then the next one.

Also the third.

The fourth seems safe, so I let out a surprised, "Oh, wow. Not even small ones?" *Are* there multiple sizes of sequins?

"No! None. Something about the… the white background and lights and ah! What am I supposed to do? We're filming tomorrow and everything revolves around my Roberto Luna gown!"

"Everything as in…?" I pause for more insight because the entirety of time and space hinging on one dress seems unlikely.

"Everything! I can't play 'Moonlight Musing' without the guitar and I can't play the guitar without the dress. How did this happen?"

None of that makes any sense to me, but she's committed enough that I know better than to argue. If my time in this industry has taught me anything, it's that you don't mess with an artist and their process. If "Moonlight Musing" requires a specific guitar that requires a specific dress, it does. End of story.

And suddenly, Chad's annoying ghost voice is in my head. *Bingo! You could sabotage this event right here, right now! Convince Larinda to pull out over something so silly and make a fool of herself. Ruin her and the event in one shot! Long live the Mer-Nuts!*

Eh, never mind. Most of that is too insightful for ghost Chad. The tiny part of my brain currently admiring the fuzzy blue pillows is probably more his influence.

No, that nefarious thought must be from ghost Marcos, Eva, Paige, or even worse—my own villainous brain.

I study Larinda's trusting expression. It would be so easy to manipulate this situation. In fact, I'd probably get in trouble for *not* taking advantage of the opportunity.

Do it! Do it! Ghost Chad chants. How is he still here?

If you don't, I'll force them to put you back on the Mer-Nut campaign for all of eternity.

Larinda blinks crystal gray eyes at me.

"What should I do?" she asks.

Drop out.

Throw a public tantrum.

Wear the dress and look like a dismembered floating head everyone will laugh about.

But I can't. Not even on pain of Mer-Nuts.

"Can you perform a different song?" I ask, stepping down into the main living area. "What other outfits do you have?"

"We tried that. Obviously," a flashy man I don't recognize cuts in. Could this be the personal assistant she was so, so sorry couldn't join us for nails and brunch the other day? "The only thing she has is the leather jumpsuit for 'Billboards and Billiards.'"

His clipped tone tells me he's not thrilled that I'm here, let alone making suggestions that have already been made. Guess I can't blame him since my presence means he bombed his portion of whatever crisis management session this is.

Larinda waves toward a rack behind us, and sure enough, there's a leather jumpsuit hanging all by its lonesome. The coordinating newsboy hat droops from a hook beside it like it's gutted at being rejected. Nothing is more depressing than a newsboy hat that thinks it's unwanted.

"'Billboards and Billiards' would be a great song for tomorrow," I say, infusing extra enthusiasm into my voice. I can't tell if it's for Larinda or her sad hat. "Honestly, with the theme of the event and the gaming community audience, a sassy anthem would probably go over better than a gloomy ballad anyway."

Please tell me I didn't just say sassy.

"Hmm… it *is* pretty sassy," Larinda mumbles, studying the leather outfit.

"So sassy!" a member of the entourage chirps.

"Like, the definition of sassy!" another adds.

I don't know whether I should be apologetic or proud that I triggered an entire moment in history dedicated to the word "sassy."

Larinda tilts her head and looks about to agree when Bitter PA pipes in.

"Sweetie, 'Billboards and Billiards' is a duet," he says with fake distress. "Obviously, we can't fly Reece Culpepper in here for one song. He plays the guitar part too, remember?"

"Crap. You're right," Larinda groans. Her crestfallen look, followed by the dude's haughty smile for me, kind of makes me hate him and his glitzy fanny pack. Why does he even need a fanny pack to sit on an ottoman in a two-thousand-dollar suite?

"*Or*," I say, staring him down. "*I* could perform it with you."

Larinda snaps her gaze to me, and I meet it with a shrug.

"You'd do that?" she asks.

No, of course not. I'd never do that. It's a horrible idea. Irritating Fanny Pack struck and I struck back on instinct. But it was a cruel joke of fate because now I have to look like a jerk and/or an idiot by backtracking. Of course I can't play one of Larinda's songs on a live broadcast. I haven't played in public for years. There's no way in hell I'm putting myself back out there with someone else's country song at an event I'm only attending as a half-assed spy. Absolutely not. Never ever. Not in a million years.

"He probably doesn't even know how to play, Larry," my nemesis says, gently rubbing her arm.

Oh hell no.

"Give me that," I say, motioning toward the white, glittery acoustic guitar beside the giant sectional.

Her eyes light up as she swipes the instrument from the stand and holds it out to me. After placing my wallet and phone on the coffee table so I can balance on the armrest, I sling the strap over my shoulder and adjust it.

As I tune the most blinged-out guitar I've ever held, something surges inside me. Fear? Maybe a little, but something else. Something older and more significant. A flutter of… anticipation. It's how music used to make me feel, a rush of something bigger than myself about to explode out and infect a room.

In this case, it will be seven virtual strangers who will hear my art for the first time. It may not be my song, but it will be my heart and soul on display, and suddenly, all I can think about is a pair of vibrant hazel eyes and dark red hair. Would I be here if Paige hadn't been pushing me lately?

No.

Because it's her voice in my head as I launch into the intro of Larinda Scott's chart-topper. It's her I'm imagining on that obscene fluffy-pillow couch, nestled among a small, impromptu audience. It's Paige on my lips when I open my mouth and release sounds I swore no one would ever hear again, but here they are, flowing over banned sequins and a room full of strangers. This moment shouldn't even be happening, and suddenly it feels like it's beyond my control.

After just a few bars, I sense Larinda's rapt attention, while Entourage Rival is pissed and does little to hide his displeasure at being proven wrong. By the time we get to the chorus where Larinda takes over the lead, her infectious grin has everyone in the room fired up except the guy I'm mentally naming Steve.

Our harmonies are tight on the bridge, and I add some ghost notes and runs to the third pre-chorus I lead. I'm not a country singer and only know this song because I've been playing around with her catalog as part of my research, but the mix of country twang and gruff rocker is actually kind of cool. The chord progression is easy and straightforward, which gives me plenty of space to add diminished variations, and even a fun walkdown on the last chorus that has her glowing with excitement. It's actually not a bad song when you take the sequins out of it.

By the time we pull together an improvised extended outro, five audience members are on their feet giving us an animated standing ovation. It would mean more if I didn't suspect Larinda gets a standing ovation for stirring creamer in her coffee from these people, but still, it's been a long time since I've enjoyed applause that wasn't sarcastic.

"That was… ah!" She throws her arms around me. "I didn't know you could sing and play like that. You're amazing! Wasn't he amazing?" she asks her friends.

Alert the press. They agree.

I force a smile, suddenly feeling self-conscious about the whole thing. It's never easy to play in front of a small audience. Even in my glory days, I would've preferred four thousand to four, and most musicians I know feel the same. There's an intimacy to situations like this that make it hard to perform, but instead of downplaying everything that just happened, I find myself absently strumming progressions from my own songs, as if my fingers can't understand why they're not always in this position.

"You played it wrong. And sang it wrong," Steve says.

Larinda lets go of me and gives him a confused look. "He changed it up."

"Obviously. I just think your fans will want to hear the original version."

Doubt flickers over her face, and now I'm really hating Steve and his absurd butt purse.

"And how exactly was she going to play an original version of *anything* with just an acoustic guitar?" I ask. "Wasn't 'Moonlight Musing' going to be acoustic as well?"

"'Moonlight Musing' is different. It's mostly acoustic anyway."

"Okay. That still doesn't solve the 'no-band' issue," I say.

"We don't need a band. We'll run the track. Obviously," he says, parking a hand on his hip. Except his fanny pack is there so we have to wait an extra two seconds for his palm to find an open location. There. Nice recovery, *Steve*.

"You know this thing is a duet and happening in a lecture room, right?" I say.

"Obviously. So what?"

"So, you don't think it would be weird to have her rocking out with a phantom Reece Culpepper in front of a projection screen?"

"No weirder than playing a duet with some nobody she met a week ago."

Ouch.

Larinda winces but doesn't respond as she considers our testimony. After several long seconds, she sighs and gives me the look I've come to expect every time I put my heart on the line. If only I had a dollar for each one.

Hey, at least I'd be able to buy Redburn's equipment.

"Maybe Steve's right," she says quietly.

Wait, his name is actually Steve? That almost makes this situation okay.

"You're so talented, Nash, but it *would* look strange for me to perform with some random person no one's heard of."

Ouch again.

"Sorry, I didn't mean it like that," she rushes out. "I just mean..."

"She means it would totally overshadow everything else she does tomorrow," Steve says. "This is supposed to be about her, and you'd be all they talked about. *'Who the hell's this rando screwing up Larinda's hit song?'*"

Geez. Do they have team meetings to practice the art of crushing people's spirits?

"And it probably wouldn't be good stuff," she adds. "That's what I meant. I don't want to see you get hurt."

Her sincerity actually isn't helping, which is probably another agenda item in the training. *How to look sincere when you destroy someone* feels like a late-meeting talking point.

"Yeah. You're right," I say, hanging her guitar back on its stand.

She *is* right. I should be relieved they thwarted such a ridiculous idea, so why is my stomach churning?

You didn't actually want *to perform, did you? This isn't... disappointment?*

"Well, I should get going. I still have to get back to my own hotel."

"Nash, wait!" she calls as I start for the door.

I turn, and her apologetic smile hurts more for some reason. She shouldn't feel bad for not wanting to share the spotlight with "some rando." I shouldn't have wanted her to. Why are we mourning a moment that isn't even supposed to happen?

She shoots a concerned look toward Steve before focusing back on me. "You know what? Let's do it. So what if it's weird and people talk? Expose ourselves, right? Show them the goods they're missing?"

Okay, we need to add *re-branding "expose yourself"* to the fake meeting agenda.

For now, I can't move as I stare at her. Every ounce of excitement that drained into hurt that drained into disappointment has now drained into clarity, because this situation is exactly why I walked away. Exactly why I stopped letting myself believe in shit. I lied that day in the salon. We should *never* expose ourselves.

"Really. It's fine," I say. "You're right. I don't belong up there."

"Nash, just—"

"Seriously. You were right about everything. I don't do that shit anymore. The last thing I want is to make a fool of myself and be the subject of all the gossip." I force another stiff smile. "See you tomorrow?"

"I didn't say you'd make a fool of yourself," she says in a soft tone.

You didn't have to.

"Seriously. It's fine. *I'm* fine."

Her teeth sink into her lip. "Okay. I mean, if you're sure."

"I'm sure."

I'm not sure.

Doesn't matter. That's why this is all bullshit.

"Hey, um, I read the notes and listened to some of the samples for that track I sent you. They're amazing," she says, adding another compulsory smile I wish we could have avoided.

I return one as well. "They are. You should consider most of them. I'll put you in touch with my buddy Val Andrews. He's the genius behind it and the one who will take your stuff to the next level."

"Val Andrews? I've never heard of him."

"He's new, but he'll be a big deal. You'd be wise to scoop him up while you can." I take a deep breath and reach for the door. "Have a great night. You'll kill it tomorrow."

"Obviously!" someone squawks.

Steve.

Obviously.

I slip out before Larinda can stop me again.

Once I make it into the elevator, I lean my head against the wall and close my eyes. My stomach sinks with each passing floor, and by the time I reach the lobby, the truth is grinding its way through my head and heart.

It's been years since I put myself out there. That also means it's been years since I've had my art thrown back in my face and remembered why I stopped doing this to myself.

* * *

"No, no, no," I whisper, scouring my pockets. This can't be happening. As if I needed this night to get any worse.

Taking a deep breath, I force myself to stay calm. Did I forget the key card or did it slip out of my pocket tonight? As I replay my movements from the time I checked into my new room this afternoon, transferred my stuff, and left again for the club, I don't remember grabbing the keycard at any point. Shit. It's probably still on the corner of the dresser where it's doing nothing for anyone that isn't a dust mite in need of a home.

Fuck!

Okay, don't panic.

Thanks to my pointless pitstop at Larinda's hotel, it's now almost one as I approach the night clerk at the front desk of my building.

"Hi,"—I lean forward to check her name badge—"Tina. I'm hoping you can help me. I'm in room 912 and I think I left my keycard in the room. Can I get a replacement, please?"

The woman's smile looks as forced as mine, but I'm guessing there's not a lot that draws genuine smiles from hotel employees after midnight.

"Of course, sir. May I have your ID?"

"Yep."

I reach into my pocket to pull out my wallet and… oh no. The déjà vu is real as I pat my jeans in a frantic search.

"Sir?"

"Yeah. Um…"

I took out my wallet and phone when I sat down to play Larinda's guitar! They're probably still on her coffee table.

"Sir?"

"Yeah, so, funny story. I just came from visiting a friend and must have left my wallet at her hotel a few blocks down."

The woman's lips press together as she scans me. "I see. Then, would you please provide the credit card that's on the reservation?"

I stare back. "Okay, well, I typically keep my credit cards in my wallet… which is at Larinda's suite. Besides, it was on a company card I don't have."

"Who's Larinda?"

"Larinda Scott. The person in the suite where I left my wallet."

Incredulous would be a good word to describe the look on her face. "Larinda Scott. The country music singer?"

I cringe as the panic mounts. "Yes. I'm Nash Ellis, her creative advisor. She called me over for this sequin emergency and—"

"A *sequin* emergency?"

"Um… yeah. It's when you were going to perform a song at an event but learn you can't wear sequins so then you have to… play… a… different—you know what? It doesn't matter. Look, I know this looks bad, but I swear I'm telling the truth."

I cringe again. No one has ever convinced anyone of anything with that line.

"So if you're Larinda Scott's *creative advisor*,"—there's no chance she believes that's a real thing—"what's the company whose card is on your reservation? Should I just look up 'Larinda Scott Incorporated?'"

Okay, now she's just being mean.

"*Noo,*" I draw out. "The company is Reedweather Media. Wait, no. It might be Sandeke Telecom or…?"

Ah!

She clears her throat and straightens with a stern look.

"I'm going to suggest that you return to *your friend* and retrieve your wallet. Once you provide ID and the company credit card, I'd be happy to assist you with a replacement key."

She adds a targeted look at the security desk to the right in case any of that was too subtle.

"Sure. Thanks," I mumble, pushing away from the counter. Now what?

I glance at the attractive glass doors leading to the street. Can I really drag my humiliated ass back down to Larinda's suite? And what? Have this same implausible conversation with the front desk staff at her hotel? They demanded ID and called up for clearance before they even allowed me on the elevator at that celebrity haven.

No. I can't. I'd rather sleep on the bench outside than show my face there anyway. Steve is just itching to point out something *obvious*.

All I can do is hope she finds my belongings and returns them tomorrow. At the very least, I'll be able to mention something when I see her… assuming I can get near her without my ID. Paige might have to be the one to get us in.

Paige. Yes! Maybe I could…

No. You can't.

But maybe…

You're not seriously considering this.

What choice do I have? Cut off a finger to get a free night in the hospital?

Not free, idiot. Plus, you'd be mad about the lost finger the next day.

Get arrested for a free night in a jail cell?

I scan the security desk and crabby front desk lady. That one wouldn't be hard.

What if your boss had to bail you out?

The thought of Chad anywhere near a run-in with law enforcement gives me hives.

So another torturous night with Paige it is.

I sigh and start toward the elevators.

"Sir? Where are you going? Sir!" Tina shouts after me.

"To see if I can crash with my friend until we can sort this out tomorrow," I say.

"Your friend *Larinda Scott*?" she asks with impressive derision.

"No. A different friend."

"You have another friend in a hotel room?"

Yeah, this just keeps getting better. I may end up in jail anyway.

"I have so many friends, Tina. So, so many friends. Probably in hotel rooms all over the world."

Her glare is not a fan of my sarcastic response but I'm all out of shits to give. Disappearing around the corner, I press the up button for the elevator and lean back on my heels to wait.

And then… oh, *come on!*

Somehow I hold my anger in check as two members of security flank me in front of the elevators.

"I'm telling the truth!" I say, clenching my fists.

"Of course you are," the one on the left says dryly. "We will be happy to escort you to *your friend*. Which floor?"

"Seven," I mumble.

The door opens, and sure enough, two night guards follow me onto the elevator. One pushes the seven button.

"Which room?" she asks.

"709."

She nods, but there's nothing in her expression to indicate that me reciting a number has changed her mind. I suppose I can take solace in the fact that she trusts my ability to make up numbers.

Fittingly, I feel like a prisoner being marched down to my cellblock as we exit the elevator and turn the corner toward room 709. The guard knocks before I get a chance, and now I'm really cringing. It takes another deafening pound before Paige finally pulls open the door, eyes squinted and… still wearing nothing but my t-shirt. Shit. Now I'm getting hard on top of it all? Great.

"What?" she asks in a groggy voice. She straightens when she takes in the sight of me anchored like a convict. "Nash? What's going on?"

Her gaze passes between the guards, and I breathe some relief that at least she's acknowledging my existence.

"You know this person, ma'am?" one of the guards says.

"Yeah. What's wrong? Is he in trouble?"

The guard scans me before focusing back on her. "Not if you claim him. Is he with you?"

She looks confused, and her attention shifts to me.

"I left my wallet and phone in Larinda's room," I explain.

"That's where you ran off to? Larinda's place? Why?"

Is she jealous? At any other time, I'd be all over that fun fact, but right now I need to not be stuck in hotel limbo between two security guards who already think I'm lying, even if I'm decent at counting.

"It's a long story. She was having an issue with her dress and then I played some song for them—"

"You played for them? I thought you didn't play for other people."

"I don't. I mean… I didn't, but… I've played for you. Multiple times if you count the studio today."

Her eyes narrow on me. "Strangers, I mean. I thought you didn't *perform.* How many were there?"

Are we seriously having this argument right now? In front of two people who are itching to call the real cops at the slightest provocation? *Please don't let Chad be in charge of securing my freedom.*

"I don't know. Six? Seven? Please, Paige, just… can I stay here tonight?"

Her lips flatten in a straight line, and I can feel the guards' excitement to use their radios for something other than alerting housekeeping about puke in a hall-way. After the longest three seconds of my life, she releases a harsh breath and steps back to wave me in.

"It's fine, Officers. He's with us," she says about as dramatically as humanly possible.

She's so convincing I instinctively salute the security guards on my transfer into her custody.

"You sure, ma'am? We'd be happy to escort him somewhere else," one says, eyeing me like I'd pick *this* scenario if I were trying to sneak into a hotel to mooch a room for the night.

"Yes, it's fine," Paige says, taking my wrist and dragging me further into the room. "Thanks for your help."

They remain in place as Paige closes the door, and I swear I hear one of them grunt "All clear" into their radio.

"Thanks," I say as I follow her into the dimly lit room.

"Shh," she whispers back, waving at Val's bed. He's out cold, which I guess is good. The less witnesses the better.

Paige's sheets are in disarray, confirming that she'd been in bed as well, and I start toward the closet for the blanket.

"What are you doing?" she asks.

"Getting the blanket to sleep on the floor."

Her venomous return look matches the violent wave she makes at the space by her bed. What had been my sleeping quarters the night before is now cluttered with… I don't even know. How could they have accumulated so much stuff in one afternoon?

"Oh. Sorry. I'll just—"

She cuts me off with another warning look and yanks me toward the bed. "Come on."

Wait. What?

She pauses at the foot, looking quite annoyed by the entire affair. "Are you getting in or what?"

"You want… I mean… Hold on."

"Just get in the bed, Ellis. We'll make it work."

I kick off my shoes, still in disbelief this is happening.

"Um, okay, but…"

"You should undress too. Your jeans will be all scratchy."

We wouldn't want that.

I watch her carefully as I unhook the button on my jeans and lower the zipper. This isn't real, correct? I'm not actually stripping to sleep half-naked in a twin-sized bed beside the person I swore I'd avoid?

But it is real, because a minute later my shitty night seems a lot less shitty when she crawls in and shifts onto her side so I can nestle in behind her. I don't fit with my back to hers, so I'm forced to turn and tuck her into the curve of my body. Her previous tension relaxes when I slip my arm around her, and within moments, the woman I'm desperate to sleep with is asleep in my arms.

16—GAMING

PAIGE

In the romance books, the first night you spend with your crush is charming and rapturous and worthy of at least a full chapter of steamy caresses and swoony spooning.

In reality, it kind of sucks.

Having another human on top of you while you're trying to sleep, no matter how sexy they are, is not a condition for recuperative rest. It's the bad kind of hot and the only kind of crowded and all the kinds of impossible to get into a comfortable position. It's also something you don't regret because every second spent uncomfortable and awake is another second aware of the amazing person tucked behind you.

For hours, warm, solid biceps wrapped me against a hard chest and firm stomach. Even better was the stiff protrusion that teased my backside every time either of us moved. By early morning, I was finding excuse after excuse to make a gratuitous adjustment. What did Reedweather call it? *Fortuitous Ambiguity.*

That works. Quite well.

Currently, it's a kink in my lower back that's forcing my butt against Nash's growing erection. I will so be adding "sharing a twin bed with Nash Ellis" to the list of Terrible Ideas, but right now, it's the best idea ever.

"Paige," he groans as I squirm against him. Gosh, he feels amazing. A girl could get used to this.

"Did you sleep okay?" I whisper in a glib tone.

"Horrible," he says. "You?"

"Horrible."

I reach behind me to run my hand along his side, then curve around to his ass. My fingertips sink into dense muscle as I force his hips into the perfect angle to grind against him.

"What are you doing?" he rasps.

"Stretching."

"Do you have to *stretch* against my dick?"

"Where do you propose I stretch?"

"Literally anywhere else."

"Does that mean you want me to stop?"

"No."

"Okay then."

I stretch again. Hard.

"Fuck, Paige," he gasps. Yeah, in that romance book, things are going very differently than they are right now.

I peek back to see his eyes clenched shut, pure agony on his face.

I start a slow, steady roll against him, loving how I can feel every inch of his growing arousal. Each brush is firmer and firmer until the rock-hard sensation of him near my entrance is wreaking havoc between my legs. I can't take it anymore and reach back for a gluttonous stroke. His entire body goes rigid, but he doesn't stop me. If anything, he drives harder into my hand, seeking more friction. I knead gently, loving the rapid increase of his breath on the back of my neck and the way my own body burns with hunger at each well-timed caress. There's nothing hotter than watching his tattooed fingers clutch the sheet in front of me to suppress his response.

He must be reading my mind, though, because soon that desperate hand lets go and slides under my shirt. His palm skims down my body, searing streaks of electricity toward the soft lace between my legs. He slips his fingers beneath it, molding them over me in a hesitant plea. I'm way ahead of him when I grind against his hand, exploding wave after wave of smoldering embers until I can't breathe or think or, ah! This is so amazing and necessary and oh my gosh I'm about to—

"Nash?"

He tenses at my brother's voice, and here we go with the odd mix of relief and disappointment when he abruptly pulls away.

And falls out of the bed.

And hits the floor with a thud.

And curses when my brother bolts to help him.

And yeah. This is bad.

"I'm fine," he says, rubbing his ribs.

"Were you here all night?" Val asks, balancing on the edge of his bed.

Nash is still on the floor between us, and now I'm worried he might not be fine. What are the signs of a concussion or broken bones?

"Most of it," he says. "I got locked out of my room."

A smile flickers over Val's face. "At least you weren't in a robe this time."

"Ha ha," Nash mutters.

He pushes himself to his feet, and ohhhh. That's why he was reluctant to move. Oops. Yeah, the tented boxers probably won't require surgery and is definitely my fault.

Val doesn't comment, but the return of a slight smile makes me pretty sure he notices. Either way, we need to get this day onto a sustainable trajectory because there is no plane of existence where I want to deal with an erection and my observant brother in the same sentence.

"Let's get dressed and sort out your room situation," I say, forcing myself up from the sheets that still smell like him. I'll make sure housekeeping doesn't change our bedding tonight.

When I look over at Nash, he's already half-dressed in yesterday's clothes and looking very impatient.

"Give me a minute to put on some clothes and I'll go with you," I say, pulling my phone from the charger. The screen ignites with several texts from Chad, including one with six exclamation points and very clear instructions to call him the second I see this like right now S.O.S.

"Uh-oh. Chad emergency," I say. "One sec."

Nash rolls his eyes and leans his head against the door to wait.

I dial Chad and immediately wish I didn't.

"Thank god!" he cries. "I think they finally got to Nash!"

He's so loud Nash winces from the other side of the room. I put the call on speaker, mostly so I can keep the phone a safe distance from my ear.

"He's fine," I say.

"He's fine?! I've been calling and texting him all night and no response until some imposter named Steve answered and said Nash was dead! Dead! I asked for confirmation and he said he'd send me his ear! What the hell would I do with an ear besides put it in a vase?"

Put it in a vase?

"Steve told you I'm *dead*?" Nash asks.

Right. That's probably the bigger issue.

"Oh my god! Nash? Is that you? You're alive?"

"Of course I'm alive. I just left my phone in Larinda's suite."

"Ah. Gotcha." Chad clears his throat. Is he disappointed? "I'll let them know."

"You'll let who know?"

"H.R. I told them you were deceased."

"You *what?!*"

"I'm kidding! Relax. Just a little spy humor. Glad you're not dead. Anyways, you didn't call in for the meeting last night. We were worried."

"What meeting?" Nash asks. "And who's 'we?'"

"The pre-mission meeting. And we is all of us."

"There was a pre-mission meeting?" Nash looks to me, and I shrug. "And who's 'all of us?'"

"There's *always* a pre-mission meeting," Chad says in his irritated spy handler voice. Guess his grieving period for Nash's loss is over. I still want to know more about the ear in a vase, though. "And the definition of 'we' is also a given. You, me, Paige, Mr. Reedweather, Marcos, Eva…"

"Were any of those people at the meeting last night?" Nash asks.

"They don't have to be. 'All for one and one for all,' right?"

Okay, even I'm lost at this point.

"Chad, I'm going to be perfectly honest with you," Nash says, picking up the phone. "Whatever espionage instruction manual you're following in your head is not in anyone else's head. Most of the time we have no clue what the hell you're talking about."

"Well!" our boss huffs. "I guess that means you don't want to hear the latest intel on the mission."

"Of course we do," I rush out before Nash can share whatever incendiary response he's got queued up that will make this ten times worse and last ten times longer. He gives me a hard look as I pluck the phone from his hand. "Whatcha got?"

"That you, Dragonfly 2?"

"Copy that." I can't look at Val or Nash as I say this.

"Okay, good. At least one of you will make it out alive," he mutters.

Nash just shakes his head, looking very much like he's fine with that.

"Well, we just learned that Brighthouse is intending to stream the entire event from their main lecture room."

"We knew that," Nash says.

Silence.

"Well, did you know Larinda will be performing a song?"

"Yes," Nash says, coming up beside me.

"And that the song was supposed to be 'Moonlight Musing' but is now 'Billboards and Billiards.'"

"Also yes."

"Oh."

After several seconds, we're both squinting at the phone. Are we done? Did he hang up?

"Okay. Well, Denver Sandeke wants you to ruin her."

Whoa.

Nash's bored expression hardens.

"I'm sorry?" he says.

"Mr. Sandeke doesn't just want to sabotage this event anymore, he wants to ruin the partnership between Larinda and Brighthouse permanently. The only way to do that is to take out Larinda." He pauses. "Figuratively, of course. Unless… I mean… You're not trained in martial arts, are you? Like that thing where you touch someone's neck and they die?"

Is that a thing?

"We're not," I say with appropriate regret.

"Okay. That's what I thought. No prob. Nash? You still there?"

Concerned by my friend's silence, I study his face for a sign. What I get is a dark cloud that makes me pretty sure he's not thrilled about a single thing that's happened in the last three minutes.

"Sure. Sounds good," he says, finally.

"Really?" Chad asks.

I can one hundred percent confirm the rest of the room echoes his shock.

"Yep."

"Oh. Um, well, great. Keep us posted, Dragonfly."

"You got it," Nash says in a chipper tone.

"Wonderful. Roger Rabbit, out," Chad says, and the line goes dead.

A tense silence settles over the room when we hang up. Val and I are both in varying stages of disbelief as we study our friend who's returned to the door.

"You coming or what?" he asks. "At the very least, can I borrow twenty bucks to grab some toiletries and stuff from the shop in the lobby?"

I open my mouth to respond but…

"What's wrong?" he asks.

"You," I say. "You're really okay hurting Larinda on behalf of Sandeke Telecom?"

"Hell no," Nash snorts out. "What a bunch of pricks. Now, can we go? I need to brush my teeth and take a shower."

* * *

Well, it's official. Nash looks good in anything, including my brother's clothing.

We didn't have time to sort out the hotel room issue, since another call to Chad revealed that Reedweather's assistant David made the reservations, and Reedweather's assistant David revealed that Reedweather has to approve any activity on the company card, including transactions David made. We pointed out that the transactions were already approved when they were made, but David gave us a long, winding explanation about the difference between verification, confirmation, and authentication, only to inform us that all three fall under the jurisdiction of Reed Reedweather anyway.

No one was brave enough to call Reedweather on a Saturday.

All this means that, for now, Nash bought what he needed, took a torturous (probably naked) shower in our bathroom, and borrowed a few things from my brother. Everything but the jeans fit okay, so he wore the same ones from yesterday.

I also learned it takes four hundred hours to stand freshly showered and shirtless while pouring through a suitcase in search of things to wear. It wasn't at all an issue for my annoying chorale of lady parts, either. In fact, it was so easy to watch, I decided to grab coffee until the guys finished their bro makeover. The fact that I don't drink coffee is irrelevant.

"Wow, they even have a green room," Nash says as our Brighthouse guide delivers us to a location many hallways and infinite doorways from the main entrance of the massive building.

"A green room? That's an entertainment industry thing, right?" I ask, peeking through the open door.

"It's where the talent can hang out and relax before the show begins."

I've never been in a green room, and I have to say, I'm slightly disappointed it's not green.

"It's not green," I say.

He smirks. "Most aren't."

"Name?" one of two large men asks.

"Nash Ellis and Paige Andrews," Nash says.

The guy scans something on his phone. "You have some ID?"

"So about that…" Nash says, drawing two suspicious gazes. "Larinda probably has my ID. If you could just ask her for it, that'd be great. It's actually a funny story."

The man stares at him with an unblinking expression that seems very skeptical about the level of humor in that particular story.

"Larinda has your ID?" the other guy asks dryly.

"Yes. If you could just ask her."

"Hey, Larinda, you know how you decided to take a break from being a superstar so you could carry around people's IDs?" the guard says in a droll tone.

Nash is definitely not feeling the humor either anymore.

"Wait, I have mine," I say, pulling out my wallet. We don't need any bloodshed before today's epic showdown even happens. Who knew having a valid driver's license would be the most important spy tool in the arsenal?

I hand over my ID and the man inspects it.

"She's inside," he says, waving me through.

"Okay, but he's with me," I say. "In fact, *he's* her friend. I'm just his plus one."

"Right," the guy mutters. "The friend who's so close she carries around his ID."

He shoots a sardonic look at Nash.

"I'm telling the truth. I was at her room last night," he says, adding emphatic hand gestures that accomplish nothing other than putting the overzealous body-guards on higher alert.

"You're saying she had you over?"

"Yes!"

"I don't remember you."

"I don't remember you either. You must not have been there. It was late."

"How late?"

"I don't know," Nash says in exasperation. "Eleven-thirty? Midnight?"

The men exchange a look that says *this guy? She's hitting up this guy for a booty call?*

I'm actually siding with the bodyguards over Nash on this one. The story is turning out to be not so funny.

"Nash!"

A woman who must be Larinda rushes toward us in a burst of human starlight, and I breathe a sigh of relief.

"He's fine, guys," she says to the guards. "Come in!"

Nash gives the men an irritated look as they reluctantly step aside so we can enter. His sour state lifts the second a fairytale-princess-beautiful woman throws herself into his arms. It's almost like… he's genuinely happy to see her. A twinge spirals through me, and I stiffen in alarm. Jealousy? No. Can't be.

I suppress the odd reaction as they do some strange kiss-half-hug thing. When they pull apart and she turns to me, I'm grateful she settles on a tight-lipped smile because that? Looked complicated.

"Oh! Before I forget," she says, clapping her hands.

At least we avoid an awkward greeting when Larinda skips away to retrieve an expensive looking tote. I feel the relief wafting from my friend as she pulls out a phone and wallet.

"You left these at my place," she informs him. In case he didn't know.

"Yeah. Thanks."

He accepts the offering, and his eyes dart to the screen like a desert wanderer who just encountered a slushy machine. I can only imagine how hard it would be to go that long without a phone. His brows scrunch in thought the longer he studies it, however.

I lean over to see unsurprising messages from Chad, along with…

"Most of those are from me," Larinda says. "You can ignore them. I was just letting you know I had your phone."

Huh. Okay.

Nash bites his lip and nods, clearly trying to keep a straight face. "Ah. Great. Thanks," he says once he can speak. "So, um, I'd like you to meet my girlfriend, Paige. Paige, this is Larinda Scott."

"Girlfriend?" Larinda's gaze sifts over me with an air of confusion, probably because I don't look like a person who could be Nash's girlfriend. He asked me to choose the least "MBA princess" of my outfits, but apparently I only managed to get myself to "MBA dropout." I thought I'd aced it with a black pencil skirt, studded belt, and casual blouse. Now, I wish I'd done more research. Is it the silver cat necklace? Probably the cat necklace.

"Hi, so great to meet you," I say, extending my hand.

In record time this woman's excitement at seeing Nash plumets to whatever level waiting for water to boil is. Pretty sure she just peeked over my shoulder, already looking for an out from this conversation.

"So glad you could make it today," she says, not sounding glad at all. Yep, her gaze is now openly in search of *anything* else.

"Thanks. It's, um, great to meet you."

Crap. Said that already.

Nash glances over with a cross between amusement and *WTF?*

I know, okay? I bark back silently.

But his subtle smile stirs all kinds of tiny, raucous bubbles in my belly. Unhelpful flashbacks of his beautiful body seducing everyone on a dancefloor and me on a bed pulse through my brain. The way it felt to run my hands over his warm, rigid chest. Breathing in the alluring scent of—

"Are you in the music industry as well?" Larinda asks, drawing me back to our present clinic on bland interactions.

She scans me with a glint that tells me she's pretty sure I'm not.

"No. I'm in marketing," I say.

"Ah."

"Well, kind of. I'm an intern." I wince at the additional unnecessary words. To be fair, none of the original words were necessary either.

"I see."

Should've gone with the secret spy from Idaho cover.

She stares off again, clearly annoyed by the lack of distractions to save her from this conversation. Her staff is probably bustling around with last-minute tasks, which leaves just the three of us: Nash and me who don't really have a reason to be here, and Larinda who has a staff to bustle around doing her last-minute tasks.

"We met at mini-golf," I blurt out.

Nash widens his eyes at me, and I wince. Right. That probably didn't help.

Larinda clears her throat. "Okay, so, I'm just gonna…"

She waves toward the other side of the room, and we watch her urgent retreat toward... a bottle of salad dressing. Yep, she lifts a container of Ranch from the snack table and studies the label with the concentration of a doctoral student researching their thesis. We've been replaced by nutrition facts. Awesome.

Until.

Sparks.

Tingles rush over my palm and up my arm when Nash takes my hand and threads our fingers. The pressure of his touch sends my pulse racing as my entire body flushes with heat. What is he doing? Doesn't matter. It feels so good. My breathing accelerates as I soak in the warmth of his skin. God, I want him. Every last inch.

I squeeze back, drawing a sharp warning in those sky blue eyes.

This is just a show. You know that, right? they say.

Maybe, but I don't care.

I cling harder and wrap my other hand around his bicep. When I lean in, I'm blasted with crisp forest air from his body wash, and now we're back in our room this morning, except this time I'm in the romance novel version.

He's naked in the shower. Eyes closed, soap cascading over mouthwatering planes and captivating ink. I surprise him with my sexy entrance, and he turns, hooded eyes beckoning. (I'm not exactly sure what that means, but it's probably hot.) *My fingers shove into his drenched hair, forcing him against the cool tile where our bodies slide together in hot, slick friction. His lips are wet when I claim them, warm and soft as mushrooming steam billows around us*—wait, not mushrooming. Um, bulging? Ew. Fine—*as regular steam billows around us.*

There are probably roses and candles somewhere too, but I don't have time to figure out those logistics.

In real life, it wouldn't take much to explode the landmine of lust currently embedded in my core. Just a few wild kisses while I yank off his jacket and rip the tight undershirt from his body. Then I'd spread my palms over the solid ridges of his torso. He'd feel so perfect, hard and hot. I'd tug his hair while he sucked on my neck, backing him into the wall...

And we're back to fantasy world again. Crap. That's what happens when you know what it's like to almost own this boy. You can't help but crave more and more. Is this going to be a regular thing? Ugh.

"You don't have to do that," he whispers, his minty breath at my ear.

"Do what?"

"Touch me. Pretend to be attracted to me. Larinda won't pay enough attention to notice or care."

He glances down at my hand constricting around his arm. The other clenches his fingers in a vice grip.

Pretending? Yeah right.

"It's fine. I have to seem clingy so it makes sense that I follow you everywhere today. We don't want to miss an opportunity."

It's a good lie. A rare true lie that even Nash accepts with a nod.

Nice cover up, Paige.

Thanks, Brain.

Welcome.

"Good point."

He casts a discreet glance at Larinda who has now switched to aligning the tray of assorted fruits into meticulous columns. Pretty sure the floor tiles need counting when she's finished.

"We have to get her attention," I say. "We have a golden opportunity for intel."

"Yeah," he agrees. "Who knows when we'll get her alone again? If Chad knew about the song, that means there's a traitor in her inner circle. We need to find out who and what else they know."

Another spy? I promise I'll care later, but for now, all that matters are the lips that are still close to my ear. The way his breathing accelerates as he lingers makes me wonder if he might be feeling this electric hum as well.

"We should try to learn more about her relationship with Jarvis," I say, barely getting the words out.

His beautiful eyes land on me, searching, pleading. My entire body is on fire.

"Yes. We need to trigger her. I have an idea," he whispers. His palm spreads over my cheek, and I stop breathing for a second. "Can I kiss you?"

More than a second.

O. M. G.

Flames rip straight to the apex of my thighs as I test his hooded gaze. (Yep, now I get it.) No question he's serious and has body parts that are wondering things too.

"Oh, um…"

My teeth sink into my lip as I try to form a response.

Please! Oh god, yes, yes, yes!

He winces and squeezes his eyes shut at my silence. "Shit. Never mind. Sorry. I shouldn't have—"

He tastes like I remember.

I grip his head and scour his lips with mine. Biting, sucking, consuming. I want everything. Right here. Right now. His unshaven scruff chafes my skin as I devour him, my thumbs locked on his jaw to hold him where I need him. It's not enough. Never enough.

He stiffens in surprise when my tongue slips out, then surrenders into matching desperation. I liquify when he invades my mouth, his tongue wrestling with mine as he threads his fingers into my hair. He backs us toward the wall and everything else dissolves.

This is Nash. And I'm kissing him. And I love kissing him. I never want to *stop* kissing him.

I pull him closer, gasping when he crowds me against the not-green wall, his hard body flush with mine. He feels like a raging fire, tastes like mint and poor decisions.

This isn't real.

It feels so real.

My hands drop to his belt, and I yank him into me. He's already hard when our hips collide and my rational brain gives up the fight.

"Nash…" I breathe out, grinding against him.

I. Need. More.

He releases a low sound in his throat, and I slide my palms around his back and over his firm ass. My thigh locks behind his at the same moment I wrench him into me again, writhing in frustration when it's still not close enough. I want everything. His skin. His heart. His soul. I want him inside me. It's like my body is trying to draw him in as it coils around him.

"Fuck, Paige," he groans, thrusting into me for several excruciating seconds before pulling back. He rests his forehead on mine, our labored breaths mingling in the small space between us. I already miss his heat and the feel of his hardness against my belly. My palm itches to run over the bulge and explore it. A gentle massage or two. Harder if he pushes for more. He'd feel so, so good.

"Wow," Larinda says, and we flinch.

Right. Forgot about her.

When we glance over, she is decidedly *not* bored.

"Please, continue. Don't let me stop you," she says, waving her hand.

She picks up one of her well-organized apples and takes a bite without looking away from us. Her brow lifts with an expression that could pass as "impressed" when she studies me. *So the stale marketing drone's got some "wild" in her after all.*

Nash grins, almost shy, as he straightens and slings his arm around my shoulders. His cheeks are still flushed, his muscles tense. Is he hurting as much as I am? I can't help a quick glance toward his zipper and I'm disappointed his jacket covers him well. And by disappointed, I also mean relieved because Fantasy Brain has just decided I'm the only one who gets to enjoy his arousal. The thought of another woman touching him the way I just did? *Hell. No.*

"Sorry," he says with a killer smile I've never seen before. What is that one? Make-everyone-melt-into-a-useless-puddle-at-your-feet? "You know how it is when things are new."

Larinda returns a coy shrug. "And sometimes when it's *not* new."

"Yeah?" Nash says, dragging me forward. I reach up and take his hand dangling over my shoulder like a good needy girlfriend. "I thought you and Jarvis broke up."

We stop in front of her, and somehow I keep my snort in check at Nash's convincing "gossip" persona. Guess he's better at this acting thing than I thought.

With a furtive glance, she leans in and says, "Can you keep a secret?"

Interesting question to ask a guy you've known for a week and a woman you've known for six minutes, but whatever.

"Of course," Nash says.

His arm tightens around my shoulders, and I take a quick peek at his face. By the clench of his jaw, something's bothering him. Is it the lie? The thought of betraying her trust? Hmm. Maybe the guy who doesn't care about anything kind of does.

"Jarvis and I..." She quiets and scans the empty room again. "Are actually still together."

"Nooo," Nash whispers. His eyes widen with exaggerated shock, and I have to force away another laugh. There's no way I get through this day without losing it.

Larinda grins and nods. "No one can know that, though!"

Except all the people who do, apparently. Nash sends me a subtle told-you-so look.

He did.

Encouraged by her big confession, she leans forward again. "Want to know something else?"

We're all nods and eager anticipation.

"Sandeke Telecom asked Jarvis to represent them like I'm representing Bright-house. Isn't that wild? At first, we thought he should take the offer, because, I mean, can you imagine the publicity?"

We can. Quite well.

She shrugs, and I look to Nash to interpret it since I don't speak *starlet manner-isms* but he's still glued to Larinda. I'll ask later. "But then we realized, it would hurt more than it would help so he turned them down."

Whoa. Hold up. He *turned down* the deal? Last we checked he signed on a few days ago. We even needlessly sacrificed a ribbon to celebrate. Why did he lie to his supposed girlfriend? Is he trying to protect her or is there some other more *deplorable* reason?

"Wow," Nash says through a damn good stunned face. "I hope you have your lawyers ready."

Her expression falls as mine twists to him in surprise. What's he doing? If I've learned anything it's that Nash in improv-mode is cause for concern.

"What do you mean?" she asks, her perfect brows scrunched.

"Sandeke Telecom and Brighthouse are direct competitors," he says. "They hate each other. They probably brought Jarvis in because they thought he hated you too. The fact that you two are actually together, well, that changes things."

"Yeah, but no one knows that."

Not true.

Nash shrugs. "All I'm saying is that both companies are known to play dirty. Expect things to get personal."

"And when things get personal, they get dead," I add in my best tough spy voice.

Nash shoots me another *WTF* look as Larinda shrinks in horror.

"You think they'll try to kill me?" she wheezes out.

Oh. Shit.

"No, no. Sorry. I just meant your career. It could kill your *career*. Not your… person."

Nash shakes his head and silently begs me to stop talking. Maybe I'll let him handle this one.

"What she means is," he draws out before sliding his attention back to Larinda. "Stay alert for ulterior motives. Once Brighthouse finds out about Jarvis, the war will be on. It won't be about a partnership between you and Brighthouse anymore. It'll be about using you against Sandeke Telecom."

The furrow in her brow does not like the idea of being used. Maybe I kind of get Nash's hesitation about this whole thing. Isn't that basically what we're doing, using her and this situation for our own agenda? Even if that agenda is ultimately for a good cause, I can't imagine he likes being on par with a lying, cheating megacorporation.

"Hmm… that's not good," she says, angling her head in thought.

"No," Nash agrees.

"W. W. A. D., right?" she asks.

"W. W. A. D.?"

"Yes. In every sticky situation, I ask myself, W. W. A. D. What Would Abram Do? He's so smart, so *competent*. Did you know he's a Gryffindor with Slytherin tendencies?"

I cough through another laugh as Nash manages a grave nod. It's not clear if he knew that, but I find it unlikely the two jaded rockers traded Harry Potter gossip at any point in their relationship.

"Yo, that crowd was epic!"

"Hell, yeah! Let's get wasted!"

"For sure! But hey, before that, I've been meaning to ask you: Hufflepuff or Ravenclaw?"

Nash's amusement fades as he evaluates Larinda's concerned expression.

"Well, I've known Abram for a while," he says. "And I can tell you what he'd do. He'd watch his back."

His tone is firm but compassionate, his expression sincere.

"Watch his back?" she asks. "And, uh, *how* exactly would he, um, watch it?"

"He'd be on the phone with his lawyer, looking for a way out," Nash says in a low voice, squeezing her arm with a warning look.

Hang on. Is he going rogue? Risking everything for a private mission that includes saving Larinda?

"Wait. Are you saying I should try to get out of my contract with Brighthouse?" she asks in shock.

Yes. He is. Which means…

I was wrong about Nash Ellis.

So wrong.

He *does* care.

He *is* incredibly bright and cunning.

He's also steadfastly loyal, and this game suddenly got a helluva lot more interesting.

Nash has no intention of betraying Larinda Scott—he's going to fuel this corporate war by protecting her.

17—BELIEVING

NASH

I shouldn't have kissed Paige. I knew it before I suggested it, as I suggested it, and definitely, *definitely* after I suggested it. Because once my lips were on her soft pink mouth and my fingers grazed her smooth skin, I forgot all about how I was supposed to be avoiding her. About how badly I was going to be hurt when all of this blew up in my face. Because it will. Violently. And I will have another scar etched into my soul.

But in that moment, she tasted like the kind of sin you don't want forgiven. The kind of sin that changes a person.

Even now, I can't stop watching her. The fluid movement of her limbs, the inviting softness of her curves, the way her lips part just enough for her tongue to wet them. She's intoxicating, and my body combusts every time I catch her gazing back with a hunger that should scare me. We will destroy each other, and apparently, instead of keeping us apart, that friction is driving us together.

Good thing we have a pointless promotional event to distract us.

Paige and I hang off-set as lights dazzle over the woman standing in front of a giant blank screen. On a large monitor nearby is the image everyone else sees on the ginormous backdrop behind her: a grid split into twenty-five avatars, a.k.a. *the contestants.*

The live broadcast has been underway for ten minutes already, and Larinda is doing an admirable job reading the teleprompter and looking like she actually wants to spend hours watching a bunch of strangers play a game she's probably never heard of.

Welcome, welcome, welcome.

Rules, rules, rules.

Prizes up for grab.

AND BRIGHTHOUSE'S UNMATCHED INTERNET SERVICE IS MAKING THIS ENTIRE EVENT POSSIBLE!

Also, Dave's Premiere Autobody.

"Premier with an *e*? Do you think Dave knows he misspelled his business name?" Paige whispers as the Dave's Premiere Autobody logo flashes across the screen.

"Maybe he's celebrating the fact that this is his first of many autobody shops," I say.

Her lips quirk up and something warms in my chest.

Not good.

I focus back on the monitor that's now a grid of barely identifiable cartoon icons again.

"Before we begin, are there any questions?" she asks the monitor.

Based on the lack of teleprompter guidance, the expected answer is "no."

But a blue square flashes, drawing everyone's attention to… is that a potato wearing sunglasses? I squint at the tan pockmarked blob and try to figure out why someone would choose "sun-drenched potato" as their representation.

"Yes… uh…" Larinda checks her cheat-sheet of the contestants' names. "Roy-Zero-One."

She points toward the blue flashing square.

"Hello, Ms. Scott," a deep, stilted voice rumbles. It doesn't sound like a real human voice, though. It sounds like… oh fuck.

My head turns at the same time Paige must form the same conclusion, and our eyes lock in horror.

"Hello, Roy-Zero-One. What is your question?" Larinda asks. Her foot taps nervously as a producer rushes to the edge of the set, prepared for a rescue.

"Yes, um, hello. I am Roy," the Hip Potato says. "I am from Idaho."

Larinda tilts her head, looking about as confused as you'd expect when a potato interrupts a live broadcast to say it's from Idaho.

I press my fists into my eyes, praying this isn't actually happening. What part of *"I've got this"* did Chad not understand? And how the hell did he get a spot in this competition?

"That's… nice," Larinda says with a polite smile. "Did you have a question, Roy?"

Another box flashes blue, and I don't know if I should be rejoicing or panicking.

"At least he's not a *Mer*-Potato," Paige mumbles.

I can't stop the snort despite everything wrong with this situation.

She's right. Small miracles.

"I do not," Undercover Chad says. "But I am a big fan. My entire family. Who are also from Idaho."

Oh my god.

Paige's eyes are giant orbs of delight as she fights off a laugh. Glad *she's* enjoying this.

"Oh, um, okay. Thank you," Larinda says, flustered.

Her cheeks are bright red as she looks around frantically. Her gaze lands on the other flashing box, and I can tell she's terrified to field another "question."

"Yes…?" She references her notes, and her agitation seems to increase. "Uh, *123456*, is that correct?"

"Yes, my dear. For the purposes of this exercise, that is my identification. As you can imagine, that is not my real name."

Wait.

Hold up.

Paige gasps at the same moment I groan. You have to be kidding me!

"Reedweather?" she hisses beside me.

I send her a tortured look before focusing back on the nightmare in front of us.

It's definitely Reed Reedweather talking, and I search the screen only to discover his avatar is… nothing. He doesn't have an avatar. It's still the default gray silhouette.

"Do you think he knows how to play Range of War?" Paige asks.

"Since he couldn't figure out how to set up his account, probably not," I say.

Paige smirks. "On the plus side, we don't have to worry about sabotaging the contest. Pretty sure they've got that covered."

"Yeah, but now we have to worry about them blowing *our* cover. If Larinda finds out I'm not legit, things will get ugly."

I try to keep my tone neutral, but by Paige's quick look, some of my inner turmoil must have slipped out. It was inevitable. I've never been good at playing games, and I've been ready to tap out on this one since it started. I love Marcos, but I hate lying, and the only thing I hate more than lying is using people.

I'm scum for what I'm doing to Larinda. I thought I'd be okay with it, that in the heat of the moment the end would justify the means. But every time Larinda blasts me with that precious ray of sunshine sparkle, I feel like the biggest asshole on the planet. I have no idea why she likes me, but it's going to make it impossible to betray her. That's why an hour ago I unilaterally reassigned myself to a new mission. The others can worry about taking down corporate tyranny; I'll be trying to take down corporate tyranny while also shielding Larinda from this mess.

And Paige.

And myself.

And Marcos because I'm still not convinced the corporate beast is finished with my principled friend.

Reedweather is now deeply invested in a story about *Reasonable Avarice*. As far as I can tell, the only link to our present situation is the shoes he's wearing. The fact that he's a gray bubble to everyone but himself seems to have no bearing on the monologue.

"Well, isn't that lovely!" Larinda interrupts as the producer waves vigorously from the side. She faces the camera with a stiff smile plastered on her face. "Keep watching for a quick preview of Brighthouse's exciting new all-home internet and cable package. And later, a special surprise from yours truly!"

My phone buzzes, and I glance down to see a text from Marcos.

What is happening right now?! Why is Chad a northwestern potato???

Me: Why is Reedweather trying to use a computer? Mysteries of the universe, my friend.

Marcos: This wasn't the plan!

Me: Nope.

Marcos: Do you see Grant?

Oh. Right. Supposedly, Grant Worthington is a bigwig at Sandeke Telecom who is *actually* a bigwig at Brighthouse. In other words, the dude is the lying, cheating leak he's pretending to plug. When this is over, I so want to be the one to tell him to "go plug himself."

Heh.

I peer around, searching for anyone who looks eerily like a Reed Reedweather clone, according to Marcos and Eva's description and the photo we found on a social media site.

"Do you see anyone who could be Grant?" I whisper to Paige.

A few seconds later she tugs my sleeve and nods toward an older man wearing an expensive suit and stern expression. I pull up the image on my phone and there's no doubt we've got our guy. A rush of excitement rips through me, and okay, maybe I was wrong about the spy thing. This part is kind of badass.

The man is in deep conversation with the producer and another woman in a suit, clearly not happy about something. Did he recognize Reedweather? He must have. It's kind of impossible not to.

The producer barks into her headset, and sure enough, square number nine suddenly goes dark. I wonder how long it will take for Reedweather to realize he's been cut from the broadcast. Four hours is my guess.

Chad's idiocy must have worked, though, because after the impromptu commercial break, the strange sunny potato is still glowing on the screen.

"Reedweather is gone," Paige says.

I nod and flicker my gaze to the angry, suit-clad man who looks no less angry now that the Reed Reedweather threat has been neutralized. "Grant must have recognized him and pulled the plug."

"Speaking of plugs," Paige says. "I have an idea of how to ruin this thing."

Her sly smile sends another frenzied rush through me, and this one fires straight to my boxer-briefs. Damn that spy adrenaline, which is what this is. It's definitely *not* the mesmerizing glisten in her hazel eyes or the seductive tilt of her shiny mouth.

You just really like plugs, Nash.

Except I don't recall having an opinion on plugs before this moment.

I'm so fucked.

"Yeah?" I ask, then clear my throat at the hoarse tone. Her eyes darken with lust when she hears what I just did. *"I'm so into you right now."*

She licks her lips, and I can't tear my gaze away.

"Yeah," she says softly. Her teeth sink into that luscious pink lip as her heated gaze lifts to mine. "How do you feel about another kiss?"

* * *

Live broadcast underway. Check.

Thick rope of power cords at our feet. Check.

No one paying attention to the nondescript couple hovering in the shadows beside the cables fueling the computers and routers. Check.

Chad is currently dead last in the competition and has done nothing to further our cause. From what we can tell his plan to infiltrate enemy territory stopped at the creation of his Idaho potato persona.

To be fair, I'm not sure about Paige's plan either as she grips the sides of my open jacket and drags me into her.

"You ready?" she breathes, gaze fixed on my lips.

My body hardens, heat flooding through me as I lean in. "Explain to me again why this plan requires kissing?" I murmur just millimeters from her mouth.

"You backing out, Ellis?"

"Never."

I brush my lips over hers, igniting when she reacts with a greedy tug on my jacket to lock me against her. We arch into the friction, and I slide my fingers into her hair to mirror her grip on me. Her mouth, her tongue, her tempting body are all mine again, surrendering in a way that feels nothing like acting and everything like sex as we stumble back toward the wall. Her faint moan is definitely not fake when I rock against her.

"Yes. Good," she pants. "Keep that up."

Behind us is the distant hum of Larinda's force-fed commentary, but all I hear is the rapid pound of my blood. All I feel is the soft heat of Paige's body. Taste, smell… it's all—*only*—Paige Andrews.

"What are we doing?" I groan against her. She has to know this is a bad idea. That once we start, we have a very hard time stopping.

Her hands move beneath my jacket and slip around to my back. Her fingertips dig into my skin below the waistband of my jeans, triggering all kinds of violent, throbbing capillaries that are making it impossible to think straight. Not sure how any of this is spy-related but it feels amazing.

"Crap, it's not moving," she whispers, drawing back slightly.

"What's not moving?" Because so much of me is *definitely* moving.

"The cords."

"The cords?"

I follow her stare down to the cables beneath our feet, and bite back a smile. "Hold on. Your plan was to unplug stuff?"

Her eyes narrow at my tone. "Yes. A blackout would ruin the event."

I force away the rising humor. She's already mad at me again. "Okay. So, um, why did we have to make out to pull a plug?"

"So people would think it was an accident," she says with a *duh* look. A blush spreads over her cheeks when I tilt my head to study her.

"Uh-huh," I say.

"Why else would I suggest it?" she snaps.

"Because you wanted to kiss me again and didn't want to admit it."

"What?! No."

She releases an indignant puff of air, but I maintain my cocky stance. She sure is clinging tightly for someone who's only using me as a prop.

"Gah! Why won't it come out?" she grunts, still kicking at the thick bundle of cables.

I watch her foot duel with the floor for a few seconds in amusement.

"Because they secure them so no one will kick them loose."

"Wait. Really?" she asks, stiffening.

I lift a brow, and she deflates.

"Well, that's annoying."

"Only if you're trying to kick them loose."

She gives me a look, and I shrug.

"So now what?" she says, leaning her head back against the wall.

I find it interesting that we're still tangled together in an unnecessary but very sexually charged knot of limbs. It kind of makes me not want to suggest what I'm about to since it involves not pretending to pretend to not want each other.

I sigh when she releases me. Probably for the best. All this acting today has been feeling a little too real.

My gaze crosses to the sour-faced Reedweather clone who is now conversing heatedly with the woman in the suit. Something's up, but I can't tell what it is. My attention diverts to Larinda who is so bravely trying to emcee this shitshow. She's wearing the infamous leather jumpsuit, and I can tell she's nervous about the upcoming performance. Of course she is. It's almost like these people have gone out of their way to make this environment as awkward as possible for her. The sequin curveball no one saw coming? The fact that she even *had* the outfit for the one song that's a duet? Steve's insistence on using a track in what's about to be a very weird performance…

Wait.

Oh no.

She's being set up! Chad said Paige and I are supposed to ruin her, but it looks like someone else is already on it!

My blood boils at the thought, and I scan the room for any sign of a traitor. Larinda's entourage, including horrible Steve, hovers by the snack table. Could it be him? I already suspected something was off with that guy, but why would he do this? Then there's Grant Worthington. If he really is spying on Sandeke Telecom on behalf of Brighthouse, he would also know what Sandeke knows. He'd know about Jarvis and possibly even the plan to sabotage his own event.

Does he know about Paige and me?

I don't think so. He hasn't given us a brush of attention. He probably thought Reedweather entering the contest was the plan, which should buy us time before he figures out it wasn't. Would he damage his own corporate partner Larinda Scott as a means to an end? I don't even need a full second to answer that.

I'm so ready to start punching things.

Larinda may not be a musical genius or a deep, layered artist, but she's honest, sincere, and kind. She doesn't deserve any of the shit that's about to go down between these corporations, let alone be the weapon and martyr at the center of the war.

What Would Abram Do? Get her the fuck out of the way.

My pulse hammers as an idea forms. Well, maybe more of a nightmare. *My* nightmare, anyway. I can't believe I'm even considering it after everything that happened yesterday. Every insecurity and fear comes racing back as I clench and unclench my fists in silent protest against myself. I must have lost my mind. It's the only explanation, but maybe that's just it. Maybe Paige is right. Maybe I've shuttered myself off so much that I have no mind left to lose. No real heart, soul, or passion. I've made myself invisible, an observer in my own life.

Maybe it's better to be hurt than to be nothing.

"What is it? You have a look," she says.

"I have a look?"

She nods. "Like you have a plan."

"Sort of. I have a plan for a plan. We need to do something first," I say.

"First?"

I nod. "Before we destroy this event, we need to do something. *I* need to do something."

"What is it?"

I suck in a deep breath and fight to silence years of doubts.

"Let's get a guitar."

* * *

Larinda is off set, tweaking her appearance and trying to calm her nerves when I find her.

"There you are!" she says, looking relieved. "You've been hiding all day. I haven't seen you."

"Yeah, sorry. I had some stuff to take care of. Look—"

"Well, you're just in time. I'm on in five minutes. How do I look?"

"Perfect. Hey, so—"

"Is that my guitar?"

I swallow my fear as I nod and hold up the sparkly white acoustic. "Yeah. I've been thinking a lot about this. I don't think you should sing to a track."

As Paige and I ran back to the green room for Larinda's guitar, it hit me. They want her to use a track so they have full control over the performance. All they'd have to do is mess with it to ruin everything. If they really wanted to screw her over, they could leave the vocals in and humiliate her with a lip-sync fail.

Yeah, not on my watch.

"I have to! What else am I supposed to do?"

"Let's do the version we played last night."

Her mouth gets stuck on the words she was about to say. "Are you… are you serious? But you said—"

"I know what I said, and I've changed my mind. You need to do a live performance."

"But the tech team already has everything set-up for the track scenario!"

"Paige is working on that now. Just… please, trust me on this. You need to do the live version."

We also need to make sure everyone is talking about *me* and not her tomorrow when this shit blows up.

"It *was* a really cool version," she says, shifting her weight as she thinks.

"It was. You sounded amazing. Your fans will love it."

"Yeah but…" She searches my face. "It really seemed like this is the last thing you wanted to do. You practically ran away."

It *is* the last thing I want to do.

Well, *second* last, so here we are.

"Like I said, I've been thinking about it and changed my mind. Please?"

"But what if people make fun of you and say mean things about you?"

"I'll deal with it." *Like I have my entire life.*

After another pause, her expression brightens and she throws her arms around me. "Oh my gosh, thank you! The truth is, I've been thinking about it too and I really wanted to do it. I just thought *you* didn't. I'm so excited. It's gonna be so great!"

Warmth spreads through me as she squeezes, and I return the embrace with my free hand. The other is still clutching a guitar that needs to be tuned in the next minute and a half.

"Let's bring down the house," I say with a smile.

Before we really *take it down.*

* * *

The producer must not be in on "track-gate" since she was fine adapting to the last-minute changes. I secure the guitar and monitor packs as we prepare to go live, and force a quick return smile to Larinda who's beaming beside me.

With my IEMs shoved into my ears, I can't hear the buzz of shocked murmurs around me, but I feel it in the sudden audience that's gathered. It seems like every person who was dutifully working a second ago has suddenly been reassigned to watch me make a fool of myself on an international scale.

This is so not how I envisioned dipping a toe back into industry waters. Not that I ever intended to allow my toes anywhere near that shark-infested swamp, but if I had, it would've been a small show in an obscure town. Some dude named Rick would be playing drums and probably screwing up half the songs. His buddy Gil would be on bass messing up the other half.

This? Have I mentioned worst nightmares?

The prompt screen in front of us is counting down from twenty seconds and my heart is scrambling its way out of my chest. I force calming breaths to still my trembling hands. They're shaking so badly I have no clue how I'll be able to play a guitar. Forget what my voice will sound like when the lyrics come out—*if* they come out. The boom stand is the same model I have at home, which feels like the only familiar thing in my life right now.

Larinda shoots me a radiant grin when the countdown reaches one, and the click-track jumps to life in our ears to start the song.

Tick-tock-tock-tock.

Tick-tock-tock-tock.

Breathe, Nash. You can do this.

Can I?

My fingers are still shaking. My throat feels clamped shut.

What the hell are you doing?! Millions of people all over the world are literally staring at you, waiting for you to choke. You haven't been tortured enough for one lifetime? You had to beg them to wreck you again? You'll never recover from this. Tomorrow you will be the laughingstock of the world. Again.

My frantic gaze scans the room. So many faces. Most curious, some concerned, a few critical. And one confident.

Paige Andrews.

The woman who just weeks ago thought I was the biggest failure on the planet is now staring at me like I finally make sense to her. That this moment answers long-held questions, not raises them. She believes. I have no idea why, but she does, and I think back to what she said at Dino's studio.

"Whenever you're ready to try again, we will be here for the highest highs and the lowest lows."

Lowest lows. There's an eighty percent chance this moment is about to be one of those.

Yet, suddenly, my fingers feel a little stronger, my chest a little clearer. All the creativity that had drained from my head a moment ago comes flooding back in a rush of anticipation. I agreed to this for Larinda, but right here, right now, in the very last situation I ever thought I'd end up, I realize I'm *doing* it for me.

Because I'm "Nashville" Ellis and music is in my blood.

"Let the waves of darkness break, and take, the pain below, purged by the undertow…"

Screw you, haters. Time to dive in and bring this whole fucking house to its knees.

18—THWARTING

PAIGE

He's magic.

I don't realize I haven't moved until I feel a sharp pinch in my back halfway through the song. Even then, I ignore it, afraid of any action that could disrupt this moment.

Nash claimed he was nervous when he went out there to rescue Larinda, but I never would have known. There was only the slightest delay before he started strumming the intro, but once he began, this stale lecture room became a world-class concert hall.

Even Larinda has come alive in a way I never expected. Given the over-the-top dramatics that define her shows, this authentic, stripped-back performance shows off a beautiful voice she deserves more credit for. She and Nash keep locking gazes and grinning through the lyrics like they're having a blast, and honestly, so are we. Everyone seemed shocked when this song started. Now they seem sold.

And Nash. Geez. Talk about potential star power. The record label that passed on this guy must have been stupid. (Well, they signed Tyler, so I guess that tracks.) Either way, there's no doubt in my mind Nash will be getting some serious atten-tion after this, and not just the kind he's fearing. I'm holding his phone for him and the thing keeps buzzing non-stop in my pocket.

But all that matters right now is Nash's haunting voice, their stunning harmonies, and whatever witchcraft he has going on with that guitar because there's no way all that sound is coming from one instrument. The guy is straight-up phenomenal, and there's not a soul in this room that doesn't recognize it. I've heard him play a few times now, but never when the stakes were so high. Heck, never when there were any stakes at all.

Nash said he was doing this so the media would attack him, not Larinda when shit hits the fan later today. This whole thing was an unapologetic sacrifice to save her from what he suspected was an attempt to hurt her. He truly believed he was marching to his execution when he walked out, that no matter how it went, good or bad, they were going to dig up the old crap and shred him all over again.

After what I just saw, "they" are also idiots.

As the song comes to a close, I'm confident I'm not the only one disappointed about trading the magic of this moment for boring coverage of cartoon good guys killing cartoon bad guys. Whatever think tank came up with this concept for a promotional event should be fired. Good thing the clock is ticking on the disaster now that Nash has accomplished his goal of saving Larinda. We're probably doing Brighthouse a favor. The worse fate for them would be letting this thing run its course.

Nash is still grinning when he vacates the platform so they can transition to the next part of the program. Larinda blows him a kiss from her cloud of assistants touching up her appearance, and when he smiles back, so do I. Man, I love seeing him smile. That can't be a good sign for a person trying to convince herself she's not head over heels for this guy.

"That was amazing," I say, drawing him in for a hug.

"Yeah?" His tone is shy as his arms tighten around me.

"Yeah. How did it feel?"

"Terrifying." He releases a soft laugh. "Incredible. I missed this."

"It missed you."

He pulls back, and I reach up to touch his face. Beautiful blue eyes search mine, anxious, unsure, hopeful.

"I'm serious," I say, running my thumb along the stubble on his jaw. "Anyone who doesn't think you belong out there is an idiot and shouldn't be allowed to think stuff."

He shakes his head with another shy grin, and I can't help it anymore. I pull him down and brush my lips over his. No acting. No strategic maneuver. No club-induced lust. Just a boy I have to kiss in this moment.

He deepens it, and my fingers slide into his hair to hold on. He's always tasted like dessert. Right now he tastes like the bread that will keep me alive.

Very poetic, Paige. Perhaps a tad dramatic?

Fine. A tad. Point is, I'm *definitely* head over heels for this guy.

"Well-played."

Nash straightens, and I follow his attention to the annoying voice that interrupted our sweet moment. A more annoying-looking man stands behind us with the ugliest belt purse I've ever seen dangling from his hand. Are those glitter-encrusted flamingos on the front?

"Hey, Steve," Nash says, a stony expression settling over his features. I can tell by the way his body tenses as he separates from me that he's not a huge fan of this person. Probably not the belt purse either, but I won't commit to that. If anyone adored sparkling flamingos for some unknown reason, it would be Nash.

"And here I thought you were a scared little puppy who ran away with his tail between his legs," the guy says. "I mean, you ran so fast you left your stuff behind."

I determine his voice is annoying mainly because it says annoying things. I wonder if that's Chad's issue as well. It would be an interesting study.

"I didn't run," Nash says in a dark tone. "And thanks for taking my messages for me. I appreciate the administrative support."

"Yes, well, your friend *Chad* seems cool."

"You would think so."

I force away a smile.

"Did you have an actual question or did you just need help putting that on?" Nash asks, waving at the flamingo pouch.

"No question. Just wanted to tell you to back off. Larinda is off limits. I've spent two years working for her and I'm not going to watch some conniving traitor use her for god knows what. I thought you were just another famewhore opportunist, but now I know it's worse than that, isn't it? Now I know who you really are and why you're trying to weasel your way in."

Nash goes pale. "Excuse me?"

"Cut the bullshit, rockstar. I talked to your handler Chad last night. I know who you are."

"Handler? What's he talking about?" someone asks.

We turn to see Larinda standing behind us, and I sense the life drain from Nash's body. My heart breaks for him as his numb stare rests on the woman he just risked everything to help.

"Nash works for Sandeke Telecom," Steve says with an air of victory that makes me want to punch him—another Chad-trait this guy possesses. Maybe every industry has a "Chad."

"He's only pretending to be your friend, Larinda. None of this is real."

Oh no.

Nash looks like he's going to be sick as Larinda's expression wilts.

"That can't be true. You don't actually work for Sandeke Telecom, right?" Her lip is already quivering.

My friend blinks at her, his mouth opening to respond but nothing comes out.

"Nash?" She swats at her eyes.

"I…"

"It's true?!" she cries.

"Larinda, please. It's not—"

"You monster! How could you do this to me?!"

"I didn't—"

"I told you he was scum. I warned you there was something off about him."

Oh god. I can't watch this. It's not fair. It's not *right*.

"I trusted you!"

"Larinda, please—"

"I can't even look at you."

"I didn't—"

"Shut up. I think she's heard enough from you."

"I thought you were different. You're just as bad as everyone else!"

"He's worse. He's a liar and a fraud!"

I have to stop this. But how?

I don't have a plan, but I've let too many people I care about get hurt with my indecision and fear of the unknown. *Nash* is the one who stood up to my parents when they went after Val. *Nash* is the one who gave my brother opportunities and reasons to believe in himself. *Nash* is the one who was brave enough to go against *two* mega-corporations. And what have I done to help anyone but myself?

Time after time I've sat back when I should have fought, not because I was being responsible and waiting for the right moment, but because I was scared. I gave him hell for being afraid to put himself out there, but I'm the one who needed that scolding. I'm the one who's never taken a damn risk in my life because I'm too afraid to fail.

And now I'm standing here like a coward, watching a hero get pummeled. He's the reason Larinda will look like a genius instead of an idiot when the video of her song goes viral and he can't do anything except duck his head and accept the onslaught.

Step up, Paige. Take a stand for the first time in your sheltered life!

"They didn't give him a choice," I blurt out.

The verbal assault stops as three sets of eyes shoot to me.

I take a deep breath and force myself to continue. "They didn't give him a choice but it didn't matter anyway. He stopped helping them almost immediately after he started and has done everything he can to protect you from them. *I'm* the one here on their behalf. I'm the only spy."

It's kind of the truth, really. There's no doubt in my mind that Nash had no intention of hurting anyone except the monsters who started this whole mess.

"They wanted to ruin you, but he wouldn't let them," I continue when I spot the seeds of doubt poking through her anger. "He just threw himself to the wolves for you, Larinda. Do you have any idea how hard that was for him? He hasn't performed in years after what your industry did to him, and he was willing to face his worst fears for you. To save *you*."

Nash meets my gaze, and the mix of pain and gratitude in those pretty blue eyes almost hurts to confront. I'd look away if I could but he's the only thing I want to see.

"You weren't wrong about him. He's special," I say quietly, searching his eyes. I feel the shift in the others and swallow the ache in my heart. "Yes, there was more to the story than what you knew, but he never lied to you about who he is as a person. He *is* the person you love."

No one seems to know what to say when I finish my speech. Even Flamingo Steve is silent and staring at his shoes.

"How were they going to ruin me?" Larinda asks, focusing on Nash.

His gaze crosses to her, and maybe there's a shred of hope in his expression.

"I don't know for sure," he says. "But you have a leak in your inner circle. Someone told Sandeke about the sequins and changing the song. I think they were setting you up to use the track, probably so they could..." He quiets and clears his throat.

"So they could do a repeat of Lip-Gate," she finishes in a dark tone. "I never would have lived down another lip-syncing disaster."

"All they had to do was include your original vocal track and it would've been Kansas City all over again," he says. "It would have thrown you off so much you wouldn't have had a chance to fake it and cover it up."

She shakes her head, looking very distraught. "But who would do that? And why?"

"Who would have known about the sequins? Who pressured you to use a track?"

Their gazes snap to Flamingo Pouch who has gotten very pale.

"Larinda, please. I'm so sorry. I didn't know! I swear! I mean. I knew, but… it was Jarvis!"

Whoa.

Also, this dude's spy game is fucking *weak* if a nasty look is all it takes to break him.

"Jarvis? What are you talking about?" she asks.

"He must have been the one who told Sandeke about the song and tried to set you up. You told me to call him about scheduling dinner tonight—"

"Shh," Larinda hisses. "No one is supposed to know we're together."

Yeah, pretty sure the cat isn't just out of the bag on that, but now jumping on the bag and waking the entire neighborhood.

"It's true," Steve continues. "I told him about the dress thing and he said not to worry about it. It was his idea to use a track. He even said he'd take care of the logistics. He's your boyfriend! Of course I trusted him."

Wow. I actually kind of hope this dude is lying about Jarvis because that? Is cold.

Tears gather in Larinda's eyes. "No. No, I don't believe you. He wouldn't do that. He loves me!"

"He loves himself and his career more," Steve says. "I'm not sure what his plan was, but there are a million things that could benefit him if you crashed and burned today. Larry, sweetie, I'm so sorry. I wouldn't have told him a damn thing if I'd known he was going to betray you. I didn't realize until just now what happened." He studies Nash, something akin to regret washing over his face. "Thanks, man. You, uh… thanks for protecting her."

Larinda bursts into tears.

"Larinda, hey—" the guy says.

"Don't touch me!" She yanks her arm away. "Don't even talk to me! You're fired! Everyone is fired! The entire world is fired! You! And you! And you!" she shrieks as she storms off the set.

"Hey! Where's she going?!" the producer cries. "We're back in two minutes!"

Nash starts after Larinda, then pauses when he sees me.

"Go fix things with her," I say. "I'll take care of the rest."

"But we still have to take these cheaters down."

"Yep. I'm on it."

He squints at me. "Really? You live for this corporate crap."

"I live for making the world a better place. There's no room for people who are making it worse."

His smile is all the encouragement I need. "Finally. Something we can agree on."

"Exactly," I say with a grin. "And right now, I *live* for breaking shit."

* * *

My idea comes quick and fast. I don't know why we didn't think of this before, maybe because we were thinking too small. We were sent in to ruin the gaming event (and Larinda, apparently), but what we really should have been scheming was how to ruin Brighthouse and Sandeke Telecom, like Marcos and Eva wanted to do all along.

While Nash tracks down Larinda to talk her off the ledge, I pull out my phone and dial Eva. She answers on the second ring, and I'm even more relieved when she tells me Marcos is there.

"We're watching the broadcast," Marcos says. "Nash *killed* it on that song! How the hell did you get him to perform?"

"Long story. Things have gone a little haywire. I'll explain later. For now, I have an idea of how to hurt both corporations but I'll need your help."

"Of course," Eva says. "Is Nash okay, though? Is he with you?"

"He's fine but he's off on his own mission. I've got this. I need you to track down one of those ransomware viruses and email it to my Sandeke Telecom address."

Silence.

Yeah. Not surprised.

"A ransomware virus?" Marcos says finally.

"Yes. I don't have time to explain. Just, please trust me. Nash said your other roommate Nate is some kind of computer genius, right? Maybe he can even find one that's defunct and will infect a network but not benefit some criminal organization. Make sure you send it from an account that can't be traced back to you."

"But if we send it to your Sandeke Telecom account, they'll know it's you," Eva says.

"Exactly," I say.

"Paige…" she draws out. "What are you doing?"

"Did you want to give these bastards a papercut or sever their freaking arm?" I ask.

"Cutting off their head would be better," Marcos says.

I chuckle and look around to make sure no one is paying attention to me. Larinda's meltdown seems to have been the perfect distraction. Everyone is in crisis mode trying to figure out how to run this event without its star, which means no one is paying attention to the non-descript office clone blending into the background. See? I knew the boring pencil skirt was the way to go today.

"Perfect," I say. "So, send me that file and let's get chopping."

* * *

While Marcos and Eva work on my assignment, I work on the rest of the plan. I'm no hacker, but I know enough from recent high-profile attacks that all it takes to bring a company to its knees is one half-asleep employee checking their morning email. *Oh, this file looks interesting. Wonder what it is? Let's open it and find out.*

That means all I have to do is connect my laptop to the main network, access my Sandeke email account, and open the file. Nefarious hacker programming will do the rest, and yeah, maybe part of me feels guilty. I don't want to do anything that could benefit criminals, and I also don't want to hurt regular people who don't deserve to get caught in the crosshairs. As much as I'd love to do some beheading, I really *am* just aiming for an arm here. I'm banking on the fact that a data company of this size must have safeguards in place to prevent complete collapse from something like this. Hopefully, it'll be enough to cause a stir and put a big dent in their public image, but not cripple the entire world and usher in the apocalypse. Because Steampunk Apocalyptic Chad? The world would never recover from that.

I sneak out of the lecture hall to work my way back to the green room where I left my belongings. The bodyguards aren't at the door, which means Nash and Larinda aren't inside. No surprise there. Nash is too smart for that. I'm sure he's taken her someplace where the vultures can't find her while they work things out. Fine by me, because I need to focus on my own task.

My phone buzzes, and I pull it out to see a message from Marcos.

Nate says he can get you a virus that will look like ransomware but won't actually execute and hurt anyone. Sound good?

I breathe a sigh of relief.

Sounds perfect, I type back. **How long?**

Marcos: He says to give him an hour or two. He's going to alter a popular one people will recognize to cause a bigger panic.

Brilliant.

I can use the time to track down the main Wi-Fi password, since all I currently have is the guest network.

Commotion in the doorway draws my attention, and I look up to find Captain Flamingo with a few of Larinda's other followers in tow. What exactly do they do, anyway? From what I can tell their only role is to giggle loudly and complain about ice to coffee ratios in iced coffee.

"She's not here?" Steve says to me, pouting.

"No. I'm Paige, by the way. Nash's girlfriend."

Wow. There was no spy reason for that announcement. Why did I say that? Do I want to be his girlfriend?

"Obviously," the man says.

"He really is a good person," I say on instinct again.

"Whatever. Not worried about that."

He tugs off his flamingos and drops to the couch with a dramatic sigh.

"Is it really Jarvis who betrayed Larinda?" I ask him.

His brows pinch as he meets my gaze. "I swear to you, it wasn't me. I love Larinda. I would never do anything to hurt her."

I study his glitzy face, and although I haven't loved most of the expressions he's worn since we met, he appears sincere now. With his ties to Jarvis and knowledge of that whole disastrous relationship, he could also be a good ally.

"Larinda said Sandeke Telecom offered Jarvis a similar sponsorship role and he turned it down," I say. "But he didn't turn them down. I was there for the pitch. And the celebration." If you can call it that.

He shudders, eyes wide. "That bastard."

"Yeah."

He cocks his head. "Do you really work for Sandeke?"

"Sort of."

"Sort of?"

"Only for another day. I'm quitting tomorrow."

"Because they're evil?"

"Because of a lot of reasons."

"Is Nash quitting too?"

"I don't think Nash ever really worked for them. Once their intent became clear, he probably did more to thwart them than help them. He's kind of incapable of being corrupted."

Hmm. It just slipped out, but it's true, isn't it? For all my critiques of Nash since the beginning, the one thing he never showed was disloyalty—to anyone, including himself. The guy is principled beyond belief.

Steve looks thoughtful as he traces the glitter on his fanny pack. "If that's true, he'd be a unicorn in this industry," he mumbles. "Everyone can be bought."

"Not Nash. But he's a unicorn in general."

And I mean it, too. He's so special in his own way. How did he go from *apathetic moron* to unicorn in two weeks?

Steve scratches at the floor with his shoe before focusing on me again. "If I tell you something, do you promise not to freak out?"

"No. And why would you tell me? You don't know me."

He glances at the others who are giggling in the far corner of the room, sipping iced coffees that seem heavy on the ice. That should keep them busy for a while.

"That's exactly why," he says. "You don't know me so I couldn't care less if you hate me for what I'm about to say."

Thanks, I guess?

He leans forward. "I messed up."

"Yeah, no offense, but that doesn't exactly come as a major headline," I say, returning to my laptop screen. Sorry, but I don't have time to be some stranger's therapist.

"Not for telling Jarvis about the song. For giving him her new ones."

My fingers stall on the keys. "What?"

He looks terrible when I focus on him again, and I allow some pity to seep in.

"I thought he was going to help her," he says in a bitter voice. "Jarvis said he was going to surprise her and work on the songs for her, so I sent him the link to her current projects. In light of the rest, now I'm afraid he's got something else planned."

No shit, Sherlock.

"What do you think he'll do?"

"Release them? Steal them? I'm such an idiot!"

Can't argue that.

"But he can't steal them and pass them off as his, right?" I say. "Everyone would know they were hers."

Steve shakes his head. "They're both country stars with similar styles. That's how they met. Normally, it would be pretty easy to prove intellectual property but they were dating this whole time. He probably has all kinds of early voice memos and notes that could make it look like they were at least collaborating. Besides, even if she *could* prove it, she'd have to go through the hell of a lawsuit and bad press. This whole time she thought they were playing a love game when he was actually playing her."

That jerk. Now I really wish my right hook was better conditioned.

"We have to tell her," I say, pulling out my phone to message Nash. "She has to know right away."

"She's gonna hate me," he groans.

"Probably."

He winces, and I shrug. So maybe my bedside manner isn't superb. Told you therapy wasn't my calling.

Me: We have a huge problem. Where are you?

What's up? Nash responds.

Me: Not through text. Larinda needs to hear this too.

Nash: We can't go near the lecture hall or green room. They're already looking for her and she's not ready to go back out there.

Me: I know. We'll come to you.

Nash: We? Who's "we"? Should I be jealous?

Me: Oh my gosh will you just tell me where you are?

Nash: *Smirk face*

Me: I hate you.

Nash: Yeah? Is that why your brilliant plans always involve dry humping me?

Me: Nash!!!

Nash: Fine. Main staircase, two floors down. Look for a room with a giant yam next to it.

Me: A yam?

Nash: Not an actual yam. A painting of a yam.

Me: That's kind of worse. Why would a company have a painting of a yam? Why would ANYONE have a painting of a yam?

Nash: Why wouldn't they? I only decorate with yams.

Me: Have I mentioned I hate you?

Nash: Yeah, but that usually ends with us naked so I'm cool with it.

I roll my eyes and push myself up from the couch. What a pain in the ass. And fine. *Maybe* I'm getting a little tingly and hot at the thought of an irritating musician naked, but whatever. That's just biology. Not my fault.

Grabbing my laptop bag, I motion for Steve to follow.

"Let's go. They're downstairs."

My phone buzzes again as we reach the main staircase, and my pulse starts its instinctive reaction to a message from Nash. It calms down once I see it's from Marcos.

Nate's ahead of schedule. Just needs another half hour or so. Also, Eva managed to get Grant's login credentials from Reedweather. We're going to send you the file from Grant's account.

Me: Awesome. How did she manage that?

Marcos: Have you met her father?

Good point.

Marcos: We also talked him and his wife into an impromptu rummy game to keep them out of the way. We tried to get Chad too but he's insisting on finishing the tournament.

Me: But he's in last place.

Marcos: Actually, he's out. He got killed off twenty minutes ago.

Me: So why is he insisting on finishing a game he's not in?

Marcos: Have you met Chad?

Good point.

"I don't know if I can go through with this," Steve mumbles behind me.

"You have to. Now help me look for a yam."

"A yam? Like, the potato?"

"I guess?"

I scan the lobby to the right of the stairs two floors down, and sure enough there's a framed portrait of a large brownish-orange blob. As much as I try to see it as anything other than a yam, I can't. It definitely looks like a glorified sweet potato. Maybe Chad was onto something with his secret identity after all.

Either way, it's the bodyguards beside the door who confirm our location, and we offer a nod on our way through. Inside, I find my friend and a tear-streaked country star huddled together. Her makeup is a mess, but she doesn't look broken anymore. Nash has his arm around her in a brotherly embrace, and I kind of feel badly about the prospect of shattering her world again. Still, she needs to know.

"Tell them," I say to Steve, skipping the unnecessary greetings.

Nash looks concerned by my tone and maybe for Steve when I blast the man with a cold look.

"Tell. Them," I repeat.

Steve draws in a heavy breath and drops to the chair across from them.

"I messed up," he says.

Confident that situation is in good hands with Nash, I move to a table and pull out my laptop so I can focus on corporate destruction. The plan is to open "the email from Grant" and infect the Brighthouse network with the fake virus. The disturbing message will pop up everywhere, including the worldwide broadcast happening a few floors above. Everyone watching will realize the data giant got hacked, which is not a great PR situation for a data giant.

When they investigate, they'll trace the infection back to Sandeke Telecom in general, and Grant Worthington, specifically. What happens next? Well, we can only hope retaliation is harsh and swift. Grant already suspects Sandeke Telecom is trying to disrupt Brighthouse's operations due to Reedweather getting caught as the worst contestant ever for anything. And when Brighthouse finds out their own secret agent is responsible for the virus, they'll be even more pissed. Guess when you're a double agent you have double capacity for angering people.

Grant Worthington is in for a terrible weekend.

The Brighthouse IT Department should figure out pretty quickly the virus is a hoax and clear the network of the issue, but by then the damage will be done. The world will know their data provider can't be trusted, and that data provider will be looking to seek revenge against the competitor who attacked them.

Commence corporate war.

All I need now is the virus and network password to connect my laptop. So... How to find the network password?

A man passes the open doorway, and I jump up to intercept him in the hall.

"Excuse me. I'm new," I say with a laugh.

He scans me with suspicion, then relaxes when his gaze rests on my leather portfolio. Not gonna lie, it's a fun superpower and has gotten me plenty of insta-respect over the years. Anyone with a portfolio must be legit. It's similar to fearing anyone holding a clipboard. Seriously. Next time you go to a grocery store pull out a clipboard, stare at a shelf, and see what happens.

"Paige," I say, holding out my hand.

"Ron," he says with a smile. "I'm in customer service."

"Great! Okay, so this is totally embarrassing but I accidentally cleared the wrong Wi-Fi network from my laptop and I can't remember the password to re-add it. I know. So stupid."

I had a flighty laugh. At least, I think it's flighty. I'm not good at those.

"No problem," he says. "Let me check."

Whew. Good thing this one likes flighty laughs.

He scrolls through his phone. "Ah. Here we go. 'S @ n d 3 k e S u x ! .' Got that?"

"Yep!" I say. "Thanks so much, Ron. Maybe I'll see you around."

I add a wink because that feels very spy-ish, but maybe not when he recoils and offers a stiff smile. People don't really wink, do they? Now that I think about it, I can't remember the last time someone winked at me and it didn't feel like I should call for help.

Winking. I add that to the list of romance novel clichés that don't actually happen.

I'm also totally buying a bodice just so Nash can rip it open. What even is a bodice?

Focus, Paige.

Once I return to the yam palace, I enter the password and release a small squeal when it connects. The others glance over at my outburst, and I duck with an apologetic expression.

"Sorry. I just love Wi-Fi so much," I say, waving at my laptop.

Nash gives me a strange look before shaking his head and returning to whatever damage control he's orchestrating over there.

It sounds like things are going rather poorly for Larinda in the *your world has crashed and burned* department. I feel for her, and it makes me want to take down some bad guys even more. Jarvis is so getting added to the hitlist.

I open my phone and send Nash a message.

You need to get Larinda out of here. She shouldn't be around when this goes down. She's got enough on her plate.

Nash: Already on it. Steve is going to tell them she has a migraine and will take her back to the hotel.

Me: Once shit hits the fan no one will be worried about her absence anyway.

Nash: I love watching you kick ass.

I glance over at him, and his subtle smile for me is almost too much.

Give us the unicorn! my lady parts chant.

Argh. Not now! Geez.

A few minutes later, Larinda seems composed enough to make her escape, and she pulls me in for a hug as she passes.

"You're a lucky woman," she whispers. "Maybe one day I'll find someone like Nash."

I swallow a surge of pain when my gaze rests on luminous blue eyes behind her. He releases a soft smile, proving how *un*lucky I am. There's nothing lucky about falling hard for someone I can't have.

You could.

Come on, Brain. You know I can't. He and I would never work. We're too different.

It's not Brain talking this time. It's Heart. Maybe you need to stop listening to that uptight bore once in a while. She's got a huge stick up her butt.

Hey! She's sitting right here *and* correct most of the time.

Yes, but not about this.

She is! I have a plan, a future that couldn't possibly include someone like Nash. He's none of the things on my list.

Yeah? Well, your list sucks.

Don't be mean.

Then don't be an idiot. Look at him. You really want a future without that in it?

God, my chest already hurts at the thought of losing him.

Larinda and Steve have made their exit, which leaves me alone with the object of my torment.

"You okay?" he asks, those soulful eyes filling with concern.

"I'm fine," I say quietly.

He shakes his head. "Don't bullshit me. You're not fine. What's wrong? Is it the spy thing?"

Tell him, Paige! Tell him how you feel.

I can't! What if he doesn't feel the same?

What if he does?

Then what if it doesn't work out?

Then welcome to being a damn human being. We're made up of our gifts and flaws. Our successes and our failures. It's how we grow and evolve and become the best version of ourselves. How do you know the best thing about you isn't still waiting to be uncovered? You'll never find it living in a box. You have to search the unknown to find something better. You can't tell me this person hasn't helped you discover another piece of yourself as a result of knowing him. Imagine if you lived your entire life like that.

Imagine…

"Nash, I—"

My phone buzzes, and I glance down on instinct.

Marcos: Incoming. You ready to do this?

"Yes, it's the spy thing," I mutter, holding up my screen.

Nash scans the message, but doesn't seem convinced. Oh well, we don't have time for teenage angst anyway.

"Right after I do this, we should take off as well," I say. "If we're part of Larinda's entourage it shouldn't raise any suspicions and then we're gone in case it *is* traced back to us somehow."

He nods, clearly forcing away whatever he really wants to say. Does he sense the war raging inside me? Can he tell it has nothing to do with corporate espionage and everything to do with what he's done to my heart?

But we don't have time, and honestly, I don't think I could take it right now anyway. I need to stay focused. I definitely need to get rid of him before I do something stupid.

"Hey, so I brought all my stuff with me, but yours is still up in the green room, right? Why don't you grab it and I'll meet you there."

"What exactly is the plan? You still never told me."

"I'll explain everything later, I promise. It's just a few quick keystrokes."

I'm already at my laptop opening a browser.

"Tell me now. I'll help you."

He leans over my shoulder, immediately distracting my brain from all the things it needs to be doing right now.

"No, really. It's fine. I literally just have to open a file. Go get your stuff and make sure Larinda got off okay. I'll meet you in a few minutes, then we can compare notes. We still need to figure out how to help Larinda with her songs."

"I'm already on it," he says with a smile.

"I'm not surprised," I say, returning it.

Our eyes lock for several seconds and my stomach flutters with all kinds of warnings. Yep, Nash Ellis is my own personal ransomware. What if there's no passcode to free my heart?

Tell him! You're crazy about him! Tell him tell him tell him.

Fine! I will. Just… not right now.

He pulls away and starts toward the door.

"You sure you're going to be okay?" he asks, turning back.

"I'm sure."

I force the brightest smile I can muster and take a second to capture how beautiful he looks right now. So talented. So honest and loyal. So perfectly flawed in all the right ways for someone like me.

It's decided. I will tell him. I will take a risk and step outside the box and brace for epic heartache or epic happiness. Either way, "epic" will be a nice change for my static life.

A few seconds later, I'm alone. A few seconds after that, the Brighthouse IT department has a huge problem.

* * *

I take my time getting back to the green room after I confirm the virus is working.

As soon as the ransomware warning popped up on my screen, I snapped a triumphant photo and sent it to Eva and Marcos. They confirmed the streaming broadcast just got hammered as well, and I took some time to bask in the ensuing chaos as I made my way through the halls and up the stairs. It seemed like every office and workspace I passed had urgent chatter and distracted employees milling about.

Not saying I have any interest in a full-time spy career, but my rookie assignment seems to be pretty darn successful, if I do say so myself. I even take a quick pitstop at the restrooms to gather my cool and prepare for the hardest part of my mission still to come: telling Nash how I feel about him.

I don't think I've ever attempted something like this. Probably because no one ever seemed worth the anxiety of pouring my heart out. I don't even know what to say, and as I stare at myself in the mirror, I realize it's because I'm approaching this all wrong. My feelings are *because* he's always accepted me as I am, because he likes that I'm awkward and honest and don't know my way around all this relationship crap. He doesn't like games any more than I do, so I don't need a speech; I just need to be myself.

He's Nash, and I'm Paige. That's all I have to remember.

I'm feeling a little more confident when I reach the green room, but disappointment seeps in when I look inside to find… no one.

"Nash?" I say, stepping further into the room. I scan every inch of the space, but he's definitely not here. Where is he? Did he leave without me? He wouldn't do that, right? Well, it's Nash so I guess anything's possible.

And then I spot his backpack.

My stomach drops as I approach it slowly. He wouldn't have left it behind. Did he go somewhere else? Maybe he wanted to watch the drama unfold from a front row seat in the lecture hall?

I'm not terribly excited about going back there but I can't leave without him either. I grab my phone from my bag and send him a text.

Me: Where are you? We need to go.

The next minute feels like forever, and when he still doesn't respond, I try calling the number.

"Hey. Leave a message if you want," his voicemail tells me.

Great.

Have you heard from Nash? I text to Marcos.

The bubbles appear right away, and I hold my breath.

No. I called him a few minutes ago, but he didn't answer. Everything okay?

I clench the phone as I stare at the response. Of course it's okay. Why wouldn't it be?

So why is my heart racing? Why is my stomach flooding with dread?

Bubbles burst to life again in the chat window. Then disappear. Then reappear. Then—my phone rings.

I answer immediately. "Marcos?"

"Reedweather just got a call," he says, and my body goes numb at his urgent tone.

Oh god.

"They have Nash."

19—AVENGING

NASH

They wanted to take me to a scary dark basement, but the door was locked and the head maintenance person said they couldn't get there for another hour. Then they wanted to take me to a scary dark closet but the first three we tried weren't big enough for all the chairs and torture and shit, so after wasting twenty minutes tossing, then reorganizing, cleaning supplies, here we are in a seldom-used conference room in a remote part of the building, seated quite comfortably in ergonomic leather chairs.

They did draw the blinds at least, so it's dark-*ish*? They also brought in a desk lamp and removed the covering to expose the bulb. I *think* that's supposed to be the obligatory "interrogation lamp" required for these types of situations, but it was designed for Fran in accounting to see her calculator better, not uncover treacherous spy networks, which means the flickering ten-watt bulb isn't instilling a ton of fear. It is mildly annoying, I guess.

"Again! Who do you work for?!" the man named Pete shouts in my face for the third time.

"Seriously, Pete. Will you stop? We already know he works for Sandeke," Grant says behind him.

"Right. Um…" Pete scrunches his nose, clearly out of questions.

I stare up at him, waiting patiently for whatever gem is coming next. The hilarious part is I don't actually know anything. Hell, I still don't even know why I'm here. Paige obviously succeeded at whatever she was orchestrating, but Brighthouse security picked me up on my way back to the green room. I don't even know what she did. Glad it worked, though.

To their credit, the Brighthouse security team is slightly more intimidating than the hotel security I encountered last night. Their uniforms even have official-looking crests that almost make you forget they can't actually do anything besides call the real police. My only goal is to keep them from doing that.

"You're in a shit-ton of trouble," Pete warns, trying a new tactic, apparently. He shoves a finger into my chest. "A *shit*-ton."

"Okay, but I'm Canadian," I lie. "What's the metric conversion on that?"

The man cocks his head, thinking.

"I got this," Grant interrupts, waving his grand inquisitor behind him. Gonna guess "prisoner interrogation" wasn't in this dude's job description before today.

"We know who you are, *Nash Ellis*," Grant says in his best evil villain voice. "We know you work for Sandeke Telecom. So just tell us everything we want to know and this doesn't have to get ugly."

Hmm. What movie was that from again? Pretty much all of them, I think.

I scan the room before settling my gaze back on Grant.

"And does Sandeke Telecom know you're a spy for Brighthouse? What do you think is going to happen when I go back to Denver Sandeke and tell him his COO is working for his competitor?"

Grant's face blazes a fun shade of red. "How do you know all of that?! How long have you been spying on us?"

Really? He didn't see that coming? I mean, it was kind of preschool hide-and-seek-level sleuthing.

"*Well,*" I draw out. "You're here... when you're supposed to be working *there*... so..."

Even Pete would've been able to put that together without much coaching. I watch the man fiddle with the lamp he brought. It appears his diagnostic strategy consists of turning it on and off repeatedly. Eh, maybe not.

Grant is still looking quite angry when I focus back on him. "Well, that's assuming you get out of here to tell them!" he says.

"Yeah!" Pete echoes, giving up on the lamp and returning to his boss' side.

I lean back in the chair. "I see. So you're, what, gonna kill me? This is a real thing?" I wave around our little pretend prison. "Shouldn't I be tied up or something?"

"We can arrange that!" Pete growls, stomping forward.

Grant throws out an arm to stop him and shoots a discreet warning. "We can't, actually," he mumbles.

"But he's a spy!"

"Yes but…" Grant tosses a look at the security guards stationed by the door. "Never mind. Just go figure out that damn lamp or turn it off. It's giving me a headache."

"You got it, boss!"

With the lamp situation under control, Grant turns to me. "I'm not messing around, Nash. I can make your life very difficult."

"Yeah? How exactly?"

I'm actually curious.

"Tons of ways. I could get you blacklisted so you'll never work in this town again. How does that sound?"

Like a line meant for *other* professions, but sure, "marketing intern" could probably be added to the list. I'm sure there's someone out there who'd find the prospect of never again making photocopies or stapling shit for minimum wage horrifying.

"Oh no. Not that!" I say in mock fear.

He glares back. "This isn't a joke. Do you have any idea who I am?"

"I thought we already established I do."

"That's not what I mean."

"Oh, then what? As in, your job title?"

"No! Like, in general. Who I am *in general*!"

"An Aquarius? Single? Vegan? I'm gonna need more clues here, Grant."

Steam wafts from his head as he balls his fists. "I take back what I said. Cuff him!" he hisses at the guards.

The three guards exchange a look, and the tallest clears his throat.

"We can't actually do that, sir. Item 4.3 of the protocol stipulates—"

"I don't care what it stipulates. Tie this bastard to the chair!"

"Um, well, we don't have that kind of equipment," another one explains.

He shrugs apologetically when Grant fires a look at him.

"What?!"

The man lifts his arms and twists from side-to-side to show off the big fat nothing around his waist except a belt. Like, a regular belt. They could prong me to death maybe. Or pool all their belts into something more useful?

"What *do* you have?!" Grant asks.

The guy looks nervous as he fishes through his pockets. "Uh… chapstick? A receipt?" He pulls them out. "A guitar pick. Don't ask how I got that."

"Oh, fun," I say. "You in a band?"

He nods eagerly. "Yeah! I play bass—"

"For fuck's sake!" Grant says, and the guard shrinks.

"*Sorry*," he mouths to me, making a zipping motion over his lips.

"*Later*," I mouth back before returning to Grant. "What exactly is your plan?" I ask him. "I know you can't actually hurt me, and I don't know anything even if you could. So is this it? You're just going to bore me to death?"

"How about getting you arrested for trespassing?" he says with a smug look.

"Hmm. Well, that's a possibility. You sure you want to bring the authorities into this, though? You and Brighthouse don't have a *single thing* you wouldn't want people with badges investigating?"

Also, technically I was invited as part of Larinda's entourage, so pretty sure I could beat a vicious *trespassing* rap, but I have no intention of bringing more people into this.

"Just tell us the damn plan!" Grant shrieks.

"You already *know* the plan," I say. "The plan has happened. We are now *post plan.*"

"I know there's more. There has to be more. I was there when Denver made the call to sabotage our event, I just didn't know how you were going to do it. I thought it was the Reedweather thing, but then the ransomware thing happened. What else is coming? Tell me now!"

Ransomware? That's what Paige put together? Hell yeah. What a badass. I can't wait to kiss her later.

"I told you already. I don't know anything else. Yes, Reedweather was a decoy," I lie. Although, gotta say, I didn't see that working out as well as it did. Another win for Zeros Being Heroes, I guess. We're like the Accidental Avengers. We're so bad at shit it goes full circle and kinda works.

"Yes, but now that the *ransomware* part happened, it's over," I say. "Isn't that bad enough?"

"You tell me."

"Yes."

"Yes?"

"Yes. Per your instructions, I'm telling you, that yes, it's bad enough. Ransomware is pretty fucking bad."

"I *know* it's bad!"

He's about to yell at me some more when his phone rings.

"What?" he shouts into the receiver. "I'm in the middle of something."

Yep, the worst interrogation of all time. They would've been better off locking me in the mailroom and forcing me to stuff envelopes until I cracked. I guarantee it would have taken six minutes. This, though? I check on Pete who's now writhing on the floor while waving the lamp over his head for some strange reason. The cord keeps getting caught on his nose at each pass but it doesn't seem to deter him. Yeah, *this* I could do all day.

"Oh. Yes, put him through," Grant says. "Pete! Get over here. I need you to take over the negotiations. They can't know I'm here."

His accomplice puts down his nemesis and pushes himself up from the floor. As he makes his way to the table, I can't help but wonder how many times in the course of history an evil mastermind has handed the reins to a subordinate who got outsmarted by a lightbulb. This should be interesting.

Grant gives me a triumphant look as he places the room phone in front of me and answers it on the first ring.

"Brighthouse here," Pete says, taking the chair to my right. "We've got your man."

"We need proof of life," a low, growly, fake-accented voice says.

Oh no. *Please* don't let that be who I think it is.

I'm scared for the first time since these goons grabbed me.

"Say something," Pete directs at me, and I clear my throat.

I really, *really* don't want to do this.

"Say something!" Pete demands.

Fine. Ugh.

"I'm here," I say.

"Dragonfly?" the voice replies. "Is that you? It's Alan."

Of course it is. *Roy* must be nursing his wounds from his Range of War loss.

"Yes, it's… um, Dragonfly," I say.

I can't look at the others. This is so freaking embarrassing.

"If it's really you, what's the code?"

"The code?" I ask, leaning forward.

"Yes! The code! What's the code?"

I squint at the phone, wracking my brain. The code… the code… oh, wait.

"You mean the pumpkin shit?"

"Yes!" Fake Alan says.

Right. So the door code is the same as the hostage code. I suppose it *is* easier to keep track if there's only one code for everything.

"Do I have to?" I groan.

"Only if you want to be rescued," he says.

Pretty sure this rescue is worse than the kidnapping. Can we please go back to that?

"The pumpkin flies at midnight," I mutter.

"What? I couldn't hear that."

"The pumpkin flies at midnight!" I force out.

Now they're really staring at me. I offer a shrug and wave a *don't worry about it.*

"Nash! It *is* you!"

"Yep. It's me."

"Are you okay? They didn't sever anything?"

"Sever anything?"

"Like a tongue or ear or whatever?"

What's with Chad and my missing body parts?

"No. Nothing's been *severed.* I guess my head hurts a little from the desk lamp."

"You animals!" Chad cries. "I swear, if you hurt him…"

He doesn't finish the cliched threat, but I suppose that's also consistent with every spy movie I've seen.

"It's fine," I say. "I'll grab a pain reliever later. Can we just get this negotiation underway? I'm kind of hungry and would love to get out of here in time for dinner."

"Right," Chad says. At least he's not using an indiscriminate accent anymore. So much for that disguise. "We know you have our guy. What do you want in return?"

"I think that's pretty obvious," Pete says, reading whatever Grant is typing on his phone.

"Exclusive rights to Kansas?" Chad guesses. "Fine. But not a single inch west of Wichita."

"What? No," Grant says, then covers his mouth. He widens his eyes at Pete who clears his throat.

"Sorry, I have a cold," Pete says, lowering his voice for some reason. "No," he repeats. "That's not what we want. We want… the…" He squints at his phone. "Pop-tart?"

Grant looks pissed and continues typing furiously.

Pete studies his screen. "Oh! Wait no. It says pop-up. Autocorrect fail, sorry. It said Pop-tart," he hisses at Grant, who waves him quiet.

"You want a Pop-tart or a pop-up?" Chad asks.

"Pop-*up*. I mean… hold on."

He leans toward Grant and whispers something. Grant whispers back, now looking very skeptical that this is about to go how he wants it to.

Pete clears his throat. "Send us the special disk to get rid of the scary pop-up thingys!"

Huh. Okay. Is that how ransomware works? I guess this is what happens when you don't include IT in your kidnapping plots.

"Hey, boss? I don't think it's really a, um, *disk* thing," one of the guards calls over.

Grant looks at him, then back to his laptop, then back to him.

"What is it then?" he snaps.

"I think you need a code. Something that will unlock the screen. They don't really do disks anymore."

Grant studies his screen again.

"Fine. Ask him for that then," he barks at Pete.

"It's seven," Chad blurts out.

What?!

"You're supposed to wait until *after* I'm freed to give them the code," I grunt.

"It's not seven," Pete says when Grant waves at his laptop screen in frustration.

No shit.

"I don't actually know the code," Chad says. "Paige did that part."

"Who's Paige?" Pete asks.

Oh my god. Chad is the absolute worst spy ever.

"No one," I say, my blood pressure rising. I'm probably also the first hostage more desperate to get my rescuer *off* the phone than on it. "Hey, Chad? Thanks for your help, dude. I've got it from here."

"Who's Paige?" Pete asks again.

"No, no. We've got your back," Chad assures me. "No way we're letting them cut off your ear or whatever. Did you tell them about Larinda?"

Oh fuck.

Grant lasers a look at me. *Larinda?* he mouths.

"Okay, fine!" I say. "I will tell you everything, just please hang up the damn phone." Before Chad gets us all killed for real. I don't even know how. Maybe they'll choke us on chapstick and guitar picks, but either way, I need to get him out of the conversation.

"Everything?" Grant whispers. "You'll tell us *everything?*"

"Yes!"

Grant and Pete study each other for a moment before Grant nods. Pete reaches over and presses the button, and the phone goes gloriously dead.

"Now talk," Grant says.

"Can I see the computer?" I ask, motioning toward his laptop.

Grant hesitates for a second before shoving it toward me. Good, because if I'm going to talk I'll have to find something to talk about. The second I see the screen, though, I breathe a sigh of relief. In fact, it's everything I can do not to burst out laughing. This can't be real.

"You better not be bluffing," Grant warns.

I'm not. I don't have to.

I stare at the "scary pop-up" and roll my eyes. Nate is such an idiot. A brilliant, hilarious idiot. I have no doubt he's involved, probably at the request of Marcos. In fact, it's kind of a given since, framed in a frightening red flashing box is the message:

"Give us six billion 'Renos' or this computer will be STRIPPED.*"*

* * *

The second I'm back on the sidewalk with my freedom and my belongings, I call for a ride, text Marcos to let him know I'm okay, and dial Paige.

She answers immediately, and all the anxiety from the last hour of captivity melts at the sound of her voice.

"Nash! I was so scared. Are you okay? Please tell me you're okay!"

"I'm fine. They just let me go. I'm grabbing a ride back to the hotel now. Where are you?"

"Oh, thank god."

Is she crying?

"I'm, um, at the hotel too," she says, sniffing. "I didn't want to leave you when I found out what happened, but Marcos said it would be more dangerous if I was there and they got me too. He and Eva told me to go back and wait for you. They said Sandeke would handle it, but when I found out Reedweather put Chad in charge, I was really scared."

Yep. Fair.

"Um, so that part wasn't great. But once I got him off the phone things went smoother. I'll tell you the whole story when I get back. We need to get my room key situation worked out as well."

"Already done. Reedweather called in with the company credit card information and they gave us a key to your room. Six, actually."

"Six?"

"Yeah, by the end of the conversation I don't think the desk clerk had a clue how many people were in the room. He just handed me a pile of keys and a brochure for a horseback riding excursion."

My brain is too exhausted to solve that one. "Great. Thanks for handling that. And the rest of the mission. Ransomware? Genius."

"It wasn't an actual virus. Well, not a lethal one."

"I know," I say with a chuckle. "Nate helped you, huh."

"How did you know?"

"Lucky guess. Anyway, I'll tell you the rest in person. It kind of worked out perfectly. As soon as I get back, I'll meet you at your room to get the key and—"

"No, go straight to your room. You're probably tired and hungry. I'll order some food and meet you there. Then you can eat and relax. I'm so sorry, Nash. I can't even imagine what you've been through. I felt so helpless when I found out they took you. I couldn't… I mean…"

She breaks into tears, and crap. All I want to do is hold her right now.

"Hey," I say softly. "I'm fine. It all worked out, I promise. Just sit tight and I'll be there before you know it."

"Okay," she whispers. "Nash?"

"Yeah?"

"I have to tell you something. I should have said it before, but… Nash, I can't do this back-and-forth thing with you anymore."

Wow. Seriously? I haven't been through enough today? I don't think my worn spirit can handle another blow at the moment.

The green Toyota Highlander I've been waiting for shows up, and I wave it down.

"Hey, my ride just got here. I'll be at the hotel in twenty minutes and we can talk in person."

"No! Wait, I—"

"You Nash?" the guy calls.

"Yep. You Lloyd?"

He nods, and I move toward the SUV. "I gotta run. I'll see you in a little bit, okay?"

I feel like shit when I hang up, but getting my heart shattered has to be easier in the comfort of a hotel room with air conditioning and a full stomach than alone on the street after escaping a hostage situation.

"You in L.A. for business or pleasure?" Lloyd asks as we pull into the street.

"Neither," I mumble.

20—HOPING

PAIGE

He blew me off. Legit hung up when I was about to pour my heart out. I'm trying not to be mad, though. I mean, the guy *did* just get kidnapped and held hostage and heaven knows what else. But still…

The next half hour is brutal. I go to the café on the second floor to grab some sandwiches and snacks, then make my way to Nash's room to wait.

And wait.

And wait.

By the time I hear a small knock, all the drama has faded, and I rush to the door.

"Thank god," I say, throwing my arms around Nash and dragging him into the room.

He hugs me back, and we let the door clatter closed behind us. I settle against his chest, relishing the sound of his beating heart. They say you never realize what you have until you lose it. In this case, I realized what I *didn't* have when I lost it.

"I want to date you," I blurt out.

He tenses in surprise, and I hold on tighter. "Sorry. I know. You have a million other things to worry about right now, but that's what I wanted to say on the phone. I want to be your girlfriend for real. I know it makes no sense, but I don't care. A lot of the best things in life make no sense."

I finally allow myself a breath and brace for his response. Sure I'm scared. There's a very real possibility he doesn't feel the same. That he's about to break my heart and say I'm being ridiculous. But that fear is nothing compared to what I felt a couple of hours ago when I thought something might have happened to him. When I thought this, right here, might never be possible.

I'd rather get rejected than never have the opportunity to have my heart broken.

With a deep exhale, I pull back to search his face, ready for anything. I'm brave and strong, and all those things I value about myself are the very things that will help me overcome even the biggest obstacles and worst fails. Our strengths aren't meant to prevent us from falling, but help us back up when we do. If Nash says no, I'll be sad, but I'll be okay. I will hurt, but I'll recover. I will eventually move on, having learned something and evolving in a way that will better prepare me for the next challenge. But if I didn't take the risk, I'd never know if—

"Weren't we already dating?"

I freeze and stare into his beautiful, exasperating face. "What?"

"You said going to seven or eight specific locations with someone and doing more than kissing is dating. I'm pretty sure by that definition we're more than official at this point."

"Yeah, but… I mean, you…" He shrugs, and a familiar wrath burns in my gut. "Are you serious right now?"

"What?" he asks, totally oblivious.

"That's it? That's your grand romantic gesture? I've been torturing myself for days over asking you out and you thought we were dating this whole time?"

"Not this *whole* time. I mean, not until this morning, I guess."

"Oh my—I can't believe this!"

I push away from him and throw up my hands.

"Wait. Why are you mad at me again?"

"I'm not mad at you!" I say, glaring at him.

"You seem pretty mad."

"I'm mad at… gah!"

"So you *don't* want to be a couple?" he asks, looking so annoyingly perfect with those stupid perfect eyes and that stupid perfect mouth and oh my gosh, I could scream.

"Yes! Of course, I want to be a couple."

"Okay, but—"

I cut him off with a kiss. And another. And another. Soon we're backing toward the bathroom where clothes start flying and faucets start running. Steam billows —no, *mushrooms*—around us as I shove him toward the glass door of the stall and tear at the button on his jeans.

"Are we doing this in the shower?" he asks as I force his pants down.

He reaches for the clasp on my bra, and I don't even care that we're not completely naked when I push him under the water.

"No. We're doing *that* on the bed. We're playing in the shower first because you've just been through hell, and I'm freezing from the ridiculous air conditioning in this place."

His grin is too much. I've waited too long and I just… have to taste it. Devour and consume it as I pull his mouth to mine. He tastes like the mint gum I both love and hate. He feels like a dream that's a hundred times better than any fantasy. Who needs roses and candles when you have wet boxer-briefs molded to a hard ridge you lose sleep over?

I run my palm along it now, finally enjoying the thick heat of him freely and fully. No one to interfere or stop me from reaching inside to grip his length in slow steady strokes that have him metaphorically on his knees and literally in the palm of my hand. He groans into our kiss when I rub my thumb over the hot tip, and I know, I just *know*, sex with him will be worth the wait.

I let go to reach around his waist and pull him into me. He cups my breasts, massaging with increasing pressure as my hips writhe against him, silently begging for more. He pinches my nipples before replacing his fingers with his tongue, and I arch into his mouth. The heat. The exquisite suction. The all-consuming fire of his closeness…

"Nash," I breathe out.

He doesn't respond with words, but I know he understands when he lifts my thigh to thrust direct, glorious friction against my entrance. I gasp at the rush, the sensation of his hard heat pushing and grinding into my screaming body.

More, more! it's pleading, but it's not just my body this time.

The rumble of his soft laugh vibrates against my throat.

"Patience," he says. "That's the second part, right?"

Crap. Yeah. Condoms and responsible sex and all that. Grr.

"Fine…" I mutter.

"Hey, I'm only following *your* instructions."

"Don't be an asshole."

"Would you even like me if I wasn't?"

I shut him up with another kiss, this one violent and filled with all the things I want to do to him. All that I want *from* him. He counters with a confident tongue that makes me burn when he tugs my head back and takes over the kiss. Rocking against me, he drives our rhythm until I'm completely lost in the cadence of his seduction. I love that he's equally secure with either role. Give or take. Push or pull. I love that he loves that I am too.

We're still locked together, our hips moving in sync at a torturous cadence. It's not nearly enough which makes it so deliciously unsatisfying. Like so many other things with this man, there is something weirdly hot about our simulation through thin, wet fabric. It's just the right amount of too-much and not-enough to make my core flare with frustrated heat and remind me that things with Nash will always be different than I expect. Fresh and new and free of the assumptions I'm so used to bowing to.

"I want to be inside you," he groans, thrusting hard into me.

I gasp and arch back against the cool tile at the sharp rush of pleasure. "I want that too."

"How much longer is this part supposed to be?"

"Um. I don't know. I didn't plan that out."

"Can we be done then?"

I grip his wet hair and tug his face toward me. *"Can we be done? Did you really just say that?"*

"What? You don't want more?"

"Of course I do. I want everything. I want you to fuck me so hard someone calls security."

That smirk. "So what's the problem?"

"Nothing!"

"There's obviously a problem."

This argument would be so much easier if my entire body wasn't on fire from what he's still doing to it with his hips and his mouth and his hands and ah!

"You're an artist," I say. "A poet! Shouldn't there be, I don't know, poetry involved?"

"You want poetry right now? You're the one who's always ripping my clothes off and shoving me into things."

He's not wrong.

"Fine. Whatever."

I pull his head down and kiss him again. And again because ugh. I hate that he's right. Once I'm kissing him I forget about all the romantic crap I'm supposed to want. Do I want it? Maybe a little, but it's fine. It won't matter once I let this fire consume me and give in to my body's craving for his. I don't need pretty words to appreciate all that he is.

His lips rest against my ear, and at first I'm not sure it's even words I'm hearing against the backdrop of pounding shower water. But when the familiar rasp of his voice reverberates throughout my entire being, I close my eyes and dissolve into the sound.

"Not a trace of the pain remains when you say my name with those soft lips that breathe my favorite air, those bright eyes that stare at my every flaw and still claw for a shred of my shattered soul worth saving.

"You'll never know all the times I cried and died a little more inside, because I can't remember the pain in the frame of your face blocking out the shadows.

"You'll never see the broken boy who barely survived and learned to hide, because he doesn't exist when he's in your sun.

"He's the one too absorbed by your light, the only reason he might... finally, finally, be okay."

Oh my god.

Tears drip down my cheeks as I pull him into me and hold on with everything I have. Everything I am and won't be afraid to be if this resilient, courageous spirit is beside me. Maybe it makes no sense, but then so many of the things that *make sense* in my life aren't worth a grain of salt. There's a whole world out there waiting for me when I'm brave enough to find it too.

"Hey, Nash?"

"Huh?" he says softly.

I smile at his perfect (and hoped for) response to my question. "I kind of love our rapport."

* * *

News flash: Sex is better than rapport.

My entire body is on fire as I sink onto him, impaling myself until I feel every thick inch of him inside me. He takes a sharp breath, his eyes flaring hot and looking every bit as consumed when I brace my palms on his chest and start to move.

"Fuck," he exhales. "Why are you so perfect?"

I smile and lean down for a deep kiss before resuming my rhythm. Low heat grinds into tiny sparks with each sway of my hips, each movement triggering another piercing burst of sensation. He grips my thighs and matches my pace, pushing further until the tingling sparks become surges of open flame. I didn't think it could feel like this, like there's an immanent explosion coming that might be too intense for my body to handle.

"Has anyone ever died of an orgasm?" I gasp out.

He smirks, but I might.

He feels so incredible, and the blaze is becoming intolerable. My body arches back as I absorb it, rush after rush after painful rush. I need more. I can't take more. But I need it. Want it. Everything. Right now.

He abruptly flips me over and drives into me, fueling the blasts of pleasure into small explosions. Stars pulse with every thrust. My toes curl, my body tenses and…

"Ah!" I cry out.

His muscles constrict as he strains harder with each push, feeding my orgasm and chasing his own. I wrap my hands around his arms for leverage, pulling with each collision, until he tenses with his own release. Eyes clenched shut and lips parted slightly, he's the picture of what I knew this moment would be. That's what it was for me, and as we both come down from the high, I'm reluctant to let him go and lose his warmth.

He rests his forehead on mine for a second, breathing hard as I shift my hold to his face. I adjust enough to draw his lips to mine for a long, sated kiss.

"You survived," he teases, pulling back.

"Barely," I mumble.

His smile grows, and I can't help but return it. Electric blue eyes search mine and project a thousand words he will probably never say that I will always treasure. Almost as much as…

"Hmm. I've never done that before," I say with a grin.

Alarm flares in his eyes as he stiffens and pulls back.

"Hold on. You're a virgin? Fuck, Paige! Why didn't you tell me?!"

I laugh and grip his shoulders to yank him back. "Relax. That's not what I meant. I've done *that* before, but I've never been a screamer. I'm definitely a quiet climax girl."

His body does relax, and I kind of love the smug look that replaces the concern. "Ah. Well, in that case, I guess you'll have to edit that description of yourself."

I scrunch my brow, considering. "Actually, I don't know. One time doesn't exactly warrant an edit. That's more of a footnote."

His eyes widen at the challenge. "Really. So how many times until an edit is justified?"

"Hmm… good question." I tap my chin, then release a sly smile. "Maybe seven or eight?"

21—DREAMING

NASH

"That's six!" I say, rolling off Paige to land on the mattress.

She shoots a glare in my direction. I can't even see it. I *feel* it.

"No. That one didn't count. It wasn't a scream. More of a… choke."

"A choke?" I push up to my elbow. "Are you serious? Did you really just imply we *choked* an orgasm out of you?"

"I didn't imply it. It was pretty explicit. And that's the perfect description for what that was."

I shake my head and steal a kiss before resuming my ire. "You know, it's not really fair when you're trying *not* to make a sound just to spite me."

"I'm not."

I give her a look, and she bites her lip with a grin.

"We should be at about fifteen," I mutter.

"Fifteen? No way. *Maybe* ten."

"I knew it!" I say, poking her arm. "You *are* holding back so you don't reach seven."

"I didn't say that."

"Nope. Admit it. I'm a sex god."

She snorts a laugh and shoves me away when I lean over her like the sex god I am.

"Whatever, Romeo."

"Was Romeo known for his bedroom skills? Isn't he more of a trellis-climber kind of guy?"

"What's wrong with trellis-climbers? I've dated a few. It comes in handy when you need to access things at the top of trellises."

I laugh and shake my head. This girl.

"Fine." I check the time and groan. "Hey, I gotta run. Val and I are meeting up with Larinda to review his work."

"I've heard what he did. It's good."

"Duh."

With one last kiss, I force myself out of bed to get ready for a long night of making other people's dreams come true.

It's been three weeks since that shitshow in L.A. I'd say a lot has changed, but that's implying there are things that haven't. I mean, I guess there are a few things that are still the same. Our armchair still has no arms. Eva still works at Reedweather Media, although the clock is ticking on that as well. Oh, and I'm sure Chad still owns the record for ugly polo shirts.

After the ransomware gaming event, Brighthouse reacted pretty much how I expected. Once I saw the "virus" and knew Nate was involved, I figured it wasn't dangerous. The passcode to "get rid of the scary pop-ups" was especially hilarious. (I told Nate about Grant's scary-pop-up-thingy-special-disk demand and I'm pretty sure my roommate pulled a muscle laughing.)

The passcode was nothing. As in, there was no passcode. You just had to press enter, but I figured it wouldn't take much to confuse (a.k.a. impress) Grant. In exchange for my freedom, I told him I'd give him the code and a copy of the virus so they could exact their revenge on Sandeke Telecom. I also promised not to tell anyone about his involvement with Brighthouse. He doesn't need to know that Marcos and Eva already knew he was a spy and his IT Department was probably about to call him any second with the magic "enter" solution.

Anyway, it worked. They let me go, I had Nate forward his masterpiece to me so I could pass it along, and thus ended my first (and only) spy mission. I put in my resignation as soon as I got back, along with Paige who insisted on having her four-page treatise notarized and spiralbound. Mine was a text to Chad, but whatever. At the end of the day, neither of us are employed at cheating mega-corporations.

As of now, we have yet to hear anything about a counterattack so the jury is out on that. I'm going to guess Grant's IT Department also told him doing the same thing to Sandeke wouldn't be worth the effort since the virus was so easy to disable it was only responsible for a surge in internet searches on "Renos."

The real damage was the publicity of the attack due to the disruption of the live streaming event. Brighthouse's network may be fine, but they took a huge PR hit when it looked like they got hacked, just as we hoped. So unless Sandeke decides to do an international streaming event Brighthouse can sabotage, the virus won't be of much use to them. It's kind of fun waiting to see when and what Brighthouse will do to strike back. Now I know how Luke Skywalker felt.

On the job front, things are looking up across the board. Eva gave Paige unofficial screaming orgasm number five when she asked if Paige would be interested in helping her execute a business plan for her own marketing firm she'd been working on for the last couple of months. I don't think Paige even asked if the offer came with a salary. Or a job title or, well, anything. She said yes before Eva could even show her the business plan she'd be executing. I can't explain any more than that because I tuned out after the screaming orgasm part. Paige is excited and happy, though, so that's all I care about.

Val had an even bigger offer on his dining-room-table desk. After Larinda heard his final production on her track, she freaked out and asked him to work on the others. We still don't know what Jarvis plans to do with the songs he tricked Steve into sending him. Maybe nothing since—I can't believe I'm saying this— he and Larinda are back together. Just to play it safe, Steve and I teamed up to form a secret society dedicated to protecting Larinda from herself. Our first order of business is to finish her album and get it released under her name before Jarvis can stab her in the back… again.

As if we needed more reasons not to love the guy, we also learned from his PA that the green bandana he wears is to show support for his own fundraiser to restore his mansion in Miami. I don't know how much he's raised so far but I'm hoping it's twelve paperclips and three mismatched buttons.

Then there's me. Yeah, we don't need to talk about that.

An urgent knock rings out on Paige's door, and I can't stop a smile from slipping out. Val is so nervous about today. It's adorable. To be fair, I've been in his shoes and it's an uncomfortable mix of terror and excitement to face your dream head-on. This meeting could change his life or send him right back to his kitchen table, so yeah. I get the frantic pound on that poor, unsuspecting piece of wood.

"Geez. Are you even late?" Paige asks. "I thought you were meeting Larinda at seven."

"We are. He's just anxious. He wants to review everything again before we head over."

"Ugh. Haven't you two listened to those songs enough? They were cool the first six hundred times."

I shrug with a grin. "Now you know how I feel when you and Eva gush over competitive analyses or whatever."

She rolls her eyes. "We've never done that."

"Uh. Yeah. Last night at dinner. Even Marcos was getting annoyed and that guy shits boring financial reports."

"I hate you."

"You love me."

"I can still hate you at the same time."

Val knocks again.

"He's coming!" Paige shouts at the same time I say, "I'm coming."

Once my boxers are secure, I pull open the door and find exactly what I expected. Yep, the guy looks like he's going to puke. How will he react to being in the same room as Larinda?

"She's gonna love it, man," I say, clapping his shoulder. "I promise."

"You can't promise that. I've never done much with country music before. These tracks are nothing like all the other stuff out there."

"That's a good thing. Trust me. Her stuff is more crossover anyway. She's *looking* for a slightly different sound, hence bringing in a new producer. You got this."

Val nods, but it's obvious my words haven't changed anything. Has telling someone not to feel a certain way ever actually worked?

"Right. I'm, um, gonna set everything up at the table," he says.

"Great. And *I'm* gonna shower. Meet you in fifteen?"

He releases a long breath and starts down the hall.

"He really respects you. You're like a big brother to him."

A smile settles over my lips as warmth fills my chest. Yeah, the kid is kind of growing on me too. Still, I can't let that comment slide.

"Gross," I say.

"Gross? That was a huge compliment."

I turn to Paige and scrunch my nose. "Yeah, but that would make you my sister."

"Oh my gosh. You're ridiculous," she groans, throwing a decorative pillow at me. I've noticed a lot of those scattered around the apartment lately. It's like she plants them in strategic locations just so she can chuck one at me.

"Yep. And you love it."

* * *

"That's her," Val hisses.

"It is," I say.

"I can't do this."

"Dude, you've talked with her on the phone three times already."

"I know! But this is different."

I've never seen Val shake so hard. Even when he met Abram Fletcher he had more cool than he does right now.

"Larinda is an angel," I say. "She will love you."

She loves everyone. Unfortunately.

"Come on."

I grab his sleeve and drag him into the studio before he can ruin his future by running away from a lifechanging opportunity. Literally, because the guy looks ready to bolt. He also looks fast and I'm in no mood to be chasing anyone down.

"Nash!" Larinda says, jumping up from the couch.

I return her greeting and motion toward Val.

"Oh my goodness! Val!" she shrieks, flinging her arms around him before I can even make the introduction.

He stiffens, looking shellshocked, until a wide grin seeps onto his face.

"Hi, Larinda. Nice to meet you," he says with legit human words. Maybe there's hope for him yet.

"You didn't tell me he was so cute," she says to me in a playful reprimand. "Look at you. You're freaking adorable. Geez."

And now Val is just a useless puddle on the floor. Great. I'm not cleaning that up.

He shakes his head with a shy smile, and I'm honest enough to admit she's not wrong. The kid definitely has some boy-next-door vibes going on if the boy-next-door also had a bit of a rebellious streak and a decent garage band.

She steps back and waves us toward two open chairs in front of a computer monitor. I see the DAW software up on the screen already loaded with the stems for one of the tracks. Huh. Interesting.

"I know you converted the midi tracks to .wav files so I could listen, but I told my people to grab all the plugins you use so you don't have to do that anymore," she says. "We'll also stick with SoundStage 4 as our DAW to make things easy."

"Is that why you asked what software I was using?" Val asks, clearly surprised. To be honest, so am I. The world grossly underestimates this woman.

"Yes," she says brightly. "I figured it'll be a lot easier to collaborate if we're all using the same stuff now that we're working together full-time."

Hold up. Did she just say what I think she said?

Val stares at her in shock.

"So you listened to what he sent?" I ask when it's clear my friend won't be speaking for a while.

She pulls up a third chair. "Of course. Why do you think we're here?"

"To show you what he sent," I say.

She snaps me a look of disbelief. "You actually think I wouldn't listen the second you sent the link?"

"So you… liked it?" Val asks.

Now she's the one looking horribly confused.

"*Liked* it?" She grunts and kicks the chair beside her so Val can sit.

Reaching for a composition book, she flips it open to a page covered with notations. "These are my notes. You're here to review them and start making final decisions so we can get these tracks mastered and released. Oh, and I *loved* your idea of adding a rock element to 'Crimson Crush.' We are totally doing that. The label freaked when I told them we're using a new producer and mixing some things up for this album, but screw them."

She giggles, and oh my god. What is happening right now?

"You told your *label* about him?" I force out. Holy shit.

She squints at us like we're the ones not making any sense. "Um. Duh. They kind of have to know I'm using someone else from now on. Contracts and rights and all that?"

She almost looks annoyed as she shakes her head in disbelief at our ignorance. "Okay, so let's start with what you did for… you know what? Let's *start* with 'Crimson Crush.' Let me just pull that up."

While Larinda searches through the folder of song files, I shoot a look to Val. He blinks at me in stunned silence, his dark brown eyes glistening with… fuck. Now, I'm tearing up too. Man, I hate this shit.

I pull my gaze away to focus on the screen before I do something ridiculous like hug someone.

"Oh, shoot!" Larinda says, pivoting in her chair to face Val. "We didn't talk about the money part! No wonder you're confused. So I'm not sure what you usually get, but I was *hoping* you'd be okay with ten per track."

"Ten?" he croaks out. "Per track?"

I hear shock in his trembling voice. Larinda hears disappointment.

"I know that's not ideal," she says quickly. "But I think we have the best chance of convincing the label to get on board if we go in low to start. After this album, they should be fine bumping it up to fifteen or twenty, especially if it does well, which I know it will. *Please* say you're okay with that. *Pleeeease.*" She even bats her eyes and juts out her lip in an exaggerated plea that's actually kind of cute. Even cuter? Val's face right now.

He's back to a blinking mannequin.

"Can he get any of that up front?" I ask. "Say, thirty-five?"

Relief washes over her. "I'm sure we can do that. If we can get you an advance, you'll accept ten per song?" she asks Val. When he still doesn't respond, she starts counting on her fingers. "Okay, well if there are twelve songs, that's one-twenty, right? So maybe we can do half up front? What about sixty?"

"You… you want to pay me *sixty*?" he says in a weak voice.

"Sixty thousand dollars, yes. Then the rest after we complete the project."

His gaze rushes to mine again and ugh. Here we go. More annoying emotions because I see everything in this saturated moment. It has nothing to do with the money, although being able to shove thirty-grand into his horrible parents' faces will be pretty damn satisfying. This is about a dream. About his soul that has just been validated and adored.

Told you this kid was going to be something big.

"I… um… think that would be okay," he says.

"Really? Eek!" Larinda says, clapping her hands. "Perfect. Then let's get started. I had this idea for the intro. You know how you had that cello? What if we add…"

My work here is done.

* * *

I end up leaving Larinda's studio long before her *producer* does. By the third song it was pretty clear they had a good thing going and didn't need my input or mediation. Besides, I have a girlfriend who keeps blowing up my phone with texts about ***GOING STRAIGHT BACK TO YOUR PLACE!*** the second I finish.

Marcos is out with Eva celebrating his birthday, and Nate is… somewhere… nursing his wounds with friends after his breakup with Myra. So, sure, I'm looking forward to chillin' at my apartment instead of hers for once too, but her excitement over a bad movie and maybe a pizza seems a little excessive.

Anyway, I text her the second I'm on the sidewalk, and twenty minutes later I fulfill my promise by returning to my apartment two minutes *before* I said. All-in-all I'd say I've had a pretty successful night in the benevolence department.

Until…

"Abram?" I ask when I see my old friend rise from the couch. I shut the door and greet him with a hug. "What are you doing in New York? You should have told me you were coming in."

"I'm only here for a few hours, and I couldn't," he says.

Wait, why does he look nervous? Abram Fletcher isn't afraid of anything.

"Why couldn't you tell me?"

"Because you would have told me not to come."

"Huh?"

He clears his throat. "Sit down, Ellis."

Okay? What's going on?

I drop to the couch and look over to see Paige seated primly on the armless armchair, legs crossed, stern look on her face. I'm about to say something when Marcos, Nate, Eva, and Kaitlyn come down the hall like some Business Casual Millennial Superhero Squad.

What the hell?

They station themselves at various points around the room, and soon I'm surrounded by my closest friends in what feels eerily like… fu-*uck*.

"Nash, this is an intervention," Abram says in a grave tone.

"Oh my god," I mutter, collapsing into the couch.

"Just hear us out," Paige says.

"Did you organize this?" I ask.

She shrugs with a crafty smile.

"We all had a part in it," Marcos says.

I groan and press the heels of my palms into my eyes. "You have to be kidding me. I don't need an intervention. I'm *fine*. Life is good. I just watched your brother unofficially become Larinda Scott's new producer."

"What?!" Paige cries. "So she liked his work?"

"Apparently, today's meeting wasn't even about that. In her mind, they're already partners and on their fifth album together."

"Oh my goodness!" she shrieks, jumping up and down. I can't help but laugh at her excitement, and yeah, maybe this part doesn't suck. She tosses herself into my lap for a massive hug, and I pull her against me. "You're not joking? You're serious?"

Her eyes shine with tears, and I'm not a fan of getting choked up for the second time tonight.

"I'd never joke about that."

"I know," she whispers, nestling against me. I hold her tight and press a kiss to her hair.

"This doesn't get you out of this meeting, though," she says.

She threads our fingers and tucks our hands against her chest. Guess we're doing this in cuddle mode.

"Your duet with Larinda is all over the place," Marcos says, drawing us back to the present nightmare.

"Yeah? So?"

"So the entire world wants to know who this incredibly talented—"

"And hot," Nate cuts in. He grins at my sardonic look.

"And *hot* artist is," Marcos finishes.

"They knew who I was three years ago and decided I wasn't worth keeping."

"No. A few assholes *thought* they knew you and convinced a bunch more assholes to believe their lies," Abram says. "The world only got a shadow of you then and loved it so much even that tiny glimpse was almost enough."

There are too many witnesses to go down this road right now. Why are they doing this to me?

"It doesn't even matter what I want. No one is going to sign me after what happened," I say, trying a different tactic.

"So what? Who says you need to be signed?" Kaitlyn says.

"*I* do! I mean, I don't. I mean… ah! I don't want it. Why can't you all just accept that? I'm fine with who I am and where I'm at!"

Paige squeezes my hand, and I force in a calming breath. They're my friends and I know they're just trying to help but they're not. Can't they see they're hurting me by reminding me of everything I can't have. They just need to stop. It's never going to happen. I don't *want* it to happen. I'm fine being in the shadows. I like it here where it's safe and easy. I'm fine being nobody. I'm so damn fi—

"You're *not* fine," Paige says. She frames my face and forces my gaze to hers. "You are not fine, and we love you too much to let you *'recite that same lie every time.'*"

"You're our friend. Our *brother*," Marcos says. "And you're so much more than *'a tragic loose end.'*"

"Or *'a deadly game of pretend,'*" Kaitlyn adds.

Wait.

"What are you doing?" I ask, tensing. "How do you all know the lyrics for my song?"

Abram shrugs. "You mean, *'this grin that's for you because mine's a joke that's been choked from lungs torn when my heart broke?'*"

"Yes! I never recorded that."

"Not true," Abram says, and I stare at him in surprise.

"What do you mean?" My heart is beating at a tempo dangerously close to the 113 BPMs of "I'm Fine."

"He means, we were recording that day you played with us in the studio," Kaitlyn says.

"You were recording?!"

"Not tracking for real, obviously," Abram says. "But we always record our sessions in case genius strikes. You never know, right?"

Shit. Of course, they do. I'd do—and *did*—the same.

"Fuck," I mutter, rubbing my temples.

"Funny, that's what I said when I listened back and found out you were doing *nothing* with that song. Or any of your music, for that matter," Abram says. "I said, 'Fuck.' Fuck you for keeping that art to yourself. Fuck you for thinking all those hacks out there deserve their pedestals while you sit around in your living room playing circles around them."

Marcos comes forward and points a finger in my face. "And fuck you for deciding you don't have a family that will have your back no matter what happens. Good or bad. Rain or shine. We"—he waves around the room—"*This* is your family. And when your family tells you you're screwing up your life, you listen."

"Billy Stanton destroyed your childhood," Nate says in a rare display of unpleasantness. "Don't let that fucker destroy your future as well."

"Technically, my future was destroyed by Tyler, not Billy. Also, Kaitlyn doesn't like the word '*fuck*' so maybe we can use more verbs."

"True," she says, "but irrelevant. Shut your mouth and listen, Ellis."

Grr. Even Kaitlyn?

"They're all Billy Stantons," Paige says, clutching my hand again. "Don't you see? There will always be a bully. There will always be someone trying to tear you down, but *you* decide what fire you're going to breathe back into the world. Know who taught me that?"

I release a heavy breath and close my eyes.

"We love you, Nash," Marcos says, softening. "We're tired of watching you drift and hide behind 'I'm fine.' You're not fine, and we won't be either until you're not just surviving but *thriving*."

I open my eyes and stare at him, all of them. Geez, they barely fit in our small, shitty living room. Seven faces shine back at me. Seven sets of eyes begging me to dream. To not just *be* but be great.

I never thought I could. Guys like me don't get to believe in shit. All we can do is hold on for as long as possible and hope the universe tosses us a scrap of one damn thing that doesn't hurt.

"I booked us time at Hive Studios near Austin," Abram announces in a firm tone that makes it clear he's not interested in debate. "It's a little out in the boondocks, but we need to keep this low profile for now. Plus, Larinda is friends with the dude who runs it. Tom, I think? He said he can get you in right away as a favor to Larinda."

"Keep *what* low profile? And wait. When did you talk to Larinda? *Why* did you talk to Larinda?"

"She's a big fan of mine, apparently," he says with a glint.

Kaitlyn rolls her eyes and smacks his arm.

"You're such a diva," she mutters.

He grins and focuses back on me. "Anyway, I reached out to see what you two were working on and how I could get you to work on stuff with me. Except, I learned something interesting."

Uh-oh.

"Yeah?" I say as evenly as possible.

"Yes. I learned you're not actually working with her. Well, she said you're her 'creative advisor' whatever the hell that is, but it's actually Paige's brother who's been producing for her."

"*Will be* producing for her," I mumble. "Technically, nothing is official yet."

Abram gives me a hard look, and I back down with a grunt.

"So then I thought, 'well, at least he's performing again' and asked her about the duet you two did. You know what she said?"

"That she couldn't wear sequins?" He cocks his head, and I shake mine. "Never mind."

"No. She said it wasn't planned. That you put that whole thing together spontaneously the night before and you hadn't even practiced. She said you only did it to help her avoid some bad publicity. That's when we realized you're not actually doing anything with your music, are you? You're still hiding your amazing gift."

"So? I don't see what any of this has to do with Hive Studios."

"Right. Well, that got me thinking, if Nash is willing to go live in front of a huge international audience to play some song he probably hates and help some woman he barely knows, what would he do for one of his good friends?"

I narrow my eyes at him, still having no idea where he's going with this. "What are you talking about?"

"This is strictly confidential. Swear on your life you won't say anything."

I glare at him, annoyed he'd even ask me that. "Of course. What?"

"We've been asked to record an original song for a huge, and I mean *huge* film set to release next fall. Kaitlyn and I have been working for months but nothing is clicking. They want something edgy, sort of rock/hip-hop and that's not exactly what we're known for."

"Ah. Yeah," I say. "It's not hard once you get over the mental block of the percussion. You have to go against your rock instinct and scale back the rhythm to give the song space for the cadence of the lyrics… what?" Why is everyone staring at me? "That's kind of my jam. Literally."

"We're aware, genius," Kaitlyn says dryly.

My gaze snaps back to Abram and my heart stops. Hold on.

No.

Nope.

Just.

No.

"The movie is about a troubled teen who keeps getting knocked down and puts on a brave front."

"Isn't he an orphan?" Kaitlyn asks in a tone that tells me she knows he is.

"Yes, I think you're right," Abram muses, tapping his chin. Smartass.

"Let me guess, this *troubled teen* is a musical prodigy whose name is *Ash*?" I quip.

"Actually, no. His name is Ryan," Abram says.

Kaitlyn nods. "And he's a football player who ends up finding a portal to another world where the trees are actually… you know what? The point is..." She waves toward Abram to continue.

"The point is, we need a rock-hip-hop anthem about a troubled kid who keeps getting knocked down and puts on a brave front. Know where we could find something like that?"

I stare at him.

And stare.

And stare.

"I still don't understand. You want to license 'I'm Fine' for your movie thing?"

I'm not sure why they're the ones who look like they want to hit me when *I'm* the one being ambushed by seven friends and a whole shitload of random information that means nothing.

"No, you idiot. We want *you* to record your song. With Redburn," Abram says.

Huh?

"Like… a collaboration?"

"Not *like* a collaboration. *As* a collaboration. As in 'Redburn, featuring Nash Ellis.'"

I open my mouth but no words come out. That doesn't make any sense.

"That doesn't make any sense." Oh good. Words. Yay.

"It makes perfect sense," Paige says. "They need a good song. You have a good song. You need a high-profile platform to launch your career. They have a high-profile platform to launch your career."

I shake my head. A lot. "You… I mean, you can't just do that, right? Aren't there contracts and producers and—"

"Trust me. We can. I'm Abram Fletcher."

"Diva," Kaitlyn coughs out.

"Let's take a family vote," Eva says. "All in favor of Nash going down to Hive Studios to record some song that will make him a big rock star, raise your hand." She even makes a show of counting all seven hands. "Great. All opposed?"

I don't even bother raising mine because this is stupid.

"Looks like you were outvoted, babe," Paige says with a shrug. "Wait, do we have to buy him a cowboy hat if he's going to Texas? I've never been there. How does that work?"

"I'm not going to Texas," I say.

"You don't have a choice. You got outvoted," Marcos says.

"That's not how that works. My life isn't up for a vote. Don't you see? I can't just… I mean… It's…"

I shake my head. It's what? Not possible? Because apparently it is. The *possibility* is sitting right in front of me, literally being shoved in my face.

Not the right time? It's the perfect time. As perfect as any other time, anyway. Time is nothing when each day dawns with the same bleak outlook.

So what is it? What's the problem? Why do I have to say no? Because. That's what I do. Say no. Watch other people live their lives.

"Let the waves of darkness break, and take the pain below, purged by the undertow."

I flinch at Paige's soft voice beside me.

"You… when did you see that?" I ask faintly.

"In training that first day. You wrote it deep within the pages of your notebook. I kind of think that's when I fell in love with you."

I stare at her in disbelief, having no idea how to respond to that.

"If not now, when?" she asks, her hazel eyes pleading. "When will you let go, Nash? When will you let the waves of darkness break and wash away the pain so you can start over?"

I blink at her, my heart pounding in my chest.

"You told me you don't get to take risks because you don't have a safety net. Look around you. You've got a fucking ocean of safety nets under you. Sorry, Kaitlyn," she says.

"No problem," Kaitlyn chirps.

"So what's your excuse now?" Paige continues. "I fight you on everything from your gum flavor to the way you hang your towels inside out. Do you actually think I'm going to sit around and *not* fight to give you the very thing that makes you feel free and alive?"

My eyes burn. Oh no. Not again.

"You wanted a family?" Marcos says. "You got one. And this is what family does."

"Family supports you," Nate adds.

"Family loves you." Eva.

"Family picks you up when you fall and pushes you when you're too weak to go on," Paige says, centering my face on hers. "Family trusts and believes enough for both of you when you're too scared to take the next step, so let us do that for you. Let us help you stop being *fine* and start being *whole*."

Tears gather in her eyes when mine cloud over, and she pulls me into her. Soon I feel another firm hand on my shoulder and more on my back.

"We love you so much," Paige whispers. "But you have to let us."

I can't breathe as decades of pain and defeat choke my lungs all at once. So many bruises and scars. So many lonely, dark nights and hopeless days. So many years of being a fraction of what I should be. What I could have been if I hadn't been cut down before I even got a chance to live.

"I'm not fine," I whisper in a shattered voice. "I'm not fine, Paige."

Her arms tighten around me, and for the first time that I can remember it feels like I'm being enveloped in a cloud of warmth. Like there's a chance in hell I could be okay. Is this what seven hugs at once feels like? Is this… family?

"We know," she says softly.

I feel the brush of her lips against my neck in a gentle kiss.

"We know, baby. But I promise, I *promise*… You will be."

EPILOGUE

NASH

"I still think this is a bad idea," Val mutters when we spot their parents in a snooty French fusion restaurant called The Hollis House. Marcos "knows a guy" and got us a reservation as a thank you for helping him out with his spy crap. He probably wouldn't have if he'd known we were going to use it to mess with Paige and Val's awful parents.

For the record, Paige and I eventually discussed "The Slap." The ensuing argument almost resulted in another slap, which then resulted in vocal orgasm number fifteen, so I'm counting that debriefing as a win.

"It's the perfect idea," Paige says.

"Yeah, but did we have to do the duffle bag thing?" Val whines.

"It's genius. Don't be a baby," Larinda says.

Val rolls his eyes at his colleague, but I catch the hint of amusement behind his irritation. Those two wasted no time going from artist and producer to laugh-out-loud besties. I don't know how they get any work done with the way they goof off every time they're together.

"Oh! We should hold hands," she whispers, grabbing his fingers.

Val shoots her a surprised look, and she shrugs.

"Wouldn't it be more fun if your parents thought we were dating on top of working together?" she asks.

I snort a laugh, and Paige smacks my chest.

"What? That would be hilarious," I say.

"And what about everyone else seeing it and rumors spreading?" Paige snaps.

"Ooh, great idea!" Larinda says, eyes widening with excitement. She tugs Val's hand. "Think about what that would do for our album if people thought we were dating!"

Yeah, no way he likes that. Sure enough, his new expression borders on horror at the thought of playing media games. Paige, though?

She glances at her parents—who are looking even more snooty than the restaurant—and relaxes.

"Yeah. Okay," she says, a smile slipping out.

"Seriously?" Val hisses. "You're okay with this?"

"Come on, Perceval. Where's your sense of adventure?" Larinda asks, shaking his sleeve with her other hand.

"I told you never to call me that," he mumbles.

"Not even possible when your name is Perceval," she says.

He casts a mock glare that results in an affectionate grin from Larinda.

Hmm. Maybe it would be fun if they dated for real. Larinda broke up with Jarvis this morning so she's single again, and heaven knows Val would benefit from some Jasmine Sparkle in his life.

Val grunts at our encouraging stares, but finally laces his fingers with Larinda's. His other hand tightens around the handle of a black duffle bag, which looks as heavy as it is. That part was my idea, and on a scale of 1 to Awesome, this idea is beyond awesome.

Paige loops her arm through mine as we move toward the table, and I know it's a gesture of reassurance as much as affection. I haven't seen her father since he hit me, and I think she's afraid I'll either hit him back or burst into tears and make a scene. She still hasn't entirely figured me out, and I enjoy the challenge of keeping her guessing about my fluctuating artist moods, especially since she keeps me guessing about basically everything else. As for this present situation, I have no intention of attacking *or* crying because, honestly, that jackass isn't worth the brain cells required for either.

For their part, Mr. and Mrs. Andrews appear about as shocked as you'd expect when your children arrive for a family dinner with an A-List celebrity, despised boyfriend, and giant duffle bag of… something.

"What…?" Mrs. Andrews stammers.

Mr. Andrews' gaze lands on me, and I return a pleasant smile which I decide is the absolute last reaction he would want. I guessed right when his eyes narrow and his lips flatten into a thin line. Yep, words are so getting repeated in the very near future.

"Good to see you, Mr. and Mrs. Andrews," I say.

Paige's fingers tighten around my bicep in warning, but she should know by now that her warnings are just rocket fuel for my snark.

"It's been a while since you assaulted me," I continue in a polite tone. "I trust your palm has healed?"

Stunned, Mr. Andrews opens his mouth to respond but nothing comes out. His wife looks speechless as well, which will enhance our interaction tenfold if we can maintain this trajectory.

The prospect of parental silence alone is worth my girlfriend's ire, but to my surprise, a small snort rises from beside me instead. I glance down at Paige who doesn't look upset at all. In fact, she looks very much the opposite of upset. She looks like she kind of loves what's happening right now.

"Anyway, we won't keep you long," Val says, drawing his parents' dumfounded shock to him.

Their gazes land on the hand linked with a country music superstar's, and I can't stop a smug grin. We were so right about this.

"Oh, sorry," Val says. "Um, Larinda, these are my parents. Mom, Dad, this is Larinda Scott. She's a musician."

"And his girlfriend," Larinda adds, lifting her free hand in a quick wave. "I love him so much too. He's, like, the best thing to ever happen to me. I mean, not just professionally, but emotionally, spiritually, physically—"

"Okay," Val interrupts, giving her a hard look.

She returns another smile, and I so wish we were staying for an actual meal. I could watch this train-wreck all day.

"Yes, we're working together," he says. "And, uh, in love, so I guess, here you go."

He releases Larinda's hand to lift the massive duffle bag and drop it on the floor at his parents' feet. No one moves as they stare at the offering for at least ten seconds.

See, now *this* is top-shelf spy shit right here. Every caper needs a mysterious duffle bag.

Mr. Andrews clears his throat.

"This is a duffle bag," he tells us.

"Yes," Val says.

"It looks full," Mr. Andrews says.

"It does," Val agrees.

"It's because it *is* full," Paige says.

Pretty sure a two-year-old could follow this conversation. Pretty sure two-year-olds have *had* this conversation.

"Just open it," Val says.

Mrs. Andrews blinks a few more times before leaning down and unzipping the bag. A gasp rushes out of her, along with a curse from her husband.

"What the…?" Mr. Andrews murmurs.

"That's thirty thousand dollars," Val says. "In cash."

"Tens, specifically," I cut in. "It was my suggestion because no one ever seems to have enough ten dollar bills, you know? Twenties, duh. Ones, too many. Fives, eh, a few. But tens? Always scarce. You're. Welcome." I even add a wink to make this moment extra special.

"That should cover *the loan,* right?" Val asks.

His parents absently stare at the bricks of bills, all kinds of unspoken awesomeness fluttering throughout this stuffy restaurant.

"We…"

"I mean…"

"How…"

There's probably a question in there… unless we're back to toddler communication drills.

"Okay, well, we're sorry we can't stay but Larinda and I have to get back to the studio," Val says.

"And Nash needs to meet up with Redburn to discuss their collaboration on the next Sunray Productions film," Paige adds.

"So great seeing you again, Mr. and Mrs. Andrews," I say.

"And meeting you!" Larinda chirps with a wave as we start away from the table.

We weave through the room and make it all the way to the sidewalk before bursting into laughter.

"You know they're gonna disown you too now," Val says to Paige through a chuckle.

I glance at Paige with concern, and she sobers herself with a deep breath.

"Do you really think so?" she asks.

Val's humor fades as he nods. "You officially took my side. They'll never forgive you for that." He reaches out and squeezes her arm. "I love you, sis. I'm sorry."

Me too, because I guess, maybe, I kind of care about this woman. A fucking lot.

Except…

Paige grins.

"Thank god," she says.

Wait. What?

"Hey, Nash," she says with a sly smile.

"Huh?"

We exchange a grin at our awesome rapport.

"Nothing. Just… I don't have a family now. You got any room in yours?"

Hell yes. I pull her in and plant a solid kiss on her forehead.

"Depends," I say softly, gazing into beautiful, intelligent, exasperating hazel eyes.

She sucks in a breath and tightens her arms around my waist.

"On what?" she whispers back.

I bite my lip and offer the most sincere, loving expression I can muster.

"How do you feel about adopting a baby Mer-Nut one day?"

* * *

Experience Nash's music with the original song "Living A Lie" by Aly Stiles and Julian Greene, available everywhere you stream music.

Link: https://linktr.ee/alystiles

ABOUT THE AUTHOR

From angsty and dark to snort-laugh funny, Aly writes romance from her soul to yours.

Thank you for taking this journey with me. I would love to hear from you! For updates, reveals, and more subscribe to my newsletter and join my fun, laidback reader group on Facebook: Aly's Breakfast Club.

Aly Stiles
PO Box 577
Trexlertown, PA 18087-0577

Facebook Reader Group – Aly's Breakfast Club
Newsletter
BookBub
Spotify
Apple Music
Facebook Page – Author Aly Stiles
Goodreads
Website
Instagram
YouTube
Twitter
Blogger sign-up for notifications about future releases, ARC reviews, and cover reveals
TikTok
Pinterest

Find Smartypants Romance online:
Website: www.smartypantsromance.com
Facebook: https://www.facebook.com/smartypantsromance
Twitter: @smartypantsrom
Instagram: @smartypantsromance
Newsletter: https://smartypantsromance.com/newsletter/

ALSO BY ALY STILES

MORE FROM ALY

From angsty and dark to snort-laugh funny, Aly writes romance from her soul to yours.

THE SAVE ME SERIES
Available on Kindle Unlimited
RISING WEST (available on audiobook)
FALLING NORTH
BREAKING SOUTH
CRASHING EAST
GUARDING SHADOWS

THE WRECK ME SERIES
Available on Kindle Unlimited
ASHTON MORGAN: Apartment 17B
CAMDEN WALKER: Apartment 8C
TRISTAN & ISABEL: Apartment 11F

THE HOLD ME SERIES BY ALYSON SANTOS
Available on Kindle Unlimited and audiobook.
NIGHT SHIFTS BLACK
TRACING HOLLAND
VIPER
LIMELIGHT
AN NSB WEDDING

STANDALONES
Available on Kindle Unlimited.
YOUNG LOVE

TRAITOR

HAUNTED MELODY

PARANORMAL BOOKS BY MOIRA HALE

Available on Kindle Unlimited

GIFTED (Gifted, Vol 1)

CURSED (Gifted, Vol 2)

ALSO BY SMARTYPANTS ROMANCE

Green Valley Chronicles
The Love at First Sight Series
Baking Me Crazy by Karla Sorensen (#1)
Batter of Wits by Karla Sorensen (#2)
Steal My Magnolia by Karla Sorensen (#3)
Worth the Wait by Karla Sorensen (#4)

Fighting For Love Series
Stud Muffin by Jiffy Kate (#1)
Beef Cake by Jiffy Kate (#2)
Eye Candy by Jiffy Kate (#3)
Knock Out by Jiffy Kate (#4)

The Donner Bakery Series
No Whisk, No Reward by Ellie Kay (#1)

The Green Valley Library Series
Love in Due Time by L.B. Dunbar (#1)
Crime and Periodicals by Nora Everly (#2)
Prose Before Bros by Cathy Yardley (#3)
Shelf Awareness by Katie Ashley (#4)
Carpentry and Cocktails by Nora Everly (#5)
Love in Deed by L.B. Dunbar (#6)
Dewey Belong Together by Ann Whynot (#7)
Hotshot and Hospitality by Nora Everly (#8)
Love in a Pickle by L.B. Dunbar (#9)
Checking You Out by Ann Whynot (#10)
Architecture and Artistry by Nora Everly (#11)

Weight Expectations by M.E. Carter (#1)

Sticking to the Script by Stella Weaver (#2)

Cutie and the Beast by M.E. Carter (#3)

Weights of Wrath by M.E. Carter (#4)

Common Threads Series

Mad About Ewe by Susannah Nix (#1)

Give Love a Chai by Nanxi Wen (#2)

Key Change by Heidi Hutchinson (#3)

Not Since Ewe by Susannah Nix (#4)

Lost Track by Heidi Hutchinson (#5)

Educated Romance
Work For It Series

Street Smart by Aly Stiles (#1)

Heart Smart by Emma Lee Jayne (#2)

Book Smart by Amanda Pennington (#3)

Smart Mouth by Emma Lee Jayne (#4)

Play Smart by Aly Stiles (#5)

Lessons Learned Series

Under Pressure by Allie Winters (#1)

Not Fooling Anyone by Allie Winters (#2)

Out of this World
London Ladies Embroidery Series

Neanderthal Seeks Duchess by Laney Hatcher (#1)

Well Acquainted by Laney Hatcher (#2)